The Altar Stone

Gerald & Moya;
Here's to many more years
at Yellow Point.
Thank you very much, I
hope you enjoy.

Bob Hardman

The Altar Stone

ROBERT HACKMAN

Goodfellow Press

Goodfellow Press
8522 10th Ave. NW
Seattle, WA 98117

ISBN: 1-891761-14-5
Library of Congress: 2001-131734

Edited by Pamela R. Goodfellow

Jacket and book design by Rohani Design, Edmonds, WA

Cover illustration by Barbara Levine

Printed by Edwards Brothers, Inc. under the supervision of Tanya Eldred.

This is a work of fiction. The events described are imaginary; the characters are
entirely fictitious and are not intended to represent actual living persons.

The text is in 11.5 point Goudy with 15 point leading.
Author photo by Roberta Gray Gaffney.

To Iola, my mother, and my brother, James.

ACKNOWLEDGEMENTS

THERE ARE MANY WHOSE EXPERTISE AND support raised this novel above what it might otherwise have been. I owe my particular appreciation to Andrew R. James, Executive Vice President, Ye Olde Curiosity Shop, Seattle Washington, not only for permission to use that historic landmark as a setting for the first chapter, but also for allowing me to present it through memories, perhaps fanciful, from my own childhood.

Mimmo Bonanni, Anthropology and Ethnic Studies Bibliographer at the Hayden Library, Arizona State University, gave his personal time to suggest many of the resources contributing to the background of this book. Marsha Schweitzerand, Graduate Coordinator, Anthropology, kindly answered many questions concerning the disciplines of anthropology and archeology.

Jose' Alberto Felix De La Cuba, research biologist, ecologist, and explorer led our all too short visit to the rain forests of the *Reservada Del Manu*. His love and dedication to the biota of that region help it endure. The knowledge he shared made this work possible. I am in awe of the Andes Mountains and the Amazon rain forests. Those who work to ensure their preservation and survival deserve the world's gratitude.

Patti, Shack, Teri, Mercer, Kae, Phil, and the Madison Park Irregulars made the long hours necessary to complete this work more easily lived. Bobbie, Suzanne, Adrian and Barbara gave their friendship and support in Peru.

Thanks and affection to the writers of Goodfellow Press who provided critique for the manuscript as it progressed and to Pamela Goodfellow who mentored both the writing and the author.

Any errors, oversights, or misrepresentations are both unintentional and my own.

BLOATED LIDS CLOAKED THE EYES AND SPIRALS of coarse black cord imprisoned any secrets the lifeless lips might have told him. For all nine-year-old Wart had learned about how you left your body to rise to heaven when you died, he couldn't help but wonder if the people weren't still trapped inside the shrunken heads.

Big dumb idea, he told himself. But it gave him the willies anyway and made the back of his neck tingle cold. He tugged the zipper of his denim jacket higher, felt the soft scuffling of Pookie, the little dog tucked securely inside, and that made him pull himself up stronger. After all, his cousin Angie trusted him with the tiny young Silky Terrier and she'd made him promise, 'cross your heart and hope to die,' that he'd keep it safe.

The glass case that confined the shrunken heads rested against the back wall of the shop. It, in turn, crouched captive of the shadows thrown down from the ceiling by row upon row of relics and remains its owner had collected long before Wart had been born. All the way through the store he'd gawked up at the ceiling and around at the walls. He'd come to a rattlesnake with its mouth open, fangs poised to strike, and the skin on his arms crawled. He shivered when he thought he could feel biting slashes across his back from the sharp-toothed shark jaws laughing down at him from the ceiling. A gun with a barrel flared out at the end like a clarinet stopped him. He raised his arms and sighted down an imaginary musket of his own at a gang of pirates snarling threats behind daggers clenched in yellowed teeth.

He stood just tall enough that he only needed to pull his head down a little to look straight in at the shrunken faces. He stared hard into the case. A fascination swelled through his body and fixed him hard to the spot. It felt like his feet had roots growing right down into the floor.

One head held his attention more than any other. It was one of the biggest and the strands that held the lips together had been used to sew the eyes shut too. Dim yellow light coming from somewhere inside the case made dark shadows around the eyes and where the cheeks had sunk. The blotchy skin ran from pale gray to the dark browns of freshly dug dirt and the straight hair had mostly faded from black to a rusty color that made him think of old orange peels. The other heads were expressionless. This one looked to him as if the owner had been mad-crazy . . . and in pain . . . and he really was still alive in there. He felt himself becoming afraid. It made the skin at the back of his neck feel crinkly-cold. He could have sworn that his hair was reaching straight up tugging at his scalp as if to get away.

He put his hands against the top of the case and pushed away, forced himself to take a step backwards. Don't let them bug you. He made himself look up at the things above the case on the wall: a row of northwest Indian masks painted brightly in red, black and blue green, the curved blade of a tarnished sword, a row of headlines about the civil war on yellowed old newspapers. It worked for a few seconds, but the heads drew him back. As he stared at them he noticed the hasp that held the sliding glassed front door of the case in place and the padlock latched through it. Relief sifted into him like dust settling in grass as he realized he didn't need to be afraid. At least not so very much.

Scary or not, the heads stuck way out front when it came to being the most amazing things he'd ever seen. Lots more awesome than his cousin Tommy's big crow about having seen Fusty Wiggins starkers. She was eleven last November and a cousin to them both. Tommy talked about how he'd seen her coming out of the bathroom without a stitch on whenever he could, which meant every time they were together and no adults were around. Maybe if he showed Tommy the heads, it would give him something new to brag about.

He nodded to himself and stuck a finger down the front of his jacket to wiggle it on top of the head of the little Silky. A cool nose touched his finger in reply. He'd zipped the animal inside his jacket because a sign on the front door of Seattle's, Ye Olde Curiosity Shop, announced, 'NO PETS INSIDE.' Angie, Tommy's thirteen year old sister, would have a snit fit if she found out Pookie'd been left to stay in the back of Aunt Clara's pinto station wagon. His aunt must have known that too, and that was probably why she let him do it. Otherwise she was definitely the type who made you do what signs said. She didn't seem to have much patience with kids and sometimes it made him nervous to be around her. He never knew when she'd make a big deal out of something his own mom may never have bothered to mention.

He let himself have a last good look at the heads then. Tucking a hand under the dog lump in his jacket, he rolled his shoulders forward and started walking through the maze of aisles toward the front of the curio shop. He tried to walk tall and look really cool, like he wasn't carrying anything at all.

Wart found Tommy and his Aunt Clara still no more than a few steps inside the front door. When they'd first come into the store, his aunt had kept Tommy back with her and told Wart to run along until his cousin could catch up. Now she held a tee shirt up across her son's chest to see if it would fit.

"It won't be boy's sizes for you much longer, young man." Tommy was a year and a half older than Wart, half a head taller and liked to brag that his dad said he was 'built like a fullback.' Though Wart couldn't understand why that was such a big deal. He'd rather be built like a quarterback. They were the smartest guys on the team.

Wart looked at the picture on the tee shirt. It showed 'Sylvester,' a mummified corpse who'd been found in the Arizona desert over a hundred years ago. The mummy stood in a special glass case of its own at the back of the shop near the shrunken heads. Writing in a circle around the picture on the shirt said, 'I Hugged My Mummy at Ye Olde Curiosity Shop.' Tommy saw him and rolled his eyes as if to say, 'this could take hours,' and Wart bounced a quick nod that he got the message.

"Hold still, young man." Tommy's mom took a firm hold on both his shoulders. Then she went back to smoothing the shirt down his front with her fingers.

Wart knew better than to interrupt. He kept quiet and tried to hold his horses, like his dad would have told him. That only made him antsy, so to kill time he let his head loll all the way back on his shoulders and looked up at the ceiling again. He fixed on a kayak made of taut stretched animal skins and suspended upside down so he could see up into it. A paddle with a blade on each end had been fastened along the deck and the opening where the Eskimo would sit had a whole slew of cobwebs inside. A gray-white skull with short curved horns and a hand-lettered sign telling him 'American Buffalo' hung in the space next to the kayak, and beside that, a cracked and yellowing elephant tusk.

"Reginald?"

Wart popped his head back up straight. He hated his real name always, but even worse when somebody said it loud like that. He glanced around to see if people were gawking at him. He pulled a face to show Tommy his dislike, then remembered to pay attention to his aunt before she said it again. She did anyway, but not so loud this time.

"Reginald, I intended to buy you boys each a souvenir tee shirt, but they seem to be out of Tommy's size in anything he wants." Her voice didn't seem to express any disappointment and he decided it might be that Tommy didn't want anything she'd like him to have. That figured. He'd do it just to be stubborn.

"Would you like to let me see if one of these will fit you, or would you rather I treat us at Baskin Robbins on the way home instead. Will that be just as nice?"

Sheesh wouldn't it? But Wart held his reply to a polite, "Yes'm," and looked on while Tommy nodded his head up and down so fast Aunt Clara frowned him into stopping.

"I'm going to keep looking for postcards for your grandma and Tommy's Aunt Phyllis in Omaha. You two run along. I'll come for you when I'm finished."

"Hey . . . Come on back there. I wanna show you something." Wart had waited long enough. He tugged his cousin's jacket sleeve. He turned and took off without waiting for a reply, carefully putting a hand back under the bulge in his jacket. After he'd gone a dozen steps or so down the first aisle, he stopped and turned back to find Tommy hadn't gotten farther than the first counter where he'd picked up a yellow plastic kaleidoscope and stood peering through it.

He headed back to his cousin. "Hey. C'mon."

"Fusty hasn't got her boobs yet."

"How'd she get that name?" Wart knew very well how, but wanted him off the subject. Somehow it wasn't fair to Fusty, and he didn't know whether that was supposed to be good or bad for a girl her age to have boobs. They'd have to get in the way when you ran.

"Cause she fussed a lot when she was a baby. Real name's Francis." Tommy tossed the kaleidoscope back on top of the pile on the counter. "Can't hardly see through the damn thing. Remember last night when my dad told us that most of the stuff in here is for dumb tourists to buy?" He paused and his expression took on that kind of slick-sly look that meant he was gong to try to start something. "You're a tourist."

Wart wanted to tell him that it was his mom doing the tourist buying, but he didn't. He could tell by the new tone of Tommy's voice that his mean would come up. At least he'd forgotten about Fustie Francis for now. They started toward the back of the store again, passing people Wart thought must be the real tourists as they sorted through stacks of one-size-fits-all baseball caps and bins of polished stones.

Wart wanted to hurry his cousin along. He led skip-walking through the narrow aisles until Tommy grabbed him by the arm and dragged him to a stop next to a player piano. It hadn't been playing when Wart had first wandered to the back of the store and he'd barely noticed it. But now keys were jerking down with each note as it plunked out a tinny version of *In the Good Old Summertime*. He wondered if there ever was a 'good old summer-time' in Seattle. He hadn't seen the sky for gray clouds in the three days he'd been here. It would be sunny and hot now at home in Spokane.

They'd come near the end of the tune and, after only a few notes, it stopped. Tommy wanted to go back and ask his mom to give him money to play another one, but Wart suggested that, if she did, she might change her mind about the ice cream.

Tommy's reply was to give him a shove. Wart grinned and started off. Tommy followed.

As they got farther back toward the rear of the store the air took on a dusty smell. They passed the mounted saw of a saw fish, a prickly spined porcupine fish all puffed up round and lacquered shiny, and an old rifle from China that leaned against a post and must have been longer than his dad was tall. Signs pointed out old coins and elephants carved into grains of rice, but he hurried on by. He recognized the last aisle he needed to turn down by the old wooden statue of a navy captain standing beside it. The statue held a lantern and peered over it as though looking out to sea. The buttons on the long blue coat were painted yellow to look like brass and the face had a full mustache and white beard. As he led them around the corner he noticed for the first time that the statue was staring right down the aisle toward the case that held the heads and the expression, especially the eyes, looked troubled. He could feel the creepies scooting up the back of his neck.

They finally got to the glass case only to find two grown-ups standing in front of it with their backs facing them, blocking the view. One man wore green and white plaid flared pants, like a pair his dad wore to the golf course, and had his hair tied behind his head in a shoulder length ponytail. Wart guessed he must be a clerk. In that instant the guy bent over, opened the padlock at the front of the case to slide one panel of the glass aside and proved it. He took something out and stood. Then he turned to show it to the other man.

"There you are, sir. The Lord's Prayer engraved on the head of a pin. Every word."

He placed the object in the other guy's open palm. Then Wart saw the clerk catch sight of them. He turned toward the boys and raised a hand as if he were about to say something but the other man cut him off.

"This is too small for me to read. If you have a magnifying glass, I'd like to see for myself."

"I believe we do, sir. Why don't you follow me?" And Mr. Plaid Pants led the other man away.

Now the boys could see them. Wart stood proudly before the glass expecting his cousin to respond with the same awe he had when he'd first seen them. Instead Tommy blurted, "I saw 'em before."

Disappointment came down like the rap of a set of knuckles on Wart's head. Then he realized what he should have known. Tommy lived in Seattle. His mom probably brought him here all the time. He felt Tommy's elbow nudge him in the ribs. "But they are pretty cool."

Tommy put his face up close to the glass and tried to read the print on a yellowed, hand-lettered card that tilted up against one of the heads. He read it out loud, "These dee-min-u-tive . . . that means small . . . heads were made the size you see by headhunters of the Upper Amazon Basin by first removing the bones and then placing stones and sand heated with lime and sulphur and . . . crapola . . . I don't know that other word." He stood to his full height and squared his shoulder and grinned. "So, what's it to ya."

Wart's curious bone really itched. He wanted to know all about how they shrunk them. That would somehow make them less scary and prove that nobody still lived inside. He did know his cousin and didn't want to get smacked on the shoulder, so he shrugged as casually as he could make himself do it and stayed gawking into the case.

Neither boy said anything for a few seconds, then Tommy took a step back from the case and when he spoke his voice came out anxious sounding and higher. "Hey look. He left the lock off."

There was a moment of hesitation and Wart turned to look into his cousin's face trying to read what was coming next. Then the tone of Tommy's voice dared him. "Betcha ain't got the guts to pick one of 'em up."

Wart turned his head back toward the case to see the padlock inside on the bottom shelf where the clerk had left it. He wished it was still in the hasp locking the glass closed where it was supposed to be. He got that petrified wood feeling again. Like he knew something he didn't really know. And scared didn't even begin to say it, but his dad had told him it's good to face your fears, so he tried just that. He put his face up close to the glass. He wouldn't back down. If he did Tommy'd be all over him. Wart thought he'd rather die than let his cousin bully him. He tried to use his oldest voice. "Sure. If you will."

Tommy looked back at him in a curious way, like maybe he hadn't thought of that possibility. Then he shrugged and dropped to his knees on the floor. Wart took a look back over his shoulder toward the front of the store to see if anyone watched. He half hoped so, because that would be a good excuse to call this off . . . but no luck. He slipped down on his knees beside Tommy. Slowly his older cousin slid the glass aside. "Scardie-cats go first."

Wart couldn't believe that Tommy didn't know that if he went first, that left Tommy to be the one afraid. So he just kind of sat there and looked at his cousin for a minute, trying to look older and not spooked. It worked until he could feel his heart beat starting to rev up like his dad's outboard motor. Wart knew it was time to make his move or he would do something to give Tommy more ammo to rank on him about. He reached in quickly and pulled one out. Tommy couldn't see his face and Wart had his eyes closed. It was only after he was holding it outside the case that Wart looked to see it was the one with both the eyes and lips sewn shut. The one with the horrible hate on its face.

A dry musty odor came from the opened case and stung the inside of his nose when he breathed. Wart wondered if dead people smelled like that. He tried to put it in his lap but Pookie started scrabbling inside his jacket and the dog frantically tried to push its way up and out. Caught off guard, Wart tried to hand the head over to Tommy who scooted back away from him with a big dumb grin across his face. Wart needed to move fast so he settled for setting it in front of him on the floor. He reached to push Pookie back down inside his jacket. He was too late and the Silky made it out and jumped to the floor. The hackles raised on the dog's neck as it stood stiff legged, tiny teeth bared, growling at the head like a mad bumble bee.

Wart reached forward to retrieve the dog, but Pookie nipped sideways at his fingers and side-jumped away to disappear under the nearest counter. Wart was about to go after him when Tommy interrupted.

"Leave him be. He'll come back when we put the head away."

Wart figured that was probably true, so he picked the head up again and held it on his knees chin tilted upward facing him. He touched the hair and it felt stiff and unreal under his fingers like the hair on one of Angie's dolls. Wart's own hair seemed to be trying its best to rise up again. The sewn eyes were puffed out almost even with the bridge of the small flattened nose. He touched the skin on the cheeks with his fingertips tentatively then let the back of his hand trail down over the lips. The skin felt cold and brittle as though he might be able to stick a finger right through it. A shiver traveled up his spine. He ran a hand along a cheek, up across the nose. Finally he looked up at Tommy and asked him. "Isn't it the most awesome thing you ever saw?"

Instead of Tommy's answer, he heard the sound of heavy footsteps tromping down the aisle toward them. Tommy glanced at him and shoved the glass door back in place. Wart jolted into action. He put the head inside his jacket and zipped it up. He leaned forward to cover the new lump under his jacket just as the clerk arrived. The man reopened the case, replaced what he'd taken out earlier, closed it and snapped the padlock. Wart could feel his body tighten all over. He wanted to squeeze his eyes shut, to make it all disappear, but didn't dare. Without seeming to notice them, the clerk stood and Wart heard his footsteps receding up the aisle.

Wart could feel his chest heaving from fear. Now he couldn't put the head back inside the case. He glanced toward the older boy who sat there on his knees kind of wilted looking. But then Tommy sat up straighter and a crooked smile came over his face.

"Hey! Let's take him home. It'll make Angie pee her panties."

That was probably the worst idea Wart had ever heard and a dread overcame him that made him want to get up and run for all he was worth. He couldn't believe his cousin would come up with such a dumb idea. "They put you in jail for stealing."

"They don't put little kids in jail. You take it, you're just a little kid. If you get caught, they'll just talk to your mom and she ain't even here from Spokane 'til next week."

"No way. And how'd we get it to the car anyway?"

Tommy clocked his head to the side. "Yeah . . . Mom would catch on in a second. She'd ground us both until we're old enough to go in the army. Ya gotta ditch it."

Wart nodded and started to pull the zipper of his coat open so he could take the head out, but halfway down something stopped it. He pulled the front of his jacket open so he could look down into it and saw that one of the strings that held an eye shut had caught in the zipper. In panic, he jerked at it hoping the string would let go. Instead the zipper tugged the string through the holes in the eyelid in one easy movement like a snake slithering through wet grass. He started to cry out, but caught himself. Tommy shook his head as if to say, 'Dumb little kid. You should'a known better.'

Wart grabbed up the head and set it down beside the glass case. He started to get up, but thought better of it and dropped back down until his belly brushed the floor. With both hands he pushed the head backward along the side of the case toward the rear. That way it couldn't be seen by anyone unless they stooped over and looked in at exactly the right spot. It bumped along the floor on the stump of the neck and as it did the newly unstitched eye lid began to raise. There was something inside . . . deep back in the open black socket. He froze, his blood pounded in his ears, scared to death of what it would be. Too frightened to get up and run. Something grabbed his wrist and he yelped.

A white-faced Tommy was trying to drag him to his feet. Wart scrambled up and they took off. The two reached the front of the store just as a clerk handed Tommy's mom change. They stood gasping for breath as she stowed it in her purse. If she noticed their discomfort she didn't show it. Just as Wart opened his mouth to tell her they wanted to leave, a plaintive yip sounded from the back of the store. In the scramble, they'd forgotten the dog. Wart was heading toward the aisle to go back to retrieve it when he saw the man in the plaid pants coming toward them carrying Pookie by the scruff of the neck. When the clerk reached his aunt Clara, he demanded. "Is this your dog?"

To Wart's surprise she didn't act the least bit frightened of the man. "Yes it is and I'll thank you not to hold it that way."

"No dogs allowed."

"Give him to my nephew."

"You'll have to take it right outside."

"You are being cruel to an animal and that is not acceptable. Now give that dog to my nephew." She pointed toward Wart.

Somehow his aunt had turned the whole thing around on the guy and Wart discovered a new admiration for her. She must be pretty smart to do that. Then a low ominous growl rumbled deep within the little dog as it hung at the end of the store clerk's outstretched arm. Wart had never heard Pookie do anything but yip and whine or make its mad bumble bee sound. Surprises were coming fast.

A startled look crossed the clerk's face and he plopped the dog into Wart's stretched arms, gave them a last scowl, and retreated back down the aisle. Wart could hear him muttering to himself as he went. Tommy broke the silence. "Can we get ice cream now?"

"D' you think your folks like you very much?" The two cousins sat side by side on the narrow bed in Tommy's room. Tommy's question didn't set Wart off. Not one bit. His cousin said a lot of dumb stuff like that and he'd toughened up to it.

"Yup." Wart knew for sure that his mom and dad liked him plenty. They'd be driving over from Spokane in six more days. He felt proud that he'd come ahead of them by himself on the Boeing 727. He knew he didn't have to miss them if they were coming that soon, yet he never went to sleep easily at night without knowing his mom was nearby. He missed his dad, too. He had a lot of new stuff to tell him.

Right after dinner Aunt Clara had urged them to, 'Run along upstairs and play quietly.' That was exactly where the boys had planned to be anyway and quietly would be a big part of the plan. They took to his aunt's request so eagerly that they'd been yelled at for running up the stairs.

His first two nights there, Wart had slept here in the same room as Tommy but the two had talked and giggled until his aunt had come to quiet them three times the first night and four the second. Starting tonight and from now on until his folks came to take it over, he'd be sleeping in the huge double bed in the guest room. It was a big high-ceilinged room that seemed empty even when he was in it. All the more reason to wish his folks would hurry up and get there.

"If they like you, how could they give you a name like Reginald anyway? Thomas is lots better. Maybe they just didn't like you when you were born. New babies are really, really ugly. I saw Mary Beth Hayslip when she was just a couple of hours old, and I almost puked. Face all red an' screwed up. Looked like she was mad as hell to be born. Now she's four and a real brat. She's growin' up to act just like Angie but she ain't so bad lookin' any more. I don't blame you for wanting to be called Wart though."

"Thanks." He gave Tommy a quick thumbs up. Tommy gave it back. It had become sort of a secret sign between them. Wart watched the other boy scoot off the bed and flop down on his stomach on the floor to work himself under the bed until only his legs stuck out. Then he wiggled his way backwards until he could sit up again and pulled out a tan colored shoebox that he picked up and put on top of the covers.

They'd been through the ritual each night since Wart had come and he knew the routine. He tugged down an upper corner of the covers to reveal a large triangle of white sheet. Tommy sat back down on the bed beside him and took the lid off. Wart saw him take out the plastic dropper saved from an empty nose drops bottle. Next came some of the bigger needles from his Aunt Clara's sewing basket stuck in a piece of cork. Then the empty vitamin C bottle now filled part way with alcohol from the family medicine cabinet and a big wad of cotton.

The precious supply of ink lay sticky in the bottom of a small metal aspirin box, the kind you had to pinch the corner of to open. Tommy had said regular ink was too thin and had made it from ballpoint pens. He'd taken out the cartridges and pinched them with pliers to force drops of the heavier ink out of the open ends.

Some of the pens had been blue and others black so the ink had an odd midnight color that Wart liked because it looked like the real tatoos he'd seen.

The two worked quickly spreading wax paper and an old towel over the exposed sheet to protect it from any spilled ink. Once that was done they could flip the covers back in place to hide things in an instant if they heard a grown-up coming up the stairs. They lined the contents of the box up in order of use, starting with the cotton, next the alcohol and the needles.

Tommy'd told him not to worry about Angie butting in and he didn't. The one truce between the two was that one of them would never barge into the other's room. Ever. He could hear Angie in her own room playing *I Can't See Nobody* from her new Bee Gee's album. The name of the song reminded him of the episode with the shrunken head and a sudden shiver trembled in the space between his shoulder blades.

He watched as Tommy pinched open the aspirin box and carefully used the nose dropper to suck in ink about a quarter of the way. After the night's work they'd rinse it first with water and then a little alcohol, to clean and sterilize it for tomorrow night. Tommy'd said the kid who worked at the gas station three blocks down and had told him, 'Or you could get an infection that will kill you.' The kid had taught Tommy all he knew about tattooing yourself and had himself learned it in reform school. Wart wished they could both finish tonight, but things had taken so much time up to this point he figured they'd be lucky if they finished by the time his folks came.

Wart pulled his tee shirt off over the top of his head and lay it on the bed next to himself so he could be put it back on in a hurry if he needed to. Tommy had his shirt off too and made a muscle as he held his left arm up so that Wart could see his work from the evenings before. They had intentionally tattooed the last letter of their names first, working away from the elbow up the inside of their upper arms. Tommy had pointed out that, if they did it the other way, they might run out of space at the elbow and make a mess out of it. In letters a half-inch high Wart saw the 'Y,' one 'M' and the second 'M' short one leg. Though they expected it for a few days, the skin around the needle marks was puffy and red and that made the letters indistinct.

"What do ya' think."

"Cool." Wart curled his own left arm to show off from the elbow working up, a whole 'T,' an 'R' that still looked like a 'P' because it didn't have the front leg on it yet, and an 'A' without the cross bar. Tonight he would finish the 'A' and the 'R' and tomorrow night start the 'W.'

"Ain't ya glad you're not doing 'Reginald'." Both of them laughed but Wart knew he wouldn't do Reginald for any reason. It was an old-fashioned old man's name and as soon as he was old enough he intended to change it. Get an alias like in the cop movies. Or maybe he'd just stick with Wart.

He waited as Tommy tore off a piece of the cotton then took one for himself. Tommy held his cotton over the open aspirin bottle and tipped it upside down. A prickly alcohol smell came into the air and he held his breath for a moment for it to spread out into the air and go away. Tommy held out the bottle and he took it. Both boys swabbed the inside of their arms like the doctor did before he gave you a shot. Wart's began to hurt at the letter 'T,' but he choked back the urge to press on it to stop the sting. He thought again for a second about the shrunken heads and decided he'd been called scaredy-cat enough for one day. "Which ones are you gonna' work on tonight?"

"Finish the 'M' maybe. And work on the 'O.' Circles are the toughest. Your lucky you don't have to do one. Betcha couldn't. What are you gonna do?'

"The 'R' is part circle and I'm gonna do the rest of it first."
The trick was to work a little bit on a letter then move to
another. That way one spot didn't get too sore. The two lay down
next to each other on their bellies and went to work.

Wart took a sewing needle, swished it in the alcohol bottle and
put the point of it up against his skin where he wanted to start the
front leg of the 'R.' He held the point of the needle in place while
he got up his nerve, reminding himself not to close his eyes. He'd
closed them a couple of times on the first night just as he was about
to poke himself and jumped when the hurt came. He'd ended up
jabbing a lot harder with the needle than he'd intended. It not only
gave him a sudden jolt of pain that made him yell, but Tommy
bawled him out because his mom might come upstairs if she heard
him. It also made him start to bleed too much and you couldn't
work the ink in under the skin if your blood was pushing it back
out. Much better if you looked right at what you were doing then
you knew exactly when it was going to hurt and you could be ready
for it. He hated the pain, but sometimes you had to put up with it
if there was something you wanted to do badly enough. He remembered that his dad said that pain was okay if you knew where it
came from and if it wasn't serious enough to really hurt you.

With what he'd done so far, he guessed he'd learned that the
skin on the inside of his arm could hurt more than almost any
place else on his body. He could feel his body tensing to flinch,
but knew he could hold onto himself. During the day he'd stuck
his chest out whenever he thought about how he'd learned to
take it just as good as his older cousin. He got the greatest feeling
when he walked around knowing that in a few more days his
name, the one he claimed as his own, would be tattooed on him
forever and nobody could take it away.

He wondered for the hundredth time if his mom would ever
notice and told himself with certainty again that she wouldn't.

After all, he'd been taking his baths by himself since his sixth birthday and it was no big deal to keep your arm close to your side while your shirt was off. If he could just keep it secret for a long time, maybe even a year, she probably wouldn't punish him for it even if she did find out. He could claim then he'd done it when he was little before he knew any better. Things like that usually worked. He'd bet his Aunt Clara would get right after Tommy if she found his, no matter how long he hid it. Wart felt lucky to have a mom like his. She'd know it was important to him and wouldn't beat his ears off for it. Just the same, he'd be careful not to let her see it until he'd grown up and was in high school.

He held the needle almost level with his skin and pushed it in ever so slowly, just far enough that he could see the point of it under his skin and just the first hint of blood. A sharp twinge came with it, but he clamped his teeth together and used all his control to keep himself from moving. He let the needle slip out and gave a sigh of relief. He glanced over and Tommy had already made a hole and now held the tip of the ink dropper against it. He squeezed the black rubbery bulb at the end of it just a bit. A drop didn't exactly come out, the ink just sort of oozed out to mingle with his blood. Tommy wiped at it with the cotton in the direction of the needle prick to prod the mixture under his skin and to take away the extra ink. The action left a dark smudge. Then he looked toward Wart. "I seen Fusty Wiggens starkers."

"You already told me that about fifty-three hundred times."

"I was upstairs at her house waiting for her to come out of the bathroom so I could go in and take a leak."

Wart rolled his eyes. There he goes again, but he didn't say anymore about it. He figured that his cousin needed a diversion to keep his own mind off the hurt. The more Tommy bragged about himself the less he'd try to find some reason to gripe at him.

"She'd just took her bath and came out to cross the hall to her room to put her clothes on. She must've thought no one else was upstairs because she didn't even bother to wrap up in a towel.

"She seen me standin' there and yelped like a stepped-on cat. And she jumped back inside the bathroom and locked the door. She wouldn't come out and I had to go out and pee in the bushes in her back yard."

"Maybe Fustie watched you pee, out of her window." Tommy elbowed him in the ribs just about the second he was going to stick himself again. Wart sensed it coming and jerked the needle back just in time.

"Her room's on the other side of the house. Anyway, girls don't do things like that."

Wart didn't know whether they did or didn't because he didn't have a sister and that wasn't the kind of question you asked your folks. Sometimes he did wish there was another kid in his family. Tommy and Angie fought a lot, though Wart liked Angie well enough and she was always nice to him. Maybe a little brother would be better. He could teach a brother how to grow up like he had. Somehow he didn't think he could do that with a sister. Or maybe he didn't need a brother or a sister if his dad would let him get a dog instead.

Wart had just made his sixth puncture, put the ink into it and was proud to see that the 'R' was beginning to look like it should, when a scratching came at the closed bedroom door. Tommy swore as he put his needle down and rolled off the bed.

Tommy hated Pookie. Wart had seen him stick a finger down his own throat and call it 'Pukey' just to get his big sister's goat. At the dinner table, Tommy'd told her that the high school kid two doors down that she had a crush on said it wouldn't fill up a hot dog bun and Angie called him an ugly toad that no girl would ever kiss and his aunt and uncle had made them sit through the rest of the meal without talking. That made Wart uncomfortable and he'd sat in silence himself. He didn't think his folks would ever make him do that.

Tommy opened the door and reached down. Wart saw him come back up holding the little dog by the scruff of the neck just like the guy at the curiosity shop. "Hey Angie, come and get your pet rat away from my door or I'm gonna' stick him in the toilet."

To Wart's surprise the usually submissive little creature let out a low-pitched rowl, like it had that afternoon in the shop. Tommy let go of the dog and Wart heard it plunk to the floor and scurry away. Another door opened down the hall. "Tommy you bring that dog to me, or I'm going to tell Mom you're hurting him again."

"The little sissy mutt ran off. Get 'im yourself."

Wart knew the battle had started and there wouldn't be any more tattooing tonight. He snatched up the needles, ink, alcohol, and cotton as fast as he could and plunked them into the shoe box just in case. Tommy and Angie kept on shouting at each other, back-and-forth. He was just slipping his shirt back on when he heard his aunt calling up the stairwell.

"Thomas, speak nicely to your sister. Don't make me come up there." There were a few quiet seconds and Wart thought he knew what was coming next. It did. "Thomas, it's getting late and you're becoming irritable. Ask Reginald to go to his room and get ready for bed. I'll come and tuck you in." There was another moment of silence, then she added, "And both of you don't forget to brush your teeth."

Aunt Clara pushed the covers down around Wart and pecked a dry cool kiss on his forehead. It wasn't anything like his mom's. The big room with the high white ceiling and the bed twice as wide as his own reminded him of the hospital room after he'd had his tonsils out and, like then, he felt alone and defenseless. The place inside his arm where he'd poked it with the needle burned hot. If you got blood poisoning it could kill you. That scared him, and he squeezed his eyes shut tight. No matter how sore it got he knew he didn't dare tell anyone about it. Not until the name he'd chosen for himself was there forever.

It took a long time to fall asleep and when it finally happened the dream started with a sharp odor, musty and grisly. Next rose the image of the dead mole. He'd found it in the alley behind Tommy's house when he'd gone out through the gate to bring back a baseball he should have caught but had popped up over the back fence when it hit the tip of his glove. He'd stopped in awe to look at it while Tommy hooted at him to hurry up. The animal lay in late spring grass, eyes gone from the flattened skull with little left but hardened skin covered by skimpy patches of damp fur. Its tiny digging paws looked like baby fingers. He'd turned it over with the toe of his shoe and uncovered the swarm of angry maggots writhing there.

Then something in the dream made a deep rumbling sound and he jerked his shoe back to let the dead thing flop back down and now the moles eyes were sewn shut with black cord and suddenly he was back in the curio shop and the light flickered as though made by flames. The shrunken heads had come alive on their stumpy necks. All the eyes gaped wide and wiggling things roiled in the black spaces behind them. Their rumbling turned to harsh low voices growling sounds in a language he'd never heard.

He wanted to run away. His muscles strained hard but his legs wouldn't move. He looked down to see that his feet had turned to tree roots that sunk into the ground. Fear turned him cold. He tried to shout to tell them he couldn't understand even though he knew in his real mind that this was a nightmare and that no one could ever hear him.

The voices became even louder and the dead faces began to twist furiously into one hideous mask after another as black shadows flickered in the creases and hollows of their dead skin. Icicles of horror pushed painfully into the space between his shoulder blades. His scalp tightened and the roots of his hair tingled.

The clerk in the plaid flared pants from the curio shop appeared and moved between him and the heads. The man glared down at him. "Run little boy. Run to your mother before it's too late." And as the man spoke his head became tiny like the ones in the case behind him. Wart tried to move again but feelings of helplessness locked him in place.

His consciousness squeezed through just long enough to tell him he did not want to be in this dream but he couldn't muster the control to wake himself. He felt himself shouting out to the real world, hoping someone would hear him. But even so he knew that no real sound had escaped. He tried again and again and finally heard himself cry out into the reality of the darkened bedroom as he jolted awake, drenched in sweat, frigid rags of terror still tangled with the bones of his spine. He panted short gasps in horror until he realized the dream hadn't been real. He moved his arms and legs tentatively. The twisted bed sheets held him as tightly as if they'd been tied around him. They clung against him with cold dampness. He wriggled one arm free and then the other and pulled the sheets down and away from his face and shoulders.

He lay back and tried to let the dream fade from his mind. A slit between curtains let a vertical band of light ride on the opposite wall. The light strip brightened and began to move across the wall only to dim quickly and jump back to its original place each time headlights reached the window from cars driving past on the street.

Something cracked like the snap of a dry stick and his body jerked in response. His mom had explained once that old houses made snapping noises as they cooled from the heat of the day. Even so, in this strange room it startled him and for the hundredth time he promised himself a brand-new house when he grew up. One without night noises.

He forced clenched fists to open and relax, straightened his arms and legs from cramped positions and wished he was home so he could slip into his parents bedroom. Maybe snuggle up between them for the rest of night . . . the thought didn't make him as happy as it should. Only little kids did things like that and he wasn't little any more. The house cracked again but he was ready for it now. After a few moments his heart calmed and he heard no other sound but its rhythm and the occasional night purr of passing autos.

Suddenly the room brightened. There were scuttling sounds and something landed hard on the foot of the bed. He jerked upright. The hall door had opened and Pookie stood stiff legged on top of the bedcovers. The little dog's lips curled back and it glared. It began a high-pitched snarl like the workings of a windup toy but in seconds the pitiful noise deepened into the same coarse growl that rolled deep within the tiny animal earlier that day at the curio shop. The same low rumbling as in his dream.

Wart considered the odd behavior for a couple of seconds and then remembered the times he'd spent with the animal that day. They were pals. The dog liked him, something else had scared him. Maybe little dogs can be afraid of the dark too. So he reached forward to take Pookie, to scratch him behind the ears, to calm him down. But before his fingers touched fur the animal launched itself silently toward his face.

In the morning, when Tommy looked over at the circular clock mounted in the side of the shiny chromed horse on the table beside his bed, he realized he'd awakened earlier than usual. He always did whenever he had a special reason to look forward to the day. It always happened on Christmas morning and his birthday. Today his mom had promised to take Wart and him to the petting zoo at Woodland Park. He caught the smell of something baking and pulled the covers back to slide his feet out onto the floor. He liked having a cousin visit. His mom cooked things she wouldn't when they were alone. He couldn't understand why she always talked about how much it meant that they were a family and then seemed to treat other people best. He checked his tattooing from the night before. One more leg on the 'M' and 'TO' to go. If it wasn't for that stupid dog he and Angie wouldn't have fought and his mom wouldn't have butted in. At this rate it would take another week to finish. There were some spaces between dots of ink that needed filling in. He'd try to fix some of that, but mostly he felt satisfied. Not many kids had the guts to do their own tattoos. He was proud of Wart too. He had guts for a little kid.

Tommy dressed in a hurry, in the same clothes he'd taken off the night before, and headed downstairs. When he passed Wart's door, he saw it was partway open though he couldn't see the bed. He was anxious for Wart to join him. Just to make sure he reached over and gave the door a single loud knock and then thumped stiff legged down the stairs so that every step was loud enough he didn't think Wart could sleep through. At the kitchen door he saw his mom leaning over the sink rinsing the last of a bowl of fresh strawberries. "G' morning."

She turned to put the bowl down beside a pan of muffins cooling on the counter top beside her. "Good morning, young man. Did you sleep well?"

He nodded with an eye on the muffins.

"I see you didn't put on the clean clothes I laid out for you. Go back upstairs and wake Reginald, if he isn't awake already after you stomped down those stairs, and tell him breakfast will be in fifteen minutes. Then go to your room and put them on."

"Mom, he doesn't like to be called Reginald. He likes Wart."

"Yes, I know dear. But Reginald is his given name and he'll get used to it. Now run along."

Tommy nodded again then thought to stick his hand out. His mom smiled and put a strawberry in it. He popped it in his mouth and tried to grin a thank you while he chewed.

"Scoot now and wipe the juice off your chin before it drips on your shirt."

He went back up the stairs, taking care to stomp each step carefully, but with less noise than before. This time he hoped to irritate his sister without having his mom get after him again.

When he got to Wart's room, he pushed the door hard the rest of the way open to startle his cousin. The knob smacked the wall and the door bounced back. He had to stop it with his hands. The covers had been thrown back and Wart wasn't in them but Pookie lay on the floor beside the bed sleeping. Tommy walked toward the dog looking around at the same time to see if Wart was hiding somewhere with the idea of jumping out to scare him. At the edge of the bed he suddenly dropped to his hands and knees, ducked his face under the edge of the bed and hollered, "Gotcha . . .." No Wart. He tried again. "Hey, if you're in the closet I'm gonna' lock you in and throw the key out the window."

He liked his own threat and giggled while he waited a few seconds to see if Wart would respond. He took a second look around the room and decided there was no place else big enough for a kid Wart's size to hide. Must be in the bathroom. He stood back up and looked down at the sleeping dog. Little shit should be awake by now. Should be running around yipping its stupid head off. He reached down with both hands to sweep it off the floor. But as soon as his hands pushed it, his muscles set hard in surprise because instead of rolling a surprised dog over on the floor he came up with it in his arms. His sister's yippie wiggly dog had become a furry stiff corpse that seemed to weigh less than half as much as it had alive. The mouth had locked in a tiny half snarl surrounded by flecks of dried foam and the eyes, lifeless and dulled by hours without moisture, stared at him accusingly. Tommy froze, unable to move as he felt panic take away his senses. Then, after what seemed like a very long time, he could hear himself screaming for his mother.

II

—[TWENTY-THREE YEARS LATER]—

BEADS OF MOISTURE RESTED ON MILLIE HELM'S perfectly formed upper lip. The flickering of more than a dozen candles made them into tiny dancing lights. Arthur leaned over her upturned face to smooth the drops away with his own lips, tasting their salt. The fragrances of her perfume and herbal shampoo mingled with the aromas of their love making and melting wax. He liked it.

The cell phone on the night stand sounded and he kissed her neck as he reached over to pick it up. With his mind on her scent, he misjudged and the backs of his fingers tumbled the instrument to the carpet. Probably another associate congratulating him on being selected to the upcoming Amazonian expedition or one of his students with questions about an assignment. Neither interested him at the moment. The phone mewled indignantly a few more times and quit. A strand of damp blond hair lay against the side of her face and he brought his hand back to brush it aside then let his fingers rest there.

As usual she'd become modest after the fact and pulled the sheet up beneath her chin. Her hands rose from under it now and she placed her fingers against his lips easing his head back until she could see into his face.

"What a delicious way to celebrate. I'm truly excited about going to the rain forest."

He brushed his lips against hers. It would be his first trip there and anticipation filled him as well, but he held it inside. "And I thought you just liked me."

She pecked at his cheek playfully. "That's certainly true. The trip will give us a chance to see if we can work out the way to bring our lives together. Don't you think?"

He felt small muscles between his shoulder blades tighten and tried to ignore them. "From the looks of things in this bedroom, I think our lives are already very much together."

He saw the smile she'd begun to make dissolve away and her tone became serious. "We've been seeing each other long enough for me to know that we'd make a great team, Arthur. We've so much in common. I love my work and the chances we have to work together. But I need children, too. And a grand old house, the older the better, to fix up and turn into a very special home for our family."

With her mention of an old house, his mind plunged away from the two of them into the dark high-ceilinged room of an old house. He didn't know where. He heard the rafters in the frameworks above him groan and crack as they contracted with the chill of night. Needles of panic stabbed wildly in his gut. He had no idea why and it took the force of will power to drive the fear away and to bring himself back into the room with Millie. Her expression became quizzical and he felt heat rising in his face. He couldn't explain what had just happened to him and tried to cover with the first words that would come.

"I couldn't live in an old place. Couldn't it be new? We'd have it designed and built just for us."

Now her smile flashed back. "Fine with me. Shall we break the news?"

He wanted to say something. To make it okay. But he couldn't find it in himself to do that. Not yet. The realization made his throat constrict and his voice refuse to work. He watched helplessly as her expression turned into hurt before she spoke again.

"We've kept things secret until now. Faculty members don't flaunt a relationship unless they mean to make it permanent or they run the risk of messing up their careers. But when we're on the expedition, there will still be time for us. We can be discrete. And we'll be seeing each other under all kinds of circumstances. Arthur, I'm not getting any younger. I need to know where my life is going and before I can make the right decisions, I need to know what you want."

There was nothing for him to do but nod. She had the right to some answers. He simply couldn't bring himself to give her the ones she wanted. But he couldn't picture her gone from his life either. He fixed his sight on his left hand while trying to sort out his thoughts and began turning his gold signet ring round and round on the ring finger.

She reached for his hand and pulled it to her. "I've seen you twist this ring for minutes at a time. What does it mean to you?"

He raised the emblem side to see it in the muted light. The worn Latin motto circling the rim of the oval face had become difficult to read. The smooth shiny center lacked adornment. It didn't recall pleasant memories, but he always wore it anyway. He welcomed the change of subject.

"I suppose you'd call it a graduation ring."

She creased her forehead as she tried to read. "*Corpus*, and what's the next word? Letter's worn smooth. After that *Spiritus*, and more I can't read. What does it say?

"It translates to *body, mind and spirit as one*. It's the motto of the boarding school where I was raised."

Her eyes expressed question. "My brilliant professor raised in a boarding school?"

"As far back as I can remember."

He hoped she wasn't going to drag him through the whole story and felt himself relaxing when she went back to the ring. "Why isn't there something on the face of it?"

"The Brothers at the school gave each new boy a plain ring like this one. They sort of guessed what our adult size would be and we wound adhesive tape around the back of the bands to make them fit. I think they wanted to give us a symbol of something to grow into. Just before graduation you could have the school name and year added to the face. I couldn't afford it. Most of the boys' parents picked up the cost."

"And yours didn't?"

"I don't have any."

"Everyone has parents. Don't you remember yours?"

"They abandoned me it seems." The admission brought the familiar black feeling of hollowness back.

"You don't remember them."

"I have a dream sometimes. Of being locked in the basement of an old house, but there aren't any parents in it." After this conversation, he could well have the dream again tonight.

Millie snuggled against him. "You tell me you 'suppose' it's a graduation ring? And for the first time you let it out that you're orphaned, more casually than someone might announce that the faculty lounge is low on tea. I've never met a man with so many deep secrets? It's a little scary."

She looked at him with a hint of reproach while he tried to put a reply together, one that wouldn't lead to more questions. She went on. "How many times have we made love?"

He looked into her face trying to figure out where she was going with the question. "A couple of dozen maybe."

She'd let her head sink back into the pillow and began a smile, but it had an odd I-told-you-so quality about it. "Thirty-one times on twenty-two occasions. Twelve sessions here at your place, nine at mine and one when we came way too close to getting caught after closing in the archives."

He grinned at the memory. That night they'd initiated themselves into the 'Sin Devils.' He'd never have suggested the idea, but she'd teased him into it. The name was a play on 'Sun Devil,' the name of the mascot of Arizona State University, where they were both faculty. It stood for the campus version of the mile high club with the library taking the place of the airliner lavatory. The night watchman had come close to catching them in the act. They had to grab up armfuls of clothing to run ducking and dodging behind rows of bookshelves, playing a naked game of hide-and-seek with the probing beam of his flashlight.

Millie poked him in the side with a finger. She was grinning too. "I'm amazed that you don't remember precisely. I memorized them because I thought you would. Did you know your students call you, Doctor Detail. You remember more minutia than anyone I've ever known. I think a big part of the reason you like me is because I can keep up with you."

"You certainly keep up very well with what we do in this room. And in the library. Or is 'keep up' the term?"

"It'll do nicely. Thank you." She raised her head and nipped at one of his fingers. "But I'm not letting you change the subject this time. You don't need to be self-conscious about your childhood.

"We'd make a great team, Arthur, and we would make a great family. No boarding schools for our kids. But I'm thirty-two. It's time for me to get a move on." She looked at him now, obviously hopeful, then quickly her face turned solemn. "I get it. That's why you always dodge the question when I've asked how old you are . . . and why its never been mentioned that you're the youngest to hold a full chair in the department even though it's seems so obvious that it must be true. You don't know when you were born, do you?"

"Some time in the early 1970's."

"If you didn't know your parents, how did you get into the boarding school?"

"My parents must have left me in a neighborhood at night. Cops found me wandering around in pretty bad shape and after a few weeks in the hospital dropped me off at the school while they kept trying to locate my folks. They never did, of course, and after a while, someone decided I was bright enough and they let me stay.

"It cost a lot of money to send someone to that boarding school. So just to provide a broader social background for the rich kids, they gave a few scholarships. Everyone knew who had them and the rich kids called them 'Cratchets' after the characters in Dickens *Christmas Carol*. It wasn't meant to be a compliment.

"The rich kids were called 'spoonies,' for the 'born with a silver spoon in the mouth,' adage. But I wasn't a 'spoonie' or a 'Cratchet.' I was at the bottom of the pecking order and no one let me forget that. I had my own name. They called me, 'the stray'."

The black hollow feeling came back and it made him afraid for her. He sensed he could never be what she needed him to be, could never keep her safe from his own torment. She deserved better. Much better. She must have read something of the turmoil in his mind for her voice suddenly became very gentle.

"Kids can be mean as hell, sometimes." She had the beginnings of tears in her eyes.

"But when you're a kid, you don't know that's all it is. I hid in the library when I wasn't working my way in the kitchen. They put me in sixth grade because that was the lowest they had. It was way over my head.

"I remember lying in my bed after lights-out, shivering and praying that God would help me keep up. I thought if I couldn't, they'd turn me back out in the street, and I'd be lost forever."

"So you took to books . . . plus you've probably always thought that if you didn't study like hell . . . .."

He saw two big tears rolling down her cheek now and took it to mean he'd overdone the sad story. He'd had enough of it himself. "Something like that. But let's not forget this is supposed to be a celebration of us both being appointed to the *Perra* dig."

"And what do you call what we just did?"

"How about thirty-two going for forty." He tugged the sheet out of her hand and pulled it away. There lay that perfect body. Blond on both ends. Probably the best woman he'd ever find. But he needed something for himself before he could commit to someone like her and he was afraid he would never find it.

She turned into him and raised a thigh along his flank. "I thought you weren't counting."

"Do you want to know how many strokes?"

As his mouth began closing over hers, she interrupted him. "No. Dammit . . . I don't." It came out muffled.

⁂

The day of the first meeting in preparation for the Peru expedition had come and Arthur strode with brisk anticipation across the Arizona State University grounds a few minutes before the appointed time. This first gathering would be on campus, to give families and the public an overview of the trip and information that would help them while their loved ones were away. Forays into the jungle always held danger, no matter how well planned or how experienced the staff. It was only fair that everyone knew what to expect and the precautions that would be taken.

The second meeting following this one would be strictly 'informal' and the location hadn't been announced. He did know it would be held off campus, because policy held that on-campus meetings wouldn't exclude the press or visitors who might be disruptive. He quickened his pace as he neared the anthropology building wondering why confidentiality had been deemed an issue.

The low salmon-colored structure had wings jutting out on each side of a taller pillared entrance giving him the impression of a boxy version of the sphinx teasing orange trees between its paws. As at most U.S. universities archaeology was sequestered within anthropology, anthro being the broader science including living humans and archaeology dedicated to the study of the past. The building wasn't nearly as impressive as many on campus.

On this sunny Saturday morning most of the people he saw were on the way to the same meeting. Janet Benedetti, another faculty member named to the trip, approached from the opposite direction and stopped to wait where the walk branched in toward the building. She offered a laconic wave, not bothering to raise her hand above her waist. An M.D. in her early fifties with a brace of Ph.D.'s in pathology and archaeology, Benedetti was likely the most highly qualified member of the team. Her foremost academic interest was diseases of ancient people as they could be identified and analyzed through remains, but her knowledge and experience were boundless. As he neared she opened the conversation. "Arthur. Glad to see you with us."

"Morning, Jan. Thanks. You too. Along with your real work you'll be keeping us all healthy, I hope."

Her lips pulled back over her teeth in a smile that always looked to him as though it caused her physical pain. He'd decided shortly after their first meeting that her smiles were more genuine because of it.

"Just follow the surgeon general's rules for jungle living. Eat a balanced diet. Get plenty of rest and exercise. Don't pet strange reptiles."

"I promise." He saw that her graying page boy lay so evenly cut across the bottom it could have been sliced with a microtome. It moved with each step she took but always fell back perfectly into position. He felt certain she'd been the deciding vote in the staff selections. Owen Lansing, the expedition chief, had been brought in from outside specifically for the job. He'd met with all the candidates but it only made sense for someone who had worked side by side with them to take part in the process. He trusted her completely. You could learn from Jan Benedetti just by breathing the same air.

Once inside the main door they took the stairway to the right and entered one of the second floor teaching labs with rows of tables and chairs facing the blackboard. A life-size model of a human skeleton, attesting to the usual subjects taught there, hung from a chrome rack a few feet inside the entry door. A girl and a boy, he guessed to be somewhere in the primary grades, stood looking at it in awe as their mother tried to explain it to them. Arthur tried to picture Millie in that role and it fitted her like a well-tailored suit. He tried to picture himself as the father. He couldn't.

A few feet away Lansing stood shaking hands with each newcomer. He greeted Benedetti warmly, then turned to Arthur, "Welcome aboard, Arthur. Glad to have you with us."

"Thank you for the chance, Dr. Lansing. I'm truly excited about it."

"It's a great opportunity for each of us and for the University."

Arthur agreed with Lansing. ASU had little history in South America and investigations there would add a new spectrum of possibilities for both staff and their research and academic programs. Voices behind him announced more arrivals for Lansing to greet and Arthur nodded his agreement as the two shook hands. Arthur moved on.

Lansing must have anticipated a crowd for the regular rows of chairs and tables had been supplemented with folding chairs in every available space. It added to Arthur's sense of anticipation. The room filled quickly and buzzed with animated conversations. Millie stood by a table in the second row. Her honey-blond hair had been pulled back to hang below her shoulders. She wore a simple gray business suit that somehow seemed both elegant and practical. She had dressed perfectly for the occasion and hadn't given up a trace of her femininity or beauty in the process. It made his heart skip. She deserved the best and she deserved to be cared for and safe. For a moment he longed to be the man who could give her those things.

She noticed him looking, offered a smile that only made his longing worse, and patted the back of the empty chair next to the one she'd selected for herself. He began to move that way but heard Benedetti's voice calling from behind.

"Arthur these are heavier than I thought. May I have your help for a moment?"

He turned to see her standing near the door holding a tall stack of thick manila envelopes and moved quickly to relieve her of the top half of the pile.

"Thank you. I intended to be here early enough to hand these out to each team member as they arrived. Would you mind helping me pass them out now?"

While Benedetti took the front tables, Arthur started at the rear of the room. When he finished and turned to walk back to the chair Millie had offered, he found it occupied by a smiling and effusive Timothy Fields.

He knew little about Fields, one of two graduate students to accompany the team. The assignment sheets for the expedition announced that he'd be in charge of most everything that had to do with communications or electronics. He'd oversee the ground penetrating radar that would use radio waves to locate buried artifacts or grave sites and you'd go to him if a computer acted up. Beyond that, faculty gossip had it he'd been a Navy SEAL. Fields never confirmed that fact but also took care not to deny it. The times that Arthur had been in the same room with Fields he'd put out an ex-military macho that made Arthur doubt they might ever be good friends.

As far as Arthur knew, he'd had little encouragement from Millie, but seemed to hang around her every chance he got. Fields was not only interested in her but also self-satisfied that he was getting his point across. This was as apparent to Arthur at that moment as the other man's thick neck and overly broad shoulders.

Millie saw Arthur looking and shrugged a what-could-I-do-about-it. Begrudgingly he had to admit she had a point. And back in some corner of his mind he wanted the freedom of not sitting with her this morning. The fact that the expedition was slated to determine their future seemed to be pulling him down. If they ended up together he was afraid for her and the worst of it was that he didn't know what to fear. He only knew that if something bad happened to her, it would be his doing.

He took a seat near the rear and leafed through one of Benedetti's manila envelopes to find ticketing information to be facilitated by departmental support staff, lists of personal items and equipment to take, weight limits for personal gear, a list of the shots that would be required and the malaria medication that they'd need to begin two weeks before departure. Last was a set of optional insurance forms in case you came down with something anyway. With only three weeks to go to end of the summer term and the departure for South America the following week, he was going to be busy.

The room quieted and he looked up to see Lansing poised behind a small lectern. Lansing began by reminding everyone to turn off pagers and telephones, then welcomed them and introduced himself. Arthur heard him say that his Ph.D. had been granted at Michigan and he'd also attended Harvard and Penn. State. Excellent credentials indeed. Lansing cited his specialty as social theory. What he left out, but what Arthur recognized as something everybody knew, was that he'd spent nearly the entirety of his post-doctorate career in the private sector. Academics were sometimes skeptical of scientists whom they considered to have sold themselves for profit. What he'd been doing for them hadn't gotten around yet and apparently Lansing wouldn't tell them today. Scuttlebutt had it that he'd made quite a good reputation for himself and had headed several successful field studies in the Amazon rain forests.

Evidently he'd enjoyed some success as the suit he wore cost several hundred dollars more than any Arthur had seen faculty wear. From his impeccable dress and classic demeanor Arthur concluded that Lansing would go by the book and was probably a stickler for detail. Arthur could respect him for these things. They had them in common.

Starting at the back of the room, Lansing added to Arthur's positive impression of the man by introducing each team member and citing from memory both their professional specialties and the unrelated duties each would assume at the site. On a dig everyone pitched in to do anything required of them. A prized colleague would be one who could not only clean and prep artifacts but might also be a good cook. Arthur was the second to be introduced. He nodded acknowledgment when Lansing noted that he would serve as the research photographer for the expedition in addition to his work with ceramics. Lansing kept his explanations straightforward and simple for the nonprofessionals and children.

Lansing also introduced the pair of young women, who jotted ceaselessly on steno pads, as student reporters from the ASU *Insight*, the campus newspaper and a slender, intense-looking man from *The Arizona Republic* who sat near them. He acknowledged the names and titles of the representatives from various offices in university administration. The expedition seemed to be under scrutiny. It raised Arthur's curiosity and made him uneasy at the same time. Lansing gave the appearance of being totally unperturbed, though he did glance toward the reporters frequently and seemed to address many of his remarks as though he was speaking to them personally. It was something that had to be done to win them over. He was grateful he didn't have those responsibilities. He much preferred working with hard evidence and finding fact supported by proof.

As he'd expected, Jan Benedetti was designated as principal scientist for the trip along with an impressive list of other duties. That likely meant she would also head the several years of research to follow if the on-site field work revealed as much as they hoped. Arthur thought he saw looks of relief on the faces of some observers when they learned a physician would be present. He let his eyes stray to Millie. Tim Fields had tilted himself sideways until their shoulders touched and seemed to be holding her attention with an animated commentary even as Lansing spoke.

He got another surprise when it came to Millie's turn to be introduced. Lansing called her name and asked her to stand.

"In addition, Dr. Holtz will assist Dr. Benedetti and myself as the principle liaison with the university and the private parties who will provide the vast majority of the funding for our work."

Millie acknowledged the announcement demurely while Fields beamed at her from his seat. It seemed everyone wanted Millie. And he was the only one who didn't know what to do about it. He'd ask her later why she hadn't mentioned the special assignment to him. She certainly must have know about it for some time and she always shared what was going on in her life. He didn't know why she'd held back and that made an uneasiness take up residence in the deepest part of his stomach.

The expedition director paused to sip from a glass of water before he continued. "Now that we've all been introduced. I'd like to tell you a bit about where we're going and what we hope to accomplish. Afterwards there will be plenty of time for questions. I promise you that no question is too unimportant to be asked and no one here is too young to ask it."

Arthur had to give him credit. He'd just won the spouses and kids. Lansing keyed a remote and a screen rolled down at the front of the room while someone dimmed the lights to put them into semidarkness. He hit another button and a ceiling-mounted projector flashed a slide map of South America onto the screen. Lansing clicked on a laser pointer to touch on the blue pattern of rivers that seemed like tentacles wrapping the middle of the continent.

"When most of us think about the Amazon River we think about Brazil. Yet the first 2000 miles of it, about forty-six per cent, lie within Peru. Because Peru was not popular for exploitation or development, either to the Spaniards or Portuguese, the tropical forests there are much like they were before the first Europeans came. Some areas remain unexplored."

He moved the laser pointer across the map again. "We will fly first to Lima, the capital city, and then on to Cuzco. This city was once the center of the Incan Empire. Now it is a modern city with a population of about four hundred thousand. It's also very high at 10,500 feet.

"From Cuzco we will go by land plane, then float plane, then by boat to the site we will explore on the *Rió Perra*. This river is a tributary of a series of rivers that find their way eventually into the Amazon. It isn't well known, yet it is more than a hundred miles long and in some places over a quarter of a mile wide. Six years ago a tourist discovered several bone fragments along this river. He also found shards of broken pottery and thought the bones might be human. Indeed they are."

Somewhere to Arthur's left he heard an adolescent's self-conscious giggle. A woman's voice hushed him with authority.

Lansing paused briefly but his features didn't acknowledge that the interruption had occurred. "The political unrest of the past couple of years and bureaucratic issues you'll hear about later delayed a return to investigate the site's potential. Thankfully the area we will explore is so remote as to make problems from bandits or guerillas extremely improbable, if not impossible. I have always found the people of Peru both hospitable and generous. There is no record of violence ever having been directed at Americans."

Arthur heard someone sigh relief before Lansing went on.

"Last year two Peruvian archaeologists were able to locate the site and have confirmed that it has the potential to offer significant finds. Perhaps the discovery of a culture heretofore unknown."

Lansing didn't dwell on the scientific interests of the expedition but instead changed to more practical subjects, attending to the interests of families and the media. As he continued, Arthur divided his attention between the expedition head and Millie. Fields had kept up a running commentary all though the meeting until Millie quieted him with a firm hand on his forearm. That would have eased the growing feeling of tension in his belly, if she hadn't left it there, until Fields tried to cover it with his own, before she took it away.

Finally Lansing concluded and opened the meeting to questions. A little girl Arthur guessed to be six or seven slid off her chair to stand and wave frantically. Lansing acknowledged her with a smile and her piping voice shrilled in the crowded room.

"My teacher says there's really big snakes in the jungle and they bite or squeeze you 'til you die."

Several adults in the room chuckled, but true to his word Lansing fielded her concern seriously.

"There are big snakes. One is the anaconda, the largest in the world. But it has no poison and is very shy. It spends most of the time in the water, and I think I can promise you we won't see one."

Arthur noted he didn't mention the bushmaster, a poisonous snake that he'd read may grow to eleven feet and was aggressive, but Lansing wasn't through with the topic.

"Most of the snakes aren't poisonous and many of them live high in the trees and never touch the ground. I've been in the jungle many times and never seen anyone bitten."

The little girl seemed to be doing her best to look skeptical and Lansing kept on. "Don't forget we'll be taking our own doctor along, and she will have medicine to cure snake bites. And we will also be accompanied by a good friend of mine, *Señor* Hector Felipe . . ." and Lansing raised his eyes now, speaking again to the entire group ". . . a biologist, who will serve both as a representative of the national government and to keep us safe from and in harmony with that very magnificent environment."

Now a little boy chimed in. "What about alligators?"

"There aren't crocodiles or alligators, but they do have a cousin there that's called the caiman. They eat mostly fish and shy away from people."

And now Lansing impressed Arthur once again. He'd foreseen the worries of the children and probably some of the adults too. He keyed the remote control to clear away the map and replace it with a slide of a pair of brilliantly colored red and blue Macaws.

"There are many kinds of animals in the forests . . ." and for the next several minutes he ran through a series of slides of toucans, parrots and other birds, spider, red howler and squirrel monkeys, a tree sloth, pig-like peccaries, and the tapir with its short prehensile trunk. When he finished, the children were enthralled and some of the teens and adults seemed so too. Arthur noticed he showed no reptiles and no insects except brilliantly colored butterflies. He guessed the adults would pick up on this. Arthur wondered for a second if anyone had protected him when he was a kid before his life at the boarding school.

As he drew the discussion to a close, Lansing assured everyone that they would be taking both shortwave radios and satellite telephones that could summon help in an emergency. They also had a contact in Cuzco who would pass along brief messages between family members. He stated that they were prepared to stay for up to three months, but that the actual length of stay would be determined by what they found.

To the staff he added a final comment. "In preparing yourselves for the trip, I don't want you to put limits on your research or ideas. Let's go at this as though we might expect anything from a new *Machu Picchu* to the recovery of Atlantis." The laughter that followed mention of the mythical lost continent was his cue to step away from the lectern.

Arthur stood to leave, comfortable that Lansing had put things on the right track and that he was probably capable of handling the myriad of administrative duties that would dog them. The man obviously had people skills and management qualities that those who preferred the lab and museum sometimes lacked.

He looked toward them just in time to see Timothy Fields propel Millie out the door. By the time he'd forced himself through the crowd from the rear of the room, they were not to be seen in the hallway. He could hear her laughing. It sounded as though they were already on their way down the stairwell. He'd begun to clench his jaw and to quicken his step to intercept them when a hand touched his arm. He looked to see Jan Benedetti.

"Arthur, the staff will be gathering at that coffee shop near the College Avenue entrance in about half an hour."

He'd been expecting to go to the second meeting, but had forgotten it in his concern over Millie. He wondered now if she knew where this meeting would be held and again thought to catch up to them to make sure. He felt his face getting hot and decided against it. Millie could take care of herself.

At the coffee shop Arthur picked up his drink at the counter and moved to a patio area outside to join the group. They pushed a trio of tables off to one side to make room for everyone and to separate themselves from the other patrons. He didn't see anyone missing other than Lansing and Millie with the pain-in-the-neck Timothy Fields. He knew Lansing wasn't coming so the meeting could maintain its informal status. He wished for a second that he'd gone on to catch up to Millie to make sure she knew where to come, but part of him rankled at the attention Fields seemed to be able to elicit from her and his guilt flitted away. Others must have noticed their absence too. If she were trying to turn attention away from their own relationship, she was doing a damn fine job. If she was trying to make him jealous, it was beginning to work. It would make things worse if he let his jealousy get out of hand. She might even walk away from him. The fact that their relationship seemed to get more complicated everyday brought a tension that continually added discomfort and that he couldn't understand.

The team members were exuberant, all talking in animated voices in the normally sedate coffee shop. Arthur let himself relax enough to join in the good humor with them. If the dig turned out to be promising, each individual stood to gain a great deal. Not money, but the kind of psychological income people who dedicate their lives to the less-commercial disciplines of science relish most. Several conversations carried on at the same time and more than once paper cups sloshed together in some impromptu toast. Arthur was about to propose his own salute when the beep of his cell phone demanded attention.

He opened it and turned aside for privacy. "Arthur Tomas."

Millie's voice sprang from the receiver like an angry cat's. "Arthur, where are you? I thought you'd follow us out of that meeting and rescue me."

He half expected the volume of her voice to raise the attention of the others and glanced around to make sure it hadn't. "I don't recall any cries for help." He regretted saying it before he'd finished.

"Has my shining knight fallen off his charger before the first joust?"

Her sarcasm tightened his grip on the phone and he had to force himself to make his voice sound unaffected by it. "Where are you now?"

"In the ladies' room at The Burrito Burro on Apache Drive. Tim said we'd all be gathering here."

"I don't think we could all get in the ladies' room."

"Not funny. Stop it." Her voice had an edge that would chip stone.

"We're at the coffee shop on College Ave. Too bad you can't make it."

"Smug bastard. I'll be there in three minutes." The phone went to dead air.

He had to admit that he did feel a little bit self-satisfied. He refolded the instrument to put it away and looked up happy to see no one had picked up on the fiery call.

One of the shiny metal flasks people take to football games appeared from somebody's briefcase. The owner held it up and announced, "Brandy. A toast." He poured some in his coffee and passed it around. Arthur saw that Jan Benedetti waved it aside when it came her way but she didn't give any indication that she disapproved. Arthur thought of passing on it too but he reminded himself of Field's campaign for Millie and, when it came to his turn, he helped himself.

Their brandy provider stood to raise his spiked coffee into the sunshine. "Here's to the dead. For without them none of us would be able to make a living."

He received a hearty chorus of boos laced with laughter. Benedetti's chair sat near the far end of the tables from Arthur and she rose from it now to address the group.

"Enjoy yourselves now for as you know there will be no alcohol allowed at the dig and you all know the risks of being caught with dope in a foreign country." Even though the no-booze rule was standard practice, she received her own round of booing, albeit, Arthur noted, subdued enough to reflect their respect for her.

Millie stayed true to her word. In what seemed to him like much less than the promised three minutes, she approached their tables with ardent strides. She apologized for being late as though it were a formally scheduled meeting. Then she looked at Arthur with her eyebrows raised. He smiled back trying to mollify the situation. It came to him that he was truly glad to see her and he hoped that the trip could bring them closer.

Benedetti came up with one of her own painful looking smiles. "Is Mr. Fields with you?"

"He's looking for parking." Millie's tone didn't quite veil the fact that she didn't care too much if he found a space or not.

She moved a chair across the table from Arthur and wedged it carefully between two other chairs before she sat down. He hoped she'd done that intentionally so Fields couldn't sit next to her and felt his shoulders relax. Seconds later Fields walked up and Arthur thought he recognized a very contrite expression on the man's face. Millie could do that.

As soon as the two latecomers were settled, Benedetti remained standing and cleared her throat to take charge of the gathering. "Dr. Lansing wants to be as open as possible but some things can't be handled well in the forum of a formal meeting. Particularly one attended by the media and we can't very well not invite them these days. I think you'll see why all the mystery in a moment."

She looked around the gathering to nods of assent. "We're going to be together in some very remote and close quarters and it's important we get along well as individuals and as a group." Her gaze shifted quickly from Millie to Fields and then to Arthur, himself. He wondered if she had sensed the triangle growing around them and shifted uncomfortably in his chair.

"First, let me tell you about Dr. Lansing. Though he'll never mention it himself, there are excellent reasons why he's been selected to head up the group rather than one of us from the department.

"He is one of the top two or three North Americans of archaeological eminence in Amazonian cultures. Just as important is the fact that he has the respect of the leaders in the field in South America and Peru specifically. He is also known to the government agencies that are necessary to our success. Our site is located in the Manu Biosphere Reserve and in that portion of it where the only outsiders who are permitted entry are approved scientific expeditions.

"He has fluent Spanish and is published in that language. He is also fluent in Quechua. For those of you not yet familiar with the area, Quechua was the language of the Incas, although it originated with another people long before that empire. It's spoken today by an estimated ten to thirteen million people in the Andean region of Peru and its surrounding countries. We will undoubtedly meet many of them and it may be that they will offer valuable information."

Benedetti pulled her chair forward and sat down again.

"But getting back to Doctor Lansing, we are fortunate to have so highly qualified a leader. By all indications the best there is. With luck we may get to keep him after the field work is over and the real research begins. I personally feel fortunate to have the opportunity to work with him.

Arthur had seen enough of the man to nod his agreement.

"If anyone has questions . . . any at all, I invite you to bring them to me and I promise that your confidence will be kept."

Benedetti paused to lean against the back of her chair and sip her coffee. Arthur realized that she really wanted to find out if anyone held resentments against Lansing, as an outsider. There would be sixteen professionals working in close harmony and early on was the best time to get past any problems. If they couldn't be reconciled, they could pose a serious enough threat to the journey's outcome that they might need to replace someone. The group sat silently for a few seconds and, apparently satisfied, she leaned forward to rest her arms on the table and went on.

"Despite the fact that my asking you to come here to let me provide you with a reading list has by now been recognized as a poorly-masked subterfuge, let me provide you with one nonetheless." She bent to lift her briefcase onto the table in front of her and proceeded to hand each one of them several pages stapled neatly together.

"This list is merely to be helpful. Some items were suggested by Dr. Lansing, others I've identified myself. You'll find the report from last years Peruvian site investigation included. You're all accomplished researchers and I'm sure will turn up a great deal more material. If there is something you think may be of interest to all of us, please get a copy to me."

Everything had been pretty routine as far as Arthur was concerned and just as he was wondering why they'd bothered to separate themselves from the group that attended the on-campus meeting Benedetti looked evenly around the group.

"Now I'd like to go over the story of how the site was discovered and the events that led to this expedition. I say story because some of what I have to tell you will be hearsay. Dr. Lansing told most of this to me and suggested that I pass it on to you embellishment and all. I'm not certain I can sort out all of the fiction from the fact but I shall do my best."

She'd piqued his interest and Arthur leaned forward in his chair as she began. Others did the same. Archaeologists liked a good story as well as anyone, as long as it didn't discourage the scientific truth. He knew that myth and folklore sometimes provided clues to important discoveries. Benedetti took the time to close and latch her briefcase where it lay on the table before her then proceeded.

"One of the boats taking a scheduled tour into that part of the Manu preserve called the Cultural Zone, where tourism is permitted, ran into trouble. The rivers there are quite dynamic and change depth and course with the rains. Underwater logs and obstructions are more than common. This particular boat had a mishap that damaged not only the propellor, but the drive shaft of the outboard motor. They managed to pull the boat in against a sand bar and when they tried to change to the spare motor, it apparently slipped into the water and couldn't be started after they retrieved it.

"The boat radioed home base, but as luck had it, their other boats were on tour. They hired a boat and skipper from the village at Boca Manu, a small river port where tours stop for last minute provisions and fuel. By the time that boat and a spare engine made it to our tourists they'd spent a rather uncomfortable night on the sand bar and . . .." Benedetti made a face as though trying to bring up just the right word, and several of her listeners chuckled, ". . . discontent reigned."

The group around the tables sat enthralled and Arthur concluded again what he had already known for a long time. The woman could charm an audience.

Benedetti went on. "According to Dr. Lansing's information, one traveler refused to continue on with the group and was permitted to return with the hired boat. As it turns out this gentleman is a graduate of our university and, it seems, one of those who've become very wealthy building patio homes and condos for the unceasing supply of snowbirds who flock to our Arizona weather."

Another round of nods from the group.

"Somewhere, back downstream from the sand bar where the tourist boat held up, they had passed the mouth to the *Rió Perra*. The river lies within the pristine area where tourism is not permitted. Apparently, this caught the attention of our alumnus. Perhaps just for the bragging rights. He waved dollars until he convinced the skipper of the hired boat to violate the law and take him up that river.

"According to the story, they ran up the *Rió Perra* for half a day and when nothing eventful happened our alum decided to call it quits and the boat turned back downstream, but not before they stopped on shore for a few minutes. The boats do not have bathrooms. During the process of walking out the kinks of the boat ride, he noticed something sticking out of the river bank and pulled out a rather large portion of a pot. In scratching around for more he turned up bones that he took to be human, and indeed it has been proven that they are. To end the story quickly, the traveler was caught trying to leave the country with the remains. As we all know this is a serious crime in most countries.

"But once again our wealthy alumnus was able to wave his cash wand, and by guaranteeing that he would fund a group of scientists to return and investigate was magically absolved of wrongdoing. We are that expedition."

Arthur wondered if these were the 'bureaucratic issues' Lansing had promised they would hear about. He'd assumed those would be the usual governmental red tape and delays or, at worst, petty officials looking for handouts. This seemed more ominous but he decided not to let it dampen his enthusiasm for the project. Benedetti concluded her comments.

"I'm afraid that's all we know. The benefactor, if you'd really call him that, would understandably prefer to remain anonymous. But the amount of money he is putting up is by the usual terms generous. Perhaps we can be grateful for that." She eased back in her chair. "And now you understand why this story needed to be told in an informal meeting, without onlookers." For the next few minutes she responded to questions and then the group began to drift away.

Arthur looked across at Millie who sat trying to catch his eye. She motioned for them to go and the look she gave him had embers in it. He already had a pretty good idea of what was on her mind. Their future. But they'd no sooner made the few steps to the sidewalk than the opportunity to bring it up disappeared as Fields' voice interrupted from behind.

"Millie, wait up." The bigger man placed himself between them as though Arthur wasn't there. "I'll drive you home."

"Thanks, Tim, but my car's in the university lot. Arthur's walking me there now."

Fields half-turned his head, but not far enough to make eye contact. "Hi, Dr. Tomas." Without the courtesy of waiting for a reply Fields turned back to bend and put his face closer to Millie's. "I'll call you later. We can go for dinner or something."

Her tone held no encouragement. "I'm sorry. Arthur and I already have plans."

"Yes we do." Arthur let his own voice carry a note of authority.

Then Arthur felt his fists begin to clench as Fields went on apparently oblivious to the inference of their answers. "Oh right. You two probably have a lot to talk about prepping for the trip."

Millie pulled her head back to glare at him from behind Fields' broad back, but changed her expression quickly when Fields suddenly took a couple of quick steps forward and spun to bounce along backwards and up on this toes like a boxer.

"Maybe I'll just run along then. Get three or four miles in before I hit the gym. Do the weights. Keeping in top shape is something I learned in the Navy. Never know when you might need it. Catch you tomorrow. We can do something then."

With that he turned away from them and began running with the smooth stride of the practiced athlete. Arthur let out a long slow breath. Millie closed the gap Fields left between them and lost no time letting him know what bothered her. She kept her voice low but it held a crisp edge.

"Arthur, it's time we gave up the secrecy."

"I thought we agreed to be discreet. To hold off and work things out at the dig."

"We did, but don't forget Tim will be there too. You can see he's going to be very persistent."

"Why don't you just tell him to get lost? If I weren't around he'd still be persistent. What would you do then?" He caught himself wondering if she was telling him to make up his mind or she'd take Fields in his place.

"Fields isn't the type who's going to take no for an answer. He'll never believe any woman isn't mad about him and putting him off will only raise the challenge. You could make things so much easier. Don't forget, we're all three in the same department. If we don't put the word out about the way things really are, it may come out in a way that hurts. I don't want it to be thought that I'm having an affair with Fields and involved with you at the same time."

He did understand and was about to agree when a feeling of uneasiness began to grow until it squeezed his throat as if it had bungy cord wrapped around it. He didn't understand his own panic and his agreement with her turned into confusion. Instead of answering he walked on in silence until they approached her car.

She stepped out ahead to unlock the door, climbed in and rolled down the window. "Stop and pick something up." She came up with a thin smile, but there was unmistakable hurt in her voice. "We'll cook at my place."

She had the engine running before she'd finished speaking and just as he leaned down to the window to ask what she wanted him to buy for their dinner, she slipped the transmission into reverse, turned her back to him to look out the rear window, and began backing swiftly out of the parking space. He had to take a quick step away and straighten up to keep from getting slapped by the rear view mirror.

Arthur had piled maps, books and manuscripts on the narrow desk and on the floor at his feet. Here in the lowest level of the Hayden campus library he'd created a home that should have been as familiar and gratifying to him as any he'd known. He'd been gathering material for the expedition for several hours by copying data and articles onto the hard disc of his laptop. The list Benedetti had given them turned out to be helpful. He'd found that she'd also called in a number of materials from affiliate libraries at other institutions. He skim-read as he covered each page with parallel strokes of the hand scanner. This procedure served him well. Under normal circumstances, he'd be able to recall enough that he would be able to relocate any piece of information without hesitation. Under normal circumstances.

This afternoon distraction thrust repeatedly into his concentration. Since the meeting at the coffee shop several days ago, his relationship with Millie had ranged between tepid and cool. They still spent a great deal of time together, they still made love, but they were still a secret as far as faculty were concerned. Somehow the closeness had given way to a deep underlying tension covered over by polite mutual accommodation. His own emotions ranged from relief that he was not under immediate pressure to give an ultimate answer about their future to fear that it might already be too late to rekindle the intense feelings they'd had for each other. He'd tried to force his emotions down, to cover them with his work, but today the effort failed him.

Neither had Fields given up, though Arthur still couldn't bring himself to go public just to be rid of the man. He had too many questions about himself and he needed answers. Millie'd said she didn't want to take the chance on making a mess of Fields' feelings by rejecting him flat out. They'd all be together for so long at the dig that any resentments could raise havoc. She reminded him that Benedetti had made it clear at the coffee shop that this would be unacceptable. She'd told him Fields wasn't her type but there he was anyway, the specter on the horizon, ready to step in if Arthur couldn't offer her the permanence she needed.

Millie had brought it up to him repeatedly that their being together at the dig site would give them plenty of time to work any kinks out of the relationship. She'd been plain about the fact that this meant deciding whether or not to announce their engagement and that there was no way she'd put up with a long one. She'd ended one discussion by saying, 'Now we'll see if you're sincere enough to commit yourself.' That night as he'd tried to fall asleep he'd pictured himself strapped down like the prisoner in Edgar Allen Poe's *The Pit and The Pendulum*, the heavy blade swinging closer and closer, unsure of what was reality and what a dream.

Now in the library he looked across the room to see a student sprawled in one of the overstuffed chairs, his girlfriend sitting across his lap. She wore an engagement ring and their faces were never more than a few inches apart. It was plain that they had no questions about their reality and he envied them for it. How simple it seemed to be for some.

In the solitude of the reading room he could almost feel Millie's urgency as he turned a page in the manuscript that lay open before him and adjusted the scanner. The trepidation tightened the muscles in the back of his neck. He realized there was no use trying to hold his attention on the material. He gave in and, to divert himself, began trying to imagine being married to Millie. He'd probably never find better. A hazel-eyed, honeyblond complete with freckles and a style about her that drew attention from both sexes. Dependable in every way, a brilliant colleague, and hard set on him as both husband and research partner. She was perfect in general and even more perfect for him in particular, but the picture he tried to conjure of their married bliss just wouldn't come to mind. Instead rose an image of Millie in mortal pain and a sensation that he had caused it. His body responded with a feeling so cold it turned his spine to blue steel and put beads of sweat on his forehead.

He stopped working and bent forward over the desk to let it pass. The reaction startled him. It fueled his anxiety and his gut clenched in response. He could lose her, or become trapped in a marriage that he wasn't prepared for, or worse, fail because of the inexplicable blackness inside him. People married all the time with much less common ground than he and Millie would have. He didn't really comprehend what marriage would mean to the life he would live. They would live.

Over it all, he felt inexperienced when it came to the opposite sex. He hadn't exactly spent his youth sowing wild oats. From the time he'd entered university, on a freshman scholarship, through to his Ph.D. he'd been nearly penniless and completely taken over by his studies. Until his faculty appointment, he hadn't exactly been a good candidate for most women. Too absorbed. Too bookish. Too poor with no great prospects to change that in the future. He'd never questioned the choices he'd made and never looked back but now he wondered if he didn't need to see more of what the world might offer before he committed himself. The thought brought him guilt but also a deep sexual desire that began to make him hard. He looked about self-consciously. The happy young couple had gone, leaving an airless void behind them.

He'd just forced his attention back to work when something popped out at him from the page he was scanning. It named the *Perra* River. There were fifteen hundred plus tributaries to the Amazon and any mention of that specific river was significant. He flipped back to the title page of the report. It was the journal of an expedition made seven years earlier by a group of Danish botanists and zoologists led by Frederik Holberg. Arthur returned to the page that cited the river and this time forced himself to concentrate as he read.

The Danish team had spent nearly three months successfully searching out new plant and animal species. They turned up a number of new florae ranging from trees to algae and molds. Several apparently had medical potential. The world had become acutely interested in medicinal plants. There was money to be made, and interest in these and the traditional medicines of the indigenous people had grown to the extent that both the forests and tribes were endangered because of exploitation.

The group had also discovered two new species of monkey, a new variety of tapir, several species and subspecies of birds, and numerous insects. None of these discoveries struck him as particularly unusual. Even in the twenty-first century any well directed exploration was bound to turn up previously unknown animals. The rainforests, once thought to be virtually homogeneous, were actually comprised of hundreds of individual forests that harbored more of the worlds diversity of plants and animals than all the rest of the planet's ecosystems combined. The story of the Danes' work seemed ordinary until he came to the brief mention of a disappointment.

The expedition had come to the mouth of a tributary to the *Perra* and had been inclined to follow it. He lay down the scanner to concentrate on his reading.

Head zoologist, Jensen, called out from the other boat that a number of unusual white birds came and went continually up the new river. Through his binoculars they appeared to be not only an undiscovered species, but exhibited unusual anatomical features that he could see even at that distance. Though the new river had a name on our charts, the Rio Gato, its course was not presented far beyond its mouth, which we soon saw to be well guarded from the intrusion of any but modern motor-driven craft by a wide stretch of difficult rapids.

When asked to turn our own boats into the river's mouth the native crews steadfastly refused, and it took a great deal of persistence to draw out an explanation. Insofar as we were able to comprehend, their story is as follows: The name of the river, though translating to the general term for a domestic cat in Spanish, did not refer to any of the four types of feline that inhabit the region. Instead it had been derived from a legend and the name itself is an evolved term relating to an entirely different word from one of the numerous Indian dialects of the area. In actuality it refers to the nemesis god of that legend, a panther, or more specifically, an all black jaguar. This deity is said to inhabit the banks of the Rio Gato where it searches out trespassers in the night and puts its own spirit into their minds in such a way as to forever hold them as slaves.

Though we tried to persuade our crews that we had no fear and that they too would be safe under our protection, they would not turn the boats. Hence the mystery of the strange white birds and the legendary black panther were in no way resolved.

Arthur started to close the journal to put it aside when one paragraph grabbed his attention.

All during our discourse with the boat crews, Jensen, whose personal distinction is ornithology, had continued to follow the white birds through his glasses. Later that night, far from the mouth of the forbidden river, he told me that, though what he had witnessed was too far away to be certain, he'd thought he'd seen them ending their flights high on the face of a cliff. This cliff itself appeared to him peculiar because at the top of it he noted perfectly straight lines and right angles as though they'd been hewn by man. The Incas came to mind, but that would be highly improbable, of course, because even though their empire was vast, some 4500 kilometers across in the prime of it, they were not known to have built structures in this region. I remarked that perhaps he had been entered by the legendary panther, whereby we *enjoyed one of the few hearty laughs that transcended the heat and constant swarms of insects.*

Arthur sat back in his chair, enthralled. These men had only been interested in animals and plants. The fact that they may have been on the brink of a significant new archeological discovery didn't seem to have occurred to them. If it hadn't given them such a good laugh Holberg may never have bothered to report it.

Arthur glanced at his ring and found himself working it around on its finger with the opposite hand. He grimaced and stopped. The Holberg journal with its brief mention of the straight cuts in stone that they couldn't check out because of the legend of a black jaguar had him snared. They had passed by an opportunity to discover something new. If the possibility was still there and if he could prove it, it could put him on a par with the eminent of his profession. Excitement quickened his heart. He thought about packing up his things to go look for Millie. It would be fun to cover the possibilities with her. Then he stopped. Their expedition had months ago been designed by others. There was no way to divert himself to goose chases and if he brought the idea up to her she'd think he was nuts. She'd be right. There was another feeling too. A deep worry gave him a pressing need to keep this to himself. He couldn't share it with her. Not yet.

ARTHUR SAT IN THE RIGHT-HAND SEAT
second pair back in the old DeHavilland beaver float-
plane. It bucked heavily along, teased by updrafts
rising from sun-scalded patches of barren granite scattered
through the tropical rain forest. The plane lugged five passengers
and all the gear the pilot would allow on board. Arthur tried to
ignore the suffocating smell of hot oil and played a pair of binoculars out the window to take his mind off the queasy feeling it
gave him.

The immensity of the vast jungle canopy brought a 'Wow' out
of him that evaporated into the engine noise. Rising smoke in the
distance reminded him how quickly man could destroy. Not only
the forest, the habitat and the major portion of the world's
oxygen supply it generated, but many of the vestiges of man's history were being burned or bulldozed, as well. It put the need to
safeguard the rain forests on a very personal level for him.

"The Amazon basin." Millie shouted over the engine noise.
"Seven countries. Five times the area of Alaska. Enough navigable river miles to reach twice around the planet."

He turned to look into the face of his seatmate. She had a clean, scrubbed look even in the heat. She'd repeated something they both already knew, just because it was so completely overwhelming to actually see it for the first time. He smiled and nodded. The strain between them remained and he appreciated the fact that today she seemed lighthearted and happy. The engine roar made real conversation impossible, so he pointed to his ear and mouthed the word 'later.' She nodded and began to study a map she'd unfolded on her lap. He went back to his binoculars.

They followed the *Rió Manu* now having branched away from the *Madre de Dios* river a few moments before as the pilot dead reckoned his way upstream toward the landing area below the mouth of the *Rió Perra*. These rivers followed such tortuous meandering courses, often almost doubling back on themselves, that they appeared to jump back and forth under the fuselage, first to be seen out of one side of the plane, then the other. Now the plane approached yet two more rivers joining the *Rió Manu*. They were of about equal size and the plane banked lazily toward the one on the right. It had no more than settled back into level flight when something poked his shoulder. He took the field glasses down to see that Millie had pushed the map in front of him and was pointing to a circle marked in red pen. She shook her head and raised her voice again. "Wrong river."

He took the map. After steadying it he studied it for a few seconds and gave her a thumbs up. He reached forward and tapped the pilot on the arm with the side of the folded paper. It gave him an irrational fear that if the man startled, he might jerk the wheel to throw the plane into some gut twisting maneuver. The pilot was an olive-skinned man with clipped black mustache and a baseball cap with phony gold braid on the bill. He looked back at Arthur over the tops of orange-tinted aviator glasses. Even though being heard was a problem and the pilot spoke little

English, he couldn't help shouting. "Wrong way, *Señor*. The other river." He pointed at the red marking and waggled his finger back and forth between the two crooked blue lines. The dark eyes raised and continued to look over the rim of the glasses at him for a few seconds in the same way he might've looked at a child who'd interrupted an important conversation. Finally he reached for the map. Arthur turned to see the other passengers watching as the pilot compared Millie's map to the chart on the clipboard strapped to his knee. Arthur watched with them until something caught the corner of his eye and he turned to the window and raised the binoculars to it.

It was a construction of some kind. He focused more sharply and saw distant layers of rectangular stones. The overall shape was a pyramid, sliced cleanly in half from corner to corner so that it had just three sides instead of the usual four. It sat perched on the rim of a high cliff at the river's edge, and one of the three sides was a perfect upward extension of the face of the cliff. He recalled the report of the botanist, Frederik Holberg. 'Vertical and horizontal surfaces at right angles.'

He sat fascinated and then turned to point it out to Millie, but stopped. Just as in the library, he wasn't ready to share it with her. When he looked out the window again the roar of the engine rose into the labors of the turn back toward the river branch they should have followed and the structure disappeared from view. He tapped the pilot on the shoulder and reached for Millie's map. In the bouncing aircraft it took a few seconds to make out the name. The *Rio Gato*. The Danes had seen something all right, and now so had he.

His felt blood rise to beat in his temples and he had to concentrate on sitting quietly, his thumb twisting the ring on his left hand round and round its finger until Millie poked him in the ribs to stop. Ten minutes later the plane dropped down to circle a portion of the river. A boat below them had taken up a position surprisingly close to a large open sand bar and he saw an orange dye marker spreading out in the current where it marked a safe landing zone. The plane banked steeply into the final turn and moments later the pontoons sloshed down and the plane slowed rapidly to a crawl behind the idling propeller. The engine coughed and went silent thirty yards before the pontoons nudged into the soft sand. The pilot reached across the passenger seated beside him to unlatch the safety catch and open the cabin door. He opened the door on his side and climbed out onto a pontoon to begin unloading the baggage compartment. Heavy damp river smells replaced those of the oil and Arthur welcomed them. He followed the passenger ahead of him, first putting a foot on the strut step and then down onto the pontoon itself. He was about to step ashore when Millie called after him.

"Hey, Dr. Tomas. Can you help a girl down?"

He stepped back to the door and by then she'd reversed her position to show a very shapely backside clothed in tan cargo pants.

"My legs aren't long enough."

He put a hand on each side of her narrow waist as impersonally as he could in the presence of their colleagues and eased her down until her foot found the step. When she stood on the float and had straightened herself, she grinned up at him.

"Thanks."

"My pleasure."

"I truly hope it was."

The remark caught him by surprise and he could feel his face coloring. He didn't want her to see and turned back the way he'd started before she'd asked him to help. By the time he'd walked to the nose of the pontoon and stepped ashore, she'd already jumped off from behind him, clearing the three or four feet of water to land on the bank easily. Her legs were certainly long enough for that and it gave him a smile.

Arthur took a few seconds to look at his new surroundings. The sand bar was almost void of growth. Where it connected to the land, a thick row of reeds standing higher than his head covered the bank in both directions. Behind the reeds stood the towering trees of the rain forest. He could see many different kinds of trees in a glance and the upper canopy showed clearly above the lower layers. The green shades of the foliage were sometimes interrupted by entire trees with leaves of dark red, yellow and orange. Numerous trees and bushes were in bloom.

One of the long narrow boats that had taken their supplies in ahead of them lay nosed into the bank nearby, waiting to ferry them upstream to the expedition site. To his surprise, Owen Lansing had come down with the boat and now stood on the opposite pontoon talking to their pilot. A somber-faced Jan Benedetti and a third person whom Arthur took to be their Peruvian shepherd and biologist, Hector Felipe, stood in a row on the pontoon. Arthur got the uneasy feeling it wasn't a joyful conversation and his senses went on alert. The pilot finally nodded some sort of agreement and the three scientists returned to the shore. Lansing spoke to the five passengers as a group.

"I'm sorry to have to report that the dig has been damaged by mud slides. It also appears that it may have been looted before the slides came down." Lansing stopped and looked around at them while it sank in. Benedetti nodded silent confirmation.

"The two groups that flew in before you this morning have already been ferried to the site and are waiting for us to join them. We will do what we must to document the conditions we've found and then leave.

"I've just requested that the pilots return in two days to begin flying us out. We'll need that much time to put information together for some kind of report and to determine if there's any reason to try to salvage something. Frankly, that possibility seems highly doubtful, and it certainly can't happen this year."

Arthur sucked in his breath, stunned. He'd expected to spend the next two months digging, cataloguing, researching and broadening his areas of knowledge and couldn't stem his disappointment. He could feel the anticipation draining from his soul. He thought back on Benedetti's story about the wealthy alumnus who had been forced by the federal government to fund the expedition. Yet even with the *federales* having demanded that the expedition take place, it had taken an unusually long time to obtain the necessary permits and permissions. He couldn't help but wonder if someone hadn't purposely held them up to give confederates time to rob the site. There was a great deal of money to be made in stolen artifacts.

He looked at Millie. Her face had paled and he wanted to comfort her but this wasn't the place. At the moment there was nothing to do but get in the boat, go see what remained, and try to come up with a plan to salvage the next two months.

Lansing had not flown in, but had come upriver by boat the day before Arthur and the others. He accompanied more than two dozen support staff hired locally so that he might oversee the transport of supplies and equipment and be on hand to direct the setting up of camp. Jan Benedetti, as chief scientist, and Hector Felipe accompanied him for purposes of their own. Tim Fields had gone with them to establish communications with the outside world and to prep for the remote-sensing that would hopefully provide the basis of a plan for the remainder of their exploration.

When the long narrow outboard-driven boat carrying Arthur and the other passengers from the DeHavilland arrived at the damaged site, it pulled up to the river bank behind the boat that had brought Lansing and Benedetti to greet them. A Johnny-on-the-spot Tim Fields brushed through a scuffling veil of white butterflies and offered Millie a hand to help her on shore. To look at him Arthur would have thought he was hosting a reception. It made him look saccharine in light of the sad news and Arthur felt himself tighten as he experienced what was becoming genuine irritation everytime he saw the man.

Millie accepted Fields' hand and Arthur supposed this was another of those times when there was nothing else for a woman to do. At least without being pointedly impolite. One thing for certain, she hadn't managed to discourage him. He studied Fields trying to determine if the time might come when they would have some kind of a showdown. Of course there wasn't a way to answer that, and he pulled himself back to the moment to become engrossed in the jumble of disembarking as he and the others transferred their personal belongings to the shore.

Their conversations were somber and terse. Even the boat crews whose colorful mixtures of Spanish and Quechua had infused the air nonstop at the other end of their journey seemed to be taking part in the wake. In the background only the sporadic calls of unseen birds continued undaunted. The dismal atmosphere only served to heighten his stress.

The new arrivals picked up what they could carry and Lansing led them up a riverside knoll to a level area where the bush had been cleared. Arthur had anticipated a small tent city set up to house the sixteen staff members, the people who worked to support them, and provide an area where apparatus could be set up and used without concern for rain. Instead he saw only several smaller individual sleeping tents and a couple for cooking and storage. Much of the equipment they would normally use remained in waterproof metal containers at the river's edge.

Half an hour later the group had moved their personal gear from the boat to the campsite. The tents sat randomly where patches of ground were most level and each bore a tag with the occupant's name on the flap. Arthur half expected to see Fields arrange it so that his and Millie's were tucked neatly together. Apparently he didn't take her for granted that much. At least not yet.

Though the day already seemed long, the sun had yet to reach its high point and once he'd stowed his gear and reinforced his insect repellent he went to join the others at the north end of the camp site where Lansing had asked them to gather. Several made it there ahead of him to form a forlorn group of a dozen or so standing in a small cleared area. They conversed in the hushed tones he might have expected at a funeral and in a symbolic way he supposed it was. Someone had erected a folding table and a platter of sandwiches sat under a wire-framed hood of mosquito netting. It had been nearly seven hours since he'd eaten and he helped himself. Just before he bit into what turned out to be plain bread and cheese, he remembered how quickly bread soaked up the dampness in the tropics and prepared himself to save an unpleasant surprise. Being ready for it didn't make the taste any better and he wolfed it down to be done with it.

Millie joined them and stood beside him. Her shoulders seemed to have gone limp with the same sad resignation that claimed them all and her dejection made his own more intense. He held back from putting an arm around her, then she leaned against him anyway just for a second and while he stood relishing the feeling of intimacy he wondered if he'd communicated with her in some unspoken way to invite it. He hoped he had. Lansing, Benedetti and Hector Felipe arrived together and interrupted his thoughts.

Lansing, his voice flat and oddly more formal than usual, began. "Our purpose this afternoon is to do our best to determine if the site is in any way salvageable. I've already used the radio to report the conditions here as we know them up to now. I'll send a second call by the end of the day and hope that it can be patched through. First I'd like *Señor* Felipe to give us a briefing on how to get about safely."

The biologist was a short lightly-constructed man with a closely trimmed black beard and mustache. A mestizo, Arthur guessed, the mixture of European and Indian that dominated in many urban areas. The man's large, dark eyes seemed gentle yet fiercely intelligent. His English turned out to be borderline fluent and he hesitated frequently in mid sentence to choose the proper words. Even before he'd spoken, Arthur liked him.

"Welcome to Peru, my friends, and especially the rain forest. I am so sorry we have come all this way to find only damage." He waved an arm toward the sparse foliage surrounding the small shadowed clearing where they stood.

"Perhaps most of you know the rules for walking in these forests. If that is true, let me just review them for you. They are for your safety.

"As you saw, we cut wide trails from the boat landing to your tents and this place where we are now has been cleaned of plants and insects. As you begin your work here that will not be the case. Most of all, please remember two things. Never use your bare hands to push vines or branches aside. Spiders, scorpions, ants, many things may be living on the sides of them you cannot see and will bite to defend themselves. And never stop walking without first looking to see where you stand. If you fail to do this ten times, I promise the ants will attack you at least twice. It is best to have your trousers tucked into long socks. If not, tie the bottoms tightly. Shorts or sandals are not good here."

"What about bigger biters?" Someone standing behind Arthur asked the question.

Hector Felipe smiled and bobbed his head in a gesture that told them he'd answered that question many times. "Our noise from being here should keep them away. I suggest you move about with two or more people at one time. Snakes hunt at night and sleep during the day. Tarantulas also are night hunters and won't harm you anyway. They only frighten you by their looks. I will bring one for you to see later and then I will return it to its nest. Just look exactly where you intend to reach and step. See carefully what you are walking under also." He turned toward Lansing to signal he had finished.

The expedition leader thanked him and returned to his own business. "We will divide up. One group will accompany Dr. Benedetti to the slide area. They will need to generate a thoroughly documented report and map locating the damage as it impacts the area we'd hoped to excavate. You can decide together how to do the best job. I think it's a good idea to measure, or where you must, to estimate slide depths in a grid pattern at say ten or fifteen meter intervals.

"Timothy Fields will try to determine if the soils in the area are stable enough after what's happened to let us do some of his remote sensing and which technique we might use. He's already getting some of his equipment together and asked for Dr. Holtz and one other person to help."

So Fields had gone right after Millie, as usual. He took a half step forward quickly signifying that he'd be the 'other' volunteer, but Lansing raised a hand to put him on hold and he stepped back reluctantly as Lansing designated one of the others. Then the expedition chief turned back to Arthur.

"Dr. Tomas, as our photographer I'll ask you to record what we find here in the clearest way you can. In keeping with *Señor* Felipe's caution to us about moving about alone, I'll give you the best companion possible, the *Señor* himself."

A moment later Lansing sent them on their way. Millie gave Arthur a look as she went back toward the river to join Fields, but he couldn't catch the meaning beyond that it was plain she wasn't having a good time. He wasn't either and the sight of her dejection made an already unpleasant day worse.

The expedition had shipped cameras that were superior for scientific work. These used large single sheets of film measuring either four by five or ten by twelve and were capable of capturing minute detail. One could be fitted with a microscope. But they were also cumbersome and required a stout tripod with special extensions so that they could be lowered into excavations from above. He'd checked shortly after they'd arrived and found them safe in their metal shipping cases with the other equipment that remained near the river's edge. He decided to leave them there and opted for his own smaller thirty-five millimeter cameras that could be hand held or braced against trees. He returned to his tent to get them. If it turned out to be necessary, he'd bring up one of the large format cameras later.

After loading film into two of them, he shouldered a gadget bag carrying a range of interchangeable lenses, flash equipment to fill in shadow, if need be, and several more rolls of film. He took a machete and returned to the spot where they'd met, then followed Felipe up the thin, recently hacked-out trail to the perimeter of the dig site. They came upon Benedetti and her group gathered around a site map made during the previous year's investigations. They were marking it into a rough grid pattern to locate where they would measure slide depths. These scientists, normally so ordered and certain of their work, seemed at odds with the unexpected atmosphere of destruction.

He'd heard the description of the damage from Lansing and some of the others, but now it became clear that they hadn't prepared him. The entire area lay two hundred yards wide along a steep section of river bank. It was built there perhaps to prevent surprise attacks from the river or to discourage marauding caimans and anacondas. When the slides had roared down the adjacent hillside much of the bank had collapsed and carried whatever artifacts it held into the river. What remained lay under several feet of boulders and mud that had already given rise to new growth. Benedetti handed him a copy of the rough site map. He knelt with them and sketched his own copy of the grid, then rose to take a picture of the group at work.

Their work progressed faster than Benedetti's group's and they'd moved on ahead before the noise of a small gasoline motor signaled that the drilling of core samples to determine slide depths had begun. Foliage had to be hacked away or pulled aside to open up unblocked views for the cameras. The biologist took charge of this, moving carefully, looking at both sides of any leaf or plant he touched, only cutting when there was no other way. It was obvious that the man loved this environment, and Arthur respected him for it.

Arthur took pains to make sure that each photograph over-lapped the previous one and he numbered and marked down the direction of each shot and its exposure parameters. It felt good to concentrate on the tasks before him so that he could push the dis-appointments of the demolished dig aside, but soon the exertion of working in the cloying heat and the ever present need for vig-ilance began to take its toll. Three hours later when he heard the irritating clanging of someone running a rod around the inside of a metal triangle meant to call them to dinner he was nearly exhausted and would have been forced to quit soon anyway.

The pair turned back and soon caught up to Benedetti's people where Arthur saw that the clean pressed khakis they'd had on when they'd arrived now displayed the trials of their owners' labors. Dark sweat stains rimmed with white salt radiated out in large circles from under arms and at the backs of knees. Long damp stripes extended down the backs of shirts between shoulder blades and all clothing was streaked by dirt and green markings from plant life. Most of them now wore wide hats with mosquito netting draping from the brims well down their shoulders. Fatigue showed deeply in every face and conversation lacked altogether.

As they neared the camp site his curiosity caused him to quicken his step when he saw Lansing in animated conversation with Millie and Fields. Millie held an empty wooden box in front of her and her features projected angry excitement. She turned toward Arthur and the group as they arrived.

"We went up the hillside to where the slides started and found this."

She held the side of the box up for them all to see. Arthur saw the words *PELIGRO EXPLOSIVOS* in red letters across the side. "Dynamite." Her voice carried accusation. Lansing stepped up beside her, took the box from her, and sniffed inside it. Next he turned it around to read every side and nodded his confirmation of her conclusion.

Millie's eyes were bright with the beginning of angry tears. "Why would anyone blow this place up?"

Lansing glanced up from the box and Arthur thought he looked at her as though he'd forgotten she'd been standing there. "We may never know. But smuggling artifacts is big business. Most likely they took whatever they thought to be of value and tried to cover up."

Benedetti concurred. "This region is rich in folklore and super-stition. Desecrating graves is taboo in most cultures. Perhaps they tried to cover this ground so some devil or an ancient god couldn't escape to punish them. Not to mention modern authorities."

Lansing nodded assent and seemed to retreat into his own thoughts for a moment oblivious to those around him. Then he looked down at his feet and left going in the direction of the short wave radio, his shoulders sagging as he walked. Hector Felipe went with him. Arthur's sympathy went out to Lansing for he knew the man would face hell back home even though there was no way he might have predicted or prevented what had taken place.

Now that they knew the slides were man made, an already sad situation became worse. They went to the dinner tables with a solemnity he'd only witnessed at funerals. To add to the insult, the camp generators hadn't started and they had to settle for cold sandwiches. Again they were soggy, but now also nearly tasteless in air heavily permeated by the stink of burning mosquito coils, an odor that only the insects seemed able to ignore. Most of the party chose to take their food and retreat to the protection of their tents.

Millie stood as one of the first to leave and went a few steps out of her way as though to be sure he'd notice. When he did look, she held his eyes for a moment before she turned and walked away into the onset of darkness. He didn't think she wanted him to follow. He glanced around and saw Fields engrossed in quiet conversation with some of the others. He hadn't tried to go after her. For once.

When he entered his own tent, he ate quickly and went to bed as soon as he'd finished. In the few moments before weariness took his mind away he remembered Benedetti's words about the superstition that would have ancient gods pursuing the dynamiters of this site. Later in the night he dreamt about himself as a young boy lost in the dark in a place he didn't know. The dream he knew well, but this time the unintelligible voices of the always present disembodied heads had a different tone. A warning.

The following morning they put aside their tasks from the day before to search for more evidence that the slides had been caused by man. They found bits of stone buried in trees like shrapnel, even tiny bits of copper from the caps or connecting wires, and there were rock and chunks of wood scorched by the blasts. Movable evidence was tagged, boxed, and located on a site map. The irony of it struck Arthur. These were the procedures they would use to remove artifacts. It was what they did best.

He and the biologist took pictures of each find though he wasn't convinced of the significance of their efforts beyond keeping their minds off the horror of the desecration. If that was a purpose, it didn't seem to be working for he saw the sadness displayed by the camp the day before turn raw as the hours passed. The offense of what had happened here ran through the group like contagion and they worked with a fever born of the need to be done with it and leave. Soon each newly-uncovered clue seemed to be followed by profanity directed at the unknown perpetrators, who these normally reserved academics now referred to almost exclusively as 'the bastards.' Arthur found his own anger rising. When he added Fields' relentless pursuit of Millie, his had an additional source.

Shortly after lunch the generator fired up to a chorus of unconvincing cheers, but there was something intrusive about that sound in this place, and within seconds Arthur was ready to shut it off and welcome back the sounds of the jungle. Lansing, whom he had come to know as the consummate scientist, continued to shepherd the wrap-up in his studied, dispassionate fashion. After eating another tasteless meal Arthur returned to the photographic documentation of the site and though they finished easily by late afternoon, he suffered the same overpowering weariness as the previous day and painfully sore muscles to boot.

He saw little of either Millie or Fields and, because there was nothing he could do to change that, tried not to let himself dwell on it. But he set his jaw tightly and resolved to spend time with her after dinner.

At four o'clock, the time the sun's rays began to slant through the high canopy and take on the yellowish hues of late afternoon, Lansing called the senior staff together to coordinate work on the draft report. They had the evening meal brought to them and continued to work well into the night under banks of generator-driven field lights. Rectangular blue-white bug lights set well back from them at the four sides of the perimeter of the work area drew insects away and dispatched them with electricity that made continuous crackling noises. The occasional calls of night birds overrode them.

Señor Felipe offered to take anyone interested on a night walk, promising they might see some of the gloriously colored tree frogs the region was famous for, perhaps even a snake. Or, if they wished, he'd lead them to the riverbank to locate caimans by the red glow their eyes would make in a flashlight beam. He stood and walked to the edge of the clearing and turned his own flashlight beam in a broad arc. Almost instantly the bright amber lights of more than a dozen fireflies answered. He caught one and brought it to the group to show them. Two spots glowing green on the back of the insect's thorax simulated the eyes of a much larger creature to keep predators at bay. The firefly was larger than any Arthur had ever seen and the *Señor's* gesture was met with enthusiasm and interest by the group, but no one took his offer of a nature walk. Fatigue was the flavor of the evening and work remained to be done.

Millie and Fields kept their heads together most of the time and Arthur began to rankle, but again had to recognize that there was every reason for them to be working together closely in order to finish their responsibilities. Lansing and Benedetti spent their time reviewing the different materials and discussing them with the respective authors with the intent of developing conclusions and recommendations. Though never stated, there was little doubt that any potential the site may have had was lost.

As the evening's work came to an end Millie stood and turned to leave in the direction of her tent. Fields rose quickly and closed in beside her. She stopped walking and though Arthur couldn't hear her words, it was obvious she didn't want Fields to leave with her. It took a second, but his brain finally clicked in and he called over to her. "Millie, can we talk?"

She put a hand on Fields chest as if to hold him back and walked toward where he sat. Her eyes were narrowed and her lips pulled back at the corners. "Thanks. That man will not be discouraged." Her tone didn't match the gratitude in her statement.

"I guess you're right. It's time for me to tell him about us."

"Too late. I told him this afternoon. It hasn't slowed him down a bit. I don't think he believes any woman he wants can turn him down."

He looked over her shoulder to see Fields standing expectantly where she'd left him and felt the hot lava flowing into his own cheeks. It was all he could do to speak in a calm voice "What did he say when you told him?"

"I anticipated the usual garbage. 'Forget him. You need a real man.' Or the wounded bull. Even some kind of accusation for leading him on. His type can go in any direction, but what he came up with was even worse than I expected. He acted as though I hadn't spoken and went right back to reciting all the things he thinks we should be doing together. I get the feeling that he's known about us all along."

With that she took a firm grip on Arthur's arm. "Take me to my tent. It secures nicely from the inside. I don't think he's stupid enough to try to force anything." As they left the group neither of them looked back to see Timothy Fields' reaction.

In the tent area a number of people had already begun the chores of settling in for the night. There were separate tents that served as washrooms at each end and Benedetti passed them with toothbrush in one hand, flashlight in the other. If she noticed that Millie held on to him far too tightly for a mere colleague, she gave no sign. At her tent Millie pecked him on the cheek and said goodnight. He stood outside until he heard her zip the front flaps into place and then returned to his own quarters.

Though every fiber in his body seemed drained of energy, he had too much on his mind to sleep. If they had thought this place would give them time together, they'd been wrong. And the problem with Fields was getting out of hand. It was one thing to have him chase after Millie if he didn't know about the two of them. If he thought she had no one in her life, it was a natural mistake, and who could blame him. But it was quite different when Fields did know and if she'd been right . . . that he knew all along . . . far worse. That meant that he wouldn't back off of his own accord. He considered Arthur someone who could be disposed of easily. It was a challenge to him personally. Fields obviously needed to be reckoned with, and he didn't have a clue as to how to go about it.

As he lay unable to sleep in the heat on the unyielding cot, he tried to turn his thoughts to other subjects to put himself at ease. He needed to free his mind from his concerns about Fields and Millie. He turned to the thing he always did when he found himself unable to cope. His work. He began to wonder what he would do with the time he'd expected to spend here at this site now that they'd all be leaving tomorrow. Then it struck him.

He rolled off the cot and dropped to his knees beside it to open an insulated metal box. He retrieved his laptop and booted it to call up the data he'd scanned into it at the campus library several weeks before. He reread the journal of the Danish biological expedition, checked the area maps he'd stored and reconciled these with his memory of the strange sight he'd seen through his binoculars when the pilot had begun to follow the course of the wrong river. It was nearly midnight and within the last few minutes of computer battery power when he was satisfied the plan to do his own investigation was sound enough to be successful.

⁂

That final morning at the *Rió Perra* site, the process of breaking camp began early. Tempers were still edgy. Nearly two hours of intense tropical thunderstorm during the night had made sleep impossible and the morning heat quickly turned the jungle into a slippery sea of steaming fumaroles. The night's rain had already begun to wash away any evidence of their work the days before.

For Arthur, however, obtaining permission to use one of the expedition boats turned out to be easier than he'd hoped. When he approached Owen Lansing, he found him acting quite differently from most of the others. He'd also changed from the somber expedition leader he'd been in the days before. He'd become the happy boy scout leader eager to return his charges to their anxious parents. When Arthur asked, Lansing almost beamed.

"Good idea. All of it, camping gear, medicines, tools, has to go back downriver. We'll try to sell some of it there to save on the cost of shipping it home, but on the way a lot can go missing. There are easy markets for almost anything along the river and the boat crews worry me. They may even feel cheated because we promised them more work here before we knew the site was ruined and they can claim any number of plausible excuses for losses. I'll have *Señor* Felipe and some of the others accompany the rest of them."

"Thank you, Dr. Lansing. I'll take good care of it. And I saw something that seems to be man-made from the plane on the way up. I'd like to stop and look at it. I hope you won't mind?"

"This river has been pretty thoroughly explored from here on down to the mouth. But suit yourself. You know enough to be careful."

Arthur didn't bother to tell him that he'd be looking up a different river.

It only took a few moments for Lansing to assign him a boat and set a group to loading it with cargo that would fare best if chaperoned. More good luck came when it turned out the man in charge of the boat spoke passable English albeit with a thick accent and mixed grammar. When Lansing waved him over to introduce Arthur, the short sturdy boatman pulled himself up to exaggerated attention.

"*Buenos dias, Señor,* I am *El Capitán.*" The title reminded Arthur of the John Phillip Sousa march of the same name.

He nodded his acknowledgment and motioned the man aside, because he wasn't anxious for the others to pick up on his idea. Leading a flotilla would cancel any chance of exploring.

"*Señor,*" he corrected himself and took care to speak slowly, "*El Capitán.* I would like to take a short side trip. There is a smaller river that empties into this one several hours down from here. I would like us to turn into that river and go upstream, perhaps ten or twelve kilometers."

The other man knitted his brows together and stared at his own feet. When he finally spoke it was as though the words were very painful to him.

"Thees will be difficult, *Señor.* All of our families expected us to return to our homes after staying here only one night. We have now stayed two. Already they worry." The boatman shifted his weight from foot to foot.

It was the beginning of a process Arthur'd expected and he leaned in close to the man and tried to speak gently but as though he held the authority.

"But if only this boat stays the extra time and the others go back, they will be able to tell your family that you are well and will be coming home soon."

"*Si, Señor.*" The answer came reluctantly.

"And if I give you extra money. U.S. dollars from my own pocket. Would it be less difficult then?"

'*El Capitán's* countenance brightened almost imperceptibly and a few moments later they'd settled on forty U.S. dollars for him, another twenty for 'his cousin' who would accompany them as crew and ten more for extra fuel and the use of the boat. For Arthur the arrangement offered an added benefit. By paying for the extras himself, he wouldn't be obliged to share everything he might turn up with the university and he sure as hell wouldn't report that site to the government and take the chance on its destruction too.

He went looking for Millie and found her with Jan Benedetti repacking some of the equipment cases. She saw him and excused herself to meet him. Her morning smile was at its best. "I understand your taking one of the boats downstream."

"Word travels fast." Her knowledge of his plans surprised him.

"Lansing mentioned it to Jan a couple of minutes ago on his way past. You wouldn't have room for one more would you?"

"I'd like that, but there will be at least two nights camping out. It would put us in a bad light with the others."

She nodded an agreement, but he could see the pain behind her eyes and reached desperately for a reply that would ease it. Jan Benedetti's voice interrupted them.

"Morning Arthur." Like Lansing, her voice also seemed unusually cheery given their conclusions that this site no longer had potential. "I hear you're doing us the favor of shepherding one of the supply boats back. Remember what I told you about not petting strange reptiles."

"I'll be fine, Jan. Thanks."

"We'll all be going back to that river lodge we stayed in on our first night. It will be kind of a debriefing spot before going our own ways. Hope to see you there."

He nodded and with that she hefted a small case of equipment and headed toward the loading area, casting an inquiring glance at Millie as she left. Millie stood on her toes to peck him on the cheek.

"I'll come down and see you off." Then she picked up another case and headed after Benedetti.

An hour later he had loaded most of his personal things in the bow of the boat and was just coming down to the water's edge with the final load, his cameras and the computer in their protective cases. Most of the expedition members were at the camp area with Lansing taking down tents and crating up the kitchen equipment, but as he approached the riverbank, Millie was there with Benedetti marking boxes for future disposition.

She came toward him and he set the cameras and computer on the ground. Her face looked as though she'd just stepped out of the dressing room for a photo shoot. Her makeup was perfect and not a blond hair out of place. She'd done it obviously, just for him, to let him know they were still a couple. He felt a lump forming in his throat.

"I wish you could come with me." And this time he truly meant it.

"But she won't be and I don't believe she really wants to." There stood Fields. Arthur hadn't seen him come up and Millie evidently hadn't either for the look on her face became pure surprise. Fields stepped in-between the two like a lion protecting his pride from the competition. His countenance had gloating arrogance smeared all over it.

His face showed the same expression Arthur'd seen on the rich boys' faces at the school. The ones who called him 'the stray'. Arthur's heart pounded and he could feel the blood surging in his neck. He turned the faceless gold ring on his finger just before he swung with all his might at the sneer on Fields' face.

Before the punch could land, something powerful grabbed his upper arm. He took a blow to the stomach that swung him off his feet and his next sensation was watching the high green canopy circling lazily over his feet. He landed hard on his back and shoulders, tumbled, rolled down the riverbank and splashed to a stop belly down in a foot of water. He tried to spring to his feet but the soggy river bottom held him to short crawling steps on hands and knees. Water blurred his vision and a mouthful of mud made him gag and spit.

As he slogged to the river bank swiping the water from his eyes, he expected to see Fields standing there challenging him. Instead he saw Jan Benedetti standing with her back to him barking at Fields in a voice any drill sargent would envy.

"Mr. Fields, if you take one step in this direction, I promise you I shall chair your thesis committee. Do you understand me?"

Arthur couldn't make out his reply, but she was apparently being obeyed for she continued.

"Go to the camp site and help there. I don't want to see you down here again for at least an hour." Then she spun to look at Arthur. "If that was some attempt at chivalry, it was very poorly timed. I believe your boat is loaded. If nothing more than your manly pride is injured, I suggest you get right in it." Now she turned to Millie. "You and I still have work to do. Perhaps you'll fill me in while we finish."

As the boat found center channel Arthur had his first opportunity to think back on his fight with Fields twenty minutes before. From his seat in the bow he cast a glance over the cargo and down the length of the long narrow boat to see *El Capitán* and his 'cousin' manning the shuddering outboard motor that growled and snorted out blue smoke like a sick and angry animal. His own rage still rode within, but it wasn't so much directed at Fields as at himself. In one petulant move he'd put his profession and any future he might have with Millie in dire jeopardy.

The two men in the stern had obviously witnessed the short-lived conflict and they looked back at him now with contemptuous pity. He knew their culture carried a strong Latin influence and any man who had let his machismo suffer damage wasn't worthy of respect. He was not only the loser, but had lost in very short order. He could feel his face burning to the tips of his ears and the stigma of that humiliation caused him to look away and focus his gaze on the brown waters idling past the boat.

In the minutes between the time Fields had unceremoniously dumped him into the river and casting off, he'd had no contact with any of the staff. Benedetti had herded Millie away and Fields had taken her direction and vanished back toward the camp site. There would certainly be a price to pay for letting his anger get out of hand. He'd broken a prime rule of conduct at any dig. Professionals got along. Period. Differences could be discussed heatedly, even mediated in some cases, but unbridled arguments were taboo and violence unthinkable. He may very well have destroyed any chance of serving with a future expedition. In an instant he'd sullied his career and given Millie good reason to walk away. He sat trying to assess the new state of his life, but the turmoil of emotions that surged and eddied inside him made clear thought impossible. Only the morning sun evaporating the river water from his clothing cooled him enough to provide distraction.

He took stock of himself. Even in the short time he'd been on the river the sun had nearly dried his clothing but for those places it couldn't reach. His boots were still sodden and he removed them and his socks to place them where they could dry. Then he tried to concentrate on the journey ahead.

The current ran about four knots, he guessed, and when he'd thought it out the night before, he'd estimated that the boat would be able to raise that to at least twelve with some to spare. If not, it wouldn't have been able to make adequate time against the current coming upstream. He'd calculated this against the flight time coming in and figured the boat's time to the mouth of the river at about five hours. They hadn't passed over any other large tributaries, so there shouldn't be any problem identifying the correct one.

He settled back as best he could against the structure of the bow and suffered being bumped against it as the boat bounced and zigzagged through the water. The boat maintained a continuous series of long sweeping curves to evade logs and branches lodged in the river bottom. *El Capitán* seemed to have a sixth sense when it came to steering a safe course. The constant swerving made it difficult to relax and then he was slammed back hard when without warning the boat bucked and the motor gasped as the propellor bit into sand. He saw the boatman stand, spin to grasp the motor cover and lift all his weight on it to tilt forward and down. The motor roared a protest when his action freed the prop but within seconds they were on their way again. Apparently the captain's sixth sense had its flaws. He grasped the edge of the boat with both hands and turned his gaze to the near bank, determined to keep his mind on the events at hand.

The river was lined with vertical banks from one to over two stories high or with low flat bars of loose sand. He knew that conditions could change within a few hours as depth varied as the result of rains, sometimes many miles upstream, and that the shape of the rivers changed almost daily.

The sand bars nearly always supported sparse low bushes that thickened toward the shore then gave way to the walls of stately perpendicular cane that guarded the edge of the jungle itself. In contrast, many of the steep banks revealed layers of canopy as openly as if they'd been sliced with a giant bread knife, evidence of the power of moving water. He picked through his daypack until he could retrieve the binoculars and concentrated them along the sand bars because they were low enough that wildlife might use them to reach water.

He began picking out birds: the dazzlingly white snowy egrets and the great egrets, their larger cousins, cormorants, the white-necked heron, a pair of pink roseate spoonbills. Many others he couldn't name. A group of monkeys, too far away for him to recognize the variety, played in the top branches of one of the tallest trees. Swallow-tailed kites swooped toward the boat and startled him. When the boat neared the banks, he picked out swarms of butterflies and moths in red and white or orange. Each color clustered to itself.

Half an hour later he spotted his first peccary, easily recognized because of its similarity in looks and size to a pig. It stood near the water waiting for them to pass before drinking, seemingly oblivious to the motor noise until it spun and headed back into the bush. As they rounded a bend a family of jabiru, the largest of the storks, ran in front of them until they found the speed necessary for flight. Several miles farther downstream they cruised near a bar at mid river and he saw a small white caiman. Only about four feet long, it faced them in low grass near the water's edge, steadfastly refusing to flee. It held its jaw up and jutted forward like an indignant dictator of that tiny island. Arthur saluted as they passed. Part of the allure of this expedition had been the opportunity it afforded to learn to know this vast forest. He regretted being forced to leave it too soon.

Exactly five hours and fifty minutes after leaving the *Perra* site he saw the thrashing waters of the two rivers meeting ahead of them and waved a signal to the boatmen. He hadn't allowed for the extra distance they would travel curving back and forth in the channel.

It took four tries in the roiling water for the heavily laden boat to make the turn to follow the other channel back upstream. That used half an hour more. It was midafternoon when they finally inched their way in, though after the boatman found the waters of least resistance, the craft moved upstream smoothly enough. It had all looked so much easier from the air.

Now instead of running with the flow and adding its speed to the boat speed, they ran upstream and the boat's forward progress dropped to a slow walk that prompted *El Capitán* to throttle the outboard to a high pitched rowl that added the speed of a bug's crawl. The new channel was slightly narrower than the one they'd left but still several hundred yards across and the water changed from brown to the green color of the surrounding jungle. Arthur could only guess at how long the pilot of the float plane had followed this river in error. Give or take four or five minutes. That would put the cliff at least six but more likely eight to ten miles farther up and an hour to an hour and a half away from them now.

He reminded himself to take pictures from the water before they landed to provide a context for whatever he might turn up and only then did he discover that the cameras had been left behind. A vague memory came to mind of him putting them and his computer on the ground back at the river's edge as Millie came to send him off. He'd done it seconds before the confrontation with Fields. If he'd just stepped up and put his arms around her as he wanted to do, Fields wouldn't have been able to come between them. It was his own selfish concern about how it would look to others that had kept him from it. He cursed aloud into the engine noise and began to worry about how to document what he might discover.

The boat pushed around the curve of a sweeping bend that allowed him to see upstream more than a mile. He knew it was too soon to expect anything unusual to appear, yet still felt disappointment when nothing did. The fear that he may not have seen anything made by man furrowed his brow. Now he couldn't even recall the scene he'd caught from the plane and the space between his shoulder blades tightened. He took the binoculars up and began to sight along the river bank and then to comb the jungle. He saw flashes of bright red and blue in the sunlight as a pair of scarlet macaws flew swiftly through the tops of the highest trees, but couldn't hear their calls for the sound of the motor. Once he thought he saw the alligator-like snout of a caiman protruding from a patch of tall grasses at the river's edge. Something surfaced in the river ahead of them and something else off to the left, caiman again perhaps or giant otter, but both were gone before he could turn the glasses on them.

He checked his watch. Anytime now but still nothing. He became impatient and more convinced that he'd sent himself on a wild goose chase. Then the riverbank began to rise. Slightly at first, but the surface of it that had been cut by moving water stood too precipitous now to support foliage. It turned from the typical tan color of the soil to gray-black of lichen crusted granite and became a low cliff rising higher. They were coming to another bend in the river, the most abrupt thus far. The waters narrowed against it and the current accelerated. He recalled the sharp angle of the river beneath the cliff that he'd noted from the air. He grasped the binoculars tightly in anticipation.

The boat began to turn into the tightest arc of the curve and he raked the top of the cliff with the glasses. Then, just as he'd begun to feel another surge of disappointment, it slid into the field of view. He let out a gasping sigh of relief, but his heart raced and pounded against his chest. The riverside wall of the pyramid stood straight up and down forming a perfect vertical extension of the cliff. Without the binoculars he couldn't have seen the seams of the cut stone that gave it away as a construction made by man. He could barely make out the stepped sides that extended onto the rock top of the cliff because branches and vines of the forest canopy concealed them nearly to the top.

Nests in holes in the cliff below the pyramid revealed hundreds of white birds, their wheeling and soaring high overhead distracting from the view. These were undoubtedly the ones reported by the Danes. No wonder this site wasn't catalogued in the data banks. Military experts couldn't have camouflaged it better. You needed binoculars to recognize it from either the air or the river and they had to be trained on precisely the right spot at the right time. If he'd been traveling upriver by boat and not looking for it specifically, he'd have been too concerned with the river bend to pay any attention to the top of the cliff. And the currents in the mouth of the river would have turned most travelers back at that point. He damned himself again for leaving the cameras.

He waved to get the captain's attention, then pushed the palm of his hand down in a sign to slow the motor. He kept at it until the boatman throttled back enough that their forward speed met the opposing speed of the river. They rode without progress at midstream, while he dug hurriedly through his gear to come up with his field notebook. He riffled to a blank page and quickly began to sketch the scene. Even with the boat at equilibrium with the current the bouncing motion of it made his work difficult and he corrected it frequently. He noted the dimensions as best he could, estimating that the cliff rose over two hundred feet and the structure another hundred. He wasn't satisfied, but under the circumstances it was the best he could do. He motioned them on again, anxious to find a spot to tie up and begin exploring on land. He tried to hold this picture in mind so that he could refine the sketch later.

Half a mile farther upriver the cliff still ran high and then the banks began to close in toward them and the current picked up speed. A few hundred yards ahead the water churned white across the entire width of the river and large rocks raised above the water. Traveling farther upstream would be dangerous. Only the first few miles of this river were navigable. Another reason why the pyramid had gone unnoticed.

The boat began to turn and he looked to the stern to see the steering lever pulled hard to the side. *El Capitán* obviously had no desire to test the quickening currents. As they came to the low sand-colored banks again, Arthur waved toward shore and a few minutes later they nosed in at the closest point where the land flattened to the level of the water. He hopped ashore to tie the bow rope to a convenient log as the motor sputtered, backfired and quit.

The silence pulled him up straight, but then the sounds of the river and the jungle rose up around them. There were the soft noises of the moving water and its gentle lap-lap against the sides of the boat. He heard the whines and drones of insects and looked about to see dozens of swarms hovering low over the water and in the sheltered air under the trees. He heard the calls of the birds he'd only seen earlier, some melodious and soft, others raucous and grating. Something grunted, but too far away to identify by sound. *El Capitán* and his sidekick made it to shore and the two stood chatting quietly in Spanish. Arthur walked to them. They stopped talking and the boatman turned to face him. He pulled himself up to his full height and squared his shoulders as he had when Lansing had first introduced them that morning, but now he seemed embarrassed and did not look Arthur in the eye. Finally he spoke.

"*Señor*, is thees the place you wish to visit?"

"Yes it is. Did you see the pyramid?"

"No *Señor*. I was busy tending the boat. The current is very strong."

"Okay, I understand. Yes, this is where I want to be. This spot looks like a good place to make camp for the night."

The boatman cast his eyes at the ground in front of his own feet looking much like he had when he'd complained about the extra time Arthur'd wanted to spend on the way down river and Arthur knew the words almost before they came out.

"I am sorry, but that will be very difficult, *Señor*."

"Look here, Captain, we agreed that I will pay you extra money and exactly how much. I don't like the idea . . ."

The captain began to look even more embarrased as he cut him off. "It is not the money, *Señor*." The boatman raised his face and his eyebrows at the same time. "I am the man of my honor. We agree to bring you up thees river, but we did not say to stay the night here."

"We have to spend the night somewhere. Why not here?" For the second time that day Arthur felt his anger rising.

"Eet is the danger, *Señor*."

"Why more here than any other place?"

"The other river is call the *Rió Perra, Señor*. It means the Dog River. Named after the certain animal that is a wild dog that has legs so long it can stand in the tall grasses of the marshes and see out over them to hunt its food. That river was given eets name many years ago, because there is a place near where the Spanish first discovered the *perra* who lived there."

Arthur knew about the *perra*, an animal in danger now because of its odd habit of stopping to turn and look back when being pursued.

"But thees river *Señor* it is named *Rió Gato*. It means cat in both *Portugese* and *Español*."

"Okay, so we have the dog river and the cat river?"

"*Si, Señor*. Eet sounds like the child's game, but it is not. You see already, it is not possible for the boats to go up the river farther than we ourselves have done. But if they could, they would not. For even so that the word *gato* means the cat, it does not name a cat of the forest. Instead it is the Spaniard's mistake of an Indian word. A word from one of the tribes that once lived below here. And the word in the language of that tribe names the immortal god that lives in the black jaguar."

"And what do the legends say, *Señor?*"

"That in the night this black animal will come while you sleep and put a part of itself into your mind. From that day forever you can do only as it commands."

A myth dealing with the loss of freedom. Common in many cultures. They were testaments to man's innate dread of slavery. The Danes had written about this one and Arthur'd just gone over it the night before when he'd reviewed Holberg's report. Hearing it again from people who lived here brought an eerie tingle to the back of his neck even though his years as a scientist pooh-poohed any prospect of truth in it. It occurred to him that to acknowledge the myth was to forgo any possibility of convincing the boatman to spend the night anywhere near here. "Surely you don't believe that, *El Capitán*."

"My cousin and myself will not spend the night on the banks of this river, *Señor*. There is a safe place to camp two hours down from where the two rivers meet. Traveling the river at night is not good. We must leave well before dark. Go looking if you must. We will wait here, *Señor*. Be sure you return at least two hours before the dark, *por favor*. *Si,* and please do not mistake. Eet would be most difficult to come back for you tomorrow. *Comprendes?*"

Foolish superstition or not, Arthur resigned himself to the fact that he had no choice.

The narrow trail followed the inside curve of the river just behind the riverside wall of reeds where the high canopy kept all but a small amount of light from reaching the forest floor and plant growth was not dense. The light that did penetrate came in the form of brilliant shafts thrown down by the afternoon sun. Arthur'd come across it as he'd penetrated the reeds to find a course of less resistance. Even though the path was clearly discernable, abundant vines and tree trunks lay across it and fronds and branches had to be ducked, moved aside or hacked away with nearly every footstep. His good fortune in coming upon the path lent energy to his efforts.

The day pack he carried held the field notebook and an assortment of professional tools he hoped very much to need when he reached the pyramid. As the path climbed it abandoned the river smells below and replaced them with fragrances of sun poached flowers intermingled with the cloying odors of decaying vegetation. The dank heady aroma played tricks with his senses. The water sounds also fell behind to leave the noises of the insects and birds accompanied by his own steady breathing and the clump of his boots on firm earth.

The boatmen had refused to come. He damned their superstitions. If they'd pitched in, the work would go much faster and much more could be achieved. He needed to do everything he could to verify the find. A coughing grunt somewhere in the distance reminded him that numbers are safer in the jungle too. But he hadn't forgotten the desecration of the *Perra* site and had to admit to himself it was probably better that they wouldn't know the details if he should uncover something of value. *El Capitán* had also made it plain that they intended to leave him if he didn't return at least two hours before dark. He checked the sun. Time to get a move on. He wondered how the men would explain it if he didn't return, or if they would even have the need. These thoughts gave him more good reason to hurry. He tried to ignore the tiredness beginning in his legs and pushed ahead, remaining ever vigilant to see that nothing lay in the branches overhead and that the foliage he navigated had no fangs.

A hodgepodge of tracks sun-dried in the occasional low spots and leftover from the rains identified this as a game trail, though it seemed logical that the pyramid builder's had used it. It must have provided their most direct access to the river. He could almost feel their presence.

Forty-five precious minutes later the trail worked its way back toward the river bank. The ground ran high above the water now and the reeds no longer blocked the view so that he saw along the face of the cliff ahead. His already pounding heart banged harder, and he stopped to stare in awe. The smooth riverside wall of the pyramid thrust upward, towering, resplendent and dazzling in radiant orange hues of the afternoon sun. It rose above the rock face as though the two were a single flat surface. Perhaps it had been erected in that way to permit the builders to sacrifice to the river below. If he could verify that and find out whether the sacrifices had been enemies, members of their own tribe, or per-haps animals, he would have achieved a major step in defining their culture.

The cliff below the pyramid housed the nests of the white birds. Hundreds rose on updrafts that paralleled the cliff face to break away high over the top of the pyramid and soar on outstretched wings over the jungle on either side of the river. Generations of excrement stained the cliff face and underlined the ledges that supported their nests. He'd never seen anything like them before. Perhaps these were one of the thousand or so species of the region that remained undocumented.

He shucked off the pack to dig out the field notebook. Nothing but to make do with what he had. He sketched quickly, painfully aware that he lacked polished drawing skills, and as he worked he jotted estimates of size and dimension. A hundred yards wide, the length of a football field, and the height of a ten-story building. Twenty stepped layers in all.

The pyramid still looked to be several hundred yards away and the muscle fibers in the back of his neck tensed with urgency as he finished with crude strokes then rose and took up the pack to hurry on. A nearby bird called loudly to complain of his coming. It gave him a start. He told himself, get a grip, and narrowed his attention to concentrate on the needs at hand. Fifteen minutes, or was it half an hour later, he almost stumbled into the lowest layer of the pyramid. It sat squarely across the trail under cover of the trees so that it looked like a single flattened layer of rock resting in dark shadow.

Each layer of the pyramid lay smaller than the one beneath it by five or six feet at three edges. Only the riverside rose upward as a smooth extension of the face of the cliff. Broad steps ran up the middle of the side opposite the smooth cliff. They were steeper and cut nearly twice as high as those in modern structures and Arthur breathed, mouth opened, his sweat-drenched shirt clinging uncomfortably, as he labored his way one step at a time toward the top.

Halfway up his fatigue became so great that bile rose in his throat. He stopped, let the pack slide from his back to the rock surface, and allowed himself a first good look around. Tired as he was, his anticipation rose to a new high and his energies grew to meet it.

The tree cover had begun to thin though he could see that the long snaking branches of the taller trees enclosed the three layered sides of the structure nearly half the way to the top. He walked the tier he was on and found that the footprint of the pyramid formed a rectangle. The two longest sides paralleled the cliff and extended twice the length of the ends. The size and the way nature had camouflaged it so perfectly gave it both magnificence and a dark somnolent beauty.

Over time soil had found ways into the spaces between the construction stones and now it gave rise to a tangle of ferns and small plants that added to the disguise rendered by the surrounding jungle. One more way of concealing it from inquisitive eyes.

The overall shape of this structure was similar to some of the Incan ruins he'd visited, yet differences he couldn't put a finger on set it apart. There were designs in the cornerstones he hadn't seen before. They appeared to be the stylized heads of a jaguar. One thing for sure. Lansing was dead wrong when he said this find probably hasn't been put into the data because it wasn't significant. The size alone made it important. And the positioning with a vertical side right at the edge of a cliff added another interesting wrinkle.

He played it through the needles of excitement in his mind. It isn't in the data simply because no one knows it's here. It's on a river the locals won't use because of a superstition and the run of fast water we went through when the rapids stopped us spoils it for any practical use. It was surrounded by jungle and really only visible from the air. He was damn lucky to have seen it from the plane. Though his legs felt sore, he stowed the notebook and resumed the tortuous climb.

As he neared the uppermost level, something began to rise into view on the riverside farthest from him. Despite the heaving in his chest, he scrambled up the last steps to stride out onto a smooth stone platform. The object he'd seen was a rectangular slab cut from a single stone, standing on end with rows of hieroglyphics carved into the face. The stonework, this general area, any of it suggested Incan, yet they had no written language of any kind. An altar stone, and though he couldn't read them, its unique word pictures announced he'd found evidence of an undiscovered tribe, almost surely an entirely new culture or even a separate race. The stone weighed several tons. The question of how the builders had gotten it up there offered a puzzle in itself. The wonder of the discovery set his mind ablaze with the possibilities it offered.

A sudden maelstrom above tore his attention away. The birds he'd seen from the trail had discovered him and their calls assaulted his ears like the swinging of a thousand rusted gates. Up from behind the altar, carried by air currents on outstretched wings, rose an unending fountain of them to soar above him. They screeched obscenities at his presence like evil monks, hunchbacked in white robes and standing on the invisible columns of air.

He waved his arms and shouted and those above him scattered to dive down and away over the jungle. But others rose from below within seconds to resume their raging antagonisms. He tried to force his focus on the glyphs carved into the face of the stone, but could not. The first moments he could remember as a child were with a brother in a dark cowled robe who whispered to him reproachfully, 'Where are your parents, young man? We can see your name is Arthur from the markings inside your arm. Now tell me your last name.' And Arthur the frightened ten year old, or was he twelve, repeated the only name he could recall, 'Tommy' he'd said. The old monk stooped to take his arm and squeezed it too tightly. 'Tommy is not a surname, boy. Do you mean Thompson or perhaps Tomas?' The boy nodded an agreement in hopes of relieving the pain of the old monk's grasp. Those were his first memories. He felt fortunate to have remembered his name for the only memory he carried of his life before the police found him and delivered him into the hands of the monk was of cold darkness.

Now, as Arthur the scientist stood using one finger to trace the Latin motto, *body, mind, and spirit as one;* that circled the barren face of the school ring, he realized this discovery was the most important event of his life. For what stood before him confirmed that he would have a future that would not be forgotten. There would be a new definition of Arthur Tomas, the man.

He checked his watch and kicked himself for letting his mind run away. Two hours at most to do what he had to do and get back to the boat or face the ominous threat of being left stranded. Dire urgency tightened muscles in his gut. He needed to work fast. He would try to make accurate life-sized sketches of several of the more unusual glyphs and do an overall sketch of them all.

He scanned down the stone face trying to decide where to start when he noticed that not all the glyphs had been done at the same time or at least not by the same carvers. In the three bottom rows the figures were slightly smaller, as if they'd had to be crowded in and the cutting was not so deep as the others. The style was also slightly different. He'd need to record samples of both types.

He selected several of the larger ones first, then drew his tools from the pack, both soft and stiff brushes, an assortment of calipers and measuring devices, dentist's picks, small scrapers and rasps in half dozen different shapes and began cleaning the detritus of time away.

Trying to accomplish as much as he could in the time he had, he worked in a kind of measured panic, though being meticulous not to dislodge even one grain of the rock that had been left in place by the carvers. When he'd cleaned them he took up the notebook and tape measure. As he sketched he recorded their dimensions in centimeters. After he'd finished six he stepped back to try to create a picture of the overall. He noted the distances apart of each word picture and the height, width and thickness of the altar stone. He cursed to himself at the pressure of time, then on impulse tore a page from the notebook and made a quick pencil rubbing of one curious looking glyph and then a second.

Just as he was beginning a third . . . without knowing why . . . his senses went to full alert . . . straining, gut tight, things prickling at the back of his neck. Maybe something he'd heard, but what? He couldn't have heard anything over the incessant railing of the birds. That was it. The birds were silent leaving a total eerie quiet now except for a light stirring of wind. He turned to look and the birds no longer soared over him on the air currents. Only a few rose at all, then just barely enough to peer over the rim of the pyramid, their heads turned to look in his direction, each a single black eye, unrevealing, not seeing him . . . somehow watching behind him.

He turned slowly to see what they saw and found nothing, yet the already tense muscles of his body hunched tighter. Carefully he began to scrutinize his surroundings. The forest closed tightly around the sides of the pyramid. The taller trees snaked long branches out and over all but the top most tiers. Below, the vegetation continued to thicken until near the base, it clouded the stonework from sight more than a few yards away.

His eyes delved the shadows underneath the interlaced branches with every particle of his concentration. Still he heard nothing. Instinctively he inhaled the air and almost tasted the flowered scents of the hot jungle. The roots of his hair tingled cold. Still nothing, and he began to feel foolish and told himself to get back to work. Instead hollow anxiety creased his back between his shoulders and he wanted to bolt, to run. His state of alert had turned to full-fledged terror. Get the hell out of there.

And reason answered. Take hold. You need a lot more information to prove you've made the find of the century. Don't leave without it. No matter what.

Then the danger warnings again. Hang around and you may not live to prove anything. Trust your feelings, dammit. Trust your instincts . . . okay. Get your things all back in the pack, but he'd scarcely begun to loosen a muscle so that he might move himself when an unmistakable noise wiped it all from his mind. A low hollow grunt, almost a cough, not loud but near. He twisted toward the sound. Only the dark green vines and leaves of the canopy shimmered uneasily in the listless movements of the late day air. Then it formed . . . slowly in the shadows . . . along a heavy branch at a level just below his feet and no more than fifteen feet away. The eyes shown first. Yellow. With the round, dark pupils of the biggest of cats. He began to see the beginnings of a form and finally to discern the outline, a shadow cradled within the shadows. A black panther well over two hundred fifty pounds, an easy leap away. The warnings of the superstitious boatman jumped to mind. He froze and stared. It eased itself closer, gliding along the branch without apparent movement of muscle or limb. It stopped, stared, moved and stopped again. Now not even a dozen feet separated him from the dark tip of its nose.

He doubted he'd have time to see the muscles tense beneath the glistening black fur before it sprang. His mind zoomed into the high gear of crisis. He tried to reason an escape. Feint one way dodge the other. He struggled for the next step. If he jumped down one side of the pyramid layer by layer, that would only take him into the jungle, put him completely at the big cat's mercy. One thing to remember, he had no practice escaping panthers, but the panther made its living killing things that tried to get away.

Something struck him as odd. He struggled to know what, and it came. The cat held its head high, erect, like a miniature version of the sphinx. Its ears were not pulled flat along the top of its head. No bared fangs or claws. The panther didn't intend to spring. At least not yet. For now it was content to wait. He kept his eyes on it and began to take tiny steps backwards, ever so slowly. When the pack slipped into view at his feet, he sank down without dropping his eyes, lifted it ever so softly, and pushed the notebook inside. The tools could be replaced. Leave them. The animal watched him, blinked, then moved its head down and forward over its paws and eased its way toward him another foot. As it pulled itself along, Arthur could see its claws working into the bark of the branch as easily as garden rakes sinking into soft soil. He lifted the pack over his shoulder, careful to make no sudden movements, aware that his sweat held the acrid stench of fear. Feral beasts went after that smell on instinct. He tried to keep from trembling.

Now he'd worked himself cautiously sideways along the stone surface to the end of the tier above the trail. Still facing the panther, he squatted slowly, braced himself with his hands, eased his legs over the side and slid down to the next level. Just as he reached it the cat sprang. A yelp fled his throat and he flung his arms up to cover his face. The nerves in his skin anticipated the rake of claws and his legs braced for the impact. Nothing came.

He lowered his arms to see it sitting on its haunches at the exact spot in front of the altar stone where he'd been standing when he'd first felt its eyes watching. It still gazed at him steadily. Arthur could see the lighter fur of its underbelly and the remnant markings of the spotted jaguar that hadn't been hidden by the melanism. He froze in place, looking back. Perhaps it was trying to herd him. Urge him into the jungle to be hunted at leisure. As if answering, the panther sank down on its belly, rested its head on outstretched forepaws. The tip of its facile tail flicked lazily against the hieroglyphs on the altar stone and its eyelids slid partially closed.

"Sorry kitty, I guess I took your favorite chair." The birds began to return on the updrafts, though unlike when he'd stood there, they didn't complain to the panther.

Less than half an hour later, he arrived drenched in sweat and breathless at the boat where the two men waited. Within minutes they were headed back downstream. He didn't tell them about meeting the big black cat of the *Rió Gato*.

IV

FIRST LIGHT SEEPED IN AROUND THE EDGES of the flowered organdy drapes that adorned the single narrow window in Elsie Hatfield's bedroom. Her eyes looked up to focus on the white-on-white pattern of the papered ceiling. Her husband Will, dead now fourteen years, was chasing her across the Old River bridge on Dalyrimple Street just as she awakened. They were small children playing together in a different town long years before they married and moved to Seattle from the Midwest. The moment of ocean-deep sorrow that always accompanied his memory flooded through her mind then ebbed quietly back into the private cove where it had bedded since she had learned to exist after his death. She loved the kids with all her heart, but they could never fill the void left by the passing of her one good man.

She twisted under the covers and looked at the hands of the windup alarm. She'd set it dutifully to the same time every night for nearly forty years, but for most of the past decade she almost always woke at least an hour before it was set to ring. It wouldn't be needed this morning either, and she reached to push down the little brass lever on the back to turn it off.

She thought back through the night and added up her sleep to three hours most. Part of getting old, not sleeping enough, waking up a half dozen times, taking too long to get back to sleep, hardly ever feeling rested. Damn shame . . . the older you got, the less you had to do, the more time to do it. And you lay awake half the night to boot. Not like when family lived at home. She didn't get enough rest then either, but more than now. She slept a good sleep and tending her family made it worth it. These days, three hours, maybe four, was the best she could do.

Missing sleep wasn't the real problem though, she'd been getting by a long time. It was just lying there with nothing much to care about that made her crazy. Too many regrets for the past, too little to hope for in the future.

Her kids seldom called her and the long distance would eat her alive if she called them even half as often as she wanted to. She didn't neighbor. They were all too young and only thinking about themselves and their kids. About the only thing she did like to do any more beside tend her garden was canning. She had a small Bing cherry tree out front and she'd buy pie cherries at the market. A row of raspberries grew next to the garage and there'd be black berries to pick from the vacant lot half a block down. She'd already stocked up on pectin to set her jellies and paraffin to seal the jars.

Her next purchase would be more mason jars for the peaches, apricots, pears, and apple sauce. She always canned more than she ate and needed to buy more jars each year. The basement held more than she could use up in two or three years and she liked the feeling of security that gave her. She always offered fresh canned fruit to her kids though and pickled beets and green beans from her garden. But they preferred the stuff from their expensive supermarkets and seldom would let her give them any. It hurt that they wouldn't take her good food, but she knew times changed and accepted the inevitable.

Canning season was still weeks away and thinking about it didn't make her feel more rested. Maybe she should get some sleepers. Better call Doc Runkle. Ain't today his day off? Tomorrow then for sure . . . if she thought about it.

The slits of dawn pushing their way around the edges of her draperies didn't offer much light, but she could make out the book opened facedown on the mattress beside her. She would have turned on the bedlamp and picked it up, but in the mornings, if she let herself lay there in bed for a while, the same things always happened. First, that little band of tension squeezing around the top of her chest and then a foreboding that something would go terribly wrong that day, though she never had any idea of what dreadful thing that might be. Next, she would get antsy and her breathing and heartbeat would start to speed up. It had already started this morning and she was beginning to feel like a cat trying to run up a tin roof. Get up girl. The only way rid of it is to get busy. Start the day.

She rolled back the heavy comforter she slept under year 'round and raised herself slowly to swing heavy legs over the side. Oh Lord, but it would be good to have kids home again. William gone fifteen years next January. She wondered how many more would there be without him? She felt ready to be with him again. Anytime. She sighed aloud. The time wasn't hers to choose.

She sat a few moments idly tracing a finger along a tiny blue vein at the top of a broad knee. She'd read somewhere that jumping right up in the morning could give you a stroke or a heart attack. When she finally scrunched forward and slid solidly to the floor, the old box spring creaked a lazy relief. She left the bed unmade. Always did . . . aired it out.

Without switching on the light, Elsie shuffled barefoot to the window and eased back a corner of one drape to peer into the backyard at the tidy rows of flowering annuals. She felt the corners of her mouth pull back toward a smile and let herself relish the pride. Her husband might be gone and the kids grown and moved-away, but the flowers were none of those things and that counted for something.

The new morning light showed a pair of robins hopping crisscross through the rainbow of blooms and buds, to struggle up angleworms brought to the surface by rain during the night.

"The early bird does get 'em." She lectured out loud to the empty house. "Right there's proof."

The weather showed better than the day before. The window stood open, but just a crack to save the temperature even though she hadn't needed the electric baseboards on in almost a month. The thin cool draft it did let in offered up perfumes of early summer. From the seat of the wooden rocker beside the bed, Elsie picked up the aquamarine robe her must-be-color-blind daughter had given her for Christmas four years ago and headed to the bathroom. Again she spoke to her surroundings.

"Maybe I'll settle for instant and do like those early-bird robins, go work in the garden. Do a little weeding. Take the coffee out and get done before the sun's too high. It could turn into a hot one."

———— ✦ ————

The boy's slack form lay motionless on the bed. Phaqutl rested it there briefly after transferring from the dog into this new body. Within seconds he made the entire nervous system his own. Soon he would know all the boy knew and still carry memories and skills from prior forms he had once occupied. This was an immense change, for the languages from the past did not help him understand these new humans and of course the puny little dog could not.

Quickly Phaqutl learned that the boy, named Reginald by his parents, preferred to be called Wart, a nickname given him by his father from a character in a favorite book he'd read in his own childhood. He also knew that the youth could not serve him well for long. He needed a body that could come and go freely among the adults, one with matured physical and mental capacities. Also, no matter the animal, the loss of its young was never resolved easily, and humans in particular, with their powers of reason and complex tribal societies, would carry on elaborate searches for many days. The lad was not only inade-quate but posed a special danger, fated to be taken because he was the only human in the house that night to whom the little dog had access.

He sat Wart up in bed. In the darkened room and through the boy's eyes he looked back at the animal he now knew in the boy's language as Pookie. It stood stiffly on top of the covers near the boy's feet. It whined, softly, plaintively, began to turn in circles as some animals will do before lying down, then abruptly lost its foot-ing and tumbled from the bed to plump down onto the carpet without sound. Surely dead, Phaqutl took no further notice.

He began the ritual testing, wiggled fingers and toes, waggled feet and arms, shook the head, flexed and relaxed muscles, regis-tering their separate and collective strengths. The hands grabbed out at imaginary forms in the air. He noted the speed of move-ment and quickness of reflex. Next he let his powers play through the mind, assessing its knowledge, its perceptions, memories, the range and depth of emotions. A pleasant improvement over the dog, many useful tools by comparison. He became aware of airplanes and helicopters, six guns and cowboys, skateboards, Frisbees, school buses, strawberry ice cream and all the sensations that they brought. For him, new, exhilarating, and frightening, though held to the perceptions of a child.

He listened intently through the ears, raised the nose to sense the air. There was no noise or odor in the house that was strange to him though he had lost the small dog's keener senses of hearing and smell. The boy had far better sight even though it was difficult to tell just how much so in the faint light. Unlike the dog with its response to being taken a singular continuous state of pitiful confusion, the mind of the little boy was aware of something terribly wrong. He wanted to scream for his mother and he put himself through hysterics of pain and anguish that Phaqutl expected might last as long as he remained inside. From his occupation of countless hosts over the millennia he recognized that the greater the reasoning capacities of the host, the greater its suffering.

The dog had died a few moments after being discarded. It was to be expected. Phaqutl gave little thought to those he abandoned, he had left so very many for whatever purpose served him at the time, and afterward they either perished or did not. Most did.

He swung the slender short legs over the edge of the bed, careful to miss the inert fur puff on the floor, and stood the body up. Time to leave. He needed to put distance behind him before morning light. Soon after daylight he would hide until it was safe to move on again and he didn't intend to be within an area that might be searched.

He walked Wart to the open door, stopping there to peer out cautiously. The hallway rested empty and dark. He started to step out of the room, then hesitated. The clothing on the little body was different than it wore during the day, a sure give away if he came upon a human adult.

When he queried the mind the answers formed instantaneously. He backed away from the door, slipped the boy out of his pajamas and let them fall to the floor, then kicked them under the bed. He knew to tug clean underwear from the suitcase resting open on the floor and took yesterday's socks from where they had been stuffed into the high top athletic shoes and pulled these on. Jeans and tee shirt came next. Then the shoes. The concentration needed to tie the strings together that bound each shoe on its foot seemed disproportionally enormous, further evidence that the boy should be temporary.

Once again Phaqutl approached the bedroom door, checked the hall, then stepped the lad into it and crept him slowly and silently along the wall and down the side of the stairs where the boy's mind knew the boards were least likely to squeak.

At the landing the dark wooden front door with narrow full length windows on each side would open to the outdoors. He tested it and found it locked, but the big iron key jutted from the keyhole. The boys mind was not familiar with the lock and it became trial and error to first turn the key one way then the other until the latch began to move and it completed its circle with an authoritative clack. He froze to listen . . . seconds went by . . . nothing.

Once outside with the door closed securely behind, Phaqutl headed his little host into the night, past the moving hut he had ridden in earlier in the body of the dog and now knew as the aunt's Volvo, down the driveway, and out onto the sidewalk. Which way to turn? The boy didn't know what lay in either direction.

One of the Volvo huts went by, its twin front lights adding to that thrown on the ground by the unending string of lights atop poles. The boy named them street lights. He turned in that direction and brought the young legs to a steady even lope down the sidewalk, observing the surroundings with the new mind until he had passed through several street crossings. Each new block revealed more rows of darkened houses on each side of the street. Another automobile, as he found it was called, came at him and he dodged onto a lawn behind a shrub until it had passed.

After several more blocks the small body began to tire, and Phaqutl eased it to a walk to let the little heart slow and rest itself. Another auto and this time he turned the boy off the side-walk onto a lawn then walked along behind a hedge to keep moving while it drove past. The boy's body startled at a single low bark and he turned the head to look behind to see a much larger, sleeker version of the same kind of animal he had discarded less than thirty minutes before. It had come up from behind and now stood just a few yards back, head low, tail stiff and throat rum-bling. Phaqutl locked the boy's eyes onto those of the dog in the classic challenge all animals know. The lithe brute bared its fangs, flattened its ears and coiled down on its haunches prepar-ing to spring.

Doberman, the boy's brain trilled. Run, it said. But Phaqutl carried knowledge from another time and knew the human child could not come close to matching the animal's speed. Instantaneously Phaqutl called on the instincts of a beast he had inhabited in the distant past. Even as the dog prepared to leap and in a single complex motion, he dropped the boy to all fours, curled the lips back over the boy's teeth, stood the hair on his head straight and raised the curve of his spine in feral defiance. From the boy's slender throat came a snarl very much like the rage of an angry jungle cat. The dog responded with a bound for-ward. Its bared teeth thrust to within inches of the young human face. Then it halted in abrupt surprise as the boy's right arm hooked out far faster than the boy himself would have been capa-ble of moving. Slashing into the dog's neck from the side, the fingers hooked together into a single claw, plunging them hard into the soft tissue of the animal's throat, tearing into fur and flesh. Now the other hand slashed out, the fingers curved like the talons of a bird, and raked nails across the animal's face and eyes. Blood foamed at the dog's throat and an eye collapsed, the socket seeming suddenly empty. The animal yelped first in stark pain and then the disgrace of the defeated and turned to run, baying shame and disbelief into the waning darkness.

A light flicked on in an upstairs window of the nearest house and Phaqutl turned the boy, still on all fours, raced him across the lawn in the rolling spine-arched gallop of the cat back out onto the sidewalk and down the street. Moments later, the animal rage began to subside, giving way to more reasoned considerations once again. Phaqutl pulled the body back up on two feet gradually without slowing the pace and kept running until the boy's reserves were almost completely expended. The heart raced, the chest heaved, there was an agonizing stabbing pain in the left side of the abdomen that caused the body to double over as it slowed to a labored plodding.

It would not do to run the boy to death, for he would place himself in mortal danger. He became aware that both of the boy's hands registered severe pain and Phaqutl held them up to see. Far too delicately formed to be used to slash and claw, they had suffered badly during the attack. The left hand had fared particularly badly. The three longest fingers were splayed, twisted and bent, at unnatural angles. Shreds of skin hung from the fingertips, some with the nails still attached. Blood ran up both the raised wrists before dropping onto clothing or the ground. Those fingernails still attached held bits of black fur and chunks of red dog flesh. Both palms were swollen and where blood had not covered them were bruised and turning blue. Phaqutl dulled the boy's pain lest it lessen his ability to control and kept him moving. He carried the mutilated hands waist high and looked down to see both the dog's and the boy's blood spattered down the front of the boy's shirt and on his trousers. When he raised the boy's vision again he noted that light had begun forming in the east.

———•———

Phaqutl sensed the need to move on as far away as he could make the boy go before the light would allow people to observe his young features plainly enough to remember them later when asked if they had seen him. Lights were showing in more windows, and the boy's mind told him it wouldn't be long before people began coming out of the houses to go about the day.

He headed the little body left at the next intersection trotting at an angle across the street and into the alley that paralleled the street he had been following. Now the view changed from front to rear yards and most were fenced with chain link or white pickets or hedged by boxwood or laurel. Wart's little body seemed to have gotten a second wind, for the side ache had vanished. The adrenalin rush and the exhilaration of the fight with the Doberman left the body in an alert fluid state bordering elation and he trotted it along as effortlessly as he would the red forest deer.

When he passed a backyard where the alleyway was open to easy viewing from a lighted window he hunched down and looked away so he wouldn't present a clear image to observe. Through one alley, across the street, up a second alley, across yet another street and into the third.

"Young man what on earth you doin' runnin' up this old alley this early in the morning?"

A smiling grandmotherly-faced woman had somehow managed to step unnoticed into the alley ahead of him, hands on hips, directly in his path. As he drew closer, the woman's large features transformed into a deep frown.

"Oh, My-Lord-A-Mighty. Lookie at you! Blood all down the front of your shirt 'n trousers. What in the world happened to you? You been hit by a car? Come let Elsie look at you."

Phaqutl stuffed the boy's fists in his pockets so the woman would not see the injured fingers, quickened his pace, and side-stepped to hurry past, but it was not to be. A chunky and surprisingly strong hand grasped Wart's arm above the elbow and nearly lifted that side of the boy's body off the ground as she turned him to face her. The large round face still puffy from sleep peered into his.

"Talk to me when I ask a question, youngster."

Inside the pockets of the trousers of Reginald, alias Wart, Phaqutl pressed both bloodied and broken hands against the boys thighs so that her actions wouldn't expose them. The boy's mind once again screamed in pain. In terror it tried to call to this woman . . . then to his own mother. Unaware, the woman continued to hold him, waiting for his response.

The frowning face relaxed and softened. "My name is Elsie Hatfield and I've raised two girls and a boy just like you. They've been grown up and gone for quite some time now, so maybe I forget how to talk to a little feller without scarin' him half to death. But you gotta forget that 'cause I don't mean you no harm. It's plain as day you've been hurt, an' a boy your age ought to be at home this early in the mornin' with his papa and mama. So you come along into my house, an' I'll look you over and call your folks and maybe call Doc Runkle too."

She paused, looking into his face. Phaqutl kept the boy motionless, still held up on tiptoe by the strength of her grasp.

"You don't understand me none, do you, son?" She raised her voice and slowed her speech. "Do you belong to one of those foreign families over by Yesler Street." Then she repeated slowly and very plainly. "Yesler Street, your mama and papa? Your folks from Yugoslavia or France or somethin'?" He nodded the head just perceptibly.

"Okay. You understand me don'tcha. You come along then."

With that, she tugged the boy with her, her strong hand still clamped gently but firmly on his arm. Phaqutl did not have the boy resist as they moved up the narrow sidewalk that led from the alley toward the small roofed back porch. The walk was lined with blue and yellow pansies, their flowers sagging under the weight of the morning dew. When they came to the porch Elsie squatted down in front of him so that her face was at eye level with his, she grasped his other arm so that she held them both and turned him to face her.

"Now," and her voice seemed to care, a maternal voice that she probably had used to comfort her own children. "Show me where it hurts, son, let's see what we need to be doin' about it. I see you keepin' your hands in your pockets all this time. Is they what's hurtin' you the most? Show Elsie now, boy. Is it the hands?"

He began to move the boy's lips, but Elsie interrupted. "Sonny, I ain't goin' to hurt you, there ain't no need for you to cry."

Suddenly the hissing voice of an enraged cat spat at her face. "Yesssss, Old Woman. It is the hands."

With a single wrenching movement, the bloody hands of the boy, now mangled into grotesque shapes like the broken talons of a bird flew from the boy's pockets and thrust into the face of the confused and astounded woman. Elsie tried to draw back in fright, but Phaqutl moved the boy much too fast and before she could react, the hands grabbed and tangled themselves in her graying hair and pulled her face hard toward his. Phaqutl recognized in that instant that the woman had reached the peak of her fear. Elsie tried with surprising strength to pull away, then to cry out, but her thin trill was cut off before the first syllable had escaped. Her face frozen, the mouth agape, the eyes of the boy flared and were answered almost immediately by a similar reaction of the eyes of Elsie Hatfield, Phaqutl's new host.

Transfer from the little boy called Wart into the body of the matronly Elsie Hatfield happened instantaneously, as always. At the precise moment this occurred, the already exhausted boy slipped silently into a coma, his body went limp and would have fallen to the ground, if Elsie hadn't already had a grip on both of his upper arms.

Phaqutl made her stand in that position several seconds, the boy's head lolling to one side, while he established the full span of his control. Then he changed Elsie's grip on the boy so that her hands grasped the sides of his rib cage as though he might suddenly awaken to wriggle free. Marshaling strength the woman could not have mustered on her own, Phaqutl had her raise the boy, tuck him under one ham of an arm, and heft him into the house. Phaqutl was still settling himself in and her initial movements were stiff and wooden though they became smoother, more supple than they had been in many years within a few steps.

Once inside her home, he moved her through the kitchen to the room she knew as the parlor, where he made the woman raise her burden and hold it at arm's length in front of her over the worn sofa by grasping the tops of its shoulders. Her hands popped open to let Wart fall, as she might drop soiled clothing into the laundry hamper. He dropped onto the thick cushions and with a bounce the small torso flopped backward and settled against the backrest. The head slumped to one side, the eyelids now raised part way and tremors jittered the arms and legs like those of a dancing marionette.

With Elsie's chunky frame unburdened, Phaqutl ignored the quivering body on the sofa and kept her standing to begin the process of assessing this new carrier. Permanent pain in the lower area of the spine, nothing to do about it, not debilitating. Knees hurting now from kneeling to work in the garden, her mind informed him it was caused by the osteoarthritis of an aging body. Medicines for pain in the mirrored cabinet over the bathroom sink.

He moved each limb, stretching, reaching, bending, twisting; and turned the head from side to side, rolled it back and forth in an arc around her shoulders. He found the ranges of motion constricted but the overall strength and state of health good. Occupying a body in deteriorating health had risks, but this one would do for now.

He settled her into an overstuffed recliner opposite the sofa and continued the inventory. Allergies to shellfish. It seemed she didn't like them anyway and he couldn't get clear pictures of what they might be. And cats. Cats made her sneeze and she couldn't stand the slinky way they walked when they knew she was looking at them.

Husband dead going on fourteen years. Car accident. He was a drunk and he'd been drinking the night he'd stalled his station wagon on the train tracks on his way back from she didn't know where. Thoughts of him seemed always present on the edge of her mind. That odd human trait.

Children, a boy and two girls, none living in-state. Sandra Mae, youngest at thirty-two, two little girls of her own, phoned once or twice a month, mostly to complain about her husband. Seldom let her mother get a word in after hello. The older daughter, never married, bookkeeper. Elsie and Marion didn't get along. Marion lived with a strange woman who always seemed to wear men's business suits that Elsie didn't like personally one damn little bit. Christmas card signed best wishes for the new year and nothing more. Oldest, Stevie, her favorite, forty-one next birthday, divorced and raising a son by himself. Sends flowers Mother's Day and birthdays, money and a card at Christmas. Even though he seemed stuck in a dead-end job, she had great hope for his future. Phaqutl read a deep melancholy surrounding the grandchildren. Elsie hadn't seen any of them for over two years.

The woman had no mating interest, no social callers, and she didn't go visiting. Now and then she had a conversation in the back yard with a nextdoor neighbor. Easily avoided. Twice a week Elsie walked two blocks to the market to buy groceries. Cashed her social security check there every month. The woman who tended the register at the grocery store treated her with indifference. Once Elsie caught her slipping a package of chicken she'd just rung up under the counter hoping she'd go home without it and more than once found she'd rung up an item twice. She was the owner's wife. Elsie wouldn't trust her with the time of day. His new carrier lived a solitary life and took care to guard herself against those who would take advantage of her. She was nearly perfect for him, for there were no other humans likely to contact her if they didn't see her for a while or if she suddenly began to behave differently than they were accustomed to seeing. This was an opportunity to learn the present, to locate the past and to locate Coquitla. If she had survived.

At the time of Phaqutl's conquest of the little dog, its mind went into the abject confusion that he expected of so pathetic a creature and it remained in that state until he cast it aside to die. Most hosts died soon after he abandoned them excepting a few of the very young who, for unknown reasons, seemed to have recuperative powers that didn't carry through to adulthood.

The boy, Wart, provided a far better host than the dog, offering much more in the way of knowledge of the new surroundings, but his mental powers were only beginning to develop. At possession, the boy's mind retreated into a whimpering fearful state, as childish instincts surfaced and the boy's thoughts pleaded for his parents to make things right again. It would have been some time before the boy's mentality would have responded on its own, with anger or perhaps the bargaining that human children sometimes applied to their prayers. Phaqutl saw the tremors wrack the boy's body through Elsie's eyes. Part of the process of dying. So be it.

The mind of the adult was very different. Now it churned. Phaqutl read extreme fright, and a panicked attempt at assessment. I can see some, but it's all fuzzy. I don't hear none at all, too much noise in my head. Sounds like a railroad train runnin' through a tunnel. God-a-mighty, it hurts somethin' awful, an' I can't move my hands? Can't feel nothin' but the headache. Must be havin' a stroke. Gonna die. Wish I'd told the kids I love'em. Ain't even made my Will. Things to do. Ain't ready to go. Didn't think it would happen like this. Thought some mornin' a long time from now I just wouldn't wake up. Where's the tunnel an' the bright light they say I'll see? I sure hope William can be there to meet me. This rambling encouraged him. It showed strong mental capability and weak resistance. Phaqutl intended to make use of it all.

Now he needed to become dormant. To replenish stamina and strengthen his ability to maintain dominion over the woman. He had been looking for a place to hide Wart, so that he could take dormant time, when he'd turned the boy into the alleys and Elsie had surprised him. Transferring hosts twice in one day and three times in two had stretched him to the limit. Taxing always, but after decades in limbo, literally dying for the opportunity to escape confinement, as iota by iota, decade after decade, his essences dissipated ever so slowly into miasma, until the little dog came. The need to draw from the energies of the woman to rejuvenate had become most acute.

On the sofa the boy's form tremored again more violently and his eyes flared open wide. He voiced a plaintiff call for his mother, but before it finished the body stiffened, convulsed, and fell limp. Phaqutl watched the features pale slowly. The chest no longer rose and fell. Should he go dormant now or be rid of the lifeless human shell? Someone could have watched the scene in the alley just minutes before. That offered the greater risk. He would replenish after.

He stood Elsie and hefted the tiny body up on her hip with an arm around its waist. He shuffled her to the cellar door and one-at-a-time sideways down the steps to drop the limp form on the dirt floor. Phaqutl took the woman up the stairs again and returned her sometime later carrying garden tools from the garage. She got down on her knees and chipped and dug in the hard dirt under the stairs until she could drag the inert body into the shallow grave. Phaqutl remained in full control of the woman's movements, but his energies had ebbed to the degree that he could no longer mask the deed from Elsie's consciousness. He couldn't stop the silent tears from running down her cheeks as she spit moisture into the hem of her skirt and used it to clean the blood from the boy's fingers. They kept falling as she moved each of the mangled fingers back into place, folded the tiny hands closed, and crossed the thin arms over the chest. Her head sagged forward when she covered the small pitiful form with dirt. She bent over him once and used the back of gritty fingers to ease the hair off the boy's forehead. She'd saved covering the boy's face until last.

ARTHUR HAD CLEARED PARTS OF THE TRAIL on his way up to the pyramid and it was downhill most of the way back. Because of this, apprehension that the panther might change its mind and come after him and his rush to be sure he wasn't left behind, he made it back in less than a third of the time it had taken to reach the pyramid. The boatmen were onboard ready to leave when he arrived. He didn't know whether they were about to go without him or were simply waiting in a state of readiness. He didn't ask.

The trip downriver from the pyramid also passed quickly for him. The excitement of his find and the encounter with the panther kept his adrenalin high and his thoughts full. He barely felt the bursts of spray that caught him when the craft veered sharply to dodge obstacles as it traveled at top speed with the descending currents. He scarcely noticed the family of capibara that watched them pass from the safety of the bank or the constant flow of exotic birds that crisscrossed around the boat and overhead in every possible direction.

Just as the sun dipped into the treetops the boat pulled in to a low wide sandbar in the crook of a sharp bend of the river. He pitched his tent on the sand and took the meal of rice and eggs hastily put together by *El Capitán*, inside. The man had threatened to abandon him and Arthur wasn't inclined to seek his company. He ate, spread his sleeping bag and lay down on top of it. The moment he closed his eyes all the recent events fell over his mind like a blanket of thorns: the fight with Fields, Benedetti stepping in, his standing with Millie, if he still had any, the destroyed *Perra* site, the magnificent pyramid and it's place on the river that hid it so successfully, his encounter with the black jaguar, the superstitious refusals of the boatmen. It was all questions, no answers, and he exhausted himself with his own mental pandemonium. Then when sleep finally came he slipped into the dream. The same one that had tormented him since he'd been a child living in the boys' home. He always lived it through the eyes of a youngster of ten or maybe twelve.

It began with the dream boy cringing under the stairway of a lightless cellar with his knees pulled up hard against his chest. His chin chattered an uncontrollable shiver in the chilly dankness and he remembered to get up and get moving to rid himself of the cold. He uncoiled from his fetal crouch and rose, stretched to relieve cramped muscles, shook himself silently to warm his blood, and slipped from his hiding place.

No wall enclosed the stairway where it descended from above and with cautious fingers he touched his way along the rough boards of the open casement, step by downward step, until he came to the place where the last riser reached the floor.

He moved around to the treads, and counting, "One," in his softest whisper, the only time he used his voice each day, stepped up. Fear touched the boy at step four as he bent in the darkness to locate the one above that he knew would groan woefully with his weight. Concentrating, he stepped up over it and onto number six. At the eighth he hesitated listening like a fawn in the jungle before going on counting his way quietly up to the twelfth. He lowered himself to sit on that one, leaned his elbows on the one above. Resting his chin in his palms, he made his eyes level with the little landing to peer into the crack at the bottom of the cellar door. A thin gray line of light confronted him, but nothing more.

As the boy stared, a numbing despair that drained away his energy settled down on him like dampness on a chilly night. He'd never tried to twist the door knob. The strip of light served as his sole companion everyday and to open the door and step beyond it would deliver him to the evil waiting there. His beginning, for he told himself he'd never existed in another place, his home, and his life were here looking to the light and in his secret place beneath the stairs.

After what seemed like a very long time the light under the door began to dim and as always at this time in the dream the dread came to overlay the dismal hopelessness. It weighed down upon the youngster, as though he wore a huge thick coat with pockets weighted with stones. And like an immense coat, the dread both frightened and comforted him. Why? This question niggled in the brain of the sleeping adult, Arthur.

In the last moments of the thin wedge of light, the dream-child raised his chin from its rest to look down at the worn boards that formed the small landing. He reached to remove a splinter from the crack between two of them, move it another board's width from the wall, and tuck it into the crack there. The splinter now rested in the fifth one from the wall. Tomorrow he would move it to the sixth and that would signal his day to bathe. The day after he would move the splinter back and begin the count again.

After retracing his way to the bottom of the steps he took two long strides forward and stretched his right arm as high as he could above his head. He waggled it in the air until his fingers touched a string that he knew hung from the ceiling. The boy stood on his toes to catch and hold it and he rolled the little bell shape at the bottom between his fingers. He knew that pulling on the string would turn on a light. He shuddered. A light in the cellar would signal to the power that dwelled on the other side of the door at the top of the stairs that he still lived and it would descend and surely make him pay for that crime. Darkness and silence held him from harm. He let the string go and for the moment exalted in knowing that for those seconds each day, when he held the bell of the light pull string in his fingers, his destiny was his to control.

With both hands in front of him now, he touched his way through familiar surroundings until he came to the square double sink fixed on the wall next to the washer. A soft voice in his head, one that wasn't his own, reminded him to wash his face and hands every day and to wash all over when the splinter on the stairs said it was the sixth day. And he did.

He searched out the handles of both faucets and selected the cold on the right. He'd turned on the hot just once and the pipe rattled and honked. He'd turned it off and groped stumbling through the murk in panic until he could hide himself. He'd stayed there, knees pulled up to his chin, cringing in the blackness until hunger and thirst drove him out. Since that time, caution had become his one true friend, darkness and silence his protectors. They, together with the jars of canned goods on the shelves along the wall opposite the stairs, and the light under the door at the top of them were the family of the little boy and with them he could survive.

Now he turned on the water ever so lightly lest the thing upstairs register the sound of it running. He made his right hand wash itself as best he could and leaned over to let the faucet trickle water up and down that arm. The boy cleaned his face and neck with his right hand also, careful to scrub the back of his neck and both ears. He held his left arm stiffly out to the side, careful to let no water touch it. There was still the pain in the fingers of his hand, but more important, his left arm must remained unwashed, though he couldn't tell himself why.

The boy leaned over the edge of the sink and twisted his head until he could cover the end of the faucet with his mouth. He drank just once a day and waited until the cool trickle filled his mouth before swallowing. He let his mouth fill again and again, savoring the feeling it brought him before turning the handle off.

The sounds came from over the boy's head and somehow in his sleep Arthur-the-adult sensed that the dream was ending. It was always the same. Slow heavy steps squeaked the boards above, then the squeaking stopped and gave way to soft shuffling sounds, a pause, and the noises of springs groaning under heavy weight and the sounds of shoes dropping, one then the other. These noises brought with them . . . prickling needles of fear . . . shining spikes of fear . . . cold slashing blades of raw terror, and just as the cringing boy knew he would scream, would give himself away to the evil in the house above, Arthur always woke himself up.

This night he lay sucking in deep breaths, relieved to be awake. The fear still tightened his scalp and raised the hair on his head and arms. The events of the previous day and the memories of the dream became all stir-fried together in the oppressive heat of the jungle night and he did little more than doze until morning.

They were back on the river more than an hour before dawn. With luck, the help of the current, and persistence the boat handlers managed to pull into the tiny harbor that intruded the riverbank at *Boca Manu* by twilight.

His crew began to walk away the moment they'd tied the boat to the single piling shared by several others and Arthur had to call them back. He'd suddenly reawakened to the fact that he'd been given charge of many thousand dollars worth of expedition gear and leaving it unattended seemed to assure much of it would be lost. *El Capitán* tried to assure him that nothing would happen, but at the risk of insulting the man, Arthur pressed until the boatman reluctantly agreed to have the cargo removed to a place where he said they could pay someone to watch over it through the night. The bargaining began again until they'd agreed upon a price to transfer and guard the goods.

El Capitán spoke to his 'cousin' who nodded and disappeared in the direction of the village, while the two of them waited. After a few moments the boatman turned toward Arthur and spoke quietly in the darkness.

"I am sorry, *Señor*."

"That you threatened to leave me alone in the forest."

"That the other man hit you into the *Rió Perra*."

The statement caught Arthur completely by surprise and he stood lost for an answer.

"He is the much bigger *hombre* and the yellow-haired woman is very beautiful. I theenk you will fight over her again someday."

Arthur couldn't see his expression but the tone seemed almost fatherly. "Would you have left me alone in the forest?"

"*Si, Señor*. We speak about it while you are away. We would leave your tent and food and my cousin would leave you his knife. But we would not stay and if we find a boat on the river that would sell us petrol, we would come back to you in the morning."

Cheerful male voices interrupted the night to confirm that the villagers were arriving. When they came within a few yards nearly a dozen flashlights switched on to play over the boat while the 'cousin' and *El Capitán* gave directions in Quechuan. Within moments four men had boarded and busily passed supplies to the men onshore. Even though he couldn't understand the words, their banter led Arthur to believe they felt they were having an adventure. Perhaps their quiet village lives made that possible.

Soon a first group loaded up and left to follow their flashlight beams to the village. As the second was about to leave, the first began to come back. A return and second loading for each man and the boat showed empty under a nearly full moon that had begun to filter its light through the topmost branches of the high canopy on the far eastern riverbank. Arthur and *El Capitán* shouldered their personal gear and followed the last of them to a large wooden shed. Like all the other buildings he'd seen, it stood on short pilings with burlap soaked in tar or creosote tied at mid point around them to discourage crawling animals and insects. Inside were several of the long narrow riverboats in various stages of construction. Arthur supervised the arrangement and packing of the gear with *El Capitán* turning Arthur's English into Quechuan as needed. Then *El Capitán* called to a lad Arthur guessed couldn't be over fourteen. He introduced him to Arthur as the one who would stand watch. The smooth-faced lad stood to beam at them while Arthur gave the boatman the agreed upon amount of money and stood by while he passed it out. Each share was accepted politely and with language Arthur took to be appreciation. The villagers waited until all had been paid and left in a noisy group.

El Capitán beckoned and Arthur followed him outside. "Where are they going now?"

"One of them is the man who owns the store. He tells them he will open it if they wish to drink. I think he will own most of the money by morning. Perhaps I will join them later, but first let me see to your stay. I have learned that your people have been taken to a lodge about six kilometers from here. It is not safe to go there in the dark. The river has many things to break the boat."

Arthur could see the man's features plainly now. Bright moonlight that laid their shadows crisply on the ground. He seemed much more at ease here in his village.

"My home is very small, *Señor,* and I have five children or you would be the welcome guest of my family."

"Thank you, I can sleep in the building with the gear."

"*Señor, por favor.*"

Arthur caught a new deference in his voice. "What is it?"

"It is my son who guards your equipment. He does this because he wishes to make me proud of him. It will embarrass him if you stay in the building. He will think you do not trust him. That he is not yet the man."

Even in the moonlight Arthur could see the pride that already crested in his features. He began to sense the void swelling in his own chest again, crowding his heart aside. Where had the father been who would have done these things for him? For the first time Arthur had a glimpse of himself standing with his hand proudly on the shoulder of his own son. A boy with Millie's eyes and hair. *El Capitán's* voice brought him back to the matter at hand.

"*Señor,* if you can do this for me? I will be very grateful. I will show you a place to put your tent. It is safe and you can watch the building from a small distance. I will bring you dinner from my home and come in the morning to take you to your companions."

Arthur put a hand on the boatman's shoulder. "Your son has good reason to be proud of you, also, *Señor.* I'll go with you.

Thirty yards away from the boatshed *El Capitán* stopped and helped Arthur erect his home for the night. Then he left to return shortly carrying an oil lantern and a cardboard box that he opened to spread the promised evening meal on the ground. The boatman pried the top from a bottle of Inca Kola, filled two plastic glasses halfway then topped them off with red wine.

Arthur had tasted this common local drink before and had little liking for it, but he accepted it and vowed not to let that show.

El Capitán set out sandwiches and fruit, but declined to join in the food, explaining he would leave to eat with his son in a few minutes. Again Arthur felt a growing respect for this strange little man, yet he still carried reservations about his conduct at the discovery site. It would likely be his last chance for private conversation and he decided to seize the opportunity. "*Señor Capitán*, would you have come back if you hadn't been able to buy more fuel upriver for the boat?"

"Yes. In one more day, perhaps two."

"If you could not stay there because of the danger, how would you expect me to survive? Did you think I would be alive when you came back?"

The other man remained silent for a few moments as if sorting out what he would say next. But finally he lifted his face in the lantern light and began speaking.

"I do not know. Perhaps that seems impossible for you to understand. Let me explain in this way.

"On the way downriver today we passed the opening to the *Rió Pinquen*. A small tribe lives just a few hours up that river and if you go there they kill you. Three or four years ago a farmer and his family went up there and only their thirteen year old daughter escaped to return. They don't kill us because they want our bodies or what we may carry with us, but because they fear outsiders. The anaconda take their children while they bathe in the river, they have horrible disease and sometimes not enough food, yet they stay where they are because they fear us more than the dangers that they know.

"People may choose to live with dangers if they know them. If you do not know them, you can only prepare yourself to fight or to run. Sometimes it is not in us to be good in what we choose to do.

"We each must know our own fears and must deal with them in our own way. I have told you my fears about the place where we took you. I think you need to tell yours to the woman with the yellow hair. Perhaps then another fight with the big *hombre* is not necessary."

The man stood to leave and Arthur thought he detected embarrassment in his movement and moonlit features. Twice his comments about the run-in with Fields had caught him off guard. Arthur could sense another night fraught with confusing thought before him. Then the boatman offered him his hand and Arthur shook it.

"I will come for you in the morning, *Señor*. It must be early."

"I'll be ready. But one more thing before you go."

"*Si, Señor*."

"You can't be *El Capitán* to everyone. What is your name?"

"A very long one compared to your American names, *Señor*. But my friends call me Manolo."

"*Buenas noche, Señor* Manolo."

"*Buenas noche, Señor* Arthur.

<hr />

In the morning Manolo woke him shortly before dawn and within the hour Arthur'd made the transfer to the lodge where the expedition members housed. The boatman told him it would normally serve tourist groups, but they'd been diverted to other locations for the few days the scientists would be there. He left, promising the expedition gear would be kept safe and refusing the offer of more money. Despite his earlier reservations Arthur trusted him all the way.

He carried his gear up the short reed-lined path that led from the river to the clearing occupied by the lodge. The sun, a shimmering yellow-orange ball, still squatted low on the eastern horizon and he saw no signs of life about. He rested his duffle against the trunk of a palm and took a quick walk around the area. There were two main buildings, both on meter high pilings like those at *Boca Manu*. The walls of the one that contained the sleeping rooms stopped short of the eaves of a palm frond roof to leave a two foot screened space at the top. The better to let out the heat. A small building, open and screened on three sides, harbored the kitchen and dining areas. A tamed crimson macaw eyed him silently from its perch on the back of one of the dining chairs.

He found what he was looking for and retrieved his gear. The showers stood in a roofless shed at the end of a short trail a dozen paces into the jungle from the clearing that held the main lodge buildings. The single overhead pipe offered a trickle rather than a spray. He found the water only slightly cooler than the morning air and, as he lathered and scrubbed, savored the feeling of the grime washing away. He'd thought he was building a tan, but most of it washed through the drain opening in the raised floor. After putting on shorts and white tee shirt he took up his gear again and returned to the clearing. The sleeping lodge still offered no indication of anyone up and about. There were soft noises and signs of movement coming from the kitchen.

On his way up the path from where the boat had left him, he'd seen lounge chairs in a grassy spot at river's edge. He went there now, straightened a chair, faced it toward the clearing to keep the sun at his back and pulled a small metal table beside it. He retrieved his log book, propped it open on his lap and began the process of trying to recall and document every detail from the moment he'd left Benedetti and the others to his arrival at *Boca Manu* the previous night. He intended to report everything and anything that might help support his discovery. Without photographs this was particularly important.

The sound of the moving water behind him provided background music to help his concentration, until the distinctive voice of Millie Holtz caught him by surprise. "Hey, Arthur. Hoped you'd be here. The woman in the kitchen said a new man came in this morning."

His spirits rose when he looked toward the clearing to see her walking in his direction. She looked every bit the girl next door dressed in shorts and brightly-colored top that gave no hint of ever having been compressed into luggage. She stood tall, glowing with health, bright-eyed and self-assured.

Apparently he'd been forgiven any transgressions. He half expected Fields to step up behind her and put a proprietary arm around her waist. But he didn't and she came striding along as if independence was her name, trim figured, flowing honey-blond hair, and fresh white smile.

"Mind if I sit."

Before he could move to help, she'd already busied herself dragging up another lounge chair and arranging it next to his.

"How was the boat trip?" Her voice was matter-of-fact and gave no hint of any hidden agenda as she sat and leaned back to cross those extra long legs he knew so well.

He didn't like holding things from her, but it wouldn't do to give his discovery away. Not yet. Not until he'd put something together from the notes and sketches to back himself up and certainly not while still in this country, where even a few overheard words could start a rumor that would send treasure hunters off in a scramble.

"Smooth enough, I guess." She seemed satisfied and now it was his turn to question. "When is the wrap-up meeting?"

"Things have moved quickly since you left us. We began flying out just a few hours after you'd gone. The boats with the rest of the gear dropped us at the pickup point and headed downriver even before the first plane load took off.

"Everyone who flew was here that night and the boats came in midafternoon yesterday. They said they hadn't seen you along the way and some of us were beginning to worry. If you hadn't checked in by morning, we were going to go looking. It's a relief to have you here."

"Motor trouble. Nothing critical." He hated the lie even before it came out.

She smiled, happy his problems hadn't been serious. He saw trust in her smile and detested the lie even more.

"We had the wrap-up yesterday afternoon. Lansing had been in touch with the university and he and Benedetti were called back ASAP. They made arrangements to pack and ship what came in by boat before they left and Lansing has asked that you stay over one more day and see to the disposition of the stuff you brought down. There's an envelope for you tacked on a bulletin board in the dining room. The rest of us are taking the boats to the airstrip to fly out in a couple of hours."

He wanted to ask, how much trouble he'd gotten himself into because of the fight? What did she really think of him now? Would Fields be flying out with her group? But he couldn't bring himself to do it. She seemed cheerful enough, as though all had been forgotten, but he thought she might be too cheerful. Perhaps she was keeping up appearances so she wouldn't have to give him bad news. Another sign that she might be holding something back was that when they were out of sight of people from the university, she nearly always stayed in some form of affectionate physical contact with him, her fingers gently touching his arm, her toes nudging the calf of his leg, or leaning against him as they walked. Now she seemed content to lie in the lounge chair with her arms folded beneath her breasts.

She was beautiful. They shared a common lifestyle and she wanted to give him the family he'd never had. Even though she seemed to be holding herself in reserve, he sensed she was offering him another chance. The scent of her circled him like the promise of things to come. He could see a future for them and he didn't intend to blow it. Not again. He looked into her face. She sat giving him that woman's knowing look . . . she knew. Tension began draining from his body as though a dam had opened its gates.

"*Buenos dias, Señor.*"

Startled, Arthur bumped his gaze away from Millie to see a slender form in a flowered ankle length dress standing near his lounge chair. She held a tray with two small mugs on it. The aroma said coffee. The tray partially blocked his view of her but he saw the top of her forehead and dark brown hair, straight with only a hint of curl where it touched the tops of her bare brown shoulders.

He took the mugs and turned to offer one to Millie. When he glanced back to thank the woman, she had turned to walk away. Her bare feet made no sound and rays of light reflecting in slanting beams up from the river dazzled her appearance to produce the impression of a silent floating apparition. Only the curve of a hip moving against the material of her dress gave a hint of the woman there.

"Arthur?"

He was startled for the second time in as many minutes.

Millie sat looking at him quizzically. "It isn't very reassuring to have you staring at the first woman who comes along, even if she is rather striking. I'm almost sorry I asked her to bring us coffee here."

He felt his face coloring and began to mutter an apology, but she continued on as though it didn't really matter. "I'm starved, but it will be a few minutes before breakfast is ready. They have one of those triangle bells. I'll have to eat and run. I've packing to do."

They continued chatting. There were rumors that the university blamed Lansing for the failure of the expedition because he should have had the site checked before they left the United States. Millie filled him in and told him details of her own journey from the *Perra* site to this place. He chatted about his experience, careful not to mention anything that might peak her curiosity and hating himself for it. When the call to the morning meal came, they carried their cups to the dining room as though nothing worrisome had ever happened between them.

They climbed the short steps to the dining area. Some of the expedition members had already seated themselves, and they greeted the two of them in the usual way. He couldn't glimpse the slightest hint of curiosity or concern in any of their features. Either the story of his debacle with Fields, who was conspicuously absent, had not gotten around, or they were studiously ignoring it in his presence. The crimson macaw he'd seen earlier walked its way slowly down the center of the table accepting bits of food from the diners with the gentle dignity of a village priest. He felt himself begin to relax.

They seated themselves at the long table that was actually several pushed together to seat nearly two dozen. Someone passed a plate piled high with dry toast in their direction. Jam and a pitcher of orange juice followed. The conversation was more cheerful than those of his last day at the *Rió Perra* site and the dig wasn't mentioned at all.

Others joined them over the next few minutes. Each time he heard footsteps coming up the entry stairs, he turned instinctively to look. He felt Millie's foot tapping his ankle under the table and he turned to her.

"He flew out yesterday with Lansing and Benedetti."

Heat began rising in his face, but couldn't let it go. "Whose idea?"

Millie shrugged an I-don't-know-or-care.

He realized for the first time just how hungry he was and reached for the plate of toast just as a noise called his attention to the far end of the table. He looked to see the young woman who'd brought them coffee at the river's edge. She stood with her back to him holding a large metal tray, placing plates of food in front of the diners. He craned forward in his chair to see what the plates offered just as she turned to face in his direction.

Millie hadn't been right when she'd called the girl striking. She'd chosen far too placid a word. He let his gaze linger for a second, but remembered his embarrassment when she'd caught him staring before and made an effort to turn his head away.

It failed.

It wasn't the contrast of her dark skin against the bright colors of her wrap-around, or the subtle movements of her breasts and soft underbelly against the material that held him. It was her face.

Their eyes met and even that far away her dark gaze riveted on his. She blinked and when her lids raised it looked as though she'd gone into some sort of trance, yet the expression of her eyes proclaimed a deep internal agony. She looked at him for a long moment then her features turned to panic and she ran back through the entrance to the kitchen and was gone.

Arthur sat literally gasping for air. His heart pounded and he could feel the hard pulse throbbing in his throat. A sudden icy chill settled into the back of his neck, as though he'd just had a close brush with his own death. He felt himself becoming aroused. He shut his eyes, made hard fists, clamped his jaw, trying to make these forced tensions reestablish control. After a few moments he opened his eyes, beginning to feel embarrassment course through him again and turned toward Millie hoping against hope she hadn't witnessed the intensity of his reaction.

Her chair sat empty.

He hesitated, taking the situation in, then a convulsive response snapped him to his feet. His chair banged over backwards to the floor, but before the noise occurred he'd already made it to the entrance and stood looking around the clearing. No sign of her.

He bounded down the steps and trotted to the building that housed the sleeping quarters. He went quietly down the single corridor, listening until he heard noise in one of the rooms. He knocked. He heard movement inside, but no one answered the door.

It had to be her. He knocked again. "Millie, it's Arthur."

Still he waited and finally she announced in a voice that warned him to tread lightly. "It's open."

He twisted the knob and pushed it in. Her khaki duffle bag stood ready by the door. She'd changed into traveling clothes and now stood beside the narrow bed with one knee on a small suitcase trying to compress it enough to latch it shut. A strand of hair dangled over one eye and her expression would have killed a snake, yet when she spoke her voice was measured, almost kind.

"Arthur I don't know what's gotten into you. Taking a swing at Tim Fields, I can almost understand. I've wanted to smack him myself.

"Riding off alone in the boat? I suppose you had your reasons and it helped the expedition." She hesitated while she snapped the latch into place and turned to stand in front of him.

"But this business with the waitress . . . what is that? Some test I'm supposed to pass?"

She didn't wait for him to respond. "Arthur is this what you're really like? Is this how you'd treat me if we were married? Whatever is going on here, I think you need to get it together. Right now I don't want to be around you. I need time to do some thinking on my own. I'll be a few minutes early, but I'm going down to wait for the boat. I can carry these things by myself. Please don't come along. And don't say anything. We'll talk when we're both back home."

"Please Millie . . ."

"Don't speak to me now." She turned abruptly to haul the small suitcase off the bed. She shouldered her duffle bag and blew past him and out the door. This was a Millie he'd never seen before. Astonished he turned to watch her go. A few steps down the corridor she called back over her shoulder. "Don't forget to pick up the envelope in the dining hall."

<hr />

Arthur watched her go. Purpose in her stride warned him not to follow. The open corridor let him see her crossing the clearing until the reeds at the sides of the path to the river bank blocked his view. A heaviness pushed hard into his chest. He retraced his steps to the dining area, found the bulletin board and took down the small manila envelope with his name on it pinned there. Only a few of the diners remained and he took a seat at the farthest end of the table from them. The envelope contained a single sheet from a yellow note pad and he recognized Benedetti's half-printed, half-cursive script.

Arthur,
We're assuming you've made it back with all the gear. Dr. Lansing is asking that you stay over until you can meet with a Señor Alverado Sanchez who will contact you at the lodge. He

will see to the packing and shipping of the equipment. The rest of the gear is already on its way. Dr. Lansing and myself have been called back to university. It appears that the gods are angry. FYI: Timothy Fields will accompany us.

—Jan

"Señor, my name is Beba." Her voice came at his elbow and startled him. He turned to find her standing there, her expression not so full of terror as it had been a few minutes before, but still frightened and somehow sad.

"I am sorry to have make your woman angry." Then without further explanation. "We must meet."

To his own amazement he found himself nodding agreement. "My name is Arthur." The pulse in his throat began thrushing again.

"We cannot meet here, *Señor*. The lodge belongs to my uncle and he would not approve of my talking for more than one minute to a man he does not know. We most certainly would be interrupted.

"There is a pathway that leaves the clearing behind this building. It goes to a small blind on a lake. The tourists go there when they hope to see the giant otter. It will take twenty minutes to walk there. I am to leave from here at two o'clock." She touched his arm briefly and darted away.

He sat staring at the unresponsive piece of yellow paper in his hand. The cold chill twisted at his spine again. Feelings stormed through him like a horde of gremlins. He couldn't believe he'd just agreed to meet a woman he'd never seen before, at a location where anything could happen. He'd embarrassed himself twice in front of Millie only minutes after he'd come to the brink of wanting to start a family with her. Two days ago he may have ruined his future in his profession by fighting with Fields and later in the same day he'd uncovered a find that could take him to the top of it only to be run off by a black jaguar. The gremlins were in a free-for-all.

⸻ ◆ ⸻

Arthur heard distant rumblings and saw dark clouds building on the horizon. He crossed the clearing and found the pathway Beba had told him to follow to the animal blind. Typically during this time of year the rain would be short but torrential. He hoped it would hold off until he could return.

He'd changed his mind just seconds after agreeing to meet her, but she'd already disappeared. The animal blind would be a perfect place to go unknowing into harm's way. Another good reason to steer clear.

After he'd returned to the lodge from supervising the loading of the expedition gear, he pondered Beba's reason for asking him to meet her. He concluded that she must know something about the failed expedition site or about his discovery that she wanted to tell him. That changed his mind. Word traveled fast through these small villages and everyone knew everyone else's business. If it concerned his discovery, he needed to hear what she had to say.

A few minutes walking and the path began to skirt the edge of a small village. He heard boys voices shouting to one another and soon came upon them, a group of a dozen or more chasing a soccer ball on a field that bordered the path. Two smaller lads, too young to play he guessed, knelt in the grass watching.

As he walked by, the pair rose and scurried to stand beside the path. One said something in Quechua while they both held out their hands. Arthur couldn't understand the request but their smiles seemed to take away the fears for his own safety and he rewarded them by handing a one *sole* coin to each of them.

Another moment's walk and he came to a mammoth tree with buttress roots like the fletched feathers of a gigantic arrow spreading thirty feet across at ground level. Here the path turned abruptly into the forest. Though it was wide and cleared of vegetation, bustling columns of ants bisected the path frequently and he took great care not to disturb them lest he suffer the consequences. A steady bird-like chirping called his attention ahead and he saw a small band of carmine monkeys scurrying away through the limber branches of the lower canopy. Ten minutes later the trail ended at the blind. It sat low, rectangular and roofless on the edge of one of the hundreds of oxbow lakes that dotted the area. It could hold about as many people as the dining room at the lodge.

He peered in, found it empty and entered. He looked back outside to view the narrow lake through one of the windows slitted in the palm frond walls that offered only enough space to accommodate a viewer's eyes or camera lens. The lake water lay mirror calm without sign of the animals the blind was intended to reveal. A green ibis walked on long thin legs at water's edge and a trio of Muscovy ducks made silent wakes as they paddled near the far shore.

A sudden blue-white flash was answered immediately by nearly as bright return reflections from the interior walls. Split seconds later thunder grumbled again. Electricity crawled on his skin. The sense of risk at being on the edge of the lake under trees during lightning strikes tightened the skin at the back of his neck. His hope of making it back to the lodge before the rain evaporated.

He felt rather than saw Beba slip in through the door. She gave no sign of greeting. She'd changed clothing and the cotton dress she now wore displayed an interlaced pattern of pale white flowers on a nearly obscured blue background. The dress almost touched the bare dirt floor and only the heels of her sandals could be seen beneath it as she stood before him. Her hair hung straight to rest on bare shoulders. The light dimmed as clouds scudded across the sun. He heard the calls of small birds warning of the impending storm. It took him a startled moment to comprehend the expression on her face . . . stark raw terror. Another flash and the deafening snap of thunder came barely a second later.

Instantly the fears for his own safety that he'd pushed aside earlier cascaded through his guts. He could almost feel the knife searing its way into his back. He jerked his head swiftly to look beyond her, out the doorway, every sense straining, searching for the cause of her fright. He saw nothing and turned back to her as it dawned on him.

"Beba, why are you afraid of me? Why are we here?"

Her voice came out small on the threshold of panic. "My uncle's lodge where you stay is the heart of our village, *Señor*. If anyone sees us together, my uncle would be told of it before the hour has passed. I have promised to him I would never be in the company with the man who is a guest in his keeping. I left there one hour ago, so they will not think we are here together."

"Right, I get the part about the small village and your uncle, but why are we here at all?"

A tear rolled down her cheek and she took it away with the back of her hand. "My worry, *Señor*, is that I do not know. I saw your woman leave the table to run away even while you did not. It is my staring at you that made her angry. It was stupid of me to do. I went to say I am sorry. When I stand before you to say that, instead I ask you to meet me here, but I don't know why. It is as if someone else speaks with my voice. I do not wish to be here also. I think the night jaguar comes to me, *Señor*, and my mind is stolen away."

If that were the case the jaguar had gotten into his too and Arthur shivered as he remembered the tale told him by the boatman at the pyramid site.

"I believe you. The same unexplainable things seem to be happening to me."

"You do not say that so to make me not afraid?"

A vivid blink and thunder boomed instantaneously. "I'm afraid I don't believe in the night jaguar. I believe in science. Things don't happen without cause."

She looked back at him with misery. "What could be the reason, *Señor?*"

His mind squirmed for an answer. "I don't know. Until now I thought I was the only one having these odd reactions and that it had to be some quirk of my own. But now you too. The possibility of coincidence here is unbelievable. And if there is no reason for us to be here. We should leave. It's going to be very wet very soon."

She nodded but instead of turning to leave she stood motionless. Her face contorted as though she were struggling with something horribly disturbing inside. He reached out to put her at ease. She stepped backward and raised a hand to stop him.

A sudden wind stirred the trees above them and the rain hit as though a gigantic cask had shattered under the weight of the water inside. Daylight all but vanished as the noise of millions of heavy drops striking broad leaves rose simultaneously to drown any possibility of conversation. He was soaked through almost as he realized it was happening, could feel the rain splashing onto his scalp and shoulders. His shirt stuck coldly to his chest.

He thought Beba might run out of the blind to find shelter under a tree and was already trying to decide whether to follow her or find one of his own, but she stood her ground.

Her shoulders began to shake and she bent her head down. He couldn't see if she was crying or chilled by the rain. He closed the distance between them intending to reassure her, to suggest they find shelter and wait out the storm. He stooped low to look into her face. Her eyes were closed and he saw no tears. She muttered softly in Spanish, words he took to be a prayer as she pressed clenched fists tightly against the tops of her rain soaked thighs.

He reached forward and at first touch her head came up and her eyelids raised wide in alarm. He took her closed hands in his and felt them tightening even more.

"Beba, what is it?"

She pulled her hands from his and reached up to push wet hair from her face. The thin wet cotton of her dress clung to the full lines of her breasts. The color of her skin shone through the white petals of the flowers patterned on it. She whispered his name.

Adrenalin detonated in every vessel and he reached for her even as she thrust herself toward him. Their lips came together for only seconds before fervor tore them apart and frenzied hands began to rake clothing aside. In an instant her dress dragged to the ground. Rain drops splashed on her bare shoulders. Droplets ran from her nipples. He felt himself freed from his own clothing without being aware of just how. Her arms came around his neck and she jumped to wrap his waist with her legs. He knelt down still holding the two of them together. He entered her in a single motion guided by her hand.

Their movements held no restraint. Only the urgency of unbridled compulsion. Her fingers dug painfully into his back as she arched her own. Her hips drove against him with an insistence that triggered his own spasms just as her body jolted for an instant, then raged in shuddering release.

They clung together for a moment. He raised his head to look down into her face. Her eyes were closed against the rain. He sheltered them with his hand. She frowned without opening them. The hard rain fell against his back and shoulders. He felt himself calm inside her. Heard the thunder moving away now and knew that soon the rain would end.

Her eyes opened and for a moment she stared up into his face unblinking as though she didn't know who he was. Then suddenly she pushed him away and rolled out from under him to jump to her feet and grab up her clothing. She hugged them to her chest and in two steps had dashed through the door into the drenched and steaming forest. He snatched up his sodden wet pants to follow, but she had gone. Only the incessant sounds of the rain remained.

VI

—[A RETURN TO ELISIE]—

AFTER PHAQUTL COMPELLED ELSIE TO BURY Wart's body in the shallow grave in the dark cellar beneath her home, he climbed her back up the stairs and sat her down in the overstuffed chair. Phaqutl needed desperately to renew. He shared a thread with all of nature, the need to rest in order to replenish. To do this he relaxed control of his carrier and entered a void not unlike sleep, though his perceptions were so finely integrated into the carrier that any turbulent emotion or action brought him instantly back to full awareness and total domination.

Now he sensed that if he didn't commence within minutes, his integration would begin to ebb. If that happened, it would wane until he lost the facility to control. Then he would be at the mercy of fate until such time as a fortunate incident allowed his transfer to another carrier where he might begin again. He'd let that happen only once through all the millennia with all the carriers he'd occupied. That lapse resulted in the predicament that left him captive for so many years inside the shrunken head. He had resolved never to let the possibility recur.

He settled Elsie safely against the back of the chair and let darkness tether itself about him like the encircling tendrils of a jungle vine.

For several minutes the two rested as one until Elsie's eyelashes fluttered and her head dipped forward and nodded. Her eyes opened and she saw her hands resting in her lap. She spread her fingers out wide, as if seeing the skin on the back of her hands reminded her of who she was. They were filthy and the nails were clotted with damp soil. She must have forgotten to tend to them when she'd come in from the garden. The dirt crusted on her skin had begun to dry to a pale gray and it made the skin feel tight. A good washing with the nail brush and some hand lotion were in order. The old refrigerator in the kitchen started up and the motor noise made her jump. She looked about at the familiar surroundings: the airy feather ferns on the window sill, television set just below them, the cream color of the floral patterned slip cover on the sofa. She took in the familiar old house smells of hidden dust and bygone pots of coffee and felt herself beginning to smile with relief. As she often did, she spoke out to the empty rooms.

"A dream. Just a bad dream. For a minute there, it all seemed so real. And scary . . . really scary . . . .."

She pressed her forehead against the back of her hand to affirm that she was wide-awake now, at the same time noting that she didn't feel the heat of a fever.

"Somethin' awful talked to me in my head. And I couldn't help but do what it wanted. Like one of those people that says a spirit talks to them inside and tells 'em to do things. They say some woman down in Oregon said God told her that her kids had the devil inside 'em and she had to get him out so she threw 'em off a bridge. An' I dreamt about a little kid too. Cute little fella. An' him passin' on right there on the sofa in front of these old eyes. Hate bad dreams like that. Sometimes I can't get over 'em for the rest of the day. It'll be even harder'n ever to get to sleep tonight. Oh Lordy, but that one seemed real."

Her heavy form shivered and her head raised abruptly. She held herself rock still. "Can't remember how I come to be inside sittin' in this chair. Last I remember was being in the back yard weedin' the sweet peas."

She held her hands up in front of her face and turned them back and forth to take another long look at the dirt on them. She pulled the knees of her gardening pants out wide and saw the patches of moist dirt drying there. Traces of it streaked her shoes.

"It all fits. But didn't I see this ragamuffin little boy lopin' up the alley and I stepped out in front of him to ask some questions? And he tried to duck around me. Bloody all down his shirt front. Can't remember what happened t'him for sure. He must a slipped on by."

The memory of the way he looked caused the muscles of her shoulders to tense so they began to ache and she stared hard at the blank screen on the TV.

"The blood coulda been somethin' else. Somethin' like tomato juice he spilt at breakfast an' his mama didn't catch it before he got out of the house. Maybe thinkin' it was blood made me dream so bad like I did.

"Okay, but then how the dickens did I get inside here in this chair? Old girl . . . you gettin' the Alzheimer's?"

For a brief moment she felt a cold fear spike up her back and her resolve of that morning, to pay a visit to Doc Runkle, came a step closer to being acted upon. For now the intention brought enough satisfaction, just as it had earlier, and the tightness in her muscles began to fade. She rocked back into the cushions of the chair to gather herself, then rolled forward again to put most of her weight over her feet and rose slowly to move into the kitchen. She washed her hands, then went through the fridge and cupboards until she'd put together a plate filled with leftovers. She put the plate down on the small table that sat against the kitchen wall and examined it.

"Haven't been this hungry since before Sandra Mae was born. 'Course, I was eatin' for the two of us then."

Just as Phaqutl predicted, Elsie Hatfield provided excellent sanctuary for the next several months. She needed to leave her home just once each week to walk three blocks to the market to buy groceries. She paid by check from the account where the benefits from her dead husband's social security were deposited automatically. The grocery clerk always took the check, looked squarely over the counter at Elsie as though she expected it to be a forgery, then stuck it in the cash register drawer without so much as raising a corner of her mouth.

The woman saw Elsie every week but for whatever reason had never acknowledged her. Elsie no longer cared about that. Phaqutl made similar observations as Elsie passed others on the walk to or from the store. He found this perplexing, for the humans he had known before, and most all the animals, even the primitive caimans that basked along the river banks, seldom came into contact with one of their own species without paying heed of some sort. Nevertheless, Elsie's chosen solitude and the fact that others seemed inclined to honor it added a measure of safety.

Between visits to the grocery, Phaqutl used the woman to initiate his quest. It was plain that he existed in a place a very great distance from the one he'd been taken from. The lower path the sun took through the sky, temperatures that required that the humans clothe themselves even when they slept, the drab colors of the birds and sparsity of plant life all verified this, but he had no reference to give him a sense of how immense that distance might be. If he wished to return to his source land, he needed to locate it in relationship to where he was now and to devise a method of travel.

He deduced that a great amount of time had also passed. The agonizingly endless blackness when he remained in the shrunken head told him that, as did the astounding complexities and over abundances of this tribe he'd awakened to. His people were far more developed than the other tribes around them and yet were many hundredfold behind in achieving what he saw as commonplace about him now.

To learn more he queried Elsie's mind but discovered nothing that could be of direct help. He did find that when she wished to know of something new, though seldom it seemed, she relied upon the television set in her living room. From that day on, every moment not needed to replenish, or for his host to sleep or to perform some task necessary to maintain herself, he kept her seated in the overstuffed facing the moving images on the screen.

From it, he first learned of those things that she considered significant, such as the host of products, each newer, better and cheaper than any other, that were necessary to bolster elemental human appetites by applying them to totally unrelated aspects of life. There were special soaps to use to clean dishes and floors if you wished to receive the love of your family and particular motor cars to drive and beverages to drink if you wished to be perceived as sexually potent. It surprised him that one as solitary as Elsie did not heed these admonitions more closely in order to improve her lot. But when he observed the contents of her home and her purchases at the grocery, she seemed most satisfied with those things she had used throughout her lifetime, and some, according to her memories, by her mother before her.

The TV also offered the opportunity to look in on peoples' lives and Elsie preferred to spend her afternoons watching the tribulations of a half-dozen different family groups that always seemed to center around the wresting of wealth from one another and infractions of a complex code of breeding rituals.

By accident, for she avoided them astutely, he discovered the newscasts that dutifully told of the malevolence these humans carried out against each other. There were wars and individual acts of savagery. Also great carnage rendered by the imprudent use of the implements of their culture, particularly the autos and airplanes that carried them about. Again he was surprised for Elsie's response to all of this was more a studied sense of detachment than concern. He began to appreciate that the television was her god in the same way his kind had been gods to be worshiped by the tribe of carriers he sought.

As the weeks passed, his early impressions began to evolve as he grasped a deeper knowledge of this culture: of the many wars that seemed perpetual, of their loathing to share with one another what seemed to be abundance beyond all dreams, of their aversion to being involved in even the most basic misfortunes of anyone other than the closest of family. He became both intrigued and appalled and as his knowledge increased so did his sense of loss, for he did not come upon even a single clue to tell him where he had come from and how he might return.

He also delved thoroughly into her memories from before she left her mother's womb to the present, but found nothing to help. Unlike the little boy, she held no curiosities. She saw no purpose in knowledge beyond that necessary to cope with the necessities of daily life.

He considered communicating directly with Elsie. It would have allowed him to shortcut his efforts considerably, but he'd recognized early on that she was far too fragile for that. On the few occasions when he had spoken into her mind, supplanting her thoughts with his words, she had come to the verge of uncontrollable panic. If he allowed that to happen she might injure herself or become ill to the point of being helpless and unable to care for herself. This was a risk he could not take. Each time he overrode her to take control of her movements her distress increased and remained. Her nighttime sleep dwindled to an hour or two and she became listless and unable to work for more than a few minutes without rest. Even when he sat her idly in front of the television her ability to perceive what was on the screen became easily clouded. He nonetheless remained content to stay with her for the time being.

The climate began to change, something he hadn't witnessed before, as he knew only the raining times and the times of great heat. The television weatherman told him of something called fall and then winter. It was early in an evening when the leaves on the trees outside her windows were beginning to turn colors that her youngest daughter, Sandra Mae telephoned. The telephone hung on the kitchen wall beside the refrigerator and the call came during an evening newscast when one of the reporters explained the consequences expected from an unusually large drop in the phenomenon that forecast their future well-being, the Dow Jones Industrial Averages. Elsie knew nothing whatsoever about them, but the newscasters acted more distressed over this event than any of the violence they regularly reported and Phaqutl sensed that dire events might be imminent. Not wanting to miss the remainder of the report he hurriedly told the daughter in her mother's own voice that she wasn't feeling well and drew the conversation briskly to a close. Sandra Mae didn't express concern and relief sounded in the younger woman's voice as they disconnected.

Phaqutl returned Elsie to the overstuffed, only to find that the program had moved on, but he knew that the subject would be taken up again on a later newscast and resigned himself to the wait. He allowed Elsie to resume control of herself. Almost immediately she vaulted into a state of high anxiety. She had begun to assign the periods her memory couldn't fill in as, 'fallin' asleep without meanin' to', and the times when her mind felt his presence as, 'one of those gawd-awful nightmares again,' but she lived for the chance she might hear from any one of her children and when she heard herself cut the call from Sandra Mae short, she stopped denying that something might be wrong and a fear of 'losing it' consumed her. For the first time she let herself accept that she truly needed help.

She also had a tremendous worry that if she revealed her plight to anyone they would undoubtedly come and take her away and 'put her in a home.' Phaqutl found her concerns eerily primitive. She lived in mortal fear of her own kind. Few animals needed to do this. True, many fought during their mating rites, but seldom did they inflict lasting damage. The old might lag behind the herd and become easy prey, but they were not driven away. Certainly this tribe must be inferior.

———— • ————

Two days later was grocery shopping day and in the morning Elsie telephoned and made an appointment with Doc Runkle whose office was just across the street and half a block up from the market. Phaqutl knew why she intended to visit him and, given her emotional state since he had caused her to cut her call from Sandra Mae short, saw no reason to stop her. She spent the morning bathing and cleaning herself fastidiously and putting on clean clothing. She even took care to hot press her underwear and dialed time on the telephone to make sure her wrist watch was on the minute.

Elsie arrived at the doctor's office at exactly two o'clock in the afternoon. She had purposely come a few minutes early and then waited a block away until the precise moment of her appointment. As she opened the ominous windowless door, the anxiety she had been experiencing was supplanted by one equally as great. Elsie feared this doctor with as much passion as she had endured in forcing herself to make the appointment. Phaqutl had seen shamans and medicine men before and remained alert, ready to defend them should the need come.

The doctor had his office in a converted home and the tiny waiting room had at one time been a vestibule. There were three folding chairs and magazines lay across a small coffee table, but there was scarcely enough light to read. There were two interior doors leading from the waiting room, one securely closed and the other a half-door with a shelf affixed across the top of it to form a small counter. Elsie went there and leaned her forearms on the shelf. A white-clad young woman smiled up at her from a nearby desk.

"Mrs. Hatfield. It's been a long time. Are your address and phone number still the same."

"Yes'm."

"And you have Medicare with Plan B? Any additional insurance?"

Elsie wagged her head, no.

"Fine. Please have a seat. The doctor will be just a few minutes."

The few minutes turned out to be over an hour, to Phaqutl's surprise once again. A morning of thorough preparation, waiting until the precise moment designated for her arrival, then the doctor did not feel obliged to keep his end of the arrangement. He must be a very powerful shaman indeed. To Phaqutl's gain, however, were the magazines. Elsie began to leaf through them, gazing at the ads and the promises they made, much as she was accustomed to doing as she sat before the TV. In the first magazine she picked up, the cover claimed articles entitled, *'Eleven New Ways to Keep Your Man,'* *'Hair Like Cher,'* and *'The Secret He Won't Tell You About Himself.'* In another that Elsie riffled through and put quickly aside, *'Hydrogen, the Energy With a Conscious,'* *'How to Reline Brake Shoes Yourself,'* and *'Important Men Who Mow Their Own Lawns.'* It was the third one she retrieved from the table that made Elsie sigh to herself and brought Phaqutl a first step forward on his quest. It was a travel magazine and on the glossy cover it displayed a full-color photo of a young woman in a bushy skirt made of some sort of dried grasses and a pastel striped top. She stood with her hips tilted provocatively to one side and held her hands off on the other in a graceful pose. The caption beneath invited, *'Come Hula with Me*, page 39.' It wasn't the girl that interested Phaqutl it was the trees in the background. The first sign of anything that bore a resemblance to familiar sights of the jungle. He took over, forced Elsie to turn to the designated page and read.

The article spoke of life in a place called Hawaii, 'among the flowers and the palm trees.' It wasn't the place where he was determined to return but it offered a first clue. The nurse poked her head over the half door, pointed toward the other door that led from the converted vestibule and announced without apology for keeping her waiting, "The doctor can see you now, Mrs. Hatfield, first room on your left."

The room she entered turned out to be an oblique contrast to the one where she'd waited. Walls, ceilings and cabinets were painted a color Elsie thought of as refrigerator white. A bank of long flourescent tubes glowed overhead. Charts in bright colors depicted graphic representations of various systems of the human anatomy. One of them showed a half-section of the human head, a location Phaqutl was totally familiar with.

In the center of the room stood a long, narrow, metal table with a padded top and a band of waxed white paper running the length of it. Strange appliances Elsie thought of as stirrups were affixed to either side of one end. The contraption made her so nervous she stood as far away from it as possible.

Contrary to Elsie's references to old Doc Runkle, the man himself turned out to be in his middle thirties at the oldest, with intense blue eyes and a shock of dark wavy hair that looked as though it had been thrown at his head. He was reviewing an open manila folder as he nudged the door open with his shoulder and slid past it into the room without looking up.

"It's been over two years since we've seen you Mrs. Hatfield. Way past time for a complete physical. We'd have to schedule more time for that, but we could get started on it today. Make it easier on you if we do it in two visits. If we do a mamogram and pelvic and take the blood today, I can schedule you for a sigmoid-oscopy next time."

Elsie froze up hard and Phaqutl set himself to destroy the man if he attacked. "Didn't come for that. None 'a them things is my problem."

Runkle showed surprise, looked up from the file as he relaxed into a boyish smile. "Sorry, Mrs. Hatfield, your appointment sheet doesn't list a specific complaint. What seems to be the problem?"

Phaqutl felt her working hard to respond. "It's my head."

"Where does it hurt?"

"It don't hurt exactly. It's more of a . . . well, maybe a mental thing."

The doctor's eyebrows raised and he closed the manila file. "Sit down please." He pointed to the long table with the waxed paper on it. "Tell me about it."

Elsie looked at the table and her heart rate increased, but she put a foot on the little step at the bottom of the stirruped end and turned to hike herself up on it. "Sleepin's part of it. I ain't slept that much for a long time, just two or three hours usually. Now I'm down to one and sometimes none at all.

"Sometimes I have real bad dreams and sometimes I find myself someplace, but can't for the life of me remember how I got there." She saw the frown creep across Doc Runkle's brow. "Then other times I seem to lose control. End up doin' things I wouldn't normally do. See myself doin' 'em but can't bring myself to stop. Like just now in the waitin' room."

"Tell me about the waiting room."

"There's this travel magazine out there. An article about Hawaii. My husband and I always wanted to go there, but never got to. I didn't want to look at an article about that place. Afraid I'd get too sad. Maybe do some cryin'. But today, even though I didn't want to, my hands just opened it up and my eyes started readin'."

"That doesn't sound too serious. Anything else?"

Elsie closed her hands into fists and pushed them together in her lap. "Sometimes . . . sometimes a voice talks to me in my head when there ain't nobody there. I just kinda stiffen up all over for a split second first, and then it starts talkin' an' tells me to do somethin'. Sometimes with actual words sometimes just with a feelin'."

Now she had his attention. "Do what kind of thing, Mrs. Hatfield?"

"Nothin' much mostly. Like turn on the TV, but just now when you was mentionin' you'd like to do a pelvic exam and that was makin' me scared, I sensed it was tellin' me that if you made a move I was to snatch up that little knife layin' beside the stethoscope there on the counter and stick it in your eye. It ain't the Alzheimer's is it?"

She saw his mouth slide open, but when he spoke it was the model of practiced composure. "No, Mrs. Hatfield, I don't think so, at least not yet. But we're getting way out of my specialty here.

I know a very good doctor over on Madison Street. I can make an appointment for you, if you like."

Elsie didn't believe in shrinks. Good common sense would get you through. But the expression on the doctor's face warned her that he might and the fear that they would take her to a home came again and put big knots in her gut. Phaqutl remained confident that would be nearly impossible. Then she realized she could always cancel the appointment from home later.

"Okay." She put her hands together in her lap and couldn't look Doc Runkle in the face.

"Good. Well then let's see what we can do for you. If you'll excuse me for a few minutes. I'll be right back."

She waited in silence, straining to hear what he was saying on the telephone in the other room, but unable to make out the words. After several minutes he returned smiling at her in that paternal way he always did. "Dr. MacAfee will see you two weeks from today at eleven A.M. He wants me to give you a complete physical first. I've scheduled you for next Thursday. Same time."

Elsie eyed him furtively, but nodded just the same. Then she remembered. "I wonder if you could give me some sleepers?"

"I can do that if you like. I'll put you down for refills, but just fill one now and we'll talk about them when you come back. If they don't do the job, or if you have any unusual reactions, I'll change them then." He eyed her over the top of the prescription pad he'd begun jotting on and sounded to her as jovial as a department store Santa Claus. "You wouldn't really stab me in the eye would you?"

Elsie could only barely recall having said that even though she knew it was only a few moments ago. "Of course not." But she wasn't all that sure just what she might do these days.

"I knew you were much too nice for that. Pick these up at the pharmacy next to the grocery and take one an hour before bedtime. They'll relax you and should help you get a little more sleep. That may be the cause of the whole thing."

Phaqutl sensed his last statement was a lie. Elsie held her hand out for the prescription. On the way out Phaqutl stopped her at the coffee table and after looking to see if the white-dressed receptionist/nurse was watching, picked up the travel magazine, rolled it up and secreted it in her purse.

Beginning that evening, Elsie took the capsules Doc Runkle had given her. That first night she got five hours sleep and the next day the tension that had built in her over the preceding months began to ease away. Elsie proclaimed aloud to the house, "Its sure good to sleep. I ain't never felt better in by life." And though it was only an hour after lunch, she took another pill and went to the sofa.

When Phaqutl finally roused her, a lassitude had set in that the old lady welcomed and accepted as her fate from then on. When he kept her rapt at the television or pouring over the magazines that were now a regular part of her purchases at the grocery store, her mind was impaired to the point that she made little sense of what she saw. Her stupor was so pervasive that his abilities to manage her were rendered nearly impotent. He tried to make her destroy the pills, but she never recovered enough from their influence that he was successful. It was time for him to move on.

Elsie trudged from the supermarket, the strap of her black handbag hefted over a shoulder of her raincoat. On each side worn canvas bags trailed near the ground. Even in the languor caused by doubling, sometimes tripling, the prescribed dosage of Doc Runkle's pills, she had seen to it that the dour-faced woman at the checkout counter balanced the heavier purchases evenly between the two bags. She wouldn't need to shift them from hand-to-hand during the walk home. She lumbered along through the market parking lot, conscious of the weight of her burdens.

She peered upward from under the wide-brimmed hat to see deeply overcast skies and spoke softly to the parked cars. "Rain comin'. Smell it plain as lamb in the stew pot." She turtled her head down into the collar of her coat to protect it from the imminent rain. Though just ten after four by the market clock, the shortened days of late fall coupled with the effects of the heavy clouds meant dusk was near. She moved along on her own, Phaqutl felt no call to expend stamina to guide her movements through this familiar weekly routine.

Years of habit turned Elsie diagonally through the lot in a shortcut to the sidewalk that led three blocks to her house. It was well past the season when turning leaves added new colors to the air and any day now the cold rains would begin. It was Friday and cars nearly filled the lot as shoppers rushed to buy supplies for a weekend of football games and holiday preparations. She had almost escaped the seductive aromas of the market's bakery goods when she reached the farthest corner of the lot and nearly bumped into him.

"Well what have we here."

Elsie popped her head back up to see a man she could only think of as huge, black leather jacket with jeans of the same color, nearly bald though he looked to be in his twenties. For the first time she wished she hadn't taken one of her pills that morning.

His jacket carried rows of chromed studs in geometric patterns. Broad heavy fists rested on his hips, elbows splayed to the side, tatoos emerging from the folded back jacket sleeves. She took a step backwards, as the muscles between her shoulders tightened and went cold. She wished with all her heart that she was still young enough to run away from him.

"Somebody's mother, Zarko." That voice from Elsie's right. A slender man with wispy strands of blond mustache hair over a pallid pouting mouth.

Now a third, laughing from somewhere behind her. "Na. She's too ugly to be anybody's mother? What the fuck d' you suppose she's got in that purse? Big enough."

She whipped her head about, eyes opened as wide as they'd go. There were four, all jacketed alike. The big Zarko took another turn. "We'll know soon enough." He stood erect, puffed his chest out, and stepped toward Elsie until it was but inches from her face. She had to look up to see it. "Maybe you'd let me have that purse old woman. No need to fall down and get hurt."

She stood paralyzed by fear. Pull yourself together old girl, ain't no use tryin' to talk sense to these bums. It worked because she felt her anger come and she brought herself up, about to give them a tongue lashing they wouldn't forget, but one of them shoved her and she reeled sideways. Hands grabbed at the grocery bags, tugged the purse strap from her shoulder. Now Elsie neared panic and instinctively opened her mouth to plead with them to let her go. Instead she felt the split second of rigidity that usually signaled the voice in her head was about to order her to do something. She became acutely aware for the first time in days. She should have fallen from the shove, but had not.

A canvas bag of groceries swung up fast and hard from ground level to catch the blond assailant between the legs. He grunted his surprise and scarcely had time to grab at his crotch before the second bag swung in a high overhead arc that brought it crashing into the back of his skull. The bag burst sending canned goods skittering along the tarmac and spinning under nearby cars. A coarse stockinged leg thrust a wedge-heeled pump high into the midsection of a second assailant. She heard a loud hissing as air expelled through clenched teeth and he dropped to his knees. Phaqutl knew satisfaction at the success of the well-placed kick he'd memorized from the television.

He righted Elsie and tuned her to face Zarko. Now ashen, the towering thug took a step backward and crouched before her, a switchblade snicked open in his hand. Then Elsie jolted forward up against Zarko. As one Elsie and Phaqutl felt the strangely painless sensation as the knife went in and up under her ribs somewhere near her heart. Elsie's arms raised, grabbed the balding man by the little hair that still fringed his scalp over his ears. The whites of Zarko's eyes widened and his nostrils flared. The rage was all that Phaqutl needed and Elsie's last movement drove their heads together.

Phaqutl melded instantaneously into place in the new body and looked back at Elsie through Zarko's eyes. The old woman had slumped to her knees and now fell backward upon the hard surface of the parking lot. A tiny red-rimmed slit in her rain coat gave evidence of her fate. Zarko looked at the knife in his own hand, at the bloody blade. Surprise widened his eyes. He hadn't intended to stab her. To frighten her yes, but not to kill.

There would be hell to pay. Time to go. He searched about for his companions. One lay writhing on the ground, the blond one sprawled inert with the back of his head misshapen and oozing fluids. The smell of exposed flesh rankled the air. Zarko didn't see the fourth man, but a familiar sounding engine roared to life and tires squealed like angry swine fleeing across the tarmac.

Phaqutl read the startled fear as Zarko sensed the danger of being stranded without the vehicle. He took that message and tried to move Zarko away, but he needed a second or two more to assert full control over the new body.

A jumble of mens' voices began shouting. "Look out he's got a knife."

"The big sonofabitch stabbed the old lady."

"Police. Drop it. Drop the knife asshole or you're a dead man. Hands on top of your head. Do it now." Someone stuck a spray canister in front of his face, sharp pain in the eyes, sight blurred instantly, lungs rasped for oxygen. The shout was in his ear. "I said do it now."

Zarko raked the air with his knife desperately, felt it drag on something for a split second. Someone swore. Before Phaqutl could respond, pain exploded in the kidneys, then came a jolting crunch on the back of Zarko's neck, another at the side of his head, and Phaqutl was trapped in blackness once again.

VII

—[RETURN TO ARTHUR]—

THE MORNING AFTER MEETING ARTHUR IN the animal blind, Beba woke at dawn from a fitful night's sleep laden with confusion and guilt. She rose before anyone and left for the lodge early. The travelers' groups came and left with a day or two in-between, but the returning scientists interrupted the usual schedule, and another tour boat was due before noon. She had to clean the rooms and to help with preparation in the kitchen.

She started first in the sleeping quarters: sweeping floors, retrieving a sock someone had left under a bed, collecting the room keys left on a bedside table. Soon she heard the voices of the villagers her uncle hired to help at the lodge and called greetings to them as she moved from the rooms to sweep the porch.

She'd tried to keep her thoughts away from the rendezvous with Arthur by concentrating as much as she could on her work. Yet when she saw her uncle emerge from the entrance to the pathway to their village his serious expression brought the remorse back to her like dropping a frog on a rock, and she had to work to keep the quaver from her voice.

165

"*Buenos dias, Tío.*"

He didn't reply, but turned in her direction and approached with decisive strides. He looked up to where she stood on the small porch still clutching her broom and spoke harshly.

"You have shamed my family name, *Señorita* . . .. Nevertheless, I am sorry for what is to happen because of this. Go now. To your aunt. She will tell you what you must do."

Before she could voice a question, he turned and began to walk away. She called after him. He stopped only long enough to answer. "I can tell you no more. Go, *por favor.*"

Beba looked after him shocked by the behavior of this gentle man. She let the broom fall, jumped the full distance to the ground, and half-ran-half-walked the path back to the only home she had ever known.

She arrived to find her aunt sitting alone on the front step, waiting. It was something she had not seen since she was a young girl coming home from school. It brought memories of a younger, smiling Aunt Eva, but the woman who waited for her now had no welcoming smile. Instead her voice commanded.

"Beba, you're finally here. Quickly. We are leaving today."

"Where are we going, *Tía Eva?*" There were deep worry lines set in her aunt's face and the sharp needles of a terrible anxiety prickled the back of Beba's neck.

Her aunt leaned forward and looked steadily into her face. "Beba, you must answer me truthfully. Did you go to him in the animal blind yesterday?"

Blood rushed to burn her face and she wanted to run into the house, to hide under the bedsheets as she had as a child, to make excuses. But she couldn't lie to this woman who had taken her in and treated her as her own.

"*Si.*" She cast her eyes at the ground.

"That is all you have to tell me?" And Aunt Eva rose to stand and face her. Beba's mind scrambled for something to say, but offered nothing.

"Your uncle carries the dishonor of a man disgraced by his own. And you haven't yet reached your eighteenth birthday."

Beba could only stare at the backs of her hands. Now the pain of anguish became evident in her aunt's voice.

"Since the moment they brought you to me, I have hoped this day would never come. I have prayed to the Virgin for as long as you have been with me to never have to say to you this."

Cold foreboding now ran the full length of Beba's body and crawled up over her scalp. She found herself feeling profoundly sorry for the woman who had raised her and who stood before her now in such misery. Her aunt smudged away tears with her fist.

"It has begun . . . the young people of our family sometimes . . . often . . . inherit the spirits of our ancestors. When they are nearly grown, these spirits begin to lead them to do foolish and dangerous things until they go to meet the elder spirit and make their peace with him.

"Dearest Beba, there is someone you must see. We leave within the hour. I have already sent word that you are coming."

"Who is it, *Tía?*" For the moment curiosity pushed aside her contrition.

"I am commanded not to tell." Her aunt clasped her head between her hands and looked down at her feet as she turned to trudge slowly back up the steps and into their home. "You must be ready. Go to your room."

⸻

Beba found clothing laid out on her bed and a canvas bag with a drawstring to close the top already packed. Once, a girl

Beba had known from the village had become pregnant under circumstances that embarrassed her family and had been sent away to a convent. When she looked inside the bag and found only clothing and the barest necessities for her personal care, she presumed that fate was her own.

Though apprehension did its best to paralyzed her and anxious questions cried out for answers, she could not disobey her aunt in the face of the humiliation she had brought to her family. She barely had time to dress before she heard the familiar voice of Ramos, one of the village boatmen, and her aunt call her to bring her belongings.

The three of them hurried to where the boats were tied and there the smallest and fastest, one that could rush to the aid of a disabled boat or carry someone from a village to the doctor, sat with its motor idling. Beba tried to question her aunt, but the older woman steadfastly refused to answer, repeating only that she had been ordered to secrecy.

While Beba and Aunt Eva loaded their belongings the stocky boatman began the process of casting off. Beba tried yet again to speak to her aunt, but before she could ask the first question the woman looked into her face and said firmly, "No." Then the motor came alive and the boat moved out. To add to the trepidation already dominating her thoughts, instead of heading downriver toward the locations of the larger villages with their churches and convents, it turned upstream where there were only the few settlements of small tribes and the unexplored rain forest beyond.

By the end of the day the small swift boat had run as far upstream as the larger boats did in more than two. Beba spent the time in deep apprehension about the fate being forced upon her, though it sometimes became mingled with curiosity and the excitement of adventure. Her aunt seemed to have placed herself into a trance-like state and sat alone staring out at the passing waters.

At last they put into shore less than an hour before dark. The place looked as though nothing more than a narrow animal trail came to the river's edge. Only traces of blue smoke lying low among the trees hinted at anything else.

When she stepped on land, her muscles were tight and her joints stiff from the long hours of confinement. She took a moment to stretch, her eyes searching for any sign of what it was they had come to see. They took their belongings and the boatman, Ramos, led them up the pathway to a grassy clearing surrounding a stilted hut that stood no more than eight meters from end to end. The words 'medicinal clinic' crudely hand-lettered on a small sign in both Spanish and Quechuan had been fastened beside the open door. The boatman called out and a tiny, stooped woman with a few strands of dark remaining in her white hair came from behind the hut wiping her hands on the front of a soiled black habit. Beba guessed that she had to be in her late seventies or older. The Sister spoke to Ramos in an accent that sounded European as though Beba and her aunt weren't there.

"The only privilege I ask of God is to raise a few chickens. If it weren't for them, I would have no meat but the monkey the Indians bring to pay for the simple ministrations I am able to perform in His name.

"Last night one of the hens disappeared. There was no sound, and no feathers or blood. It had to be a constrictor. Another animal would have left chaos and probably murdered them all. I can't see how anything could get into the pen, but snakes are so very clever. I can't even keep them out of the clinic.

"I know I must love all of His creatures, but I have learned that not all are deserving of equal respect. And it was the serpent who tempted Eve into sin."

Then she stopped and raised her head as a look of suspicion rose over sharp sun-creased features. "You are not due to bring supplies for eight more weeks, *Señor Ramos*. Why have you come?"

Ramos ducked his head in greeting. "Sister Brigga, we hope you will let us stay the night. I believe you received a message." Then he introduced Beba and her aunt by name.

The sister eyed them for a moment, as though she were trying to remember if she had indeed gotten a message, then said curtly, "*Si*, now I must finish with the chickens," and turned to go back the way she'd come.

Ramos smiled at his charges as though this was exactly the response he'd expected and motioned them up the steps to the clinic. Inside the only light came from the door opening and a single small glassed window. The hut contained one large and one small room with the smaller displaying neatly arranged belongings that proclaimed it the quarters of the nun. Apparently no one was ill in Sister Brigga's province for the four narrow beds in the larger room held only thin, striped mattresses. A brightly painted crucifix on the wall looked down on them. The remainder of the room stood neat and barren and made Beba feel cold even in the jungle heat.

Beba heard tired footsteps climbing to the porch, and Sister Brigga's humorless voice came through the doorway behind them. "*Señor* Ramos, the ladies will sleep here, you will sleep under the building. Take a cot down there but place it away from the cooking area. There is a pot of soup on the fire. I've added more beans. Bring some up for the women. I have eaten already. It is fortunate the snake will not eat again for more than a week, or he might visit you tonight."

Sister Brigga then passed them and entered her own room to turn and pull a curtain over the door. "Eat quickly for the sun is nearly gone, and I must save the lamp oil. *Buenas noches, Señora.*

After they had eaten and settled in for the night, Beba lay on her bed listening to the faint snoring of the sister in the adjoining room. It had been a day full of guilt and self-recrimination for the disgrace she'd brought upon herself and family. She had been banished from her home and had no knowledge of her future. Tears leaked from the corners of her eyes, but then everything fell into place. She had been sent to stay with this woman. She would keep the chickens safe and help tend the sick. The sister would demand repentance through study of the scriptures and hard work. The woman seemed stern, but not unkind. When *Señor* Ramos returned in eight weeks to bring the supplies, she would return to her village with him. Surely her aunt and uncle could remain angry no longer than that. Relieved and now armed for the adventure, she slept.

At the first sound of movement in the morning, Beba rose determined to make a good impression on her new teacher. She found her aunt also rousing, smelled food cooking in the area beneath the clinic, and dressed quickly to go there. Ramos tended tea made from coca leaves steeping in an open pan and Sister Brigga spread bowls on a small table nearby. Their meal turned out to be a thick porridge-like soup made of potatoes and corn meal. Beba had never eaten it before and like the bean soup of the night before, found it tasteless. Surely she could help the sister to a more pleasant diet.

Beba had decided to accept her penance and to do her best to abide by whatever terms were required of her. This gave her the first light-hearted feelings since morning of the previous day. She owed a great deal to her aunt who had served as her mother since her real parents death before Beba's memory began. Aunt Eva looked unbearably forlorn at breakfast and her eyes and cheeks were reddened as though she had cried in the night. Beba tried to cheer her aunt, but the sadness remained.

When the meal ended, Ramos excused himself to ready the boat. Within minutes Aunt Eva had gathered her things and Beba walked with her to the river. They gave her things to Ramos to stow and her aunt turned to her.

"Be careful, my niece, and may God treat you well." Her voice broke and she fell silent.

Beba reached toward her, but her aunt held her away.

"Go now, Beba. Don't look back. You may not love me as much as you think you do at this moment, when you meet your fate. But I beg you to remember, I was given no choice. It is only by accident that I did not receive the same birthright as you and I would give my life to take your place now."

Her aunt threw both arms around her and held her in a grasp so tight Beba could barely find the strength to breathe. Then the motor started and Beba watched the boat pull away. She stood listening to its fading sounds trying unsuccessfully to take meaning from her aunt's parting words and she wept.

When Beba returned to the clearing, she had already become homesick and renewed her vow to herself to serve in whatever way she was asked in order to assure her return to her village at the first opportunity. She went to the cooking area where the nun bent over the small table clearing it after the morning meal.

"What may I do to help, Sister Brigga."

The tiny woman eyed her oddly for few seconds, as if deciding whether or not she could be trusted, then spoke. "Can you wash dishes?"

"*Si*, I do them at my aunt's home every evening."

"Begin there."

A yellow plastic pan with soap and water already in it sat on a wooden stand near the fire and she dug into the task. Only the tea cups remained to be washed when she saw the sister stop her work to stand erect listening. Beba listened too and heard the sound of something coming through the forest. Seconds later two nearly naked men stepped into the clearing. They stood taller and had lighter skin than the Indians she had seen before. One carried a machete, the other a long pole, and both had large rolls of belongings slung at angles across their backs. They came almost close enough to reach out and touch her and then stopped.

Beba felt the desire to back away, but stood fast lest she seem impolite. She had been taught as a young girl that if she should encounter people from the remote forest, never to smile or show them her teeth for that would be seen as the snarling threat of an animal and they might harm her, and she remembered that now.

"Have they come for medicine?"

Sister Brigga gave her the odd look again before she spoke. "No, my child, they have come for you."

She spun to look at the sister, not believing what she'd heard, and it gave them the chance that they needed. They moved quickly to take positions on either side of her before she could recoil. She was strong and much younger, but the strength of the two of them overcame hers more quickly than she could have imagined. She shouted for the sister, but no help came. They pushed her down on her back and held her fast and the frustration of being unable to move added panic to her struggle. They tied her hands in front of her and her ankles with rough rope. They laid out a blanket beside her and moved her sideways onto it. She watched in horror as they wound the blanket around her then tied the ends of it to the pole so that it made a hammock hanging down beneath it. They lifted the pole between them to their shoulders.

Beba continued to writhe and struggle though the rope began to chafe her wrists and ankles. She kept shouting to the nun who stood nearby watching passively. "Please don't let them sister. Make them stop."

Finally the woman walked to place her face near Beba's. "Struggling is of no use, child. Make it easier on yourself."

Beba's voice had terror and desperation in it now. "Where will they take me. What will they do to me? Why is this happening?"

Sister Brigga put her face closer again. "Where? I only know it is into the part of the forest where no one is allowed to go. I do not know what they will do there. But why? Because you were born with the evil."

They placed a cloth with a vaguely sweet odor to it over Beba's face so she couldn't see and carried her between them hanging under the pole like a slaughtered animal. She continued to cry out and to struggle, to no effect. Eventually she became weary and let her movement cease. They had the slow steady pace of those who knew how to make their energies last and the cadence lulled her. She could tell that they carried her up over hills and down again. Some of the hills must have been high for it seemed to take them a long time and she could hear their heavy breathing.

Frequently during her ride, her captors communicated with one another in a language she'd never heard. She knew many tribes living in the forest shunned outsiders and that some remained undiscovered. That brought her curiosity up and when she tried to speak to them, it quickly became clear that if they understood her at all, it was very little.

When they finally laid her on the ground and pulled the cloth away, she saw the sun had traveled late into the afternoon. One of them stripped the blanket away and untied her ankles and wrists. Shouting had made her throat raw, and she accepted water. When he helped her stand, she began to feel nauseous and lost her balance. She fell up against him and she could smell the sweat of his daylong ordeal. He helped her to sit. She rubbed the raw spots on her wrists and ankles, massaged muscles sore from her struggles and worked joints stiffened from the hours of being bound. After a few moments she began to feel better. Strength started to flow again into her arms and legs and she let them relax.

Though she still felt the pains of her ordeal, she concluded that she had suffered no damage. Her head began to clear and she took stock of her surroundings. Her captors had begun setting up camp for the night. The younger of them took a small bow and several very long arrows from the roll he carried across his shoulders and walked into the bush. When the other turned his back to her to prepare a fire she saw her chance.

She stood quietly and moved her arms and legs to limber them. She watched every move her remaining guard made from the corner of her eye, so that if he turned to see her she would seem unconcerned. Adrenaline began to rise and muscles tensed. Then the moment came when he rounded his shoulders and hunched over cupped hands to blow on the first sparking embers. She moved quickly, shoved him from behind to sprawl across the beginning flames, took the direction opposite from the one who left to hunt and dashed into the forest.

She ran with all the speed she could muster, ducking vines and trees, leaping over logs. Something she didn't see tripped her and she came down hard to scramble up and run on. Underbrush tore at her skin and clothing. She could almost hear the flight of the arrow that followed her as it came through the air. On and on until her heart pounded and she began to rasp for air.

Finally she had to let herself slow down, but even that wasn't enough. Her wind had gone completely and her strides began to falter. Soon she fell and this time it took great effort to rise. Her chest heaved. She stepped behind the wide trunk of a tree and stopped. She leaned against the trunk and tilted her head backward as she tried to regain her breath. She strained to listen through her own panting to hear if anyone followed . . . nothing.

Satisfied, she allowed herself to stand there, waiting for her heart to slow, surveying her surroundings. She hadn't heard the noises of the river since they'd taken her from Sister Brigga's clinic. The cloth covering her face kept her from keeping track of the direction they'd followed. Dense forest surrounded her on all sides. With growing horror she realized that she couldn't find her way back. Even if she knew every step of the way, it was late in the day, and she would be forced to spend the night unprotected in the jungle.

She looked up, trying to take direction from the sun, and he stood there. Silently, a few paces away, the one she'd pushed. He watched her as a father might watch a wayward child. He'd come without sound and breathed as easily as if he'd only walked across a room.

He watched her for another moment then turned and moved away. Her shoulders slumped. She had no choice. She followed.

When they arrived back at where it all began, the other man sat on his haunches pulling feathers from two brown and white birds the size of small hens. A pile of crushed leaves lay beside him on the ground and several bunches of red berries had been placed beside that. The little fire flamed brightly.

When the birds had been cleaned he stuffed them with the leaves and roasted them on a spit made of branches gathered from the forest floor. When the birds had cooked, he tore them into pieces with his hands. He offered her a breast and it tasted as good as anything she'd ever eaten.

When the fire began to die away, the man who'd been their cook handed each of them a branch of the red berries. Beba picked one off and popped it into her mouth. When she bit down the bitterness of it seared into her flesh and she felt her entire face contorting. She spat it out and shook her head. She wiped her lips forcefully with the back of a hand and then looked up to see the two men convulsing with laughter. One of them took his own sprig of berries, stripped the branch with a single swipe and crushed them in his palm. Then he began to stain his skin with them while the other one imitated the high-pitched whine of a mosquito.

Beba blinked several times and shielded her eyes as she stepped from the dense bush into the bright sunlit grassland. The older of her two captors led the way, the other walked behind. They followed the first indication of a trail they'd come upon in three days of trekking through the rain forest.

The clearing opened to spread hundreds of yards to either side and ranged so far in front that she couldn't see it end. The vegetation consisted mainly of sun-burned grasses intermingled with occasional flowers in a variety of shapes and colors. Wisps of wind dipped into the grasses making them frolic. Occasional trees stood like stern lonesome sentinels.

During their travels she had slowly gotten over her fears of these men. For even though they could not communicate verbally, they had proven to be kind, almost affectionate in the ways they treated her. She had been well-fed, her cuts and bruises tended, her clothing mended where she had torn it running away, and she was allowed privacy whenever she indicated the need. The final remarks of the sister and her banishment from the home of her aunt and uncle weighed heavily upon her, so as her fear of the men abated, it was replaced by a growing sense of alarm attending the uncertainty of her future.

The path widened and wound onward as clusters of small stone ruins began to appear. They passed a circular court surfaced with stones more than half a meter wide, each cut and sized so perfectly they formed concentric circles diminishing toward an empty pedestal at the center. Stone shards of differing colors testified that a monument or perhaps a statue had once occupied the spot. The pervading odor of rotting vegetation in the forest had given way to the sweeter smells of the grasses and flowers. She breathed them in deeply and for a few moments felt a tranquility that eased her weariness.

After perhaps a kilometer, the ruins came to an end and her eyes followed the pathway as it rose steadily up the long slope ahead. Now she could see the far side of the grassland defined by an abrupt wall of forest. Close-by she spied a row of more than a dozen long stone walls. Near the midpoint of the row two had tilted together in a way that formed a roof over the cone-shaped opening beneath. A few more minutes walking and it became apparent that this opening was their destination.

As they approached it, all reason gave way to a monkey of fright that climbed screeching, hand over hand up her spine.

Her instinct once again ordered her to run. But again where would she go? Apprehension or no, Beba needed to answer the terrible mystery of why the roots of her life had been torn away so abruptly.

The man ahead of her walked directly into the opening and as she followed she felt the screeching monkey stick icy paws into the back of her skull. Battling to call upon reluctant muscles, she clasped her arms across her chest and went in.

Several steps inside, the suddenly diminished light forced her to pause. As her eyes adjusted she became aware of a woman a few paces ahead, seated within a shaped mound of robes. The robes rose about her to form the high back and arms of a throne. Those who had abducted her had taken places behind it on either side.

Light flickered from two small oil lamps set in niches cut into the granite of the nearest wall. The woman's face remained in dancing shadow. Beba stood paralyzed.

"Come toward me, child." Beba started at the sound and the echoes of it that rebounded from the hard stone surfaces, then stifled a shiver and let herself move forward. The voice seemed young, but streaks of silver in shoulder-length black hair, deep creases surrounding high cheekbones and crisply chiseled features told her that the voice belied the woman's age.

"Farther into the light, Beba. This will be our only chance to speak and we have little time."

Anxious to look more closely herself, Beba began tentative steps forward. "How do you know my name?"

"I have known it always."

Beba stopped abruptly. The fright monkey's paws were climbing her spine again. "Why do you say always?"

"You will know soon. First stand tall before me. Let me see you well. What I have to tell you will call upon all of your understanding."

The woman waited. Beba sensed a great sadness in her. She straightened herself, as much in an effort to quell her own fears as in heed of the woman's instruction.

"Why have I been kidnapped?"

The woman's eyes crinkled with pain. Beba sensed that she had suffered deeply for very long and she saw tiny tremors moving her lips as she fought to maintain control.

"Before this time, I was the Queen of our tribe. Your tribe."

Beba stiffened as if she'd been slapped. The woman went on.

"In our language we call ourselves the Sacred Ones. Today, for reasons I shall tell you later, I inform you that hence forth until the time comes when you will pass the title on, you are our one living Queen, and you alone carry the privileges and burdens of this, our highest honor."

Beba had to hold herself from backing away. "I am no Queen. I have never heard of a tribe called the Sacred Ones."

The woman leaned forward and narrowed her eyes. "We were once a tribe of nearly two hundred souls, a people of peace. We tamed the land, and the animals, and lived at one with the nature about us. We traded and shared our wealth with the other tribes nearby. Now we are only five. We three you see before you and the one who took you soon after you were born, to live in the village, to raise you until the 'time had come' and then to send you to me here."

"Auntie Eva?" Beba clasped a hand to her chest.

"That is how you know her. The remaining member and the only one of your generation is yourself."

Beba let her voice raise. "Why would I want to be Queen of a tribe of only five? For what purpose? What happened to the others?"

"Hush now . . . hear me.

"Our people worked hard over the generations and developed many skills. We were artisans and artists, we took metals from the rocks and formed them to our will. We learned to melt them together so that they held a keen edge for tools and weapons. There were gifted souls who could take the medicines from plants to heal the river sickness and the red burning that enters wounds. Others quarried stone and made the design of our great temple. And yet others understood the movements of the sun, the moon, and stars to predict the seasons and the proper times to sow the seed and mate the animals. Because we traded with those about us and made their lives better, they revered us, but there was also envy."

The woman tugged at the robes to pull them more closely about her. Beba felt herself relax. Let this woman tell her story.

"As the many raining seasons passed, we lived in peace. The conquerors from Spain, exploiters from Europe and the Americas, all passed us by. We were too deep in the forest and there was nothing they knew of that they wanted from us.

"Then a band larger than our own, who had been driven by their greed from a land far away, settled nearby. In their years of travel they had come to know the white men. Some even had lived among them. One thing they learned was that a metal the color of the morning sun could be taken to the white men's villages and traded for many wondrous things that did not exist in the forest. They brought cloth of shining colors none had seen before, longer knives with keener edges than any of their own, axes and other tools that performed tasks they could not do . . . and the gun. This tribe did not have our skills, they did not know how to give the metal its freedom from the rock."

Flickering shadows rendered by the lamps revealed the character of the woman's beautiful features. Beba stood where she was and watched in fascination as the story continued.

"Late in a night at a time when the moon had gone away to slumber at the home of the jaguar, they came to hide outside our village. They brought many leaves of the bush of dark dreams.

When these leaves are heated until they smolder, the smoke brings a sleep so deep, that the snake could put it fangs into the softness of your belly and you would not waken.

Before our people went to sleep that night the women, as was the custom, put the embers of our cooking fires to rest by covering them with freshly cut leaves of the river reeds to keep the heat in through the night. In that way flames can be wakened by a mother's breath in the morning.

While the fires were resting in this way, they crept into our midst and lay the devil leaves upon them. When the leaves smoldered they placed them quietly inside each sleeping house. All but a few of our people were found murdered where they slept, even our newborn babes. The few that wakened and tried to fight were found but a few steps from their doors."

Beba heard the horror resonant in the woman's voice and shuddered down her spine. "If all of them died how do you know these things? How is it you live?"

The woman raised her hand to stop Beba's questions.

"Our Queen and her husband had taken we four children to a village close by to offer trade between our two tribes. Our parents feasted with their friends and toasted with the happy drink, chibuku, as was the custom, and slept there that night. When they returned in two days, they found our village quiet, our fires out, the animals gone, and our people murdered and left as they lay."

"Do you remember this?" Beba frowned beginning to believe the sincerity in the woman's solemn manner.

"I was very young. Only a little girl." She cast the back of a hand toward one of the men behind her. He nodded stoically. "But our eldest brother had already lived twelve raining seasons and the second eldest eleven. Their memories are vivid and still visit them in the night. Our mother taught us what we did not remember every day of our lives until she left."

"She died?"

"Perhaps, I do not know, child. She left us as I must leave you when our time together is over."

"Your father, the king, where is he?"

"When he saw the bodies of our people he was overcome with grief. First he hid our mother and we children in the forest in a large nest he built so high in a tree that the leaves beneath made it impossible to be seen from the ground. Together he and our mother stocked it with foods and items left in the village."

The woman began rocking herself slowly back and forth. Now Beba had become captive to the story and stood rapt.

"Our most sacred alter stood nearby the village atop a pyramid with three stepped sides and a fourth straight up and down so that it was an extension of the cliff that overhung the deepest part of the river. Our wise men had it built in this way to be nearer the sky yet in full view of the river, so that the Gods of both would have no cause to be jealous.

"Together our parents carried the bodies of our tribe up the stepped sides of the pyramid to the altar where they let each fall to the water below, so that they might rest in the home of the fishes without the shame their bones would bring to their souls if left to bleach white on the land.

"This task took many days, and the stench of the rotting bodies of his friends and our family lay in our father's clothing and on his hands. His grief turned into the darkest rage. He lay in the nights in our nest home with his head pressed to the breast of our mother and cried out to the night sky for revenge.

"Our mother, who was his Queen, forbade him to take up arms to punish the murders, giving as her reason the need for the safety of their children.

"Then on a day when they were finishing up the affairs of our dead village, a gang of the murderers returned. Most likely they came to see what else they might take for themselves. Our father hurried us up into our hideaway and, disregarding the wishes of our mother, returned to take vengeance upon them. He was as swift and strong as only a man gorged with craze can be and he was filled with purpose worth more to him than his own life. The gang of murderers were cowards taken by surprise. Our father dispatched the lives of six to their evil gods, but not before a seventh could flee to their people to carry the word that one of our tribe still lived."

The woman paused as if near exhaustion and Beba watched as the older of her brothers stepped forward to bring a robe around her shoulders. She clasped the back of his hand as he placed it there.

"Our father knew that they would bring all their warriors to seek him out and he feared that we would be discovered when they came. Our mother ordered, then begged him to take us away, but the rage that burned within would not suffer his running from them. He left us and did not return.

"Much later our mother heard a story, already a legend, from members of wandering tribes. They told the tale of a bird spirit in the guise of a human, who flew down into the murderers' village just as they gathered for the last meal of the day. They spoke with great wonder of the spirit whose marauding arrows and flashing knives took life after life, whose feathers caught fire and set their huts to burning, whose cries deafened the ears of their women and children for days to follow.

"The legend tells that fear gripped these cowards who had already been banished by their own people and for the second time they fled. Each time they settled the spirit bird found them and took his vengeance in the night. Over many rainy seasons the weaklings ran. Then one day they returned to those who first cast them out. They begged and pleaded and were allowed to remain.

"Soon one night the human form of the spirit bird came again to serve them their just due. But now these offal of vultures numbered more than the berries in all the bushes along all the rivers, and their warriors came at him as one.

"Finally they took the human life from the spirit, and gathered about the fallen form to consecrate that most costly victory. They cut open his chest for they intended to eat his heart before the warmth of it left, so that it might make them stronger for the next battle. As they held his body open so that the organ could be removed, a bird made only of fire emerged from it, and it was larger than any bird they had ever seen, larger than the whole of the man that gave it up. Its talons clawed the eyes from those nearest, and it rose into the heavens and was gone.

"Those murderers lived in horror of its return and to protect themselves against this spirit bird, they ate the flesh of the fallen warrior, and, as was the custom, made his head into the size of a man's fist. Instead of displaying it as a trophy of battle as they did all others, they put it on an altar in a place of worship. And the wandering tribesmen who first told these things to my mother said they had seen this head in a visit to that village and it was indeed the likeness of the face of my father."

"Over the years the neighboring tribes were forced to move on, because we were no longer there to teach and help them when the Gods did not provide. They have all been gone for a very long time and when you go there now you will see few traces of them, only the ruins of our own village for we were the ones to know the skills of hewing the stones and who thought endurance divine."

The woman paused now and rubbed at the base of her throat. Beba looked on steeped in uncertainty. The story about the tribe could be true, perhaps. She had known since she was a little girl that she and her aunt did not carry the features of others in their village. She and her aunt were tall and the women of the village shorter, with darker skin tones and less sharpened facial features. Standing there, she had begun to see those features in the two men and the women before her. But the story about a bird dwelling in a human? Preposterous. No more than superstition.

Then it came to her and she stood erect. "There . . . are five in your tribe and you are Queen. Your mother was Queen, and now you say I am to be Queen. Then you are . . .."

"Your mother."

Beba sank to her knees, looking up at the woman now. Her voice beseeched. "No . . . my mother is dead. Aunty Eva has always told me . . .."

"Your aunt is my sister. You know her as Eva. Her Indian name is Attua, the men behind me are her brothers the same as they are mine. She took you to your village, married, raised you, and told the stories of my death. She did so, because she was required to do so by her Queen and for strong reasons you will soon understand."

Beba couldn't hold back the color rising in her face. "If what you say is true. There are no reasons good enough for the lies you have had her tell your child."

"Perhaps not. But now it is time to decide for yourself."

———— ◆ ————

Beba coughed as she awoke. Her throat felt dry and her temples throbbed dully. It took a moment to sense her surroundings, but when it hit, she jumped to her feet and gaped about with alarm. This place where she had met her mother for the first time stood barrenly empty. Not even the oil lamps that had flickered in the niches in the stone walls remained. The dirt floor had been swept clean.

Vague visions of the night before returned . . . hands seizing her from behind . . . the sight of burning leaves out of the corner of her eye as her senses began to fade . . . the peculiar smell of the smoke. The two men, her uncles, had somehow gotten behind her. The burning leaves must have been of the same 'plant of dark dreams,' used in the murder of that tribe. Her tribe.

She remembered her mother's face looming closer to her own as consciousness slipped away and knew she would never forget the creases of deep sorrow or the tortured anguish in those eyes. If she weren't standing in the reality of the place where they had been, it would all have been a dream.

She called out and was answered only by the echoes of her own voice. There was so much she wanted to know. Much more than just the strange legend of murder and an avenging warrior. If her mother had been a little girl when all this took place, how had she spent her life, where had she gone now. The night before her mother had said, 'I have always loved you, Beba.'

She wanted to know why the woman had hidden herself all these years and had wished Beba to think her dead. And the one thing she'd forgotten to ask and her mother had not volunteered, who was her father? Of all the things her mother had felt the need to tell her, she had avoided that.

They'd taken everything except a roll like the one the men had carried when they'd taken her from the medical clinic. She stooped to open it and found the personal things her aunt had given her to bring from their village, clothing similar to that her mother had worn, and a blanket. Next to it lay a long machete and a large piece of bread beside several pieces of a strange fruit.

She took the food and went out into a high morning sun. A light breeze brought the clean fresh scent of drying grasses. She sat and leaned back against the outside stone wall and began to eat. The first bite brought her hunger into full play and she finished all of it quickly and rested against the warm stone trying to understand why she had been sent here. Certainly not just to hear those fables and be told she was now the queen of a tribe that no longer existed. Nor simply to meet her mother and then be drugged and abandoned.

You have a strong healthy body. It will make our time together easier.

Beba yelped and twisted in both directions looking for a source of the voice. It sounded very near. Almost as if it had come from inside her own head.

You are correct. I do indeed dwell inside of you. I communicate with you directly. It will feel to you as though my statements are your own thoughts, though you will know the difference.

"Who . . . who are you? Where are the others?"

You need not speak aloud to me. Merely think what you wish me to know. I shall understand.

Beba couldn't stop herself and her voice raised to a panicked shout. "Where are you hiding? Come out where I can see you. It is not possible to be inside another person."

But I am. Calm yourself. Remember that your mother told you she would pass the throne of the Queen to you, and also that the gods of your tribe dwell within you and guide your living. I am Coquitla. The God who guides the Queen.

The seed of my posterity was made to lie within you while you grew within your own mother. As you flowered, so it did also. When your mother's sister found that you had lain with the foreigner, Arthur, she knew the time had come, and called your mother here. She did so to save your life, for if I had not left your mother to join my seed soon,

it would perish and you with it. Now I live on within you until the time comes for me to, in the same way, join with your daughter. That is how I am immortal.

Beba struggled to understand what was happening. She must take hold of herself.

Yes. That is a good idea. We have far to go today.

It struck with a jolt when she realized she hadn't spoken aloud. Something inside her had actually heard her thoughts. Terror surged through her like frigid water. Her lips and fingers trembled and ice glazed over the back of her neck. She jumped to her feet and began to run, but without her intending it, her body halted to freeze in place after only a few steps. Then her head began to tilt down and when she tried to stop it nothing happened. Despite herself, her eyes focused on her feet and she could only watch as they pivoted her about until she faced the opposite direction and then took long deliberate strides to return to the exact spot where her running had begun.

I see there is a need for me inform you of my powers and what I shall require.

If Beba's mind had fingers it would have clawed its way out of her skull.

Long ago we left animals to dwell in humans.

I can't be hearing these things. I must still be asleep and dreaming.

You are quite awake and alert. I shall repeat . . . when we joined into the humans, humans gave us a new future. Few jungle animals live in groups finding that the need for safety or the constant quest for prey prohibits this. Those that do, birds and some small animals like monkeys are in constant danger and have very small powers of the mind.

Living in the tribe permitted us to live well in a group for the first time. To be near enough to one another to become more powerful than we could have otherwise. Humans offered an intelligence animals do not. These two things helped to assure our survival. While humans, in their everlasting search for entities to claim as gods accepted us easily. Honored us. Served us well and did not complain even when we brought them hardships.

Beba took in the message. Heard it in her head. Tried to accept the fact that its source did indeed exist within her. Was repulsed by it, but saw no choice. She would not accept the possibility that she had gone mad.

No. You are not insane. Let me offer proof.

And instantly Beba heard her own thoughts in another language. The language she had heard her mother use the night before when she spoke to her brothers. Only now she understood every word, recognized that she knew the language in its entirety, and when she tried it, could speak it aloud clearly. And with the language came knowledge. The lore of her tribe, how they lived, their fears and values and those things they revered. Then came the images: of a river, the jungle, a village and a stone pyramid high above the river on a cliff.

We must leave now to travel to the village you picture in your mind.

The trail to the river led her back into the forest, but it had been cleared of growth only hours before. The presence of Coquitla kept her in a turmoil of anger, frustration and fear for her own sanity. Each time she tried to resist, to reverse direction, to stop, to blank out the voice in her head, even to fall down, Coquitla prevailed to force her away from where she had met her mother with long strides.

The sound you hear is the moving of the river. You will travel upon it soon.

How can I travel on a river?

A boat waits.

Who will take me in a boat?

You will take us. I shall guide you.

No, por favor, I cannot do this. My head is too full. I am certain my mind will burst.

This is not unusual. The strong ones often feel this way. You will adjust.

Where are we going?

To the village where you will be Queen.

How many live there now?

Only you . . . until he comes.

I am to be queen of an empty village. This is madness.

Pay heed to where you go. The boat is near.

The trail had begun winding downhill and Beba could see the broad slow river moving below. At the bottom a boat lay nosed snugly into shore at water's edge, held in place by a growth of reeds. It was a single log, crudely hollowed out. A long pole lay inside jutting out over the stern. Bundles of some kind had been tied securely inside.

A new apprehension began to rise, but her attention was drawn by a flash of pale green that launched into the water as she neared it. The long tail of the caiman propelled it rapidly into the currents to submerge. Beba shuddered.

Do not fear the animal or the boat. I shall inform you of what you must know to be safe.

Gracias. But Beba was far from convinced.

You may feel assured, for it is what I must do to insure that I also suffer no harm.

Coquitla took her now: stepped her into the shallow water, dropped her roll into the dugout, stepped her over the edge and into it to kneel and then to take up the pole and hold it ready.

Do not try again to resist. It would not do to unbalance the boat.

Beba felt the muscles in her arms and chest flex and move. The pole dug into the soft river bottom beside the craft and it nudged backward a few centimeters. Two more thrusts and the dugout backed into open water. Another push and the bow turned downstream and the current began to move the boat along. Now the pole served to keep the dugout a proper distance from the river's edge, sometimes by nudging into the bottom, at others by serving as a rudder.

Twenty minutes into the journey, Beba began to accept that Coquitla could be trusted to direct her. Then the river began to narrow and she spotted rougher waters ahead. Her reflexes responded instinctively to move the boat toward shore, but even before the pole could be set for the first time, Coquitla acted to steer them toward midstream.

Do not allow yourself fear. Your emotion may hamper what must be done.

Abruptly, faster currents took the boat and swirls and eddies began to work at the narrow hull. Again she could only feel her body working as she settled low in the boat and took a grasp at the midpoint of the pole to use it as a double ended oar: steering, paddling, back paddling to keep the boat in balance. It was like watching the cinema at the school two villages downriver from her own. Seeing the perils unfold before her, anticipating dangers, experiencing the fear, only to see her arms use the pole to deliver her from harm at the last instant. But unlike the cinema she could feel the canoe pitch and toss, taste the spray on her tongue. She felt the harsh strain of exhaustion scalding hot in her back and arms. Felt it burn away her strength until she sensed her muscles beginning to fail. Then as panic took her, black bands circled tighter to narrow her vision and she opened her mouth to scream . . ..

When she became aware again the canoe moved easily. *Did I faint?*

You became unsafe. I took your consciousness.

Beba saw that the river had widened again and that the smooth waters had taken on a polished silvery sheen.

See ahead.

She looked and there was a cliff rising along the left bank. At the top rose a dark shape that she first took to be the peak of the cliff itself, but then she saw the stepped sides of the pyramid.

Our journey nears the end.

THE CHAIR ARTHUR OCCUPIED IN THE OUTER room of Owen Lansing's office seemed even harder than he remembered and he readjusted his body yet another time trying to manage some comfort. The receptionist who had occupied the desk near the inner office door before the failed expedition had apparently been reassigned, for the one material on the desktop was a coating of dust made plainly evident by the swipe of a fingermark through the center of it.

The only other occupants of the room were two young women sitting beside the open door of the private inner office chatting over notes on a steno pad. He vaguely remembered them as the student reporters he'd seen at the orientation meetings for the *Perra* dig. His mind was on his proposal asking the university to fund an expedition to the pyramid. He'd given copies to Benedetti and Lansing and then asked for this meeting. He hoped to be convincing and do what he could to move the request along through the cumbersome chain of university hierarchy. He tried to review what he wanted to say in his mind, but his adrenalin level wasn't making that easy.

He'd purposely asked for his to be the first meeting of the day anticipating that Lansing and Benedetti would be able to give him uninterrupted attention. The presence of the young women seemed oddly out of place, because he'd requested a full hour. If they'd also scheduled a meeting, they'd arrived very early.

The wall clock marked twenty past eight when Lansing accompanied by Benedetti finally passed through the room to enter his private office and Arthur noted ruefully that his hour was already a third gone. Lansing greeted the two student reporters by first name and beckoned Arthur to follow. Two things stuck out as Arthur entered the familiar office. First was the copy of his proposal atop a stack of documents on the corner of Lansing's desk and then the bare walls and boxes strewn about in various stages of being packed. His apprehension increased.

Lansing waved a hand at a pair of hardback chairs and Arthur and Benedetti pulled them up close to the front of his desk. Then Lansing began.

"Arthur just so you understand the climate within the department right now, let me tell you that as soon as we filed our report and had a meeting with university administration and our alumnus benefactor, all remaining funds that had been provided for the *Rió Perra* site were withdrawn."

Arthur felt his heart sinking. Between the packing boxes and what he'd just heard, a turndown was already in the air.

"I know you believe your discovery may be important, but the fact is that funding from this university simply isn't available.

"And you've most likely heard there are a number of people who believe the expedition should have taken precautions to make sure we didn't waste our resources on a disastrous trip. In retrospect I'm not sure that their complaint is entirely without merit. If that is the case, the responsibility surely rests with me."

Lansing leaned over his desk toward them and his voice quieted to little more than a whisper. "The details aren't worked out yet, but there is a very good chance I'll be leaving quite soon."

Arthur couldn't help shaking his head at the injustice of it. He'd learned to respect Lansing and hearing him accept responsibility even though the disaster was not something he could have prevented only added to it. He felt truly sorry for the man. "Dr. Lansing, I can't believe you should be blamed for anything that's happened."

"Thank you, but I'm afraid those who would disagree with you have already cast the final votes."

Benedetti turned in her chair to face Arthur. "The department is rethinking the whole idea of committing resources in South America. We will strengthen our interests in the other areas where we're already involved instead. At least for the time being. It could be a matter of months or even years before South America is put back on the burner."

He suddenly felt selfish bringing up his proposal in light of the circumstances he'd just heard, but there might never be another opportunity. "Did you have a chance to look over the material I left with you. Even if there isn't funding, I'd appreciate your thoughts."

Lansing reached over and put a hand on Arthur's proposal. "I took the time to study it in fact. Your work is good. Very thorough. But there isn't sufficient data to support the scientific value of an expedition. Even if money were available. Sketches, rubbings, descriptions. Not concrete enough in today's world. You need photographs at the very least. Satellite work. You know the possibilities there.

"Arthur, your reputation is established here. But we've just suffered one very big flop. You can imagine how skeptical administration is liable to be even if the department supports you."

Arthur could only nod understanding. It suddenly felt as if he had a fever and his ears were burning. He was sure his complete disappointment could be seen by the crumpling of every fiber in his body.

Lansing gave no indication that he'd noticed, but turned the discussion to the content of the proposal and for the next few minutes he and Benedetti offered constructive comments. Although he'd asked for their critique and followed along politely, most of it was lost on Arthur. He'd gone ahead with the proposal because he'd been there. He'd seen the pyramid, knew the truth and had somehow managed to tell himself that should be enough.

For a brief moment the story the boatman had told him came back. About the rain forest tribe that would kill you if you entered their territory and who hid from civilization because they were afraid. They chose the hard life of the jungle because it was easier to live with the fears they could understand. His jaw seized and his hands clenched. He'd just received a lesson in how unfair the world of academia could be and he didn't like it.

The entire meeting lasted about fifteen minutes, then Lansing walked them to the door of his office and called in the two reporters. Arthur realized with dismay that Lansing had never intended to give him the full hour. He clenched his fists as he and Benedetti started down the hallway away from Lansing's office. She took him by the upper arm and pulled him to a halt.

"I'm sure the pyramid is an important find, Arthur. And you did the right thing bringing it up as a proposal. Personally, I think the hands-off South America policy is knee jerk and will go away soon enough.

"I could be wrong, of course, but if it does, I still have a little bit to say around here. I'd be willing to push for you. But realize that from approval to the time you board the plane is probably at least two years. If I were doing it, I'd go after other sources. You know how to find them. Drop by my office and I'll give you some leads I have tucked away."

He'd begun thinking about outside possibilities even before they'd left Lansing and the fact that she stood willing to support his work gave him the first real lift of the morning, but Benedetti had more to say.

"When you deal with strangers you won't have the reputation you have here. You've got to consider going back for more evidence. Everyone of us walks around with one of the small point-and-shoots in a pocket every time we go on a dig."

The fact that there were no photographs gave his proposal the credibility of a UFO sighting. "I know you're right. I wish I hadn't forgotten to take the cameras."

"It's going to be hard to sell the story that the expedition photographer went off and left his cameras because he got knocked into a river, Arthur."

Her mention of the debacle with Fields heated his face up like a fireball, though her willingness to stand up for his proposal told him he'd been at least partially forgiven for taking a punch at Fields. Time to clear the air.

"About that last morning at the *Rió Perra*." He heard himself stammer.

"You're not off the hook." She interrupted and gave him that uncomfortable looking smile of hers. "I'll think of some suitable sort of penance for you on a dig we're on together in the future. But I did have a chance to speak to Millie after you sailed away from the *Perra* site. It seems you were provoked to the point where your actions are somewhat understandable, if not entirely forgiven. But let's get back to your discovery."

He felt relieved she didn't need to dwell on it and even more fortunate to have her in his corner. The hallway they stood in seemed to take on more light.

She moved her hand to his shoulder. "Photographs can be doctored too. Corroboration. Take someone who has expertise with you and preferably someone not too close to you personally. An impartial witness so to speak. Do anything you can to cast your proposal's data beyond the shadow of a doubt."

He nodded agreement and was about to thank her, when she gave him her quirky smile again.

"And how is Millie?"

"Off to New Hampshire visiting family."

The day he'd returned he'd telephoned and that had been about the only information she'd been willing to give him. She'd made it clear that she wasn't ready to go beyond light conversation until after she'd returned. He'd even told her about his discovery, but she'd only passed it off saying that she'd had enough of that part of the world for a while and that it might do more to hurt his professional standing than to help it. His behavior in the animal blind convinced him that he wouldn't be the husband she needed and he couldn't bring himself to push for more. But a sadness and longing remained as part of him, because of that.

Now Benedetti's voice took on a gentle quality. "She's a fine woman, Arthur. It would be a great mistake to let her get away. If you want her you'd better let her know.

The Monday morning following their meeting in Lansing's office, Benedetti phoned him at home while he was still getting ready to leave for the university. She asked him to meet her off campus. She offered no reason, but her tone of voice made the request an order. She wouldn't even settle for the coffee shop they'd used for meetings before the expedition, directing him to a place a good five miles farther away from campus.

Thirty minutes later, and with a head full of questions, he pulled into the dusty parking lot beside a pastry shop and went inside to find her sitting at a small round table with two cups of coffee in front of her. She pushed one toward him as he took the chair across from her. Without further greeting she unfolded a newspaper and placed it on the table for him to see. She had the expression of someone ready to go to war and her tone was brusk. "Did you have anything to do with this?"

An ominous feeling took him as he held the paper up and checked the banner. It was that morning's edition of the campus newspaper. The lower right-hand quarter of the page ran an article headlined, *Science or Silliness*, and under that he saw two small but exact copies of the rubbings of glyphs he'd taken from the altar stone.

"How bad is it?"

"Keep the paper and read it for yourself. The gist is that the reporters played up the criticism of the trip to the *Rió Perra* and infer that the department is about to go off on another wild goose chase. It cites your request to use the leftover funds and some of the same things we talked about in our meeting in Lansing's office, lack of photographic evidence, that sort of thing. It ends up suggesting that the department has wasted funding and is giving the university a bad name."

He glanced up to see Benedetti's eyes flashing anger at him. "I repeat, did you give that information to the student paper?"

His own anger matched hers. "Of course I didn't. Who would do something like this?"

Benedetti slapped her palm down on the table top. "It's all bullshit, Arthur. But people who are uninformed or who just want to believe it, will do just that. It's the kind of thing that starts investigations. The kind that substantiate conclusions made in advance."

She paused for a moment to take a breath and spoke again. "Who had copies of your proposal aside from Lansing and me?"

"No one even knows about it but the three of us."

"And now the entire campus."

He folded the paper and dropped it beside his coffee cup. "Have you spoken to Dr. Lansing?"

"He left us even sooner than he thought he might. Friday was his last day. He stopped by my office to say goodby. Said something about getting away for a little soul searching in a cabin on a lake somewhere. We'll probably have to tough it out for a few days, before I can reach him. In the meantime all hell can break loose.

"But he's too good a man to be the culprit even with the disappointment he has to be feeling over the way things turned out for him here. He couldn't do such a thing. I don't think I've ever met a more upstanding man."

"Then how?" He pushed his chair back and it complained as it scraped across the floor. "The student reporters. The proposal was sitting on the corner of Lansing's desk."

"Of course. That must be it. How careless of us all. To be honest with you, Arthur, if it had been you who gave it away, I was ready to throw you to the wolves. As it is, I'm afraid your colleagues are going to be hard on you. People, even those the quality of the people in our department assume guilt whenever they see something in the media. Freedom of the press may have ruined as many lives as it has saved. And it's almost certain the story will get picked up by the city paper, maybe even one of the archeological journals.

"If I were you, Arthur, I'd find some research to do in the library today. Let me try to do a little damage control before you have to answer a lot of questions. Call me tonight, I'll tell you what I find out. Then you can prepare yourself."

ZARKO LOOKED AT SOMBER FEATURES IN THE plated steel rectangle that served as a mirror over the sinks in the communal washroom. Years of inmate's polishing had worn through the chromium surface in about half the area and left the duller metal beneath showing through. It gave a blurry gray complexion to the face reflected in it. Nearly bald now, it had been over twenty-three years since he'd been sentenced to life for the murder of an old woman named Elsie Hatfield. He contended to this day, he hadn't meant to hurt, let alone kill her. Deep creases lined his forehead and furrows rose between his eyes to give testimony to the cares of prison life. A man stayed wary every moment, outside his cell or in, for the predatory and deranged waited should he let his guard down for even a minute. The place had a code of its own that he'd learned well.

After wearing a full beard for over a dozen years, until it turned white, Zarko had gone back to shaving and began lathering his face with hand soap in preparation. Phaqutl slumbered in his dormant state.

"Ain't the same tough-ass white boy shared my accommoda-tion, when he first come here way back until they gived me a cell to my own."

Winkie Washington, well past seventy and hunched by age and the fact he'd never exercised for one second from the day they locked him up, still rose nearly six feet under recently clip-pered snow-white hair. Winkie weighed almost as much as an average man half his height, and Zarko thought whoever'd said Winkie's shoulders didn't stick out any farther than his ears could have been talking about the most obvious characteristic of either of those features. Zarko caught the other man's hazy burnt-honey reflection peering over his shoulder, eyelids working up and down in the rhythmic pattern that gave him his name.

Despite his age and frail stature, Zarko'd known since the day he'd met the man that nobody got tough with him. And that Winkie knew he knew it, for he was protected by the largest and by far the most powerful of the gangs that ran the inside of the prison. There were several, but Brown Sugar, Winkie's guardians, The New Nazis, Damian's Disciples, and a quasi-religious mean spirited bunch that called themselves The Cellblock Saviors were the biggest. Over the years they had split up the turf; the guards, inmates, suppliers from the outside, all of it and controlled every-thing but the keys to the world outside.

Officially, Winkie was a Brown Sugar, his race offered him no choice, but he also had the respect of the other gangs, because he got favors done in many ways for anyone and didn't ask too much for them. For two packs of cigarettes you could get your dentist's appointment at the infirmary moved up a week and for a carton, enough chloral hydrate to put you to sleep every night for a week. When your aching tooth went way beyond the one aspirin morning and night the infirmary gave you, relief a week sooner and sleep was worth the cigarettes and a hell of a lot of respect. Winkie could get most anything, but he didn't do weapons or drugs. The felons got them dozens of other ways.

After Zarko'd known him for about six years Winkie'd finally opened up to a white boy for the first time in his life.

"The ghetto weren't no good. No way a man like me could make it there and you couldn't get out from it. Least not in my day. An' in here ain't no good neither, but here I's with the power an' the majority. An' because I do good for folks, I gets respect an' those things is somethin' good. Reckon that's why I let 'em keep me in so long."

Remembering all that, Zarko said it anyway, because he was the only man in all nine hundred plus, in a prison built for five hundred inmates, that could get away with it without fear of reprisal.

"Might just come down to that cell someday and kick your rickety ass, old man."

The eye lids went up and down, up and down. "After all I learnt you when you first come to Chainville, 'n took all those years doin' it, an now I sees I ain't did no good." Winkie stepped to the basin next to Zarko and began the ritual. His movements were painfully slow and deliberate, carefully timed to let him remain out of his cell for as long as the guards would tolerate.

Zarko liked the old con for a lot of reasons, one of them his complete obsession with working the system every way he could: a few more seconds on the yard, an extra boiled potato at lunch, sheets without stains or sewn up tears. Zarko smiled a grim half smile, the maximum allowable in open areas under the code unless you were looking for love. He saw it returned by the other's reflection in the metal mirror. Zarko didn't have friends, but if he had to chose one, Winkie could maybe do.

"How's Mister Phaqutl this mawnin'?"

"Sleeping. He doesn't come out much anymore unless it's library time or when I'm readin' in the cell. It's gettin' closer to the day we'll be leaving and he says he wants to build his reserves. Whatever the hell that means."

"Every con in here thinks they's leaving' real soon. Some does, but you ain't one of 'em unless you plannin' to kick the bucket'. Why'nt you wake Mister Phaqutl up, I wouldn' mind talkin' to someone a lot smarter'n you for a spell.'"

"You know I can't."

"Less'n you starts actin' up. Then he comes up quick-like and turns you into a real nice fella almost. If it were'nt for him you'da spent the last couple 'a decades in solitary. Instead you a trustee like me, though it took you long enough. You a real split-down-the-middle like that Dr. Hyde and Mr. Jekyll fella. You is both Zarko and Mister Phaqutl an' the better off for it."

Zarko slowed his movements, watching in the mirror, matching Winkie's shaving stroke for stroke, trying to take advantage of his ability to keep them away from their cells that few extra minutes. Not being a patient man, it wasn't all that easy. Then he felt the telltale half-second of stiffening through-out his entire body.

"Good morning, Mr. Washington."

"Mornin' Mister Phaqutl. Zarko said he couldn't get you awake. How is it you come out?"

"I am nearly always alerted when Zarko shaves. He cuts him-self and the sting triggers my danger response."

"How you doin' in there? I wuz just tellin' Zarko about all the good you done him."

"Fine thank you. And yes, I did hear. I appreciate that. Do you suppose you could let us have some more copies of *National Geographic* and whatever other magazines you can spare for me to keep in the cell a few days? At your usual fee."

"I'd do this one for free. Ain't no danger in it fer me no more. Guards don't care none. I told 'em how readin' keeps ol' Zarko's bile from risin.' Anyway I'm getting plenty extra to eat, an' you don't look like you can spare none. Next time you can pay."

"Of course. Thank you."

"Zarko tells me you thinkin' to leave soon."

"My education has gone about as far as it can here."

"I remembers. Onc't you got interested in books, ain't been nuthin' could turn you off 'em. How come you didn't study law like most folks do? Get you a *writ of habeas corpus* or somethin'."

"Because I was not ready yet. I do not know where to go."

Winkie openly broke the code and laughed out loud. "Mister Phaqutl, you an' Zarko plainly is a pair."

The banter continued as the two men finished up, turned their razors in to the guard at the washroom door and moved in opposite directions toward their cells. After a few steps Zarko turned to watch the other man shuffle away.

It was his hour on the exercise yard and the high wispy clouds blocking the sun made Zarko's shadow barely visible on the hard packed ground. Twelve foot stone walls plus another ten feet of cyclone fencing topped by razor wire formed three sides of the three acre enclosure, and the prison building enclosed the fourth. Most of the hundred seventy odd prisoners outside this hour either played basketball, lifted weights, or strolled around the oval track in small groups smoking and chatting. Here and there singles stood by themselves. They were the loners, solitary by choice. Over the years Zarko had noticed that the hard core loners weren't usually around all that long. When they got crazy enough they transferred them to the prisoner's wing of the state mental hospital. Today Zarko stood alone. Not for solitude, but for safety.

He stood under the wall opposite the main building equally distant between two guard towers. He wanted to see and be seen, though he questioned whether the guards would intervene if he needed them. He'd wanted to skip the yard, to stay in his cell until things calmed down, but doing that would seal his guilt in the minds of the inmates and assure that he'd die at their hands. He didn't kill Winkie Washington, but the defenseless old man had been found in the infirmary where he worked with his head twisted until his neck had broken. He wouldn't mind too much busting the neck of the sonofabitch that done it.

Obviously, a powerful man had killed Winkie and Zarko more than qualified. The way he and Winkie bantered with each other, though born of years of familiarity, could easily have been taken as animosity.

Proof that he'd been marked as the murderer came soon enough. Hundred Stevens approached slowly. He was a squat wide-shouldered white man. Self-named as a brag that he'd broken all the ten commandments at least ten times. He walked with his hands open and away from his sides to show he carried no weapon. Crude black swastikas, prison tattoos, decorated the backs of his hands and each thick knuckle rose through the out-line of a star. He sat number two in command of the New Nazis.

Zarko stood pat, trying to look unimpressed, but rising adren-aline and the increase in muscle tension roused Phaqutl.

Who is this coming? Why are you afraid of him?

I ain't afraid of nobody.

Your body shows that you are.

Then the Nazi arrived. "Yo, Zarko. How you doin', man?"

"Okay. Good. You?"

"I'm cool. Came to say we're behind you, man. You did good to kill the sonofabitch. Less niggers the better."

Zarko wanted to reach out and tear off that smug face. He knew for a fact Winkie was a thousand times the man who stood before him. "Winkie was a good con. I didn't off him."

"Gotcha. 'Course you didn't. Keep in touch anyway. Word has it Brown Sugar's gonna pay you a visit before this hour's done. They won't try nothin' out here. Too many witnesses and some of the guards belong to us."

"I figured that."

"But I wouldn't take a shower for the next week or two, the guards in there won't see nothin'. An' don't come up sick and check into the infirmary. Winkie wuz a homeboy there. Not a one of em' wouldn't kill you an' they got all the ways to do it. You know, pills, needles, scalpels, the whole shittin' lot."

"Thanks. I take care of myself."

"We'll be workin' out a plan. Maybe take down another one or two of 'em. Scare' the shit out of 'em. That'll take attention off you. We'll be keepin' in touch."

And with that Hundred snapped to attention, clicked his heels, did a quick military aboutface that left him tilting off balance like a willow in a windstorm until he hung a leg out to the side in midair to rebalance himself. Zarko didn't try to keep from laughing. Finally the Nazi returned to upright, shot him a look that would have been a warning if his face hadn't been so pale, and strode away in a version of the Nazi goose-step.

Zarko watched him go until Phaqutl posed a question.

Do we need their help?

Only if I want to die for sure. Those bastards are all bark, but they're crazy enough to stir up one helluva mess. Anybody thinks I joined 'em and I better kill a guard just to be sent to another prison. Better alive on death row someplace else for ten or fifteen years than dead here by the end of the week.

Zarko looked out to see Hundred's goose-stepping cease abruptly and drop into the familiar slammer shuffle of men who'd walked for years with no place to go. Phaqutl took the clue and intervened to turn Zarko's head to the right to see four men emerge from the prison building and make a beeline in Zarko's direction. They weren't normally on the yard this hour, but the guards seemed not to notice.

Wrench Crescent led, followed by a man that called himself Peters. Both close pals of Winkie's. They brought two hard looking men with them. He didn't know their names, but he did know them as enforcers for the Sugar. He could see the guards in both towers paying close attention. One moving to get a full view from an open window, letting his rifle barrel swing out of it intentionally. Zarko forced his shoulders to relax, spread his feet apart, clasped his hands behind his back.

He kept his eyes on the approaching foursome and informed Phaqutl. These are the ones to watch out for. As they arrived Wrench and Peters took places side by side in front of him, the two enforcers took stations on either side.

"How you doin', Zarko?"

"I didn't kill him, Wrench. Call your men off."

The broad-shouldered black man put out a laugh that Zarko was sure he meant to sound forced and raised his voice so loud it made his intent to draw attention fully clear. "Why yassa Missa Zarko, we jus' knooows you didn't hurt ouwa' lil' fren' Winkie. It mussa been some otha ol' chicken shit white ass."

The four moved in closer. Zarko's every muscle tensed and his heart began to pound so hard he thought the others would see it beating in his chest. Phaqutl interrupted in his mind.

We shall fight.

Not if they don't start first. I'm not committing suicide until they push me off the bridge. Just listen in. We'll know in about a second.

Wrench stepped closer and lowered his voice. The phony patois disappeared. "We know you didn't, because we know who did. We're going to take care of him and you're going to help."

Zarko's head jerked up to meet the other man's gaze full on. "Who?"

Wrench held his reply and Zarko's tension turned to anger. "Tell me who the sonofabitch is."

When Wrench spoke again, he kept his voice so low that Zarko had to strain to hear it. "Cul-de-Sac."

"Holy shit. The boss of the Sugar."

"He thinks Winkie was gettin' too big for his britches. Too well-liked. Doing favors for folks didn't deserve it. Like white folks. Getting respect boss should of had for himself, taking down the big man's power. He knew you'd be easy to finger. Done it already."

"What do you want from me?" Zarko didn't feel relieved, only that the problem had changed. Maybe gotten bigger.

"The Sugar has its own golden rule, Zarko. If one of us gets killed, we off the guy that did it. No matter who. Even if he gets outside. Somebody out there can do it for us."

"Most gangs have their rules."

Wrench drew himself up to his full height and pulled his shoulders back. "No Sugar kills another, no matter what the cause or how good the reason. Kill a brother, die by a brother. Nobody in the Sugar can kill Cul-de-Sac without taking his own turn. But Cul-de-sac killed Winkie and it is our duty and a pleasure to return the favor."

"I don't get it."

"It's a good rule, Zarko. Makes fighting among ourselves the worst sin. It's our eleventh commandment. We have one more than the goose-stepping simpleton that left you as we came out. It keeps us strong. Holds us together."

"Where do I come in?"

"You aren't a Sugar. With our blessing, you cut Cul-de-sac."

"The hell I do. Why would I?"

"Three reasons, my friend. One: you do the job and we make sure everybody knows you're in the clear. So you get to live. Two: Winkie would have wanted it this way and we know you care about that, whether you say so or not. I might add that he named you a white boy could be trusted a long time ago. Don't break that trust now. You need it. And the big number three: we ain't giving you no choice."

"Bullshit."

"No shit about it, man. You do it right, or we let Cul-de-sac and maybe one or two of his friends do it to you. That way you take the fall, then we let the Nazis go for Cul-de-sac. But if that happens our folks will start a war and we'd have to let 'em or the Sugar would come apart. You know prison war. Somebody breaks his legs today. One hangs himself next month. Guy gets out and gets a cap busted in his ass a few days later. Worst part Cul-de-sac might just make it through without a scratch."

Zarko looked up at one of the guard towers for a moment, glad to see they were being watched. "I got no way to do Cul-de-sac. He's bigger and meaner than a pissed-off rhino. I got no weapon. He don't go no place alone. I'd have to be crazy."

"You'd be a lot crazier not to. Listen up. We got you a weapon. A shiv. Homeboy made, an damn good. We'll deliver it to you right here. In a minute or two. Then we'll set Cul-de-sac up and let you know where. It'll all have to be done quick or we won't be able to hold 'em off you."

"If this shiv is Sugar made, doesn't Cul-de-sac know about it? He'll be careful as hell."

Wrench scuffed a toe in the hard dirt of the prison yard, the three men with him had the expression of those who saw and heard nothing. "We always keep one on hand. Cul-de-sac knows this one's gone. He thinks the guards found it on a surprise inspection after they found Winkie's body. He already donated five hundred to the 'guards retirement fund,' so nobody will put the heat on us for it, but he's been tipped we can't get it back. Its supposed to have already been turned into the warden's office by a green guard.

"I figure two days is also about how long we can keep your ass from gettin' killed. We'll tell 'em to hold off, but it won't keep 'em down long. Can't let out what we know and what we're doing about it until after Cul-de-sac goes down or the word will get to him and we got us a big problem. When he's gone, I'm the new boss, you're home free, everything's okay again. We'll be obliged to you."

"How are you going to pass the shiv to me with both towers watching."

"That's the fun part. Mr. Peters here will step back from the rest of us. Then we're going to shout at you some. When the hollering gets heavy, me and these two boys will close in tight, jostle you up a bit, and Jerome there will slip the shiv inside your shirt. Then Peters charges in yelling 'not now, not now,' and we'll break it up before a ruckus starts and the guards get involved. We walk away cussing back at you to make it look good. Should all be over . . . fifteen maybe twenty seconds. Guards won't hurry to get here that quick. Some of 'em hopin' we give it to you for Winkie anyway. Your hour's about up. Five minutes and your back inside, no one the wiser."

"How do I know I'm not being set up to get the shiv in my gizzard right now."

Zarko saw Wrench almost smile and the phony accent came back. "Why you doesn' missa white boy. You jus' gonna haffa trus' us."

With that one of the enforcers shoved him hard from the side into the one called Jerome. Zarko gritted his teeth and let it happen. The shouting started with Wrench screaming.

"Gonna fuckin' kill yo' ugly ass."

Zarko felt the hand inside his shirt front, and before he could respond, Peters was there, pulling them off him, shouting for them to back off. They stopped, anger and hatred looking all too natural on their faces.

Zarko felt sweat pouring down his face. He hoped they'd take it for good acting, but he wasn't. He hunched over at the shoulders, stuck a hand inside his shirt over his gut as if feeling to see if any damage had been done and pushed the implement far-ther down, so that the waistband of his dungarees held it securely in place.

When he looked up again, Wrench and the others were thirty yards away, Wrench was walking backward and there was a man on each of his shoulders pushing him along. Wrench looked crazed.

"Seein' you again real soon, Mothafucka."

A guard came up, someone he recognized, but couldn't name. "You okay, Zarko?"

"Yep. Just a misunderstanding. No harm done."

"Maybe this is a good day for you to go back to the cell a little early."

"Don't mind if I do." Zarko took a look at the sky. The clouds seemed much darker.

———— ·•· ————

Back in the cell, Zarko dropped down on his lower bunk, laced his hands behind his head and stared up at the wire springs and stained gray mattress over him. His cellmate worked an extra shift in the bakery two days a week for a few more cents to send home for his kid and Zarko had the place to himself. Phaqutl hadn't interrupted since before the episode with the Brown Sugar in the yard and he assumed he'd gone dormant again. He seemed to be most of the time lately, content to leave him at peace unless there was something to read. At first Zarko rebelled at anything that smacked of schooling, never having had any truck with it before prison, but he softened on the idea when he found it could take up a great deal of time. On the inside a lot of time needed filling. With more practice in any one week than in his lifetime on the outside, his reading skills improved, and his prison alter ego somehow made sense of things he wouldn't have understood otherwise. As far as Phaqutl being there was concerned, having a double personality didn't bother him much. There were a lot of men crazier than him in prison, slam did that, and Phaqutl sometimes seemed saner than Zarko himself.

He wished he'd wake up right now. They ought to talk out the issue of Cul-de-Sac Jones. First of all, if Zarko, the real Zarko, started something like that and Phaqutl didn't approve, he'd just stop him anyway. That could be deadly in a fight. Then too, his Phaqutl personality came up with some pretty smart stuff now and then and could come in handy. He could raise a little hell and wake him. He'd have to jump up and down or smack himself with something hard enough to hurt, and it didn't seem like a good idea to do anything that would give them an excuse to come in and search him and the cell with the shiv still tucked in his pants.

Now was a good time for special caution, but before hiding it he thought he'd better give it a good look. If it hadn't been made right and couldn't do the job, now was the time to find out. He turned his face to the wall and took it out.

As promised, it showed excellent work: stiletto shaped, about nine inches long: six of blade, the handle a little short for hands the size of his. Carved from bone, the blade had been polished until it looked like ivory and reflected the image of the square barred window even in the dim light. It had a keen double edge and the blade was made thin to give it the slicing capability of a razor. So thin Zarko worried about it breaking. Obviously its maker intended it to be used only once. The very end of the handle had been cut at right angles to the blade and given a smoothed out little hollow that would just accommodate the ball of the thumb. The shank had been roughened. These features were intentional so that the user's hand wouldn't slip down onto the blade when he shoved it in.

He could guess how it was done. The bone had been smuggled from the kitchen. A leg bone, more than likely ham. They ate a lot of ham. Even though bones were counted in and counted out, it wasn't all that tough to get one. This one probably laid in the bottom of a stew pot for a few days. Another slipped into the out-count twice by some slight of hand. If the trick was noticed, the real bone would be produced and the ruse tried by another con a few days later. Pulling a trick like that could lose a con a good job, even get him a stint in the hole, so it would have been one of the cooks that did it. They had no special immunity, but raise hell with one and the others would see to it the food tasted like shit for a month. That always caused a big attitude problem the guards didn't want to deal with and, of course, they ate the prison food too. Some even took it home. Once the bone had been officially written off, the rest was safe enough. The big ends of it would be cut off and ground into the food. Probably the regular Thursday night meat loaf. The shank of the bone could then be stuck down the front of somebody's pants, like a real boner, and walked back to the cell to be worked on. It could have been abraded into shape a number of different ways, against the rough underside of the toilet, with a smooth stone smuggled in from the yard, or a bit of a nail file from the infirmary. Polishing would have taken time, but toothpaste worked better than some of the stuff you could get on the outside. Just tuck a little bit under your arm at the morning washup. This shiv had been worked on for hours and looked to be the result of prideful effort, possibly while the con who made it fantasized about cutting the heart out of someone hated, a particular guard or the man now fucking his wife.

He waited a few more minutes trying to think through what had happened in the yard, and when it seemed safe enough, he still gave it another ten. Then he slipped quietly off the bunk, checked as slyly as he could to see if anybody watched, then knelt before the small stainless steel sink on the cell's back wall. Reaching beneath it with both arms, he twisted the drain pipe and worked it down into the 'U' shaped trap. It took some doing, but he was able to pull it to the side far enough.

Carefully he worked the blade down into it and then slipped everything back into place.

His cell mate kept his dope stashed in the sink drain too and it drained slowly. It would drain even slower now. They'd have to take care not to let the guards see that and he hoped the edge of the shiv hadn't cut the tightly rolled plastic baggie. If it had, he'd have to buy him some more to keep him shut up. Stupid weed ass claimed he couldn't live without it. He ate the shit, because they'd smell it if he smoked. Zarko'd put a stop to that the first time he'd seem him starting to roll one. He wasn't giving up any privileges so some hemphead could suck rope. Phaqutl figured that one out for him a long time ago.

He rolled back onto the bunk and assumed the position he'd left a few moments before. There wasn't a real variety of comfortable positions to be taken in a cell and men established favorites just like men outside often have a favorite chair.

So, what would he do about Cul-de-sac? Brown Sugar tried not to leave him much choice, but no matter what they said, his best interests would be second to their own. He'd keep his own council and make his own decision. The point was to come out of it alive and not hurt too bad. Not an easy task. Check it out, think it out, get the best odds.

Isn't the answer obvious?

Glad you woke up. Tryin' to figure out what the hell to do here.

I repeat, isn't the answer obvious? You just summed it up yourself. Get the best odds.

How's that?

What are the chances you can kill Cul-de-sac without being hurt?

Pretty good to a hundred percent.

And what are the chances that you will be hurt, if you don't?

If I don't off him, big odds they'll get me.

There you see, the answer is obvious.

Kill him.

Correct.

How?

If you are sure the odds are favorable, then you must already know how.

How to do him? Sure. That way the Sugar will leave me alone, but the 'man' will know I did it, and they don't like people adjusting their rules. I'll have a life like Bambi in a forest fire after that.

Don't let that trouble you too much. It is time to leave here anyway.

Okay and I suppose you know how to just up and do that?

I always have.

That revelation stunned Zarko for a few seconds and then he sat up hard in the bunk and rammed his head into the flat springs above. He grunted with the pain.

"You bastard. I coulda got out a here years ago an' you didn't say nothin' about it."

Become calm. Noise will only result in someone looking in, perhaps a search. Now is not the time. You won't be able to do what you must do if you're locked in the hole.

Zarko wiped his forehead with the back of a hand and looked at it. A smear of blood confirmed that the pain was the result of a cut from the springs over his head. Damn chickenshit split personality. He forced himself under control. If nothing else, prison taught you to handle your emotions. A display of any kind could bring reactions from guards or inmates you didn't want. He worked at it, but his breath wouldn't slow. Too much going on. He had after all, just been ordered to kill somebody by inmates who didn't really give a rat's ass if he died in the process.

The magazines.

What th' hell are you pissing at me about. What magazines?

You question the obvious again. The ones you stashed far back against the wall under this bunk. The last delivery from Winkie.

Forgot about them.

Obviously. Get them now.

He had and now it bothered him. To forget Winkie's last act told him he was hiding from the loss. Being a con's all about loss. You can't care, not about anybody. No matter what or why.

What the hell for? We'll look at magazines later.

Get them now. We must have a place to go when we leave.

He knew that if he didn't retrieve them Phaqutl would force it. Fuck you. He rolled heavily off the bunk, checked again for an observer and dropped to his hands and knees to reach underneath for them. There were three.

Back on the bunk he rolled to face the wall keeping the magazines from view from the window in the cell door and looked them over. The first was a travel magazine. Small wonder they were popular inside. He leafed through it quickly, stories about Europe, the Arctic, a Louisiana Creole food tour. He knew Phaqutl had no interest in these. For some reason he went nuts over anything about Central or South America. Probably the same reason that made him call himself that damned odd name. Got it from some magazine too, most likely.

The second magazine, the May issue of the American Journal of Archeological Research, mentioned the Amazon rain forest. On the lower corner of the cover he saw the teaser, "*Inside . . . Discovery or Fraud . . . Arizona Scientist Claims Discovery of the Hidden Ruins of an Unknown People. But Are They Real? . . . page 64.*

Zarko saw his fingers riffling hurriedly through the pages as Phaqutl took over and rushed to the article. There opposite the lead-in page of the story, he saw a full-page sketch of a stepped pyramid with a large rectangular stone centered on the topmost level. Two insets showed an artist's version of carvings supposedly made into the stone.

Zarko suddenly had the sensation that his mind was being buffeted in a high wind. He dropped the magazine and clutched his forehead when Phaqutl interrupted.

Do a pass-the-word to Wrench Crescent. Tomorrow.

On the yard the next day Zarko waved the goose-stepping Hundred Stevens over. The Nazi swaggered his way with his shoulders rammed back and his butt cheeks sucked in tight enough to pull water through a straw.

"Herr Zarko, you have decided to join us? Hiel the Aryan Race."

"Hiel a hairy asshole to you, I have not. You said to call on you for help, so I'm calling."

"You want us to take out some niggers for you." The squatty man inhaled deeply, puffed himself up, standing even more stiffly than before. Zarko thought he looked like a blowfish making himself look big to keep from getting swallowed.

"I want you to do a pass-the-word to a Brown Sugar. Wrench Crescent, no one else."

"I don't do no errands to niggers."

"There's two things in here can get your ass offed even by your best buddy. Rat on a con and refuse a pass-it-on. I need to send the message in by somebody who isn't one of them. I'd guess most everyone will know you ain't."

Hundred's lips smiled and his head nodded as though acknowledging a grand compliment, but the tiny wrinkles around his eyes told Zarko he was scared shitless, and he played to it.

"Out with it. You in or you dead?"

The pseudo-Hitler wagged his chin back and forth and started to whine something, but Zarko cut him off. "The Sugar owns the laundry. I need a man in the laundry. You tell him that. I need other things too. Tell him I need to talk. Him. Nobody else. He names the time and place." Hundred had his hands clasped behind him and was waving his butt back and forth like a little boy needing to pee.

"I get an answer by this time tomorrow or the word is out you refused a pass-it-on then gave it to the screws. Believe that. Wrench doesn't always move real fast, so maybe you better beg him to hurry up a little bit. Might save your ugly ass. If it don't seem like he's willin' to move, tell him you'll be his bitch."

Hundred opened his mouth, but it didn't seem to work. Zarko took pleasure in his discomfort. The guy more than deserved it.

"I guess you don't need to answer now if you can't. I'll know by tomorrow won't I?" Zarko spun on his heel and left.

—— • ——

The Brown Sugar set him up to do Cul-de-sac Jones just the way he'd laid it out for them. In the shower room, during the regular time with three other guys going in with Jones, so he wouldn't be too suspicious. Then the Sugar started a ruckus at the door to the outer dressing room that kept others from going in and took the guards attention. Zarko slipped past the fuss at the door, walked through the dressing room without stopping, took a glance into the showers to see Cul-de-sac and slipped in behind him.

Zarko meant to reach around from behind and jerk the shiv across his throat. But as big as Zarko was, the greater height and bulk of Cul-de-sac made the reach more difficult than he'd anticipated and he bumped into him with a forearm when he tried it. His target spun out of his grasp to face him. An ordinary man would have been scared shitless when he stood naked and unarmed to face a man with a weapon, but Jones gave Zarko a come-to-papa wave like he might give a little boy taking his first steps. Suddenly all of Zarko's planning and mental preparation got sucked down a drain in the shower floor.

His heart pounded in his ears and he knew he had to move fast or end up the one dead in the prison shower. He figured his adversary for more powerful but slower. He feinted and then moved forward to do business only to find a quickness that wasn't supposed to be and he took a sledge hammer smash over the heart from a fist half the size of his own head. Darkness welled at the edges of his vision and the strength in his legs betrayed him. For a split second he could sense the end coming and every muscle in him felt like it had locked hard to never move again. He watched an eerie welcoming smile spread from ear to ear across his opponent's massive face. But then Cul-de-sac made a mistake and let the smile turn into a sneer and that pissed Zarko off way too much to die. The paralysis in his muscles turned into hard fight, a cold resolve replaced the fear, and Phaqutl took control.

Without conscious effort his hip slid under Cul-de-sac's arm and when the bastard tried to wrap him up with the arm, Zarko used the bigger man's momentum to throw him. Cul-de-sac hit the floor on the back of his shoulders with a convincing splat, but bounced up onto his feet and was in the process of driving a fist towards Zarko's balls when the shiv slipped into him just above the pubic bone and didn't stop going up until it lodged under his breast bone.

Cul-de-sac Jones popped open and dumped out like tomatoes from a wet paper bag. Things spilled out Zarko didn't recognize, and the man's effort to push the wound closed with his hands proved quickly futile, yet his sneering smile seemed to broaden. Then Cul-de-sac went over backwards and the only noise he made this time was a dropped watermelon sound when his head hit the concrete floor. It reminded Zarko of a fruit stand he'd tipped over when he was a kid, but it gave him no appetite for apples. Vapors began to rise from the exposed viscera and the acrid stench of violated intestines steamed into the air.

He wanted to run out as quickly as his legs would go, but instead dropped the weapon on the floor and turned on the nearest shower faucet to let the spray wash away prints. Blood spread into the puddles that formed on the floor and began the trip to the drains. Without another glance at his handy work, he turned, strode out past the guard, who was still distracted by a quartet of Sugar seemingly about to start throwing punches at each other, and entered the main hall. He let out a long breath of relief and forced himself to walk with the nonchalance of the seasoned con.

Two Sugar broke away and took positions on each side of him, another walked in front. One inmate they passed developed a sudden all-consuming fascination with something on the floor on his side of the hall. The only other stopped before they came to him and remembered that he had business behind him he'd forgotten to attend to. At the third corridor they turned him to the left and went on until it ended at the door to the prison laundry. His escorts broke away and left him. He stepped inside. The noise from the rows of sterilization vats, commercial washers and mangle irons drowned out any possibility of normally-spoken communication. Steam escaped from flawed pipes along the wall and overhead as well as from the vats and irons making the air nearly unbreathable with cloying, hot dampness.

A bone-skinny man with closely cropped hair, that he'd seen hang out with Crescent, seemed to appear from the mists. He offered the new arrival an expression of intense hatred and pushed a clean pair of regulation orange coveralls up against his chest. Zarko looked down and for the first time saw the stains of Cul-de-sac's blood on his own.

His one-man welcoming committee literally pulled him out of sight of the door and the other workers and behind one of the huge steel vats. He watched fearfully impatient as Zarko changed. His bloodied coverall disappeared into the vat before he had the clean pair pulled up waist high. While he buttoned, his reluctant host pointed to a large institutional laundry cart of white canvas suspended inside a steel framework and pushed him toward it. He barely had time to crawl into the confined space and pull himself into a fetal position on his side before full bags of laundry began jolting down on top of him. When he was nearly covered, the gaunt, black stickman leaned over and pushed two half gallon plastic jars along side him.

"What are these for?"

The man leaned down into the cart and spoke loudly over the noise. "One got water in it. T'other ain't. You drinks out of the one. You pees in t'other. Don't make no difference to me which, an don't you do nothin' else in that cart else I cut you myse'f."

Zarko looked up to see the man fumbling in his coverall pocket. He withdrew two small boiled potatoes and dropped them down on him.

"Them's from Winkie friends. Wuz me, you could starve. I'm goin' off shift now. Don't make no noise. The brotha on after me went huntin' around to kill your ass today." Something akin to a chuckle followed the words.

He had no way to know how much time passed. As it dragged on the apprehensions that had begun to build since the moment the Brown Sugar had first approached him in the yard rose to fester inside him again and new trepidation crept in to cloud his consciousness. He began to hear the voices of guards and antici- pated the feeling of the laundry bags being drug from the cart. He knew his mind played tricks on him, but couldn't quell the hair prickling on his neck and arms or the clenching of his hands. Phaqutl seemed content to let him face his own problems.

He tried to force his mind toward easier thoughts but instead became haunted by the benign smile of Cul-de-sac just before he collapsed to the shower room floor. He couldn't banish the horror of the scene from his mind until it slowly dawned that his victim was also the artisan who had made the shiv that had killed him. Had Cul-de-sac Jones' last expression been pride in the results brought about by his own handiwork? He knew men had done stranger things in prison.

When Crescent and he set it up, they'd anticipated that the killing and Zarko's disappearance would trigger extreme precau- tions that would make it inconceivable to try to slip him out for at least the first day or two, but they could slip out a pair of orange coveralls. A pair that conveniently had blood spatters on it, courtesy Winkie's friends in the infirmary. They considered using Cul-de-sac's blood, but if things went wrong, they didn't want to provide something that might become evidence against him so the blood type was intentionally different. The two had laughed at the opportunity to put one over. The coveralls were to go out a prison supply truck window into a ditch about a half mile from the prison gates within two hours of the death dance in the shower and a few minutes after that a phone call, supposedly from a passing jogger in a phone booth, would tell the police. They figured the warden's men would have poached egg on their faces for the murder and apparent escape. The possibility of a trick and that Zarko might still be inside wouldn't occur to them.

Zarko tore material from the collar of his coveralls and pulled it into two pieces that he rolled and worked into his nostrils. Snoring could bring unwanted visitors. He slept fitfully and never for more than a few minutes if his perceptions were correct. While awake he planned his future on the outside over and over again to keep from falling into the mind trap he'd suffered before. It seemed like an eternity before he felt the weight on him get lighter and his keeper looked down, this time with his arm and hand extended. Zarko looked up.

"I need to get out. I'm damn near starved." He tried to raise up on an elbow, but couldn't.

"Jes' gimme them jars."

"I really need out of here for a few minutes."

"Pass 'em up or keep 'em. Makes no mind to me."

Zarko blew air out of his mouth and handed them up. "You got anything more to eat?"

"You goin' on a little trip firs'." And with that came the dreaded bags again and the cart began to move. He felt the double bump as it passed over the doorsill out of the room into the hall. Even in the confines of the cart, he could feel the cooler air and he welcomed it into his lungs. A long bumpy ride later, he felt the cart glance off something and come to a halt. This time when the weight lessened, the hands that reached down for him took him by the arms and shoulders and hauled him through the laundry to his feet.

Lying cramped for two days left him unable to stand up on his own and the two men who helped him up had to support him. One put a hand behind one knee and helped him lift it until his foot rose over the cart frame and eased down to floor. They lifted his other leg out and once both feet were on a solid floor he could ease himself erect. Every joint complained, every muscle ached, he was hungry and he needed the toilet. One of his helpers must have read his mind and pointed to an unmarked door.

After taking care of business he washed himself using paper towels from the machine on the wall, a luxury not found else-where in the prison. Then came a rap at the door as it opened a crack and a faded pair of jeans and a black sweat shirt were thrust in. His ribs still ached from the blow Cul-de-sac had awarded them. Trading clothing proved painful and difficult. When he left the toilet he looked about for the first time at the small morgue attached to the infirmary. Now he took in the cloying odors of embalming fluids. A stainless steel gurney stood to one side. On it was an unzipped white canvas body bag made inside the prison for this special purpose. Wrench Crescent stood beside it waiting.

"You did what you said, now we'll do ours. You leave in about ten minutes. Don't envy you the ride. Hearse will drive you to a mortuary about a half hour out. It keeps the bodies from here until relatives comes and claims 'em. Cul-de-sac Jones is goin' there. You goin' with him. Driver is a Sugar. Once he wheels you inside, you're on your own. It'll be okay to get up. Someone will come by to put the body in the cooler an hour or so after you gets there. The mortuary folks ain't in on it, so don't be seen. Don't leave no marks of you bein' there. Hide out 'til dark, then go."

"You get me the car?"

"In the parking lot. Same one the hearse takes you into. Car key over the door as you leave the building. Got it at the airport this morning and we know sure the owner's gone for two weeks. Tank's full. Two brown envelopes in the glove compartment. One's got the passport, the other's all presidents. A little shy of what you asked for, but enough. We got costs too. Chainville ain't goin' to miss you."

Zarko was about to respond but saw the door of the morgue push open behind Crescent and the pallid face of the posturing Nazi, Hundred Stevens, jabbed inside. Crescent must have seen the startled look come over Zarko for he spun and crouched like a man expecting attack, but then he relaxed, stood erect again and slipped into the feigned accent Zarko'd heard before. "Yo, bitch. I tol' you wait 'til I come out. This gonna' cos' yo ho' ass big time."

Hundred's face took on a contrite look and disappeared. Crescent glanced back over his shoulder at him, nodded just perceptibly, then turned back to the door and walked out.

One of the morgue attendants handed Zarko a cold fat chunk of corned beef and a Styrofoam cup of tepid water. He gulped the water and handed it back for a refill, then went after the meat. The attendants didn't try to hide their impatience and as soon as the last of the beef was in his mouth, they half ushered and half carried him to the gurney, took his shoes off and got him up and into the body bag with his head at the bottom end. Then they laced the false bottom over the top of him and all light disappeared.

Seconds later Zarko heard them wheeling up another gurney. Then the realization of what was happening came and his old place on the bottom of the laundry cart would have been welcomed. They lifted the weight of Cul-de-sac's cadaver into the upper portion of the body bag head to toe with Zarko. They conferred the dead man a great deal more deference than he'd received.

The mass of the inert body bore on him. As the zipper pulled shut, the odor became stifling and brought bile up in his throat. Fluid seeped down onto him through the lace holes at the sides of the false floor. The gurney began to move and he felt the jolt as the wheels collapsed under it automatically when they pushed into the back of the hearse.

When the hearse pulled to a stop at the prison gate, zipper noise told him the body bag had been opened no more than two or three inches. Just far enough for a quick peek to verify that it indeed held a body inside, then it zipped closed again. He heard the nasal twang of a guard's voice.

"He's sure as hell a big'un, weren't he?"

"Biggest man I ever seen." Came the answer from the baritone voice of the driver.

The vehicle accelerated and Zarko let himself heave a breath of relief. The rest of the ride to the funeral home turned out to be uneventful. At the destination, he felt the gurney pulled out of the vehicle and wheeled inside. Within seconds he heard a door close and a key turn in the lock.

Getting out of the bag was the one thing they couldn't manage to set up in advance without a good chance he'd be discovered as well. He had to set himself free before he could be discovered by the mortuary attendant who was to come and refrigerate the body. No time to lose. The lacing at one side of the false floor came away easy enough once he located the loose end just above his head. The zipper turned out to be a different story. First he had to worm out from under the cadaver and work himself around and up on top of it.

The body lay naked and cold and though he hadn't thought the odors could get worse, they did. He thought back to the scene in the shower, Cul-de-sac smiling even as he died. Dead and beneath him now. The flesh eerily soft. He could almost feel the lifeless hands reaching for him now to take their revenge. Heard himself gasp. Fought not to lose it in panic. Worked the underside of his heel against the inside of the zipper pull. A dozen, two dozen times until finally he could feel it give half an inch, then another inch. He worked it until he could get his heel out, then his whole foot to the ankle and things got easier. He forced the zipper to knee level with the calf of his leg and then he could reach down and pull it open to get out.

When at last he stood erect in the sterile room, he looked down to see the lifeless face disappear as he zipped the bag closed. Cul-de-sac Jones lay, still smiling.

My plan has served well.

Zarko rushed to a nearby sink and lost the corned beef.

ZARKO HUNG UP THE PAY PHONE AND walked back to get into the Chevy. Finding the home address of the archeologist mentioned in the journal article he'd read in prison had been a snap. When he'd gotten to within three or four miles of Arizona State University, he'd stopped and looked up the name in the phone book. There had been two Arthurs. A phone call to the first one listed brought the voice of a young woman on the line. When he'd asked if he'd reached the residence of the university professor Arthur Tomas she replied, 'Oh, you want the other one,' and hung up.

Less than ten minutes later he slowed the Chevy to a crawl and ducked his head to hunch forward over the steering wheel for a better look through the open passenger window. Muscles at the back of his neck ached from sleeping in the car the past two nights since leaving the mortuary and he took a hand from the wheel to rub some of the stiffness out of them. The small one-story the phone book told him Arthur lived in had forest green shutters guarding narrow-paned windows, the only feature that distinguished it from all the others on the block. The curtains had been drawn closed.

The smells of someone's backyard barbeque came through the window and he realized he'd forgotten the aromas free men took for granted. He inhaled, trying to take in all of it. This neighborhood looked like the place he'd dreamed about all his years in prison. A place where people mind their own business and leave you alone. Maybe he'd try to keep straight. His luck had taken a definite change for the better. Don't push it, he told himself. Stay cool and figure things out. Winkie would have told him to do that and in a way, Winkie had made it possible for him to get out, to be here, free. He guessed he could owe him that.

Move the car around the block.

Okay. Let's get this over with. He pulled himself erect and eased down on the gas. At the end of the block he twisted the wheel to the right and pulled onto the cross street.

Stop. Drive in there.

The nose of the sedan dipped like a bird drinking water as he braked hard to keep from missing the turn. What for? It's just the back alley?

Yes. We will view the house from the rear before we enter.

Looks like nobody's there.

Perhaps not. Let us see.

Five houses up the narrow alleyway, he saw the dark green shutters again. The rear yard had neither fence nor garden, only threadbare grass in need of water and a flagstone walk leading to a small roofed porch. Zarko guessed it was a rented house. Owned homes got more attention. An older compact sedan with buffed wax finish offering contrast to the state of the yard, sat on flattened grass parallel to the alleyway. A rear window of the house had been raised and only a closed screen door guarded the rear entrance.

There it is. Now what?

Someone is inside. We shall go in.

What if it isn't him, a wife or somebody?

It does not matter. We shall wait.

And then you're going to leave me. Right? And I can go wherever I please. You said you would.

Yes. After our business is finished. You will be free to go where you can.

Today?

Have you forgotten the passport? Ask no more questions.

He had forgotten and although leaving the country didn't appeal to him, it would be far less likely the cops would catch up to him. One thing for sure. The bastards'll never take me back.

I, too, am certain of that. Now drive back around and park in front of the house.

———— ◦ ————

Arthur sat at the desk in the bedroom he'd made into his home office, fussing with the details of a plan to return to the pyramid site. It had been almost two months since Jan Benedetti found the article in the student newspaper. He'd developed the plan easily enough, coming up with the money and someone with the right credibility to accompany him, had proven much more difficult. He'd tried every source he could find, but the publicity in the prestigious *American Journal of Archeological Research* seemed to have frightened everyone away. The frustration only made him more determined.

The front door buzzer gave two short rasps, sounding like the wrong answer signal on a TV quiz show. Arthur rolled the desk chair back and stood. As he walked from the office the buzzer nagged him again. People here weren't usually impatient without reason. He quickened his step and called toward the front entry door. "I'm on the way."

He swung it open without bothering to glance out the side window and felt his eyes grow wide as he bobbed his head up to see a man nearly as tall and wide as the door frame. The stranger wore faded jeans and a black sweat shirt, both badly stained, and several days' growth of gray beard. A draft swirling in through the opening cloaked Arthur in the acrid-sweet smell of formalin. It was an odor common to university science labs and he stood trying to recognize the man as faculty from campus when his surprise guest interjected.

"Dr. Arthur Tomas?"

It sounded accusing. He gathered himself and gave him his best I'm-sure-we've-met smile. "Have I had the pleasure?"

"I am Phaqutl. You are the professor who located the Pyramid of the White Doves."

It took Arthur a second to realize he referred to the hostile birds he'd seen at the site. Curiosity nipped at his ribs. "Is there something I can do for you?"

"I hope you will agree that there is something we shall do together." The journal article seemed to appear from nowhere. The magazine had been folded open to the arty renditions of his rubbings of the hieroglyphs on the altar stone and fastened open along the side with a row of paper clips.

The man held it up in front of himself and worked carefully at smoothing the pages. Arthur's hackles stood up. Since the article had been published, he'd lived through hell. His standing among his colleagues in the department had fallen to zero. He'd been approached by literally dozens of people ranging from journalists to palm readers, all with their own agendas, some crazy, others just disagreeable. With the disheveled appearance of the article, this guy looked like he'd be one of the nutty ones, and

Arthur didn't intend to waste his time.

"Look Mr. . . .." The name. What did he call himself? ". . . Phaqutl. I don't mean to be rude, but I doubt . . .."

The man held up a hand and smiled as he interrupted. "I know I'm intruding, but I think I can be of valuable assistance. This article insults a man of good standing in our profession. There is reason to make them regret their words. Let me help you."

Arthur felt his interest climbing as he watched the strange-looking Mr. Phaqutl look down over the top of the journal and put his finger at the top of the first glyph.

"Acclaim the Gods who dwell within. As they counsel our lives, so do we provide their desires in . . ." he stood even taller and cleared his throat ". . . in unity and veneration."

Arthur took an amazed step backwards. The man obviously had knowledge and understood his professional predicament as well. "You read that like it's a newspaper. Yet it's only one glyph."

"This one is part of a pledge to their Gods. It is in my memory. I am familiar with this culture. I learned it from their lore. The original was decreed to them by the Gods and cut into stone at the top of a pyramid in a village that served as the home of their Queens and the center point of the universe as they saw it.

"Until I found this article, I did not know where that pyramid might be. You have discovered it and your find is important."

Arthur began to think this giant of a man might be exactly the right person to take to the pyramid. "Won't you please come in?"

He led his guest back to the office bedroom and offered him a chair beside the desk. He took out a small tape recorder, clicked it on, and put it and a note pad on the desktop.

The man with the curious name started to recite again in an oddly cadenced monotone, beginning precisely where he'd left off.

"Their guidance is divine . . . their insight uplifts us. They are the givers of all wisdom . . .." He bowed his head and continued his recitation as if he were pulling it from someplace deep inside himself. Sometimes he used a word or phrase in a language Arthur hadn't heard before, then its counterpart in English.

When he'd finished, Arthur wanted to ask what else he knew of the culture and its origins, but the man glanced at the clock on the desk and shrugged as if to call the questions to a halt.

"In time. We have other matters to discuss."

Arthur couldn't rein in his curiosity. "Mr. Phaqutl, that was truly marvelous. Where did you learn that language? Why did they name it the Pyramid of the White Doves? I'm no ornithologist, but those birds are definitely not doves."

Mr. Phaqutl interrupted. "How soon can you return?"

"I had hoped to put an expedition together here at the university, but that can't happen soon. My guess is three or four years and nothing is certain. I'm seeking funding from outside sources, but I have been made painfully aware of the fact that I need to obtain more viable proof before funding is at all likely to become available."

"Then I am your good fortune. How much will it cost for just the two of us?"

The man seemed too good to be true and Arthur's hopes began to rise with anticipation. He took a file from a desk drawer and leafed through it.

"It'll depend upon how long we stay and the sophistication of the equipment we take with us. I've written down some estimates. I think we need a minimum of about three and a half weeks. That will put us on site for twelve to fourteen days."

He extracted several sheets from a file and pushed them across the desk for Mr. Phaqutl to see. "These are the numbers I've come up with so far."

The other man scarcely glanced at the papers before him. Instead he began fumbling in a front jeans pocket and pulled out a fat brown envelope. One end had been torn off. He tamped it against his hand until a thick pad of bills jutted out. He ruffled them with his thumb to show nothing smaller than a hundred.

"Will this be sufficient?"

Two hours later Arthur ushered the man back to the front door. He'd kept their discussion hypothetical because he wanted to describe the odd Mr. Phaqutl to Jan Benedetti to get her opinion for good measure. Even so, he felt an exhilaration unlike any since his first sight of the pyramid itself and they had discussed nearly every aspect of a return visit.

As his guest stepped out onto the porch, Arthur thought to ask, "Mr. Phaqutl, do you have a given name?"

"My other name is Zarko."

"Zarko is your first name?"

"Zarko was my name first. Now I am Phaqutl."

"Uh . . . I'm sorry, but it's important for me to be clear about the name if I'm going to get our visas. By the way, do you have a current passport? That could hold us up."

"Yes I do. Would you like it?"

"Might be a good idea."

He watched as the dark blue passport was produced, then accepted it and opened it to see DeMers written on the line next to a front view of the man who looked baleful enough it could have been taken at a police station. Zarko showed as a first name and nothing was spelled out where the middle name should have been. It struck Arthur that he had the answer.

"I should have picked it up right away. Phaqutl would be your Indian name. Am I right?"

"It translates to 'Father of All the Gods'."

"That's quite a title. Why didn't you just tell me that earlier?"

"I needed to convince you that we must go to the pyramid."

Arthur eyed him for a moment. It seemed his new backer had a spiritual commitment to the culture that went beyond his desire to study it.

"Goodbye, Zarko. See you tomorrow." He clicked the door shut, turned and lay back against it, feeling oddly relieved that Zarko had left. Benefactor or not, he was definitely a curiosity.

He went immediately to the telephone and had begun to listen to Benedetti's recorded voice inviting him to leave a message when her real voice interrupted. "Caller ID says it's you, Arthur. How are you and Millie doing these days?"

"Fine. Just fine." But he knew it wasn't true. Their relationship had fallen into a strange limbo since she'd returned from the visit to her family home in New Hampshire. They still dated, but the intensity seemed to be fading little by little. Although he felt her slipping away, he couldn't give himself permission to do anything about it. Not with the confusion his tryst with Beba left in him. If he and his new benefactor could make the trip, he'd see Beba again. Try to clear things up.

"You still there? Glad to hear it. What can I do for you?"

"I've just met a man I think may be the kind I need to take back to the pyramid and he's willing to finance the trip."

Arthur went on to recount Zarko's visit in detail. It was only when she asked about the man's academic credentials that she stumped him. He'd asked Zarko, but the man brushed the question aside as he did anything that did not bear immediately on the planning of their trip. When Arthur explained that to her, she didn't seem particularly concerned.

"What you need is a credible pair of eyes. Training and expertise are good to have, but as long as someone goes who can see your pictures later and say, 'These are the real thing, because I was there', you are okay. I'm not sure I want to have heard all this, but I say, go for it young man, and come see me right away when you come back."

———————

Three weeks almost to the day after Zarko came knocking, they motored upriver to the pyramid. The heavily laden inflatable dogged its way through the currents as the scorching sun and motor noise intensified Arthur's already acute eagerness to arrive at their destination.

They'd used two float planes to accommodate their gear, following the identical route of his first trip, and landed at the spot below the site of the ruined *Rió Perra* dig so their pilots would believe that was their objective. Instead they'd run downstream to the confluence of the two rivers and now up the *Rió Gato*.

This time, Arthur steered from the stern, in place of the superstitious boatman who had refused to remain at the pyramid after dark. Twenty feet in front of him Zarko lay back against the bow, eyes closed and motionless. Between them they'd stowed the boxes and equipment intended for obtaining scientific data and supplies for the three weeks they planned to spend. They packed double in case of delays or emergencies. They also carried a wide assortment of tools including axes, shovels, coils of rope, canvas and plastic tarps, picks and sledges, in the event their discoveries required them to excavate, erect retaining walls, or build protective coverings.

As Arthur glanced forward at the inert form of Zarko he recalled how at first he'd been frightened by the man. There was a certain menace to him he couldn't put a finger on, but he'd spent much of his life learning not to make conclusions based upon mere intuition and when Benedetti had blessed the opportunity, he'd let himself believe that Zarko was the answer to his prayers.

Their plan had been worked out thoroughly and meticulously. They would concentrate on the pyramid until they had it measured and recorded and then search for the village Zarko cited from the lore. It only made sense that one would have been built nearby. Zarko himself had insisted that Arthur would be the leader and that he would also receive sole credit for the discovery.

The only point of disagreement between the two had come when Arthur wanted to schedule a visit to the village where Beba lived before they flew to the site. He'd written her three letters now that had gone unanswered and though the pace of his preparations had kept his mind from dwelling on it, the mystery surrounding her was still very much with him. Zarko insisted that they continue straight through to their destination and Arthur'd been hard-pressed to come up with a reasonable justification for a delay. It would be a different matter on the way back.

He tugged the steering arm of the outboard to take them around a log floating toward them in the current. A black cormorant stood on one end of the log and the two skippers eyed each other as their vessels passed. He readjusted the course of the inflatable to center it at midstream.

Despite the fact that he'd let himself trust him, there was also no doubt in Arthur's mind that Zarko was an eccentric, albeit a wealthy and adventurous one. The fact that he slipped in and out of his alter ego, Phaqutl, like some people flipped TV channels had taken some getting used to. The odd part of it was that with Phaqutl turned on, Zarko seemed to be less agitated and more intelligent.

Tawny flashes in the afternoon sunlight distracted him as a pair of deer at water's edge turned to bolt into the bush. Now the inflatable approached the river bend that concealed the pyramid and he spotted the beginnings of the bank that gradually grew to be the cliff supporting it. He throttled back, heading the boat toward the right-hand bank at the point where he'd landed before. The abrupt change of course brought Zarko to a sitting position and he craned his neck toward shore. He looked back at Arthur and began shaking his head emphatically and pointing farther up stream. Then he called loudly above the noise.

"Go beyond. We will land at the village."

For a moment Arthur thought he hadn't heard him correctly, and when he realized there was no mistaking what Zarko had said he could feel his heart speeding up. Arthur had only been able to assume that there would have been a village located near the pyramid. Zarko had assured him there would be one and now he claimed to know the location. Arthur had taken a chance on this man and Zarko was proving him right. Then he remembered the dangerous currents they'd run into before. His enthusiasm waned, and he shouted back.

"Can't go much farther up. Water's too fast."

"Not at this time of year."

A scowling Zarko waved them upriver again. Arthur had seen him disagreeable before when he didn't get his own way, but he'd never known him to be wrong either.

Another minute's running time and the cliff neared its maximum height. The pyramid came into view towering two hundred feet above the water. The strange white birds wheeled and soared in the currents above it. Arthur held his breath as his excitement rose higher than the first time he'd seen it.

When they reached the place where the river narrowed and the currents had roiled so dangerously before, he saw that the water level had lowered considerably and moved far more placidly than he remembered. The boat nudged into the fast water and slowed to a crawl, but without danger. The channel grew wide again and the water flowed flat and shining in the light of the sun.

The cliff had dwindled in height until all evidence of it disappeared and the forest bordered the water's edge. His companion motioned toward shore and Arthur headed in.

Chalk another one up for Zarko. It crossed Arthur's mind that it was odd that the man who claimed he was aware of the village from his studies not only knew the location of the village, but could also choose the exact place to put in from midriver. Zarko knew the seasonal conditions of the river as well. As they neared the river's edge, Zarko pointed to a deep column of trees standing on stilt roots that held them high above the water. A slow eddy behind the trees had made a shallow cove that lay almost completely hidden from the river itself. Arthur idled the motor and slid the boat in.

Fingers of sand sheltered an area large enough to land half a dozen boats. Even before the inflatable could pull into it, Zarko grabbed the bow rope and jumped knee-deep into the water to thrash ashore. Arthur cut the ignition and grabbed an overhead branch to pull the side of the boat over against the land. With the motor silent the noises of insects and birds could be heard. He straightened himself and raised his arms over his head to stretch and ease muscles cramped by the confining ride, then his eyes grew wide. A boat made from a single hollowed log rested a few yards away and the damp earth surrounding it had captured the footprints of hard-soled shoes. Zarko took it in too and turned to show the first genuine smile Arthur had ever seen on the man.

XI

SOUNDS, PARTICULARLY HARD SOUNDS, TRAVEL great distances in the forest. As Beba brought firewood to stack inside the shelter of her hut, she heard the sound long before she could identify the source. It was clearly man-made and the thrill it sent through her stopped her short with the full load still in her arms.

According to the marks she scratched daily in a corner of the hut's dirt floor, it had been over eleven weeks since Coquitla had forced her to the ruined village and the noise came as her first reminder of civilization. She dropped to her knees and began to slide the wood piece by piece on top of the pile, listening with her heart.

It became louder . . . and finally loud enough that she could identify it as a motor. She waited, not moving until it became clear that it was the motor of a boat. Excitement and anticipation rose in her like fountains of lights.

Forgotten in the moment, Coquitla broke the euphoria. **There has never been such noise here.**

A boat is coming up the river. I am going to call them in.
**I shall not permit you to bring them here. We wait for
only one and that one will know the way.**

Beba dumped the last few pieces on the pile and started to rise
anyway, but Coquitla held her fast in place. The frustration of it
made tears come to her eyes. The steady drone of the motor continued to grow louder, then abruptly it softened and took on less
ardent tones. After a few more moments it ceased. The silence
seemed to numb her senses.

Arise. Take up your belongings and go into the trees.

Again Beba tried to resist, but her efforts were futile. Under
Coquitla's control, she gathered everything in the hut and pushed
it into the same cloth bag she had carried it in when she first
arrived. At the fire pit she took the small cooking pot and at the
edge of the clearing she snatched up the short-bladed machete
from where she'd chopped the wood. A few steps more and she
melted into the bush as she had learned from Coquitla, silent as
mist moving through the trees.

Arthur pointed at the footprints in the soft ground beside
the dugout canoe. "Someone's here. This could be trouble."
The smile he'd seen on Zarko narrowed but did not disappear.

"You worry that this will come to be like the desecrated
Rió Perra site, but it will not. Look at the footprints. There is only
one set. Only one person. The prints are small. A woman, even a
child."

"Certainly, you don't think a child brought that canoe here?"

"It does not matter. It is not someone that can harm us. We
shall go to the village."

He admitted to himself that Zarko had a point. After all there
were two of them, Zarko stood the size of a small truck and they

both carried heavy-bladed machetes. Zarko seemed to be right about everything he said and without reluctance Arthur agreed. "Okay. Lead the way."

He followed a few steps behind Zarko, who moved quickly and more lithely than he would have expected of a man of his size. To his surprise, the cut ends of branches and vines testified that the trail had been maintained recently. Whoever was there had been there awhile and likely planned on staying.

Ahead, the trail widened into a clearing. Zarko halted a few steps before he reached it and motioned Arthur to stop beside him. They peered into it intently . . .. Empty . . .. The only sound was the high-pitched chirp of a tree frog. Zarko's head raised as if to test the air for scent. Arthur looked about them, scanning the bush, acutely aware that they were exposed and vulnerable. An eerie sensation anticipated the sting of an arrow in the back of his neck.

He wished they had rifles. But smuggling them in would have been the only way and they'd had neither the time nor the desire to take the risk.

Gathering courage, Arthur called out. "*Olla. Buenos dias.* This is Dr. Arthur Tomas. We are scientists. Is anyone here?"

Zarko lowered his head and turned to look at him as he might a child. "Do not shout. No one is here, though there has been. See over there, the fire smolders."

"How do you know that no one is here now?" He pointed the blade of his machete across the clearing. "Maybe in those huts beyond the far end."

"The air moves from that direction. It brings no scent."

"Are you serious? Your nose must be much better than mine."

"Precisely."

Arthur looked back at him and cocked his head. This intense man had let his voice become strident, as if he'd suddenly taken command. It gave Arthur his first indication that the man may not be as he wished Arthur to believe. Zarko ignored his look and moved into the clearing to walk one side of the perimeter. He motioned for Arthur to take the other side and the gesture was that of a general directing his troops into battle. Arthur began to feel tautness in his gut.

"Hold up. If we both go out there, we'll be sitting ducks."

"If someone wishes to harm us, they have already had more than enough opportunity."

Arthur nodded without conviction and moved into the open area. It proved to be more than a simple clearing. An oval, perhaps forty yards the long way, thirty the other. Paved with imperfectly rectangular stones precisely fitted together, affirming they were hand-cut. Probably a long time ago. The stonework was similar to some he'd seen that the Incas had done, but different in ways he couldn't pin down at the moment. This discovery alone was scientifically significant. It thrilled him even in light of his present perception of danger and the new imperious role Zarko seemed to have assumed.

Arthur could see that the riverside of the oval, the side that Zarko walked, offered entrance to two trails, the one they'd followed up from the boat and another, at the opposite end, leading away in the direction of the pyramid. Set back in the bush near the trail to the pyramid, he could see a large hut built of vertical poles laced together with palm fronds and with a palm frond roof. Two smaller huts sat side by side a few yards behind it. Because the forest would reclaim them in a matter of a few months, it was obvious they'd been erected recently. Whoever had built them intended to stay. The bush had been cut back to make vertical green walls at the edges of the paving stones and surrounding the three structures. The layers of canopy above formed lofty arches that filtered the afternoon light into scattered tilting shafts and held off the direct heat of the sun.

On his side of the clearing, he walked passed a pile of branches in the process of being hacked into firewood and a table made of straight poles laced together with vines. Next to the table a firepit had been set into the stone surface. An almost invisible wisp of smoke rose out of a mound of leaves from the reeds that edged the rivers. The embers had been banked carefully so that a blaze could be restarted several hours later. He stooped to touch the stones around the pit, then stood and turned to see Zarko approaching.

"Rocks are hot a foot away from it. There's been fire here for at least several days and it seems whomever set it planned to come back. Likely still does. What did you find?"

"Nothing of concern. Let us go to the huts together."

"Didn't you say you already know no one's in them?"

"Yes, but we shall stay together nonetheless."

There was his damn posturing again. Arthur realized that sooner or later he'd probably have to challenge it, but it should be over something more important so that the issue, not personalities, would be the deciding factor. "Okay. Lets go."

Zarko led as they walked the thirty feet from the clearing to the first hut and the big man pulled the door open with the tip of his machete, while Arthur stood by trying to be ready for a surprise. Again there was evidence of someone there not long ago. Outside the door, he saw the same small footprints they'd seen beside the dugout. Inside the empty hut more prints as well as rows of marks in the dirt floor, a series of four vertical lines with a diagonal slash across them. The universal way of counting. Seventy-eight in all.

"Maybe we scared him off."

"We will see the other huts."

Those were also empty and he couldn't understand why one person would build three huts. Not for food storage. There was plenty of food to be had year-round. The only answer he could come up with was that the builder expected others to come. He hoped they weren't already on the way.

"As I have said. No one is here. We shall bring the supplies from the boat."

"I'm with you on that. I'd like to have them here where I can see 'em. And it'll be dark in an hour."

It took the rest of the daylight to unload and carry most of their gear up the trail to the huts. They left a few less essential items to be retrieved in the morning and divided what they had carried up between the two huts that stood farthest back from the clearing. The surrounding vegetation grew thick enough to offer protection from surprise on at least three sides. One man would sleep in each of the supply huts as an additional safeguard. The doors could be tied with rope from the inside so that each man could exit quickly to respond to a call from the other.

Zarko brought the fire back to life, while Arthur rummaged to find the coffee pot and meat stew that they heated in the can. As soon as he'd finished eating, exhaustion rolled over Arthur like a sea fog. He said good night and dug out the sleeping bags and mosquito netting. After his was rolled out on the floor, he hung the netting from a ceiling pole to drape it on all sides and crawled under it and lay down.

His bed was no more than a sheet on a thin foam mat on the hard dirt floor. Uncomfortable as hell. They'd brought canvas cots, but he hadn't located them yet and had thought to wait until the next day to bring them up from the boat. Forty minutes later he realized a decent night's sleep would be impossible without one. He rose wearily, resigned to finding a cot.

He took the machete and a flashlight and stepped out into the night. The sound of deep breathing told him Zarko was doing fine without a cot. The trip down the trail turned out to be more unsettling than he'd imagined. The flashlight beam left all but a narrow sliver of his surroundings in pitch blackness and he remembered the huge panther he'd met before. By the time he reached the river, the hackles on his neck warned him of watching eyes.

He played the light about to prove to himself that his fear was unfounded, but instead of relaxing, his heart went into hyperdrive. The boat was gone. His first thought was that someone had taken it, but as he raced to the spot where it had been, he saw it had collapsed and sunk. He aimed the beam down into the water. The stern with its motor lay in water over his head. Only the bow retained air enough to hold the tip of the rubberized material above water. Long slashes had been cut in each of the separate inflatable compartments as far down as he could see. He slammed the blade of the machete into the soft ground.

Since they'd arrived, he'd carried a growing apprehension that whomever had run off when they'd come didn't want them there. He'd worried about them returning, fearing they'd be hostile. Now he realized that even worse, they were being prevented from leaving. His foreboding turned to unbridled fear and he retrieved the huge knife from where he'd stabbed it into the soil.

He turned in a circle to cast the light beam about him. He sliced it into each dark spot in the bush, into the stilted roots of the nearby trees, behind him and back up the trail into every conceivable recess that might conceal an enemy.

Still afraid but satisfied for the moment that no one was within easy striking distance, calling upon all his control to keep from fleeing back up the trail, he inspected the ground beside the mutilated craft. He expected to see footprints similar to those they'd seen beside the dugout and at the door of the hut, but he didn't. Only his own and the oversized prints of Zarko were evident.

As he considered the scene he became incredulous. There were a great many more of Zarko's prints than of his own. Though he didn't want to accept it, his years in science had taught him to believe the evidence and the facts before him were convincing. Zarko had destroyed the boat.

He needed time to think. The flashlight located a thick root at the edge of the area where he could sit with his back safely against the tree trunk. He flicked the light off to conserve the batteries. It was as though turning off the light had turned on the silence. Only the soft river sounds remained. All traces of daylight had gone. The darkness had always been his friend, as far back as he could re-member. Tonight it hid the sight of the devastation and helped clear his mind. He put the light and his machete down, one on each side of himself, and worked the gold ring around his finger.

The inflatable was dead. Any one of the long slashes in it would take more repair material than they had. The motor could be raised, but getting it to run again was another thing. The dugout was still there and the route to safety was all down river, though it took a skill he didn't have to stay upright in any kind of fast water. Perhaps he could add outriggers or build a raft.

Zarko, the man with two personalities and a name like an oil company, posed a different problem. He'd pretty much taken him at face value until now. He'd thought him to be an eccentric scholar with enough money to make the trip possible. Now it became obvious that he'd been here before. How else would he have known the exact location of the village and where to land the boat.

Yet back in Arizona it had clearly been true that Zarko didn't know where the site was located. He couldn't pick out either the country or river system. What had been proven to Arthur today beyond doubt was that Zarko had gotten him to lead him here and for his own separate and very frightening agenda.

"Do not turn on your light. Identify yourself to me now?" It was a woman's voice.

The startling interruption set him upright. The voice seemed familiar and even while his mind sorted out the words he grabbed up the flashlight and reached for the machete. The first blow hit him across the tops of his shoulders, the second in the back of the neck. Then a flashbulb went off inside his head and all light vanished.

———

His knew his eyes were open because he could see the silhouettes of branches and leaves against the faint light of a night sky. The back of his shirt was damp and uncomfortably cool. He lay on wet ground. Head aching, back hurting, blood thrushing in his ears. Something heavy on his stomach and chest. It moved and sobbed. He moaned.

"*Madre de Dios*, Arthur, you live. Tell me I have not killed you. That you are all right. I shall die, if you are not." And her crying started again.

The pain in his head didn't let him think clearly. He only knew he wanted to stop the crying. Didn't understand how she knew his name. "I'm not dead."

Her hair had a scent he'd smelled before. An image began to form in his foggy mind. The girl from the lodge. For a moment he thought he must be delirious, then he tried her name.

"Beba?"

"*Si*. I thought I would never see you again. Then before I knew who you were, Coquitla made me to hit you. I am so sorry."

"What's a Coquitla?"

"She is not with me now. Have I hurt you badly?"

He touched a lump forming at the back of his head. "Headache. Bruises."

She retrieved the flashlight and placed it in his hand. He turned it on. Her face seemed much thinner than he remembered.

Then he saw the outlines of her arms and shoulders in the dim light and reached to touch them.

"You've become thin."

"It is only the work I do."

The haze inside his head began to lift, and a flare of realization put goose bumps on his skin. He hadn't told her about his discovery. Or that he planned to return.

"Why did you come here? How did you know of this place?"

When she replied, he couldn't mistake the anguish in her voice. "The people of my village know what we did in the animal blind. I have disgraced my aunt and uncle. They sent me from their home."

He had his own pangs of guilt from that experience. Now he found that he was the cause of her punishment. But that didn't answer all his questions. "How did they know to send you here? What are you supposed to do here?"

"I am told my ancestors lived in this place. That most of them were murdered. And that if they had lived, I would be their queen. I am made to build back a part of their village, in the hopes that one day more of them will return."

She put fingers to his lips and held them there. "I will tell you more later. Let me help you back to the village. You need rest."

He hurt in too many places to argue.

He walked with his arm around her for support. About halfway to the village, they stopped for him to rest. The events of the day had his head spinning and the lump on it didn't help.

While he waited for his strength to return, he told her everything that had happened to him since they'd parted at her uncle's lodge. He described his disappointment in not being able to locate funding until Zarko came along and their arrangements to make the trip together. He gave her the entire story right through to his discovery of the slashed inflatable and the evidence that Zarko'd done it. He couldn't see her face clearly in the darkness, but she seemed oddly interested in Zarko and asked a number of questions about his past that Arthur couldn't answer. He didn't know what to make of it, but it put a small cold stone in the pit of his stomach.

In turn, Arthur tried to get more of the story of how she'd come to be there, but Beba remained steadfast in her refusal to speak more about it. His curiosity rankled, but he felt responsible for her being forced to come here and couldn't blame her if she didn't want to share everything with him. Perhaps in time he could help her trust him.

Inside the clearing, he played the flashlight about and found it empty. "Zarko was sleeping when I left." A picture of the sunken boat came back, and it brought his hackles up. "I don't think it would be wise to confront him tonight."

"Do you think he will try to harm us?"

He recalled a statement Zarko had made earlier and echoed it now. "If he wanted to hurt me, I think he would have tried by now. He doesn't know you've come back, though he knows someone left as we arrived. Perhaps we should stay together tonight to be safe."

She stopped walking abruptly. "*Señor*, sleeping together would be a bigger mistake."

"Beba, I'm not going to repeat what we did in the blind. You're safe with me."

"*Si*, I know." She stood on her tiptoes and pecked his cheek. "*Buenas noches.*"

He went to his own hut, but as exhausted as he'd become, sleep evaded him for hours. The fact that Beba had come here ahead of them was troublesome and more coincidence than he could embrace. And the destruction of the boat by Zarko made it certain that the man not only had lied about his purpose in coming here, but could well pose a danger to their lives.

Voices . . . Beba's and Zarko's from the court yard, rousing him while soft bird sounds still greeted the dawn. No sooner did his eyes open than the discoveries of the previous night erupted through him like hot steam through empty pipes. That brought him scrambling to his feet. His first thoughts were for Beba's safety, but even though he was too far away to understand the words, he realized that they carried neither anger nor menace. In fact, the conversation seemed no more threatening than two acquaintances chatting over breakfast. They must have introduced themselves and waited for him to join them.

As his concern for the immediate situation diminished, he became aware of aches and pains fanning throughout his body. Not only did his head and shoulders hurt from where he'd been hit, but the bone-hard bed on the ground had added its own share of sore joints and muscles. He did his best to stretch and ease those he could while he pulled on pants and socks and scuffed into his shoes. He passed on shaving and grabbed his shirt to slip on as he walked. Less than two minutes after waking, he headed toward the clearing.

On the way he remembered his final resolve last night before drifting to sleep: get the research data, get it as fast as he could and get Beba and himself the hell out of there. Zarko had to be both dangerous and crazy. They'd take the dugout and stop downstream beyond Zarko's reach to add outriggers and whatever else they could to make it the rest of the way safely. With any luck they'd be gone by midafternoon. To hell with Zarko. Let him fend for himself. He'd made his own problem and they'd be leaving him most of the supplies anyway.

He found Beba and Zarko seated on opposite sides of the table at the far end of the clearing. They turned to face him as he marched toward them and their conversation snapped off like somebody had thrown a switch. His curiosity rose again. It wasn't as if the two of them were old friends who didn't want him to hear what they'd gotten him for his birthday. There were too damned many questions and he wanted answers. He'd nearly reached them when Beba offered him a smile that was neither as broad nor as beautiful as he remembered. And just for an instant before her face changed, he thought he'd seen the beginnings of a far different expression. Fear or anger, perhaps. Or was it something else?

"Good morning. I see you've met." There was that odd flicker of darkness from Beba again. Zarko nodded but remained characteristically dispassionate. Arthur tried again. "Coffee smells good. May I?"

Neither of them responded. He went to the fire and poured his own. He looked at them over the top of his cup. So far he was still the only one who'd spoken. Finally Beba started.

"*Señor* Zarko and I have been talking of the mine. It is nearby. My people once took gold from it."

There it was. The explanation he'd spent half the night searching for. Zarko had come back for gold. The oldest story on the planet. With any luck they'd leave him to rot with it. Maybe that also answered the question of why he'd destroyed the boat. He wanted to somehow make it possible to keep the gold all for himself. He must have planned to get rid of them. Now that Arthur understood clearly, conviction that his plan to leave was right added to his purpose.

He checked to see the look on Zarko's face now that the secret was out. Not so much as a blink, but the big man finally broke his silence.

"I will bring the tools. The first thing is to make a new trail. Then we can explore the potential of the mine itself. The two of you will help."

Arthur had seen him try to take command the night before and thought now was as good a time as any to bring him up short.

But Beba turned so Zarko couldn't see her face, to press her lips together and shake her head in a way that told him not to push it. He reined himself in. She was probably right. He nodded to show he understood, but he had no intention of feeding Zarko's greed. The mine might be as precious a find archeologically as the altar stone. It could go a long way to explain the people who'd once lived here, and he couldn't let it be defiled by this fool. But he decided to go along for the moment.

Now Zarko turned his attention to Beba. Arthur felt his jaw go slack as he addressed her in a language he hadn't heard before and she responded in kind. Soft and melodic when she spoke it, throaty and harsh from Zarko. She'd said it was her tribe who'd lived here. They spoke the language of her people.

The whole thing was making him crazy. His thoughts were interrupted by Zarko, who spoke to them both. "I will bring the tools. Eat and be ready to work when I return." He evidently believed they'd both obey him, for he turned without waiting to be acknowledged and left in the direction of the supply huts.

Arthur went to Beba and dropped to his knees in front of her. He took both of her hands in his. "Beba, the man is dangerous. He destroyed the boat. He only came for gold and he doesn't intend to invite us to share it with him. We need to get out of here quickly. Without him finding out. Do you understand?"

She looked at him without indication. He firmed his grip on her hands. "Do you?"

Slowly she nodded.

"Good. Come with me to the pyramid. I'll only need three or four hours. We'll be out of here by afternoon. We'll leave in your dugout while he's cutting the trail."

Were those the beginning of tears in her eyes? If they were, they were gone before he could be sure. "I cannot come with you. I must work with Zarko. I know him in a way you do not."

He couldn't believe she'd said it. "Are you afraid of him? Has he threatened you?" He sat back on his heels and looked into her face for a clue.

Nothing. The back of his neck became hot. He insisted. "You have to believe me. We are in danger."

She looked at him as if trying to decide how to break sad news and when she finally spoke her voice had taken on a strange quality, she'd become a very young girl exhausted and somehow defeated.

"Go to the altar stone now, Arthur, before Zarko returns. When he does it will be too late . . .." She started to say more but seemed to choke on it and stopped.

"Beba, I'm responsible for your family sending you here and I'm not leaving without you."

She pushed his hands away, seemed to gasp for breath, and then her back arched and stiffened and her voice became passionless and flat.

"Phaqutl requires that we work with him today. Wait here until he returns."

Arthur sat back, incredulous. Something was terribly the matter with Beba, but what? She was scared to death. He remembered her fear in the blind That's it. She'd just said she knew something about Zarko he didn't. Right now the last thing he wanted was to be in the clearing when Zarko got back. He'd do his work, load the dugout and then come for her. When he did, he wouldn't take no for an answer.

Two hours later, the morning sun had already seared the dark stone surfaces and the heat radiating back from them made sweat stand out on his face and trickle under the back of his shirt and down his spine. He worked at the same spot where he'd been when the panther sent him packing several months before. He pitied the beast if it showed up today, he was ready to take it on barehanded. The only animals he saw, though, were the white birds that screeched and wheeled overhead. He'd shouted at them more than once since he'd climbed up to the altar stone, but it failed to daunt them.

The work he had to do was the painstaking chore of cleaning the glyphs and altar stone with dentists' picks and a small wire brush, so that every minute detail could be observed and photographed. He'd have to forgo the witness unless Beba could be of some help. He'd try to work that out later. Today he intended to take enough rolls of film to at least lessen the possibility of being accused of altering photographs. He'd brought slide and print film and he'd use both. He had a small video camera as well. Prints could be altered, but slides, negatives and video tapes were much more difficult. He'd not only shoot the altar stone, but also the pyramid at different levels and from the trail on both sides. He'd get the stonework in the clearing and the pyramid from the river. That should make a pretty solid case.

Nonetheless, after the morning's discoveries, he couldn't bring himself to feel like being meticulous at all and had to fight to force himself to exercise the care the work demanded. He stepped back to view his work. Nothing much had changed since his last look just a few minutes before. He told himself to stop gawking and get on with it. He went back to work, but the joy he'd anticipated during the weeks before he could return, was lost.

The screechings rose to a new crescendo and he looked to see the birds responding to something behind and below him. He turned half expecting to see the huge cat gathering itself to spring, but instead saw Zarko at the base of the pyramid beginning to climb the steps toward him.

Here came a new problem. How should he treat the man after what he'd found out? He could feel anger rising inside, but decided not to confront him about the gold or accuse him of destroying the boat. To do so would serve no purpose now and would only tip his hand. He worked the gold ring around his finger and stood waiting.

Zarko moved off the steps onto the stone tier one level lower than Arthur and came to stand below him. He stood tall enough that his head rose to Arthur's waist. His voice commanded.

"Come down. You are to clear the way to the mine. You may not take time for this."

Zarko's brazen insistence took Arthur off guard and his astonishment took the chains off his anger. "I came to research, have you forgotten? As soon as I collect the data to prove the scientific worth of this site, Beba and I are leaving. Then maybe the university will put an expedition together with proper staff and equipment to come back here and do the job this site deserves."

"You will not bring others here. You will not leave. I have made the boat unable to float on the river."

He took an ominous step forward, but Arthur stood firm and looked down at Zarko's huge upturned face. "Why in hell are you trying to keep us here? We won't help you steal gold."

"You think it is the gold I came for? I have returned to rebuild the village."

"I found your mining tools, Zarko."

"The tools are to cut and shape stone. The soft stone that is in the mine. Years ago enemies came and raided the village at night. Those who slept here did not survive. It shall not happen again. The huts will be of stone. A wall of stone will protect them. I, Phaqutl, with Coquitla will make a new tribe."

Now he could feel adrenalin pulsating through his arteries. "Get off it, Zarko. If you're trying to convince me your nuts, you're doing a damn fine job."

"You shall not deny me." Zarko reached a huge hand out to grab at Arthur's leg, but Arthur saw it coming and side-stepped. Even as rage swept across the other man's face and with his own anger barely throttled, Arthur's impulse was to hold back, to rely on a lifetime of training and call reason into the situation. The hesitation cost him as Zarko drove his other arm in a powerful arc that swept him off his feet.

He came down hard on his side, tools flying from his hands to skitter across the stones. His breath left him and darkness squeezed in on his vision. Even as he fought to clear it, he saw Zarko pulling himself up onto the tier where he lay.

All reason gave way to the will to survive and his instincts took over. Both his hands gripped the stones under him for leverage and a foot thrust out hard to catch Zarko high on the chest. The big man's eyes widened in surprise and he disappeared back down the way he'd come. A guttural cursing followed the sound of his fall. As Arthur forced himself to his feet, he realized that only the winner of this fight would leave.

Zarko outweighed him by at least a hundred rock-hard pounds. Arthur needed all the help he could get. He glanced around quickly and realized that none of the gear he had with him could serve as a weapon. The only advantage to him was being above his adversary on the pyramid.

He looked down to see that Zarko had either rolled or fallen down an extra tier and was now two below his own position. One tier down and perhaps Arthur could have jumped on him landing with both feet where they would do enough damage to end it. Two tiers was too far to jump without risking an injury that would make him easy prey. Arthur dropped down one level to prepare himself, but Zarko was already moving and just as Arthur lit and stooped forward with the impact, Zarko reached up and drove a fist into the side of his head that put him down again. Before

Arthur could get his bearings he felt himself being dragged down to the next level and sensed a terrible end coming if he didn't do something fast.

He did the only thing he could and wrenched himself out of Zarko's grasp to tumble down another tier and then scrabbled over the edge of that one and down one more to prevent the possibility that Zarko could reach him. He gathered his feet under himself and looked up to see it was now Zarko standing two tiers above. If they were playing King of the Mountain, he'd already lost. He saw his enemy preparing to do what he had contemplated just seconds before. He intended to jump his full weight down eight feet onto Arthur's body.

Zarko let out a monstrous roar and sprang. For a split second the sky seemed to turn dark with his huge form blocking the sun. Arthur instinctively spun, ducked and drew his back against the vertical surface of the tier above. As Zarko sailed over him heading for the exact spot where Arthur'd just been, he drove himself upward and rammed into Zarko's massive back from behind.

Even before Zarko's feet touched stone the thrust propelled him off balance over forward and down to smash headfirst into one level and then to roll and fall another. Arthur stepped to where he could see down. Zarko lay on his back, head twisted unnaturally to the side, eyes closed. The body spasmed and a moan gargled low in his chest. A line of blood began to trickle from an ear, adding bright color to the dark stone.

For the first time he became aware of his own body, that his heart thrashed hard against his chest wall. He couldn't seem to get enough air into his lungs. His head hurt where Zarko'd hit him, and there was blood on his clothing. He bent forward at the waist to catch his breath, putting his hands on his knees for support. It wasn't enough. He sank down on the hot stone and closed his eyes. Gradually his heart calmed. He waited to feel elation or triumph from the victory, but all that came was a quivering relief that it was over. He'd been lucky. By all odds, he should have been the one lying down there.

But one problem had been solved. Since he'd left Beba in the clearing, he'd been trying to come up with a plan to break her away from Zarko, so they could leave without him following. No need for one now.

Then slowly it came over him that he had to do something about Zarko. There was no doubt that the man's injuries were serious, perhaps fatal. It wasn't in Arthur to leave him. He must do what he could. He pulled himself up, descended to where Zarko lay and knelt beside him. Zarko's face had grayed to the color of wood ashes. His lips quivered. Arthur leaned forward to open the man's shirt to ease his breathing. At first touch the huge form stiffened then the eyes snapped open and Arthur started and began to rear backwards with the shock it gave him. Not soon enough. The arms came from behind him and huge hands grabbed his shoulder and the back of his head. Tremendous force pulled his head down at the same time that Zarko's rose. As they clashed, it all went black . . . ..

He heard the white birds keening as his senses returned. He sat up and saw he'd been slumped forward across Zarko's torso. The face had drained of all color now and the eyes were half opened, staring upward at the complaining birds. Arthur put a hand on a lifeless cheek and even in the hot sun it felt cold. He sat back and braced himself with his hands, preparing to stand. **Now Doctor Tomas, you will heed me. I am Phaqutl.**

WHEN BEBA HEARD SOMEONE COMING she expected Zarko, but a battered Arthur lurched into the clearing. She sprang to her feet and cried out. From his stumbling walk, his stiffened features, the frightened horror in his eyes, she recognized what she dreaded even more than her own desolate future. She would have given anything to warn him, but Coquitla had been alert every moment she had been in Arthur's presence and thwarted each attempt. In her heart she knew he wouldn't have believed her, if she had succeeded. She couldn't have expected to convince this man whose life's work demanded that he be skeptical of anything he could neither measure nor test.

The frustration of helplessness seemed to suck her strength even as she hurried across the clearing to him. His eyes caught hers and a flicker of recognition registered just as they rolled back into his head and he pitched forward. She dove to reach him and his weight nearly took them both down, but she managed to hold his limp form until she could ease him down slowly. Gently, she turned him on his back, knelt and took his head in her lap. He looked up at her, eyelids half closed, conscious but plainly unaware. Coquitla intervened.

Question him.

But she needed no urging. "You must not let yourself sleep. Speak to me. Tell me where you hurt."

Then Coquitla took her spoken voice. "Phaqutl, it is you. What is the condition of this body? Where is the human, Zarko?"

Arthur's form tensed, his legs stiffened and quivered, then all of him went slack. "This body has been heavily exerted and is overly fatigued but in no immediate danger. It needs rest and then food. The one called Zarko is dead and has been given to the river from the altar stone. As was the custom. The change came under difficult circumstances. I too must replenish soon, though this one attempts to resist every outcome and that may be difficult if I must maintain constant dominion."

As Phaqutl reconfirmed her worst fears, Beba heard herself respond. "It would have been better to keep the other one. He learned long ago not to resist our way and his strength would have been useful."

"It could not be avoided. This one will do acceptably. Let her bring water to him now."

His eyes closed as she took his head from her lap to place it gently on the stone surface and rose to fetch the water. She gave it to him in small sips, then left him again to bring clothing to fold and place under his head and a cloth to wipe the moisture from his face and to fan away the heat. After a time his breath seemed to come more easily. Then Coquitla manifested her will once again.

"Phaqutl, he will listen to this one. He will accept what she tells him. She will speak to him and inform him of our ways, while you take time to regain your energies. I shall remain alert for the two of us."

"That is agreeable to me."

And a moment later Arthur's frame quivered almost imperceptibly and his eyes opened. He blinked and looked at her.

"Did you hear?"

He nodded silently, but the look in his eyes told her of the agony he suffered.

"Arthur, I am so sorry for what has come to you. I wished to warn you but I could not. Now it is too late. They make me tell you what it is that you must suffer."

She helped him to stand, move slowly across the clearing and sit at the table. She took a place across from him and began at the beginning. She told him that because they had been seen together, her aunt had sent her from the only home she had known. Of meeting her mother whom she had been taught to believe dead. Of her tribe that once flourished in this village and of their massacre by another in order to steal the metal 'with the glow of the morning sun.' She told him of the death of her grandfather, the enraged warrior king, who sought vengeance but in achieving it had died at the hands of those same murderers and of the legend of the bird of fire that rose from his breast.

Upon finishing that much of her story, she paused and leaned across the table to him to take his hands in hers. She dreaded what she must say to him now, but when he opened his mouth to speak, reached quickly to place her fingers over his lips and went on.

"My mother was our queen and now I am queen of a tribe that today has only four other living souls. *Tía Eva*, my mother and the two brothers who attend her. It was they who drugged me and left me in the night, so that I could not know where they have gone."

She paused again, gathering the will to continue and after a moment raised her head to see into his face. "My mother, gave me . . . forced me . . . to receive from her . . . a god of our tribe. One called Coquitla. She dwells inside my body just as surely as the unborn child lives inside its mother. Coquitla has great power and I cannot defeat her, nor can I stop her from what she wills me to do."

Regret strained her voice. "When you came here, it gave me hope that together we might find a way . . .." Her throat clenched hard and she couldn't speak.

Do not give him false beliefs.

Slowly her throat released. "When you came here, you brought Zarko. And within him Phaqutl, the one who once dwelled in my warrior grandfather. Now Zarko is dead and Phaqutl has taken you.

She squeezed his hands gently. "The whereabouts of Phaqutl has been unknown since my grandfather followed the murderous tribe back to their lands to take his vengeance. Every year since then Coquitla made first my grandmother and then my mother travel here. To rebuild, what the forest had claimed in the preceding months, in preparation for Phaqutl's return. Each time a message was left at the base of the pyramid to tell him when Coquitla would return again and the women were allowed to go to a safer place to live until the next year for it is difficult to live here alone.

"Coquitla ordains that I do the same. That is how I came to be here when you arrived. But also Phaqutl returned and together they plan to remain and to rebuild the village. Because of what happened here before, Phaqutl would rebuild the huts in stone and erect a wall of stone around them."

Her teeth pressed into her lower lip for a moment before she resumed. "Now that Phaqutl resides in you, perhaps you can understand why I was not able to tell you these things when you first arrived. To warn you so that you could run from this fate."

Finally she gave in to her tears, grasped his hands more tightly in hers. Arthur sat across the table looking at her and she couldn't tell whether it was he or Phaqutl in control. When he spoke he seemed to be in awe.

"I didn't know what was happening when the voice spoke inside my mind. Zarko and I fought and at first I thought I'd taken a hard knock and was having some sort of auditory hallucinations . . ... Hearing things. Then it made me drag Zarko's body the rest of the way up the pyramid to the altar and push it over the back side to fall into the river. I couldn't believe I was doing it. I tried to stop and couldn't." He sat shaking his head slowly from side to side.

She took the same cloth she'd used to wipe the moisture from his face and used it to clean the tears from her own cheeks. "You cannot fight Phaqutl by willing your body to move or your mind to respond as you normally would. We must find another . . .." Her body stiffened as Coquitla prevented her from finishing. This time she saw Arthur's eyes widen as he realized what was happening to her.

Tell him to obey us now.

"You have already seen that Phaqutl can take control and move your body as he wishes. And that he can observe through your senses and speak with your voice." Tears began to form in the corners of her eyes.

Keep yourself composed and instruct him in the most befitting ways to respect our counsel.

She took a slow deep breath, but couldn't keep the anguish of resignation from her voice.

"It is not possible to fight or ignore him when he commands you. Yet they do prefer to remain silent. It is as though they become dormant . . . to somehow renew their energies. As much as you can, hear what Phaqutl tells you in your mind and do it.

It is often difficult, but that way you can move, use your senses, and feel as you wish. If you try to say or do something against them, they will take you again instantly."

She waited, but Arthur didn't respond. "They have skills we do not. I was able to bring the dugout safely through the rough currents even though I had never paddled one before. Knowing which plants to eat, how to catch fish, to be safe from snakes and insects, all came from Coquitla.

"If you become overly excited they will awaken. Their first response is that you are in danger. Phaqutl can use your body to defend you in ways beyond your own ability. This is what gave rise to the legend of my grandfather."

She stopped then and let her head bow forward, her shoulders shaking in sorrow for what she had been made to tell him.

"Astounding."

She looked up to see Arthur's glazed eyes staring off into the jungle, a smile half formed on his lips.

"The scientific community will be amazed. A whole new form of being."

Once Arthur had blurted out his dazed response to Beba's explanation of their captors, she'd helped him to her hut, and he could only recall falling into a bottomless sleep that lasted until the following dawn. Then Phaqutl woke him and both humans had been compelled to begin work cutting a new trail to the promised mine. By the afternoon of the second day, the newly-cut route extended well over two hundred yards from the village in a line opposite the direction to the river.

Droplets of sweat jumped from his hair and torso with every stroke of his machete as others ran down to sting his eyes and force him to pause frequently to wipe them away. Plant juices from the severed vegetation injected acrid odors into the dank unmoving air and left green streaks across the blade.

The long knife seemed to grow heavier with each swing and he still ached from the damage he'd taken fighting Zarko. His feelings for Zarko had run from awe and respect in the beginning, to suspicion when he'd found the sunken boat, to unbridled anger even hatred as they fought. At first the man who used the two strange given names appeared to be spiritually connected to this culture. Instead he'd been a captive of it's malevolent tyrant. Now Arthur pitied him, for he knew firsthand that the man had no choices in what he did. His own attempts to defy Phaqutl had proven Beba's advice correct. The most difficult feat had been accepting the existence of Phaqutl as reality and not delusion or madness.

Beba worked just behind him, making the trail even wider with her own machete and tossing the cuttings from both of them into the bush. From time to time one of them paused to move along a day pack of supplies their tormentors forced them to bring. The strenuous labor discouraged conversation. In what Arthur now recognized as customary, Phaqutl had set him to work and then withdrawn. In that way the discomforts of his labors weren't Phaqutl's to deal with, although should Arthur slack off, he'd emerge quickly enough. Arthur's only chance at jurisdiction over his own faculties lay in being compliant and he'd learned to relish his moments of freedom as his only hold on life itself.

In another hour he began to see the high layers of forest canopy ahead of them thinning to let wide sloping bands of sunlight stream through to the forest floor. It signaled a clearing ahead. A few moments later they came across a path that seemed to skirt the clearing. One of several game trails they'd found in the area, but when Arthur started to cross this one the large tracks of a jaguar were plainly visible in the soft earth. He felt the hair rising on his scalp, and his fingers clamped hard on the handle of the machete.

You have no need to fear. The tracks are many hours old.

How do I know it isn't coming back?

He sleeps in the day and hunts at dawn and dusk.

I wonder if it's the black one I saw at the pyramid.

They claim a wide domain. We are within his. Finish the trail to the mine.

———◆———

The clearing they entered was about half the size of the village courtyard and had been paved in a similar way with stones cut and fitted so expertly that little vegetation found root in the cracks between them. Only the occasional vine encroached from above. Now that the disturbance they'd made hacking through the bush had ceased, the jungle dwellers returned to their own sounds. A flock of tiny green and yellow birds swarmed into the nearest bushes where they hopped among the branches twittering fussily. In the distance he heard monkeys throwing contemptuous challenges through the treetops. Beba came up beside him and he took the pack from her and slipped his other arm around her shoulders.

She looked up at him through grime and fatigue and motioned toward several structures on the far side of the clearing. "Is that what we look for over there?"

"We'll soon see."

They walked over to them. It didn't take him long to recognize the purposes they'd served from similar ruins he'd studied.

"It's a kind of primitive smelter where they took metal from the ore. The Indians mined metals in this area before the first Spaniards arrived in the early fifteen hundreds.

"They probably crushed the rock into pieces over there and then heated it to temperatures high enough to melt the metal and release it. There's the pit where they heated it. You can still see soot burned onto it.

"That broken framework beside the firepit could have been covered with animal skin or something woven to make a kind of bellows. That mound over there seems to be leftover slag. Modern methods could probably take much more metal from it."

"Sí, but where does the rock with the metal come from?"

He looked around. Nothing more to see but a rectangular outcropping, half again as tall as a man, and next to it a mound of stones at the edge of the clearing.

"Doesn't seem to be here. I hope that doesn't mean there's more trail to cut."

Go to the stone pile. Remove it. The entrance is there.

Beba had already moved in that direction. It seemed she had orders too.

Pile them to your left. So that the door will open without hindrance.

The stones had been selected carefully, each about as large as one man could lift. Beba tried and her features contorted with the effort, but she managed to lift one and after that she worked beside him. He looked at her. A thin determined smile told him she did it by choice and not merely as Coquitla's captive. She had pride and he admired her for it. By the time they'd finished the backbreaking chore, he guessed they'd moved two or three tons.

The door lay level with the earth, a foot and a half above it, and supported by a heavy frame made of thick straight timbers that still bore tool marks. Neither the door nor the frame showed signs of deterioration. The wood hadn't weakened in the decades since the mine had been used. Neither had the same wood where it had been stacked beside the fire pit. Obviously a wood very resistant to decay.

The timbers ran the long way of the door and wide thick strips of dark metal near each end banded them together and extended past the edge to form crude but massive hinges. He ran a thumb over the metal, then turned to the stones they had just removed to inspect the places where the years of dirt had been scuffed away to leave clean metal in the process.

You waste time. Open the door.

I don't see a handle anywhere.

The door is too heavy for that.

I was joking.

A wasteful practice of your kind. Look at the holes cut into the wood under the ends of each of the metal bands. They have been placed opposite the hinges. Put a wooden pole into each so that it extends out beyond the door edge. They shall provide leverage.

You're the boss.

A dispensable observation.

He turned to see Beba returning from the far side carrying an armload of poles from the firepit.

"Coquitla told me that we must use these to open the door and then to make a torch."

"I'm getting messages like that myself." He checked the diameter of the holes under each band, then took a pole with ends that looked as if they'd fit from Beba. The first slipped in easily and lodged tightly when he struck it with the other. It left an end sticking out past the edge of the door frame about two feet long. The second was less compliant but a few sharp raps with a stone secured it.

He'd no sooner set the stone down than Beba stood at the end of one pole, ready to lift. He set himself then nodded, and they both pulled upward at the same time. Their first try ended in failure.

Repeat that again.

This time he squatted down to get his legs into it and Beba watched and followed suit. At his count of three they strained against the poles and the door resisted for a moment then gave a loud tormented sound of groaning hinges and raised. As soon as it cleared the frame a few inches he reached to stick one of the spare poles in the opening so they could let the door down against it to reset themselves. Then another moment of straining and the door lifted up and over until it tilted at a steep angle away from the opening and stopped of its own accord.

Arthur and Beba looked down into the black rectangle below them. A wide wooden stairway made of the same resistant timbers led down ten or twelve feet to the mine floor.

Make a torch now.

Why not just use the flashlights?

Make it. Flashlights cannot test the mine for safety.

The flashlights are much brighter than torches, and . . .. He felt himself moving to the poles.

Do not waste more time.

Why so anxious all of a sudden?

There are no considerations for you to negotiate. Nor shall there ever be.

Arthur'd tried to reason with him before with similar results. It made him angry, but there was nothing to do but repress it once again. He turned his attention to the poles. Beba was ahead of him. She'd gathered an armload of long narrow leaves and proceeded to wrap them around the larger end of a short sturdy piece. She tied the leaves in place with strips of cloth torn from material brought in the pack. He dropped to his knees beside her and poured oil that had been intended for the outboard engine over the cloth and leaves. Then he took it to a shaft of sunlight to hold it under a magnifying lens he'd brought to use in his work. It soon began to smolder and he blew it into flame.

Take the torch down the steps. Place it on the mine floor and quickly return to the top.

I don't think you want to kill us both.

Do not underestimate my wisdom. By placing the torch on the mine floor you will see if the air is sufficient for you to breath.

Or if the air is made up of the wrong stuff, maybe just set off an explosion.

There was no reply.

Arthur lay the torch on the stone surface, motioned Beba back and went to peer down into the mine. Then he stepped back several paces, picked up the torch, and tossed it into the opening toward a place where he thought it would clear the stairs. Nothing . . . at first . . . then after several moments, a tiny curl of black oil smoke rose through the door frame. They went to the opening to see the torch lying at the bottom of the stairway burning brightly.

"Well nothing went bang, and there seems to be oxygen down there. Shall we have a look?"

They took the flashlights and Arthur led. He tested each step carefully before putting his full weight on it. Still several from the bottom he stopped. Some dreadful instinct refused to let him put his foot down onto the next step. When he'd reached his foot out over it intending to test it anyway, fear froze him solid. He pulled his foot back and the tension eased. Curiosity made him try again. This time he had the sensation that his hair was standing on end as his heart pounded hard in his chest.

I sense your fear. It is unfounded. Continue down.

For some reason I can't bring myself to stand down on that next step.

The solution is obvious. Step on the one below it.

Arthur didn't expect that to work either, but as soon as he had his intention clearly in mind the sensation relaxed and stepping down over the dreaded step to the next one below gave him no problem.

He turned to Beba and pointed. "Don't put your weight on that step. It's dangerous." He hadn't managed to keep alarm from his voice.

"How are you certain of that, if you did not step on it first?"

"I don't know. Humor me."

She had curiosity on her face, but she smiled and followed his example. When they reached the mine floor, he picked up the burning torch. The yellow light grew to make shadows flicker on every surface.

The floor was stone, chiseled flat. The shaft itself had also been cut into solid stone. In contrast to the smoothness of the floor, its walls were jagged streams of alcoves and outcropping, evidence of the position of the ore vein. The mine sloped down and away from them and in most places was barely wide enough for them to walk side by side.

"The vein must have surfaced where they built the stairway and they followed it as it ran into the ground from there."

"Do you think there is more to take from here?" Her voice sounded as if she was shaken and he remembered that she thought her ancestors had been murdered because of this place.

"Lets have a look."

He kept the torch well out in front of them above eye level and they both switched on flashlights. Even though the torch continued to burn brightly, the air had a dry empty smell to it, as though it wasn't really there at all. He decided he didn't want to stay long. They walked the tunnel together, but there was little to see. It ran about a hundred fifty feet maintaining the same easy slope and ended abruptly. There were two places where side tunnels had been cut, but the flashlights showed both to be no more that twenty feet long.

"Probably cut to follow branches in the vein that petered out."

Except for tool marks in the cut surfaces, nothing remained as a sign that man had been there. The ceiling became lower as it progressed until there was barely room to stand. He had to drop to his hands and knees before he could see what they'd been after, a mineral band running yellowish to olive green roughly three inches thick about two feet above the floor. He scratched at it absently with a finger, then returned to his feet and led her back toward the stairway.

Beba took the torch from him, rubbed it against the floor to put it out, and rested it against the wall. He led them back up the stairs. When he came to the step that had upset him before, he stepped over it without hesitation and didn't look back. On the surface they left the doorway open to let the air inside improve.

He sat on the ground and leaned back against the massive framework. She came to sit beside him and leaned her head against his shoulder.

"We have uncovered their secret. This is where they made the gold. This is the place that caused them to be murdered as they slept."

Arthur could feel her anguish, but there was more for her to know. "Gold didn't get them killed. Though I imagine that's what the murderers thought they would find. The legend your mother told you called the metal 'the color of the morning sun.' Perhaps they meant the very early morning sun, just at dawn when it can be red before it turns yellow."

She was looking at him now and there was a deep furrow in her brow. "I do not understand?"

"The metal door hinges are dark brown. Oxygen in the air causes that. Gold doesn't tarnish. It would be too soft to use for hinges anyway. I'm no geologist, but the vein in the mine appears to be atacamite or one of the other copper chlorides. It may even offer a mix of metals, but I don't see any signs of gold here.

"The legend your mother told you spoke of using the metal to make stronger better tools with sharper cutting edges. Gold wouldn't work for that. Gold has never been part of the culture of your tribe. I'm afraid your people died for something that didn't exist."

He saw rage in her face and feared what it might bring her when she spoke.

"I'm glad my grandfather made them pay with their lives"

I T HAD BEEN OVER TWO WEEKS SINCE ARTHUR
began working the mine and each day had been much like
the one before it. He swung the heavy sledge against the rod
end of the star drill to drive the cutting edges a fraction of a millimeter farther into the stone. He worked an outcropping on the
face of the right wall near the stairway to the mine entrance. So
much for the idea that Zarko smuggled these tools to the village
to mine gold. He rotated the drill a quarter turn and hit again.
This time a narrow fracture-line opened and instantaneously
connected with a number of other holes he'd drilled. The stone
dropped away and only a quick jump backwards saved his toes.

Each morning he came to the mine to hack out forty to fifty
pound chunks of stone until the open door to the entrance no
longer admitted enough light for him to see. When a stone had
been cut he carried it up the steps, always driven to avoid the
ominous fifth step, and loaded it onto the travois Phaqutl had
obliged him to make out of cut poles and canvas. When the
travois held four or five stones, he would haul them to the village.

Each evening, after a quick meal, Arthur sharpened the drills and chisels and went to his separate hut to collapse into sleep until Phaqutl intervened before dawn. The dream of the pitiful little boy imprisoned in the darkness returned most nights, but he'd been living in hell and driven hard, and chalked it up to stress.

He lay down the sledge, stooped to the newly cut piece at his feet and took up the smaller hammer and one of the chisels to knock off an odd protrusion before struggling it up the steps into daylight. Bending over to arrange it on the travois brought a twinge of pain to his lower back. He clasped a hand over it, dropped to his knees and sat back on his heels to begin massaging it away.

You suffer no damage. Return to your task.

Only one more stone will fill out this load and that should be the last one today. I'm going to rest for a few minutes.

Do not disobey. After you load the next cutting begin another. If it is not completed before the time to return to the village, you will finish in the morning.

My body needs a break and I'm taking it. With that Arthur grabbed the water bottle, moved to lean up against the stone face and stretched his arms out wide to inhale a deep breath.

His lungs had barely begun to take in air when they collapsed with a noisy whoosh. His body rolled forward, scrambled up on unsteady feet, then tottered to the open mine. He stood looking down into the black hole.

He'd been forced to do this without being allowed to breathe, and now it took real effort to pull air back in. When he finally managed it, he'd already begun to get lightheaded. Even so, he used his first whole breath to shout into the jungle.

"Damn you. Leave me alone."

You are aware that I feel your thoughts. There is no purpose in using your voice. I gladly leave you alone, but

you must obey. I find it curious that a human with your broad knowledge is unable to recognize the futility of resistance. Now go down the steps and work.

Though he felt his cheeks heat up, the rage that filled him couldn't erupt, because Phaqutl locked every muscle in him up tight until Arthur managed to stow it away inside like a hot ember shoved into damp grass. When the anger had been stuffed aside, it was replaced by an overpowering sense of dread and despair. He couldn't recall the number of times he'd tried to resist and lost. He'd tried to reason and bargain too, but none of it had worked. Beba's warnings had been correct, but if he couldn't find a way to go up against Phaqutl, they were lost.

Okay, I'm ready.

Proceed.

The trick was to take off each piece of stone in a way that made the next ones easier by taking advantage of the natural fractures and splits and having each of the holes he drilled serve more than one cut. He'd become better at it day-by-day and guessed he'd have the next one free in little more than an hour. That would be the last load of the day and he'd take the tools with it for Phaqutl refused to leave anything unattended, afraid from experience of the past that marauding tribesmen would happen upon them, and they would be lost. Arthur had been unable to convince him that the tribe that once raided the village was long gone. In fact, all the old tribes in the area had moved on and had not been replaced.

Instead Phaqutl intended to turn the village into an impenetrable fortress. The plan was to drive the two of them to surround the huts and courtyard with a dry stone wall and then to build living quarters of stone. A dry wall would take several times the amount of stone of one using mortar and the construction of dwellings without it would require that each piece be cut to perfection. Precise stonework was important to the history of the region and from the looks of the pyramid, Beba's ancestors had been as good at it as any. Coquitla had already passed the skills on to her, and while he worked to quarry, she did finish cuts and fitted the stones into place. These thoughts brought his curiosity up. Diversion might help him pass the time.

Tell me about the pyramid and the altar stone. Why were they built? How did they cut stone without the tools that we have?

It is not necessary to your purpose here to know. Spend your efforts cutting stone.

The response made him angry, but it was pointless. He'd tried before to obtain answers to some of the questions that brought him here, but Phaqutl refused bluntly each time. Gradually he let himself calm down.

In the weeks they'd been working on the wall, they'd only been able to complete a short portion of a section bordering the courtyard, and he felt certain the work would take years. They were being forced to work toward unattainable objectives under impossible circumstances and Beba had already suffered harsh consequences. When he'd seen her here for the first time, she was thinner than he remembered. Now she'd lost so much weight that the features of her face had become sharp from the bones underneath and the joints of her knees and elbows protruded beyond the surrounding flesh. Though she hadn't complained, she'd been losing strength day-by-day, and he feared for her.

He looked at his own arms. He'd lost weight too, but he'd started with more and hadn't been here as long. Instead of losing strength he'd actually become more fit. His body reflecting the forced work with new hard muscle. As long as he had the extra body weight to call upon, he'd probably be all right, but after that his fate would follow Beba's.

Somehow he had to protect them both until he could find a way to end the possession. The state of Beba's health made that urgent. If he had no answers, they had no future. His frustration with their dilemma made the next blows of the hammer harder than they should have been and the vibrations up the shaft of the steel drill rang through his wrists and chest. He kept it up until the stone came away and had barely enough stamina left to carry it up the steps and haul the travois to the village courtyard.

When he did manage to drag it onto the paving stones there, his concern for Beba rose even higher, for she hadn't managed to keep up with the supply of stones he'd brought, for the second day in a row. When she came to greet him her smile had turned thin and her movements seemed leaden.

He forgot his own weariness and dropped the poles of the travois to go to her. As he came nearer he saw new bands of darkness surrounding her eyes. He put his arms around her and it was like embracing her clothing without the woman inside. There was a frightening darkness about her sometimes, yet he missed the strong radiant woman she'd been before and wanted her back.

"What's happened, Beba. Are you okay?"

Her laugh seemed forced and not strong. "I am only very tired. It will be good to sleep tonight."

"I'm worried. Your color isn't good. Last night you hardly ate."

"Please do not concern yourself. It is as it needs to be."

"What do you mean needs to be? Coquitla's working you into sickness. Bring her out. Let me talk sense to her."

Beba raised a hand as if to quiet him, but her lips quivered and the hand fell back.

"I am here, Dr. Tomas. What is your question?"

"Can't you see you're ruining her health. She needs more food." Arthur stared at Beba's now expressionless face. "We have few medicines here. If you make her sick there's no way to help."

"I do not keep her from it. She eats as she wishes."

"See what's on her plate. That's not enough. Her appetite must be gone, because you're working her too hard."

"Sometimes she works more than I command. Phaqutl has decreed that we build the wall and the huts for protection so that what happened here before cannot happen again. He is the adored Father of Our Kind. Our children must be safe."

Arthur suddenly got a strange crinkling in the pit of his stomach. "What children?"

"Has Phaqutl not informed you?"

Arthur stiffened and heard his own voice speak as he was taken over. "I have determined not to. This one would ponder over it to excess. It is his nature. He is sometimes troublesome. It will accomplish more if that does not happen."

"Perhaps it is time that he knows."

And with that Beba's frail form turned and walked toward the fire pit. She looked back over her shoulder at him as she went, and there was an expression of mortal agony that seemed to warn him away, but he couldn't be sure if it was Coquitla or Beba herself who sent the message.

First the two of you shall build the wall and huts of stone. Then you shall bring us children.

You forgot to mention children. Damn you.

In the years I was away, Coquitla could only pass from generation to generation by moving to the human offspring of the woman she dwelled within. This was true even though each offspring carried our seed inherited from her own mother. Now that we two are together again, her seed may be mated with mine. The human children who follow will carry new and separate entities of our kind. As it was

done here before. As with your species and all others, it guarantees that our kind will survive.

Arthur's breathing was still harsh from dragging the travois and he let himself slump down to rest on the stone surface of the courtyard. You're going to try to remake the tribe?

When the tribe grew here before and replaced their old people with young, we also became many. That must be again.

Beba and I are only two humans. That will take generations, if it's possible at all, and there are so many things that can go wrong. She is already suffering.

Unlike humans, with your short life span, we do not perish so long as we have healthy creatures to carry us. Time means little to us. Therefore we do not perceive the urgency that humans do. I remained with Zarko in prison for over two of your decades. There was no reason to move on until the future became clear. Only survival matters. Increasing our number is necessary to insure that. Humans offer us the most and suit us the best. And we will bring others here to bear more children as that suits us.

If time is unimportant to you, why are you forcing us to work so hard?

For our safety. Until the village is safe from attack.

I have tried to reason with you before. All the old tribes have disappeared. There's no one within miles of this place.

You cannot be certain of that. I must assume that your lives are at risk.

And yours too?

There is little risk to us. We always survive. I once moved from the deer that was its prey into the panther, then when the panther had been hit by the arrows with their poison, into the human who came to claim his kill.

Zarko was already dead by your definition, when I discarded him for you.

Only once have I come close to fatality, when the grandfather of Beba suffered at the hands of the murderers. They feared his corpse because of the ferocity with which he fought them. Ferocity that I gave him.

When they took his head to make it small, I wished to enter the shaman who would do it, but the man also lived in fear of her grandfather's spirit and sewed the eyes shut quickly, without allowing himself to see into them. His fear also made him alter the methods he used so that he could be rid of the head sooner and in some way that permitted me to survive until I escaped. But that cannot happen again.

If there was danger to her grandfather and thus to you, why did you let him chase them for all those years?

There was no longer a large enough group of people here to make our posterity grow. He killed only the warriors. Soon there would have been many women to help our need.

You're a little too sure of yourself.

I am certain.

The problem for you then is that one of us may die before we make this place safe for Beba to have children.

As I have said, we will bring others.

But she is already ill. She may not live until then.

Again you attempt to bargain with me. Stop. We keep you apart now so that it will not be necessary for her to do heavy work when she carries a child. When the work is done we will put you together each time that her body may hold a child.

What makes you think that just putting us together will bring children? Arthur started to stand, but Phaqutl held him in place.

We know what makes your children. The two of you have been together already. I can cause it to happen whether you wish it or not. Let that be clear to you.

Now Arthur felt himself released. He stood and moved to the firepit where Beba was putting the finishing touches on the evening meal. Her plate had very little on it.

"I know what they're planning to do now."

Then before he could continue Phaqutl took his voice.

"The procedure is now revised. Beginning tonight, Beba will increase her food intake. If she refuses again, Coquitla will force it. From now on she will eat three times daily instead of two. At midday she will sleep, but will rouse to work stone in the afternoon."

Beba looked back at him and blinked back tears. "They will breed us like pigs."

He saw the stiff little tremble that meant that Coquitla had taken charge. Beba's hands reached out, took his plate and dumped it onto hers.

She finished her midday meal in the shade, leaning back against the altar stone. Since Arthur had convinced Phaqutl that she needed to improve her health, Beba had been forced to take rests. Now her day consisted of no more than nine or ten hours work cutting and fitting stone with the remaining daylight hours spent at less strenuous chores. She rested or napped for about an hour during the hottest part of the day.

In the three weeks since these changes, it seemed to her she was regaining strength and had perhaps gained back a little weight. To compensate, Arthur's hours had been increased and he worked not only in the mine removing stone, but also at the village finishing and placing what stone she did not.

Though she couldn't tell Arthur because of the risk of informing both Phaqutl and Coquitla, she had resolved that her own children would never carry the seed that had been left inside her by her mother. She would make that true even though the only way open for her to prevent it was to assure they couldn't be born at all.

They had not yet been moved into the same hut at night, but it was increasingly plain that it would be soon. Even though she had been with Arthur and had felt the excitement and desires of a woman then, she knew now that the causes had come from the germ of Coquitla and not from herself. The idea of their being forced together again made her cry in the night. That it might happen again and again brought a horror that caused her to shudder and wrap her arms closely about herself.

What is it? I read no danger through your senses. You are thinking about being with Arthur again. You should be happy. Phaqutl has brought you a fine mate, though perhaps the larger one would make better children to live here in the forest. You should be grateful to us.

Stop. I beg you.

Then rest.

Do you love, Phaqutl?

Not in the way you think of it. We have an intense drive to make our kind multiply and survive. We do anything to make that happen. Phaqutl is the Father of Our Kind, a term that shows respect and reverence. We do not feel the emotional joy you call love or the pleasures of your sex. Rest now. Or I shall give you no choice.

She forced herself to relax and finally was able to drowse on the verge of sleeping. This was part of the ritual to which she had let Coquitla become accustomed. Then purposely she let her eyes open and without excitement of any kind rose to her knees to hold the cloth she'd wrapped her food in over the edge of the river side of the pyramid to let the up-drafting winds whisk the crumbs away.

The motion of the cloth caused the soaring birds to increase the intensity of their screeching rebuke. She'd feared them the first time she'd seen them. Now she loathed them as well. It would have been easy to avoid them, but invoking their wrath was a necessary part of her plan. She needed to experience the apprehension and fury they awoke in her here at the top of the pyramid, so that Coquitla might expect it without affect at a decisive time here in the near future.

She folded the cloth and placed it at the base of the altar stone beside the two long coils of nylon rope she'd brought on previous days and the third she'd carried up with her lunch. Since she'd put the ritual into place and maintained it without deviation, Coquitla had remained somnolent through the entire midday break and remained unconcerned about the growing rope supply.

Now Beba brought her mind to the ritual. One brief thought on the business at hand and immediately several others on something unrelated. She'd fallen onto the scheme while putting dinner together several nights before. She'd brushed her hand against a pot just off the fire and burned the back of two fingers before she'd realized what was happening. She'd snatched them away and grasped them tightly with her other hand to squelch the pain. It came on anyway and to distract herself further, she'd repeated a bedtime story in her mind that her uncle recited to her over and over when she was a child. It told of a little girl and a huge jungle snake with very persuasive powers that wanted to hug the little girl as a ploy to swallowing her whole. At the end of it her uncle would grab her up in his arms and squeeze and Beba would squeal and try to squirm out of his grasp. The hurt from the burn and Beba's initial reaction brought Coquitla up ready to take charge, but when she'd heard a harmless children's story she'd gone back to the dormant state without attempting more.

Beba'd become so elated by this, she'd aroused Coquitla again within seconds and was able to shift her thoughts back into the children's story quickly enough to achieve the same result.

Since that moment she'd tested and retested Coquitla in different ways, almost always with success. It even seemed as though Coquitla's response time slowed and her interest dimmed with repetition.

If the ruse continued to work over the next several days, Beba would be ready to bring the misery to an end. She began her thoughts for the day.

I may be able to delay Arthur in the mine tunnel . . .. I will pick some of the dark red berries for us tonight. The best bushes are along the river by the landing. Six big handfuls should be enough. I wonder how long the season is for them. Perhaps there is some way to store them for later on. I should ask Coquitla about this. She paused. There was no response.

I'll follow him when he goes down there . . .. Perhaps the same berries for tomorrow morning too. They will be gone soon. And so it went. After a few more minutes she had thought her way through a simple plan to keep Arthur from stopping her. It would be in her memory when she needed it and Coquitla was none the wiser.

The process seemed daunting and painstakingly slow at first and she was certain she would make some error, like getting carried away by her emotions, to be discovered. Now it came almost automatically, like using polite language in front of the guests at the lodge and with nearly as little effort. The real test would come when she tried to carry her plan through to its end.

She turned to the three coils of rope. She'd tied the first two together yesterday. Today she would add the third. She selected the rope ends that she wanted, took one in each hand, pulled them together, then looked up quickly to see out across the expanse of jungle on the far side of the river . . .. The mists are unusually dense today. I wonder if that means a change in the weather. I hope we will not have thunder storms . . ..

She did not look down at what her hands were doing. Right hand over left and tuck the rope under . . .. The last one kept me awake much of the night. To say nothing of the roof leaking. She concentrated her eyes on the tall trees . . .. And the opposite: left over right, tuck it under and pull it tight . . .. The tall ones are magnificent, I could look at them all day, but I must return to the village to work. She stood, still looking outward toward the trees, then glanced down quickly to see the square knot lying at her feet. Good. Tomorrow I must tie a loop in the end large enough to throw over the altar stone . . .. Perhaps I shall go pick the berries on the way back. She began the climb down.

XIV

ALFWAY DOWN THE CRUDE STEPS THAT
led into the mine, he heard the hinges of the massive
door release a tormented groan, and it pounded shut
above him. The frame had been built parallel to the ground
above so that the door dropped flat and if he'd still stood a step
higher it may have killed him. Instead it struck the top of his
head, lights of pain flashed before his eyes, and Arthur fell the
rest of the way to sprawl dazed on the rock floor. A wave of nausea
cautioned him to stay put, to take inventory. The door sealed out
all the light. He couldn't see any part of himself, but his palms
burned hot from trying to catch himself on the hard surface and
the joints of his wrists and shoulders ached from the shock of
impact. It took several moments for his senses to sort themselves
out and as his head cleared it began throbbing.

"Beba?" he called into the black void, his hazed mind voicing
vague concern that she'd been hurt. She didn't answer and it
took several seconds for him to register that she hadn't followed
him down the steps and a few more to realize that she'd been the
one to slam the door. Certainly not by accident, it would have
taken all her strength to lift it from its open position to the point

where it would roll over and drop the rest of the way into the frame. He wondered what she was trying to do. Anxiety raced to fill his mind. He cautioned himself not to go out of control now. There were things to do. He fought the pulsing headache and tried to paint meaning on what had happened. He sensed he wasn't painting with a clean brush. A strange foul odor invaded his nostrils, one he couldn't place.

It is dark. Yet only midday. You became unconscious. What is the danger?

Just dazed. I'm in the mine. The door slammed shut and cracked me on the head.

You have some pain. The injury has no consequence.

Thanks a lot. It still hurts like hell.

I have informed you before. Pain is merely a primitive warning mechanism. Do not pay it heed when there is no urgency. Why have you come here?

Beba said she wanted to look for a particular shape of stone.

Was it she who slammed the door?

Yes. Coquitla must have forced her.

Rise. There are things to be done.

He braced his knuckles against the floor and raised himself to full height. It made him dizzy and he waited for his head to clear. A booming thunk reverberated overhead, quickly followed by another.

She's piling stones on the door. Making it too heavy to open.

Quickly then.

And Phaqutl took him over physically, walked him back up the steps, turned him to brace the backs of his shoulders and his hands against the underside of the door like the statue of Hercules supporting the weight of the world. He made Arthur push upward with an adrenalin rush stronger than Arthur himself could generate, giving him greater strength than he could muster on his own. Sweat broke on his brow, stung in his eyes, and rivulets of it ran down under his arms leaving cold trails on hot skin. Phaqutl forced him harder until Arthur sensed cartilage and tendon compressing as the amplified power of his legs forced him against the immovable weight. Pain seemed to flood into his brain from everywhere. His head jarred against wood as dropped stones continued to jolt the door from the outside.

Stop . . .. Too late. Can't budge it. Keep this up and you'll do real damage. This is no time to go down with an injury. The strain became even more intense for a few seconds and then gradually eased as Phaqutl relinquished command.

Arthur cupped his hands at the sides of his mouth and turned his face upward to the door. He called to Beba with all the volume he could muster, heard it echoing behind him in the mine, called again . . . and yet again. Only the thumping sound of stone falling on stone came in detached response. Arthur pulled his elbows together in front of himself, trying to stretch his arms and shoulders to relieve cramping from the failed attempt to lift the door.

We must assess the situation.

It's certainly fruitless to strain against an immovable object. Arthur stooped to feel his way down until he could sit on a lower step, put his elbows on his knees and rested his chin on the laced fingers of his hands.

She left you to die.

Who? Coquitla?

You still fail to understand us. For Coquitla that would be impossible. You call us parasites. Even if we were, one of us could not do such a thing. We do not kill those who carry us, for to do so is to assassinate one of our own.

Didn't I learn from you that each time you abandon one host for another, the first dies. Isn't that really what killed Zarko?

We move to new carriers to survive as you eat to survive. It is true that many die. That is not our choosing. Whatever it is you eat, plant or animal, all perish. That is not your choosing either. But for us at least some do not die. The young are able to adapt physically and most always live on. Those we join within the mother are born as any other and survive when we move on. Your Beba's mother lives on. It is only the adults who cannot survive.

Like yours truly. He didn't like the sick feeling growing in his stomach.

A child could not have brought me to this place.

Am I somehow supposed to approve of that?

You would not suffer the pain if you would accept what you cannot control. As I have said, we will not kill our own kind. Coquitla will force Beba to free you as soon as she becomes aware of this predicament and it is certain that she soon will.

If you're so certain Coquitla will rush to the rescue, why did you have me try to force the door open?

It is time to attend to the present.

Arthur wiped at the feeling of sweat on his brow and brushed grit into his eyes. He blinked them in the dark and moisture came. And so did anger.

How did Coquitla allow this in the first place? You must have lied when you told me one of us couldn't do something or even think it without your knowing.

Arthur expected a blunt denial and when Phaqutl didn't respond, it gave rise to his first feeling that the situation might be truly desperate. Muscles at the back of his neck tightened and he worked the signet ring in circles with his thumb.

Coquitla doesn't know what Beba's done. If that's true, Beba's found a way to mask her thoughts or her actions or both. She can fool Coquitla. If Beba could trap him in the mine without Coquitla knowing and if she intended that he die, she would also know she must hide her actions until it was too late for Coquitla to stop her.

He wondered how long it would be before it became too late. When the oxygen ran out his face would pale and his fingers and lips would turn blue. He wouldn't see that in the darkness. It would take him quietly. His mind would simply lose reality and drift away as he slipped toward death. Beba had chosen one of the least painful ways for him to die. He wondered if she'd planned it that way. He wanted to believe that she had and so he let himself. Somehow it made him feel better. Strangely, he was proud of her.

Concentrate on the problem at hand.

Let me then, damn you. He had no way to calculate the volume of air in the mine or how long it would sustain him. The main tunnel wasn't more than a hundred fifty feet long, scarcely tall enough to stand upright, and about nine feet wide. A couple of short side tunnels? Inconsequential. He could only guess how long that gave him. Hours . . . half a day perhaps. Just an hour or two would be a long time for Beba to hold something from Coquitla, even if she had found a way to deceive her.

He realized she had a plan. Then the answer caught him and brought his dread to full flower. She had no way of knowing how long before the air went bad either . . . so it couldn't matter to what she intended to do.

Then he remembered how thin she'd gotten and Coquitla saying that Beba worked even harder than she'd been forced to and cut back on her eating herself. She'd been starving herself. He remembered the little warning look she'd given him at the end of that conversation. At the time he couldn't tell whether it came from her or Coquitla. But now he realized that she'd been doing what she could to warn him that she would not let herself bear a child with the seed of the parasite inside.

She wasn't trying to kill him now. Only to get him out of the way. A delay. He smacked a fist into his palm. She meant to free her children in the only way she could. By taking her own life.

I will stop her. We have faced such things before. We shall always survive. Though for once your thoughts are relevant.

Shut up. Let me think. Beba's going to kill herself. She'd tried to warn him. And because he hadn't heard her plea for help, didn't even let himself recognize it, he'd forced her to go it alone . . . and to leave him to die in order to make it possible. Irony. Regret and shame tightened his eyes. He tried to push the feeling aside and replace it with anger toward her. It wouldn't work. He tried to turn the anger toward himself, to embrace the guilt, but it served no purpose either. He felt heartsick because he'd been blind to her and for a fleeting moment remembered that he'd been blind to Millie too.

A noise from far back in the mine shaft interrupted. A low rumbling rasp like the night cough of an old man. Arthur snapped up rigid where he sat.

The panther. You are not alone. If you had used your senses, as I have tried to teach you, you would have recognized the odors, heard it sooner. You would have learned from these observations that it is feeding. Since the door has been left open many weeks, it may have learned to come down here to hide its kill from animals who would steal it from him.

Will it attack?

Almost certainly, though it has no need to hurry. There is no enemy it fears. It will wait until it finishes. Perhaps even rest first.

How will it? With the door closed I can't see my own fingers.

It will move so that you cannot hear it coming. It can see you with its nose, pinpoint your precise location by the sound of your breathing, while its own instincts caution it to breathe silently. The first you will know is when its claws rake your body. And there is a second concern. It breathes your air and uses more than you. You must leave here soon.

Easier said . . ..

Give yourself what safety you can until there is a plan. Move behind and below the steps.

Good idea.

He stood and felt his way around to the underside of the steps. With an odd sense of *deja vu*, he put his back to them and crouched down into the 'V' they made with the floor. He waited listening in the dark, put a hand behind himself to touch one of the thick notched poles that supported the steps and at once an odd sense of belonging settled over him, strangely comforting as though he'd come home. Then the feeling that he'd lived this all before became clear. Just like the dream.

Give your attention to making a plan.

Without the strength to lift the weighted door, he'd need leverage. Some kind of tool. Without his tools there were only odd pieces of broken rock, nothing that might do to pry the door open. If only he had a torch now.

You do.

I do what?

When you left here the first time, Beba put the torch out and left it behind.

I have no way to light it.

You made it from wood from the pile near the fire pit. The same strong wood that makes the steps and the door.

It has dried many years and become very hard. There may be another use for it now. Find it before the panther finishes its meal and comes this way.

Arthur moved from under the steps with his hands held out to protect against bumping into things. He stood at the base of the steps facing into the shaft and thought back to where Beba had left it. It should be on his right, fifteen to twenty feet ahead, on the floor leaning against the wall.

Play it safe. Can't get disoriented. Think it out. Make sure I can get back to this spot. He moved slowly to the right until his outstretched fingers brushed the wall. Though only a few feet from the steps, he began to feel vulnerable and exposed. The big cat could take him from any direction at any second.

He placed himself full length against the mine wall, sank down on hands and knees, felt himself become smaller, feeling safer, and began to creep along the wall. He kept a hand out in front of himself, sweeping back and forth against surprises. He estimated the forward movement of each knee at about a foot. At twenty feet he began to worry that the torch had been moved. Perhaps Beba had taken it away.

At thirty the uneven rock floor had begun to hurt his knees and at forty he became certain it was gone. He'd turned himself about, intending to retrace his journey, when his hand brushed against something in the darkness. He reared away from it slamming his back and head against the wall, heard his startled shout echo back through the tunnel. He expected the panther to snarl in reply, but heard nothing. His heart jumped hard against his chest wall and his pulse throbbed at his temples, his breathing rasped in the stillness. The bruise on his head protested the new insult. He cursed and another echo rewarded him for it . . . then silence except for faraway crunching sounds made by the dining cat.

If you really wish it to come for you, let it know how
frightened you are.

I think I just did.

My point.

He gave himself a few seconds to calm down and settled back
into the same position he'd been in before the incident. He
reached forward gingerly, involuntarily tense and ready to recoil
a second time. Again his fingertips contacted something in the
blackness. This time he held himself in check and let them feel
that the object was hard and cool to the touch. The torch. He
took it and stood, then after listening to reassure himself that
the panther was still occupied, turned about and retraced the
distance along the wall and back to the steps.

He sat on the bottom step as he had before to run his hands
over the torch to brush away the remnants of the dried leaves
that served to hold the oil it had burned. His action released the
smell of these to thin the repugnant odors of the panther and its
kill. Twelve to fourteen inches long, he guessed, and thick, over
three inches and a bit through the middle. He tried to push a
thumb nail into the wood and couldn't. The wood was strong.

How will it work for you?

Read my mind. I'll take it up to the door.

With that Arthur stood to turn and climb the stairs and
there it was again, that horrific apprehension that made him skip
the fifth one up from the bottom. Then it dawned: hiding under
the stairs, skipping one with the knowledge that if he didn't he'd
be in big trouble, the damn dream again. It made him feel foolish,
but he had more important things to think about and wiped the
back of his hand across his forehead as if brushing the whole thing
aside.

Near the top, he lowered himself onto a step, lay the torch
handle aside and rested his elbows on the step above. He lowered

his chin into his hands and looked where he expected to see light coming from the crack the door made with the frame. There wasn't any and he heard the beat of his heart accelerating. Something was terribly wrong. He knew, that before he could do anything to help himself escape, he had to see light at the bottom of the door.

Of course. He wanted the smell of fresh air.

Check it out. He raised himself and reached to run his fingers over the interior of the door. It opened outward and so the hinges weren't available to be loosened.

The inner surface was smooth and he could feel how each thick board joined tightly with the next. The tribe had been good craftsmen. He ran fingers along the crack at the side then at the bottom. Here and there he felt a gentle coolness on his fingers. Tiny air leaks, not enough to feed in the oxygen he needed to live.

Near the bottom and opposite the hinged side, a short section of one of the boards had been lost to leave a rough groove in the facing of the door a couple of inches wide. He pondered it for a moment and the web of an idea began to spin in his mind.

He placed the smaller end of the torch handle into the groove and the other end on top of the step beneath it. The torch was longer than the distance it spanned between the step and the door, so it tilted to the side at an angle. Good. If he could force it along the step to stand upright, it would lift the door. Perhaps no more than an inch or two, but that might be enough. He could force it if he could pound it hard enough. He needed a hammer.

His lay the torch handle aside and hurried back down the steps, counting compulsively again as he went, stepping over the one that was taboo. This time hope generated urgency and he chose to overlook the strange behavior. When he reached the mine floor, he held onto one side of the steps with one hand and bent to sweep for loose rock with the other. Several stones, nothing heavy enough. He switched quickly to the other side of the steps and again stooped to reach out in all directions. He muttered an oath when the backs of his knuckles raked hard against a rock, but when he picked it up he'd found what he'd been searching for. Up the steps once again, counting and stepping over, breathing heavily in his haste.

At the top, he grasped the torch handle with one hand, placed it in position and held it there. He intended to strike the torch near the bottom where it touched the step. That would drive the bottom end of it along sideways until it straightened upright under the notch in the door above and pushed the door up. He had to swing the rock parallel to the step just above it and his first try glanced off it and hit the torch handle with little affect. The second proved more accurate and drove the torch over nearly half an inch. The next moved it another quarter and the echoes returned solid notes with each contact. Encouraged, he increased the power in his swing and the next smashed into his hand. It jolted him, but this time he squelched the impulse to shout. He bent his head forward, clamped his jaw and eyes shut, and held the injured hand against his chest. As the initial shock of the pain eased, he raised himself and waved the hand back and forth in the air, shaking it out to veil the hurt. He felt warm droplets against his face.

You have indeed injured yourself this time.

Always first with the news.

You have smashed a knuckle, fractured a bone in the smallest finger. The bleeding is unimportant. Proceed.

Piss off.

It took all his will to force the injured left hand back on the torch handle. He grasped it gingerly and swung the rock more deliberately now, each blow sending white electricity through the injured hand. After several more, the torch handle had wedged firmly into place, and he could let go. He put the stone down and tested the crack with the fingers of his good hand to find it had widened and the door had raised ever so slightly.

A dozen more blows and the first thin rays shone through followed by the heavy, cool, sweet smell of fresh air. He stopped to stare at it, let himself inhale deeply, then returned to the task. The slit of light continued to grow until it was an inch high and the sturdy torch pole stood upright and unable to lift the door farther.

The brightness shocked his eyes and he looked away from it back down the steps to find the full length of them and a circle of the mine floor visible now accept for his own shadow. He moved and the shadow moved with him, and it startled him even though he had known it would do that.

He moved his hand into the light and inspected the swollen knuckles, tried to straighten crooked and bent fingers that resisted with sparks of pain. Just looking at the hand brought the whole of it to life and it flared hot in response. The palm and back of it had swollen, the skin scarlet and taut.

The pain invaded his consciousness and in the faint light the picture of the hand first blurred then began to grow anew in his mind. He saw that hand, but transformed now into a child's hand injured in a different way. Swollen too, but gashed and bleeding with broken fingers splayed. Then a rush tore through him and he gasped as he realized that the image in his mind was real. He had actually injured that hand before, had felt that pain before. The memory became vivid and tormented him.

It seemed important to know what had compelled him to perform the eerie dream ritual here in the mine, counting his way up and down the steps, avoiding one as though morbid danger lay manifest within it. He had a feeling that his need to force open a light at the bottom of the door had nothing to do with wanting fresh air.

He turned back to face the slit of light and sat staring and bewildered by the hold it had over him. None of this was new . . . he'd seen it before. He'd sat at the top of darkened stairs like these, looking into light under a door. Absently his thumb turned the ring on his right hand and the old ritual twisted open the spillways of his mind and memories surged through to rise and fill him. The little boy in the recurring dream had sat like this. But he wasn't dreaming then. The dreams had been a trick played by his subconscious to make him relive those hidden memories. A ploy so he would see Arthur the boy and reunite that tormented child with Arthur the man.

Now trapped and dazed with pain, in the mine, his guard fell away, and he saw himself as that boy again. As clearly as yesterday. For the first time he recalled the days before the orphanage. Lying on his back somewhere unable to move, a terrible weight holding him down . . . choking out his breath. Frightened . . . so very frightened. Trying to call out. Coughing and gasping. Struggling to sit up. Can't lift the weight. Trying to kick . . . uncontrollably panicked . . . lungs crying for air . . . the weight getting lighter on his legs . . . kicking freely now, but the weight still pinning his body. Raising his knees up, pushing down hard with his feet, heaving, thrusting upward with his hips, desperately, with every ounce of a little boy's strength. The weight on him growing lighter, spilling off his chest. Now raising himself to sit and the rest of it running off him. Dirt . . . he could smell it now. He had lain in it, been covered by it.

Standing now, shaking himself, shaking it from him. Small fingers digging it from his nose and ears. His hand hurting so badly. Causing his eyes to tear through the crusted dirt. Sucking in damp cool air. New odors of wetness and mold. Alone in the cold darkness. A darkness just like the one Arthur the adult sat in now. And the adult remembered back to that other slit of light. It too came from a crack under a door. The boy hiding under the stairs, frightful noises above his head, eating from the canning jars, the fifth movement of a splinter of wood from the wall serving notice of the day he bathed. Washing himself in the cold water from the faucet, being careful of the left arm. That child remembered nothing before rising from the dirt, but instead believed he was born from the dirt and in doing this, keeping himself from the memory of Arthur, the adult.

He'd always known there had to be more. Until that moment he'd only remembered himself at the orphanage. Now he recalled that he'd lived in darkness in a . . . cellar. Had awakened in the dirt and survived. But that couldn't be all of it. His mind had repressed the memories of the boy. That boy had lost all of himself before his resurrection from the dirt of the cellar floor.

And there were other things that boy held over from before being buried. The wounded hand. Yes, and something else. The need to protect the inside of his upper arm, his left arm. On the stairs in the old mine, Arthur the adult caressed the inside of his left arm with the knuckles of his right hand. Then memories from earlier times before the basement roiled through him. An old woman calling to him in an alley, the boy fighting the Doberman, something inside him in his mind controlling him, making him hurt that dog and there was another dog too. A little dog that the boy loved.

Another boy too . . . .. His cousin. They were hiding in his cousin's bedroom. The inside of his arm hurting. The cause of the pain . . . making a tattoo. Putting his own name on the inside of his arm, but the name wasn't Arthur.

He had a different name. That boy was called Wart. And the thing had come into Wart's head and it made him watch horrified as the little dog turned in circles beside his bed, foaming at the mouth until it died. Arthur took his eyes away from the light under the mine door to stare blankly at the dimly lit steps below him. The thing had come into Wart, the boy, just as Phaqutl was inside him now. And then it all became clear to him and the emotions of the years welled monstrously inside him. For moments he thought he might lose all control. Then the knowledge he'd kept from himself all the years gave him the beginnings of a plan.

You have stopped. Why?

We need to be out of here.

There is much to do. Do you oblige me to take control?

When you brought Zarko for me at the university, was that the first time you knew me?

I learned of you from the magazine article.

Are you certain you didn't know me as a young boy? Twenty years before.

Would you remember what you took for sustenance that long ago?

Call the panther.

You wish to die? If I am forced to leave you, it will be your end, as it always is for the adults.

You say that the young survive. Do you remember a little boy called Wart?

That boy died.

He lived, no thanks to you. I was that boy. I have his chance to survive.

And so.

You said once the panther has the strength of six men. Is that true?

Nearly.

Use my voice and call it. When it comes, leave me and go into it. If you can make it do work, then together we may be able to lift the door.

The plaintiff yowls and hollow grunts that came from Arthur's throat didn't sound all that much like the noises he'd heard from the black jaguar and the contortions Phaqutl put him through rasped painfully in his throat and hurt his chest. He was about to complain when a reply from the big cat rolled through the tunnel.

Is he buying it?

It has acknowledged your presence as its own kind. I sense question, but no challenge. That may come when it discovers the sham.

Call it here.

It already comes.

I don't hear it. How do you know?

Its only alternative is to act. It has only two choices, to face you or to leave, and it will take whichever poses the least threat of harm to itself. Unlike many humans, it does not believe that ignoring danger will make it go away. In this mine, it knows it cannot fade into the safety of the jungle. It will arrive to face you very soon.

How will it come?

A predator knows the value of surprise. If it springs, your human reactions will not be quick enough to provide the opportunity I shall need to go into it.

Talk to it again. Hurry.

The muscles of his chest swelled and contorted and he could feel his neck arching. A coughing grunt followed by a series of higher pitched rowling sounds echoed into the mine tunnel. The effort was exhausting and painful.

What did you tell it?

It now believes you are with young. A female.

Fine, you're counting on its paternal instincts. I suppose it'll come to play with the kittens.

It has no fear of man, but if it accepts there is a mother here that will kill for the safety of its young, it will approach with great caution.

And then what? A noise interrupted him and he looked into the circle of dim light at the bottom of the stairs. His body tensed as it reflected back to him from the round yellow eyes of the panther.

Beba timed the trek to the mine with Arthur to be just prior to her usual noon break, so that on the trip back she could pass through the village and on to the pyramid without raising questions from Coquitla.

Even though slamming the mine entrance door and piling rocks on it took intense physical effort, she had become accustomed to that, hence Coquitla had also accepted that level of activity without rousing. Now that Beba knew how to do it, she was surprised at just how easy deceiving Coquitla could be, as long as she herself remained composed and without internal commotion. What came next would take much more control than she had tested herself with so far. Resolve stood like a cold granite pillar inside her. Odd that self control turned out to be her only active weapon rather than a form of constraint.

If only she could have told Arthur, but there was no way to communicate to him without giving herself away. She couldn't let herself think about the danger she had put him in.

Now, as she labored up the tall steps, her lungs began to ache, and her pulse made thrushing sounds in her ears. Normally this wouldn't have happened and she took it as a warning sign that her tensions were building and that she needed to exercise even more effort to hold herself in.

But by the time she reached the top, her legs shook, and she barely made it onto the area where the altar stone stood before being forced to stop. She had to stand for several moments with head down, hands on her knees, panting, while her heart rate slowed and the midday sun drove hot fangs into the backs of her shoulders. To keep her mind safe from Coquitla, she recited a rhyme she'd once been taught in her efforts to learn to speak English.

"Columbus said, 'the world is round.'
Wasn't he a Dilly.
'The world is flat,' the wise men said.
'Columbus is quite silly . . ..'"

Her glance drifted as calmly as she could make it to the three coils of rope lying along the vertical cliff side wall of the pyramid next to the altar stone. She walked to the last one and pushed at it with her sandaled foot. The largest of the loops began to sag over the abrupt edge. A second push and the entire coil tilted then slipped over the side and disappeared. In seconds the weight of it had begun to pull rope from the remaining coils. She turned her back, stepped away and tried to concentrate her gaze into the sun drenched canopy of trees extending away from the pyramid.

It would be so much easier if she could simply walk to the edge and step off, but she knew she couldn't make it work without rousing Coquitla, and if that happened there would be no second chance. She forced herself to inhale the fragrances of the jungle in the air.

" 'Three boats I'll give thee,' said the queen.
'Come bring me what you find then.
The wealth you'll bring to Spanish Isles,
So much the worse for England.'
"He sailed away the wooden ships,
Those gifts got from the queen.
'Take one last look,' the wise men said,
'He'll n'ere again be seen . . ..'"

The uncoiling rope made angry sounds as it grated with increasing speed over the harsh edge of the stone into space. Screeches from the birds railed in insult at the invasion and she could hear them in growing numbers as they rose from their nests in the cliff face below to soar and swoop over head. Then abruptly the rope noise stopped and only the bird sounds remained.

The time had come. She scuffed off her sandals, placed them meticulously side by side. Felt the muscles in her jaw tighten and concentrated with all the energy she could muster upon the rhyme.

"Through storms they sailed, til death drew nigh."

Still facing away from the edge of the cliff, she stepped over the rope so that it lay between her feet, then bent to pick it up. It was far heavier than she'd imagined and for an instant she thought she'd come to a deadend. She felt the pain of fatigue still in her legs, as she worked her way backward in small shuffling steps. The rope scraped through her hands.

Sooner than she'd expected, she came to the edge, felt it beneath the heel of her foot. She dropped forward onto her knees and then worked along farther until she lay on her stomach with the rope still clenched in her hands. Her legs began to stick out over the edge as she worked her way backwards using her elbows, still reciting aloud. When she could, she let her legs drop down and circled them around the rope. From then on it happened all too quickly and within seconds she had slipped over the edge and was sliding down the rope beside the vertical riverside wall of the pyramid, still concentrating upon the rhyme.

"'Land Ho!' He heard the sailor call
From perch atop the mast.
"Thank God,' the careworn captain roared,
'Tis India at last."

The yellow eyes of the panther gleamed at the bottom of the steps below him. Arthur saw the round pupils of its eyes grow as the animal stepped into the light. The acrid stench of it attacked his senses. Its sides moved in an out silently with each panting breath.

It took another step and he watched the sleek ebony form glide silently in the dimness. It seemed more a hovering shadow than a two hundred fifty pound beast. The urge to run was overwhelming, but there was no place to go even for a futile try, for he sat wedged at the top of the steps. The door already touched the hair on the back of his head.

Control your fear. If it senses you are afraid, it will attack.

Easier said than done.

If you wish to survive you have no choice.

The huge cat stopped and turned its head up, apparently content to stare at him for the moment. Muffled guttural rumblings from deep inside it warned of the enormity of its power.

Check mate.

Do not concern yourself with a board game at a time like this.

We can discuss idioms of speech another time. Right now I'd like to know how you can move into that thing without my being slashed to shreds in the process.

I cannot, perhaps.

The first time you have ever shown me doubt about anything. What happened to Mr. Perfect?

It is not doubt. It is an accurate assessment of the potential outcome.

But not an outcome either of us like, is it? What next?

The animal opened its mouth to began a rasping pant . . . evenly, slowly, as though well aware the choices were all its own.

Its pink tongue extended out between needle sharp lower fangs. The smell of it had become asphyxiating.

We . . . I will force it to attack. When it springs, it will come with its paws extended well out front, claws unsheathed. The intent is to knock the prey down or off balance while it selects the most vulnerable place to strike with its fangs.

Its usual prey would either freeze, if caught by surprise, or dart away. An enemy would pull back or duck to the side looking for its own opportunity to lash out. But I shall take our best defense from the prize fighters I observed on your television. When the blow comes, you will duck inward toward it to let the power of it go behind you.

Can that really work?

Once its paws have passed by your head, one on either side, I will drive your body upward until I can make the contact I need.

And if it's a bit faster than you believe and it tears my throat out?

Then I shall have a solitary existence in a human head, once again.

Forever.

That was not the case before and it shall not happen again. Sooner or later something will come along to eat the head. But enough, We should wait no longer.

Okay. Let's make our move.

Arthur felt his chest muscles tighten and his throat and rib cage contort as more animal sounds came from deep inside him. The panther tilted its head sideways for a moment as though questioning what it heard. Then Arthur saw muscles harden beneath black fur and the animal moved backward on its haunches preparing to pounce. Arthur's every instinct shrieked for him to flee and he would have tried that, but he no longer had control. He could only watch as the animal uncoiled silently with a blurring speed that thrust it upward toward him like the strike of a giant viper. A quick stripe of searing pain traveled the full distance of the side of his face then he felt his legs driving his own body upward. He caught an instant's sight of the redness in an open mouth, then the yellow eyes, then his head exploded into pain and nothing more.

Beba clamped her legs around it the way she'd learned to do climbing ropes as a child, pressed her eyes shut, and began to pick up speed. The friction of her descent brought hot pain to the palms of her hands and she tightened the grip of both hands and legs to slow herself and ease it.

The seconds went by and she had no idea how far down she had gone. She dared not open her eyes for the sight she would see could cause her to panic and rouse Coquitla too soon. One thwarted attempt would put Coquitla on guard and make a future try impossible. Subterfuge had been her only weapon and in a few more seconds the battle would be over. She couldn't just let go yet for the same reason she couldn't have just stepped off the top. There was too great a risk that in the final split second, her emotions would climax to waken Coquitla to stop her.

She felt the wind tugging at the full length of her tether and realized she'd begun to swing, could feel herself twisting in a slow circle, and felt first a shoulder then a knee graze the stone surface as her descent continued. Even though she'd slowed herself the burning in her palms grew worse until she had to stop the sliding altogether. This was more difficult than she'd expected.

With eyes still closed she began to let herself down hand over hand. She counted each handhold as she went. The verse started again in her mind to the rhythm of the counting: one . . .. *The world is flat*, two . . . *the wise men said* . . . three . . . four . . .. *Isn't he quite silly* . . .. Carefully, with all her concentration on maintaining control, she worked her way down. At one hundred she let her eyes open. The rope spun her in a lazy circle.

At first she looked out high over the jungle's green canopy, and as she continued to turn, saw that she had descended below the base of the pyramid and faced the cliff, now half a dozen feet away. She clamped her eyes tightly again, and forced herself downward again, "One-hundred-one . . . one-hundred-two . . . *Columbus claimed the Indian's land in the name of Isabella . . . .*"

At one hundred twenty a high pitched hissing scream startled her eyes open to see that she'd come down to the level of the first nests. The narrow ledges they rested on were strewn with bleached bones and the partly eaten remains of small birds and animals. Beba saw a foot long green and blue lizard writhing its last throes as a bird pinned its back against the ledge with curved stiletto talons. Others tried to snatch the prey away. She grimaced. The rockface looked as though it had been stained white for centuries, but it wasn't smooth and pretty as she'd imagined it when she'd first seen it from the riverbanks below. There were streaks of yellow and the reddish browns of years of the blood stains of their prey. The acrid odor of feces and the rotting smells of decay rose too strong to be washed away by the swirling currents of wind.

The birds shrieked again and again to summon others. They erupted into the air by the thousands like giant plumes of steam from a volcano and the fear and loathing they evoked in her returned. She hoped these feeling that she had nurtured in her daily trips to the altar stone would seem common to Coquitla today, but suddenly her hands locked themselves in place.

Something is wrong? Where are you?

The noise of the birds became deafening as they closed in a boiling cloud about her. Turning, twisting, diving. Each pass closer than the last.

"We are where you can do nothing about it." Beba shouted it out loud. "Our time together is over."

Absurd. That is not yours to determine. Have you not learned? Phaqutl must retrain Arthur from time to time. I thought that you knew better.

Beba felt her head turning taking in the scenery again, but for Coquitla's benefit now, and this time her sight was handicapped by the swirling mass of birds. Under Coquitla's control, her head tilted up and she could see the top of the pyramid, now well over a 50 meters above.

"You're through teaching now. The one last thing we will do together is fall to the river."

Climb to the top.

"It is much too far. I haven't the strength left to climb back up and the rope ends at least thirty meters above the water."

You will not go against me. Are you so ready to die?

"My death came the day you took my free will. My mother had no life. She was only the vessel of a parasite. No child of mine will come to that fate."

I shall force you to reconsider when we are back at the top.

"Don't you understand? I have come much too far down the rope for my own strength to pull me back to the top. Even you can't force that. I'm already beginning to weaken. The more you try to make me climb, the sooner it will be over. When I'm no longer able to hold on, we both fall. If you release me I will let go. There's no way you can prevent that.

She felt her muscles tense as Coquitla took command and she began to climb. Her body pulled itself up hand over hand at first, then using her legs also. She rose rapidly and the strength that Coquitla managed to call forth alarmed her. But as she neared the base of the pyramid once again, her energies began to diminish quickly and in a few more seconds of hectic attempt, it failed altogether. Coquitla fixed her body to the rope by wrapping it tightly around and between her legs. Beba felt the hot burning of exhausted muscles and the pain of stretched tendons as she hung desperate for air.

Impossible. You could not have planned this without my discovering it.

Before Beba could reply, pain stabbed into her shoulder.

His head began to clear, but Arthur couldn't remember where he was. He lay on his back with his eyes closed taking in something that smelled bad . . . very bad. A quick dash of warm wind hit his face and the odor got worse. He blinked his eyes open to look up squarely into the face of the panther. He started as if to jump back, but that was impossible against the floor and he banged his head against it to add pain upon pain that was already there. The huge beast stood over him, head tilted to one side in the pose animals sometimes take when they are trying to understand what they see.

He thought he should be afraid, but for a reason he couldn't place, he wasn't. Overhead above the animal he saw the wedge of light shining down from the opened crack in the mine door and he began to come back to the present. He concluded he must have blanked out and rolled down the steps to the mine floor when Phaqutl had clashed his head against the big cat.

Then he remembered and felt his eyes open wide. Phaqutl had gone into the panther. Arthur was free. He'd survived.

"Your breath would scrape the moss off a log." He got the questioning head twist again.

"Back off."

The head twist became even more exaggerated, but the animal backed away.

"Hey. You understand. You're in there?"

It sat down on its haunches and opened its mouth to pant in the warm air.

"And you understand what I'm telling you?" He felt foolish saying it. There was hesitation . . . then the head bobbed impatiently

"Absolutely amazing. I'm actually speaking with a animal. What a tremendous opportunity to learn."

A low rumble came from back in the panther's throat and its upper lip curled to expose ominous teeth.

"Right, we've got to get out of here." He looked up again at the door. He'd been able to prop it open a bit more than an inch. That allowed enough light in so that the area around the steps was dimly lit and enough air in so that running out of oxygen was no longer a threat. But he had to wonder if the two of them could lift it together.

Phaqutl knew the plan and was ahead of him. The big cat took the steps in one bound. At the top it turned and glared as Arthur scrambled up behind it and for the first time put his weight full onto the fifth step. Phaqutl wedged the huge body underneath the door with it resting on top of the shoulders just behind its head.

Arthur took a stance three steps below with bent knees and his own head and shoulders rolled forward to put the door across his upper back.

He looked sideways at his unlikely partner. "On three."

In the dimness he saw the muscles beneath the black fur gather into knots and his own tensed in anticipation. On the count he drove his legs upward and pushed against the door with everything he had and saw the panther also forcing itself up against the heavy load. Seconds went by and for an instant it seemed as though the door might relent, but it didn't. The reward was no more than the rasping groan of wood tormented by the stress of their efforts.

Finally, his strength ebbed and he realized he no longer pushed with any relevant force. They'd failed. He stooped until the weight left his shoulders, then moved down the steps until he could stand erect and stretch. His back ached and his shoulders had cramped from the awkward stance he'd taken. He heard the animal panting heavily above him and glanced up the steps to see it sink down to rest its head on it paws. There was no victory in taking back control of himself, if his fate was to perish here in the mine. He turned away from the cat and sat down, rubbed his eyes and lay back against a step.

He sat wrestling for answers. But had none. His thoughts wandered, now only searching for the means to face defeat. A jolting blow between his shoulder blades sent him to his feet, trying to keep from pitching head first. He jerked around to see the panther standing behind him. It raised its eyes to glare intently into his.

He stared back. "Why the head butt? It surely can't be time to feed the kitty? It's been back there gnawing on something that stinks since we came in."

The panther continued to glare for a moment then its head wagged emphatically up and down.

"What are you trying to tell me . . .? We gave it our best and didn't even come close. There's no use unless you can come up with a better idea and I doubt the brain you're in offers much in the way of reasoning power."

The big cat backed up the steps slowly until its haunches squeezed into the angle the steps made with the door. With hind legs bent, it pushed its butt upward against the door, bared its fangs and nodded the head again. Then it stopped and waited.

"Got it . . .. You can push harder with the hind quarters than you did with the front. Makes sense. The hind legs are what it springs with. The movement is right . . . one more try."

Arthur crowded up against the panther and took a stance. "On three again." The knowledge that it was his last chance caused him to count slowly gathering himself for the effort. At the mark, he put everything he had into it.

This time the door raised perhaps a quarter of an inch, but no farther. The panting of the panther had stopped and he thought he could hear claws digging into the wooden steps. He inhaled deeply and forced himself to push harder. The door held fast. Then without warning he felt the teeth of the panther clamp down on the back of his thigh.

Arthur shouted and stiffened violently to brace himself for the attack. Instead he heard a grinding sound and then a thump as one of the stones piled on top of the door fell from the stack to the ground. Then the sounds of a second and third and instantly the door became lighter and began to raise. With each inch he heard more stones topple away and more light flooded into the mine.

"Painful, but a nice trick."

The panther offered a brief grunt, then the door was open and the two of them wrestled over each other scrabbling to get out.

※

She jerked her head back in time to see the bird that grazed her wheel away to begin circling upward for another assault. They were all about her. Screeching, whirling, diving from above with opened talons thrust stiffly below them only to slip to one side at the last instant passing just beyond reach to brake with outstretched wings and begin the climb back up. Tactics to intimidate an intruder. But one had dared to hit her, and she sensed that within moments others would gain courage from it, and the mock attacks would turn real until suddenly the entire swarm would descend to rip at her with claws and beaks.

They will attack.

"I've beaten you."

A wing brushed her face. She hadn't seen it coming. Then, all her bravery and resolve whisked away in an instant like her panting breath in the winds. The horror of her predicament overwhelmed her with panic. She froze and locked onto the rope, every muscle taut. She caught sight of the river below. It was time to let it be over, to let herself go, but she hung there paralyzed with fear.

The bird noises turned into high-pitched keening that sent tremors through her back and shoulders. Talons raked her hair. She felt a warmth run down the side of her face and a body brushed her head. She flinched violently and sent out a scream of tormented horror.

Then her eyes snapped open wide as Coquitla took her and she caught sight of a marauder closing to strike at her face. She felt her legs clamp tight on the rope and watched her arm shoot upward to snatch it by the legs and take cuts from its claws in return. It stretched its beak down to tear her at her fingers, but before it could, her arm swung it in a looping arc and let it go to dash against the face of the cliff. It crumpled and there was a sound like a footstep on dry twigs. Now a disarray of broken feathers, it fell away out of sight below.

Where has your defiance gone? You were willing to plunge to your own death just to kill me with you and now

you cower at the plight of the bird. You cringe and dangle on your rope like a baby clings to its mother.

An attacker came close and her arm grabbed out again, this time only to catch a wing. She heard it snap as her fingers clenched then let go. It tried vainly to fly, but the others saw it falter and dove to tear it apart in midair.

You are correct. It is indeed impossible for you to climb back to the top. You are doomed to fall to your end in the river or to end up in the bellies of the birds. You are no longer suitable to me.

Beba heard the cry of an impending assault and felt her head turn to see the attacker plummeting toward her. This time she sensed that Coquitla had timed the strike and found herself holding back until needle sharp talons had already begun to puncture skin. Then the arm snapped out and took it squarely by the chest and her fingers worked themselves upward along the torso until the head and neck were immobilized by her grasp.

I go.

And Beba saw the head being rushed toward her own and felt feathers and bone hit just above her eyes. Then for a moment she could neither see nor hear.

When her senses returned only a few seconds must have passed for she still clung to the rope with all her strength and her reflexes had pulled the bird up against her body and held it tighter than before. She felt claws scrabbling at her flesh as it fought to gain freedom.

Then she realized that Coquitla had gone . . . now inhabited the animal struggling in her hand and the torment of her mother and of her grandmothers before and of her children to come, melded together in her mind, and she couldn't let go. Her finger tips dug into yielding flesh and tiny bones bent then gave way. The orange beak opened wide and a high pitched squeal, not unlike the death scream of the lizard she'd heard moments before, rose above the noise of the savage flock only to fade as the black beads of its eyes glazed over. And as the lifeless body trailed limply in her grasp, she still hung on. Then the anger in her drained away, as the bird's life had ebbed from it and she could let it go and watch as it became smaller and smaller. It nearly disappeared beneath her before it splashed into the river to float downstream as a tiny white dot carried on the surface.

She watched, for the moment forgetting where she was. Relieved and satisfied to know that Coquitla had died with the bird and that she was free of her for all time. Then as happiness began to flood through her, it suddenly shrank and withdrew, for she faced the fate she had made for herself.

XV

A RTHUR ROSE TO PUSH HIMSELF THROUGH the door the instant the two of them forced the opening wide enough, but the huge cat jousted him from behind and crunched him through to pitch out onto his back. He landed beside the mine entrance, eyes dazzled by sun streaming through the forest canopy above and heard the big animal bounding across the clearing to crash into the bush. No sooner had he hauled in the first welcome breath of fresh air than reality hit him and he rolled over to lurch to his feet.

She'd trapped him for a reason. Not to cause his death as he'd first thought in the mine's blackness, but to delay him. To give herself time to accomplish her own death. He couldn't figure out where or how. The questions tolled in him like bells.

He began moving toward the trail. Unsteadily at first as balance and muscles readjusted, but gaining equilibrium with each step and by the time he'd reached it, he could run. Scarcely a minute later he burst into the village shouting her name, though a dark intuition told him there would be no response, and none came.

Everyday she'd gone to the pyramid, but had no work to do there. She'd said it was to be closer to her past. Now the realization of her real reason sank into him like a hot iron into cold water. He sprinted toward it, hoping he wasn't too late. More than once along the rough trail he stumbled or tripped and fell to claw his way up and plunge ahead. By the time he reached the base of it, thorns had torn skin and clothing and his sides heaved from exertion. He stopped and cupped his hands, fought to control his breath, and shouted up.

"Beba, wait. Phaqutl's gone. I'm coming."

As he began the race to the top, he hoped to see her silhouette rise against the sky to wave down to him, to signal that he'd come in time. He saw only the movements of the roiling birds. Each step seemed higher than the last. Hard pain cramped in his side. His heart pounded.

Finally his eye level rose above the top step. The platform was empty but for the altar stone. She'd jumped already, or he'd come to the wrong place. He slammed closed fists against his thighs. But then the next step up raised his view enough to see the white nylon line circling the base of the altar stone and her sandals beside it.

He scrambled across the platform to its riverside, saw the loop tied at the rear of the altar with the line running taut over the cut stone edge. He dropped on his stomach and put his head out over the cliff to look down. So far below she could have been a child's doll dangling on a string, Beba twisted slowly in the wind while the birds swooped and dove about her.

He called to her, but she didn't look up, and he knew she wouldn't hear him above the shrieking birds. His only chance was to pull her up and hope she'd realize what he was trying to do. And that she'd allow it to happen. As the quandary began to steal his attention he reached to twist the gold ring, stopped when he saw what he was doing, wrenched the talisman from his finger and threw it out over the river.

His efforts had to be consistent and steady. To let the rope slip back even a few inches could jolt her hard enough to make her fall. A task made more difficult because his own strength was nearly spent.

He took the nylon, pulled and worked it around the back of his shoulders until it formed a U shape running from the altar stone to him and returning again to the riverside edge. He walked himself backward using the strength of his legs to thrust against the rough stone, hauling the rope up as he moved. Slowly, deliberately across the platform toward the opposite side, talking aloud as he strained against the weight. "Hang on Beba. Be strong a while longer . . .."

Then he stepped backward, working down the vertical face of the tier, forcing his body to lay back into the taut line as a mountain climber would, feeling it burn as it creased over his flesh. He repeated the procedure across and down the next. Tier by tier the mass of the pyramid rose above him and the length before him grew, but the strain was taking a toll.

As he neared the base of the pyramid, he wondered if she'd let herself down so far that he'd reach the bottom and be forced to continue backing his way into the bush. The dense vegetation posed a new problem. He'd turned and craned his neck, trying to see what he'd be dealing with when something slipped and exhausted muscles collapsed. He felt a sharp jerk and the line went slack. The sudden release spun him and he sprawled over the edge of the bottom tier into the dirt. There was a sound like a swarm of raging bees and he lifted his head to see the rope, carried by the force of its own weight, slithering toward him, faster and faster until the end of it fell at his feet.

Her breathing shallow and fast, Beba sensed it would be no longer than minutes before exhaustion would win out and the burden of her own weight would wrench her fingers from the rope. She knew well she could have made no other choice and had accepted this outcome days before. Even so, she couldn't bring herself to open her hands and let it be done. Coquitla was gone and these were a final few moments of freedom. A few seconds of triumph to hold aside the dread of her own death and of what she had done to Arthur.

All about her the keening birds took their calls to a deafening pitch as they gained boldness from their numbers and began diving near enough to rake at her flesh as they passed. She felt the biting stings of their slashes on her back and shoulders, the tearing of her hair and scalp. She clung with her body and legs hugged tightly around the rope and face turned down, but it gave little protection and the pain grew more intense. For a brief second she thought she heard Arthur's voice calling from above and ducked one then a second plummeting attacker before she could hazard to look up. No one and she added it up to the cruel trick of a desperate mind. Then the rope quivered like a plucked string.

The turn of events set the birds to shrilling even louder, but they reacted to avoid her now. The movement confused her at first, but slowly the face of the cliff began to slide downward before her eyes and she realized that the line was being pulled up from above.

The certainty of death gave way to the rise of a restored hope. At least she knew that Arthur lived. No one else could pull the rope. But he could tire or Phaqutl might force him away. The sooner she could get back to the top, the more likely she would survive. Warily, fear that her actions would end in a fall trying to turn her rigid, she began to climb. One hand reaching up and over the other, resetting her legs on the rope each time. She barely had strength, but the weeks of working with stone had drained away every ounce of unnecessary body weight and made her stronger. Minutes went by and she watched the crude nests strewn with the torn carcasses of prey pass downward, next came the cleanly cut stones of the pyramid.

As she neared the top she looked up, waiting to see Arthur reaching down to pull her to safety. He did not come. As her own hands neared the place where the rope ran over the abrupt edge of the topmost stone, she suddenly understood it would rasp the line from her grip. She felt her jaw clamp tight as every instinct dreaded what had to be done and she whispered a plea that terrified muscles would respond.

At the last second she released the first hand, heard herself cry out, thrust it up and over the edge to grab the line again where it stretched across the flat surface. The moving rope scraped skin from her knuckles. She had no choice and repeated the action with the other. At last her head rose above the surface and again she expected to see Arthur there hauling up the line and again disappointment. There was only the thick white nylon running across the surface to disappear down the opposite side.

Now the edge came up against her chest and she could feel the sudden extra tension that put on the rope. It frightened her and she tried to ease the problem. She tightened her grip, walked her elbows across the surface, flattened her face to it and tried to pull herself along with her chin.

She felt the granite edge working slowly down her body, pulling at her clothing, scraping at her breasts and then her stomach. She let her legs free of the rope to bring a knee up, but before it could happen, the line jolted and the force of it began to yank it through her grip. Though she tried with the last of the strength in her hands, she couldn't hold it, and it began to run faster. Already sore hands burned so that she cried out for it to stop.

Suddenly she felt the end of it pull up over the edge beneath her stomach and even before that sensation was complete the end shot through her hands with a release that sent it flying into the air to disappear over the far edge.

With her heart racing she gasped as frenzied fingers scrabbled against stone but failed to hold. She felt her torso sinking back over the edge and in final desperation tried once more to swing a leg up. Her heel landed on top, slipped, caught, slipped again, then held as she strained to lock bare skin against the hard surface. Her fingers caught and she pulled with the dregs of her reserve. Half inch at a time, she worked her body up and over the edge, until she lay panting on the hard hot surface. She stayed there face down, too spent to rise, sobbing quietly into the stone.

<hr />

The smell of the inside of the mine roused anguished senses from sorrow. No . . . not the mine. He'd remembered falling at the base of the pyramid. It was the stink of the panther.

Arthur bolted upright and looked about himself fearing the worst. He'd nearly forgotten that the big cat and its new boss might still be in the neighborhood. He raised his head to see it sitting several tiers above him, lips curled back to expose yellowed fangs. It moved to set itself to spring. The hair on his neck crinkled. He needed to act fast.

"I'd stay up there, if I were you."

The big cats ears flattened and its head twisted sideways.

"You still understand me. Good." He needed to think of something that would get him out of this.

A low rumble told him Phaqutl wanted answers too and the one he had to give twisted his guts. He lowered his gaze until he could make the words come out. "Beba . . . fell from the top to the river . . . they're gone."

The big head above him shook from side-to-side so violently the animal's front paws did a macabre dance on the stone.

"It's true. I don't know why Coquitla didn't stop her."

The panther snarled and drew back farther on steel haunches. Arthur tried to set himself to duck when it came. He'd protect his face with his arms. Then the voice came from the top.

"I deceived her. She went into one of the birds."

The sound of her voice brought him up straight, arms in the air, the panther forgotten.

She shouted again. "It fell, and I saw it floating away down river."

She'd given Arthur the answer he needed. "You'll need the panther, if you hope to find her. It's faster in the forest. And a much better swimmer."

He heard Beba scream just as it slammed into his chest. The air went out of him and he went down, tumbling and rolling, over and over, anticipating the feel of its claws and fangs. Instead he heard the howl of its rage as it crashed away into the bush.

He lay panting . . . trying to catch his breath and to shout to her at the same time. Then he heard her jumping down from layer to layer and turned just as her arms went around him and her cheek pressed hard against his.

XVI

*T*HEY SAT SHOULDER TO SHOULDER, LEANING
back against the altar stone under a fresh morning sun.
It had been nearly three weeks since they'd climbed the
pyramid. It had been a time for healing body, mind, and spirit.
They'd stayed away from this place to let the memories of the
terrors they had suffered there slumber. The dugout Beba had
arrived in had outriggers now and the few things they would take
with them were stowed safely inside. Soon they'd walk the path
to the river to leave.

They'd let themselves be carried in the moment by an intimacy that pretended their lives together would go on without
interruption. They both knew that couldn't be. They were at different places in their lives and each had tasks before them that
would make sweeping changes in their futures.

As much as he looked forward to going back, he knew he'd
miss Beba and a hint of sadness colored his voice. "Where will
you go when we've returned?"

She looked at him for a long moment before she spoke. "All of my past is here. I have touched it, smelled it, lived it. Felt the glories and the agonies of my ancestors."

"Yes. And you've made it so that the glories needn't be forgotten and the agonies won't be suffered again."

"*Sí.*" She said it matter of factly, then got to her feet to turn and put a finger on the face of the altar stone at a place where slightly smaller glyphs had been added, apparently at a time after those above them.

She concentrated for a moment and when she began he realized that this was a portion Phaqutl hadn't bothered to translate for him that day they'd first met.

"*What comes before was written in the hope . . .*" She spoke to him in the old language, a legacy of their ordeal. "*. . . that love of our gods would provide our needs, bring us happiness and fullness inside. We let them direct our minds and souls, to find they took but gave little in return. Please, Wise One of the Skies, send to us those who will drive them away to let our people strive for themselves once again.*

"I must search for my mother. It will help her to know that her child and her grandchildren will live freely to provide for themselves and to find a better god."

"How will you find her? You said she left without a trace."

"*Sí*, but I believe *Tía Eva* will find it in herself to help me now. If not, I shall search on my own."

He nodded and smiled, he had every reason to believe she'd succeed. He'd seen her courage and strength and knew she was capable of using it in ways most could never achieve. And maybe he'd grown too. At least he no longer had to protect himself like the little boy, Wart, hiding under the stairs in the lightless basement, relying on blind ritual to survive. Even the rituals of science.

He thought he might look up his own family too. All his life he'd told himself they'd abandoned him. The dream that had truly been reality didn't tell him who they were, but it told him that he'd been stolen from them. Perhaps they had suffered even more than he. Knowing that made him also know that the harm he feared he might do to Millie or their children was no threat at all.

"One thing about these past few months that disturbs me. There seems to be too much coincidence. First I was Wart . . .."

She interrupted him, "Reginald. *Si.*" and giggled. "I adore that name and will use it only from now on."

He looked down at the backs of his hands and had a fleeting memory of someone asking him, why if his parents had really loved him, did they give him that name.

"Okay . . . first I was Reginald and Phaqutl came along. And then I became Arthur and came across the woman who carried the spore of Phaqutl's mate. Next I discover this place, the one Phaqutl wanted to return to and came here to find you with Coquitla and end up Phaqutl's victim all over again."

"And you think this happened by some strange chance? Perhaps there was never coincidence from the time he took you from your family as a boy. Ask yourself, how it is you grew to become this man of science who studies the history and people of this particular place in the world."

He pursed his lips, letting it sink in, then took a quick look at the sun. The heat had begun to rise and the time had come to begin their journey. He stood and even before he could speak she took his hand and matched his first step away from the altar stone.

"And you? You will go back to the woman you were with at the lodge?"

"If she'll still have me."

"How could any woman turn away a man named Reginald?"

EPILOGUE

*T*HE TINY OUTBOARD THROBBED PLAINTIVELY as the two worked the small boat in a lazy circle below the confluence of the rivers. They knew the larger river well, though none from their village dared travel the other. The fish waited where the waters came together to take advantage of the food washed by the one into the other and more than a dozen clung to threads of life in a small tank built into the bottom of the boat between them. Juan, the younger by more than two decades, glanced into it, then straight overhead at the sun and finally at his partner in the stern.

"We have caught nothing for almost an hour. The fish must be sleeping. Perhaps we should follow the example."

The older man cupped an ear as though he hadn't heard, but at the same time turned the motor to head toward the near bank, while Juan busied himself bringing in the lines. Moments later the boat nudged the shore and they climbed out to pull it up and out of the currents before moving away from the water several yards to a small shaded clearing with an open view to the river.

They ate lightly and slowly for the heat thwarted their appetites. The older man's mouth was still chewing when he settled back into the grass and pulled his hat down to cover his eyes. Not ready to close his own just yet, Juan eased back against a convenient log and looked up and down the river seeking nothing in particular.

He'd almost let his eyes sweep by, when its tail twitched and caught his attention. A jaguar a hundred or so yards upstream stretched out on its belly at waters edge on a low sand spit. Juan had seen them before, but never a black one, and this one at an odd time of day for them. A female, with the conventional spotted coat, glided from the bush behind it to stand at its side.

Juan leaned sideways until he could tap his partner's knee and spoke in a hoarse whisper, "*Eh hombre*. Look up the river. At the sandy spot. Tell me what you see."

His partner lifted his hat and looked back at him balefully. "Why don't you just tell me what I will see?"

But he lifted himself anyway and looked in the direction Juan pointed. After a moment he nodded then frowned quizzically. Juan turned back to look and the two watched as the big male stood and waded into the river to within inches of where a fish larger than any they had caught for several months circled slowly with its back and dorsal fin well above water.

Juan expected the cat to pounce and capture it for its dinner, but instead it waited, and the fish circled closer. The lad whistled softly. "I see a foolish fish teasing a very big jaguar. They will be taking it to their lair to feed their young soon."

Just at that instant the male took the fish in its mouth, but to Juan's surprise, it lifted it gently almost lovingly as a mother might take up its kitten and carried it to lay on the sand. Then it walked backward several steps and raised its head. All through this the fish remained motionless. It did not struggle.

For a moment the female seemed reluctant then it moved to the fish as if to sniff it. The fish came to life, writhed violently, then seemed to launch itself into the face of the spotted female. The big cat swatted at it furiously and rowled in anger. Juan started at the surprise.

"I think the fish waited too long to go on the attack, old man."

The other chuckled, "Si. You are right," and Juan turned away from the scene to see him shaking his head in mock amazement. The two exchanged grins, but when they looked back at the sand spit, it lay empty.

Juan watched for a few moments half hoping they'd return. He looked at the sun and it was time to get back to their work. He was about to rise, when from nearby he heard an odd cough that set his blood cold. The female had suddenly appeared from the bush between them and the boat, its fangs bared. Next came the deep throated grunt of the male behind them.

Goodfellow Press Catalogue of Titles

The Quest
by Pam Binder.
Time cannot destroy the tapestry of
a life woven with love and magic.
ISBN 1-891761-10-2
$19.99/$23.99 Canada

The Dalari Accord
by Matthew Lieber Buchman.
Memory is the alien within.
ISBN 1-891761-04-8
$19.99/$23.99 Canada

A Slight Change of Plans
by John Zobel.
Sometimes the answer is right
in front of you.
ISBN 1-891761-01-3
$12.99/$13.99 Canada

Matutu
by Sally Ash.
To find healing and love, an English
violinist and an American writer
must explore a Maori legend.
ISBN 0-9639882-9-8
$12.99/13.99 Canada

The Inscription
by Pam Binder.
An immortal warrior has conquered
death. Now he must conquer living.
ISBN 0-9639882-7-1
$12.99/$13.99 Canada.

Cookbook from Hell
by Matthew Lieber Buchman.
One part creation. Two parts soft-
ware. Season lightly with a pair of
love stories and roast until done.
ISBN 0-9639882-8-X
$12.99/$13.99 Canada

Ivory Tower
by May Taylor.
Does the scent of lilacs herald
a soft haunting?
ISBN 0-9639882-3-9
$12.99/$13.99 Canada

White Powder
by Mary Sharon Plowman.
It's hard to fall in love when
bullets are flying.
ISBN 0-9639882-6-3
$9.99/$10.99 Canada

Bear Dance
by Kay Zimmer.
A man betrayed and a woman
escaping painful memories struggle
to overcome the barriers keeping
them apart.
ISBN 0-9639882-4-7
$9.99/$10.99 Canada

Glass Ceiling
by CJ Wyckoff.
Facing career and emotional upheaval, Jane Walker makes a bold choice to explore east Africa with an unorthodox man.
ISBN 0-9639882-2-0
$9.99/$10.99 Canada

This Time
by Mary Sharon Plowman.
A man and a woman with differing expectations and lifestyles take a chance on love.
ISBN 0-9639882-1-2
$7.99/$8.99 Canada

Hedge of Thorns
by Sally Ash.
A gentle story unfolding like a modern fairy tale, of painful yesterdays and trust reborn.
ISBN 0-9639882-0-4
$7.99/$8.99 Canada.

2001 RELEASES

Howl at the Moon
by Polly Blankenship.
On a dusty country road in Texas, a woman and a boy come face to face with a nightmare.
ISBN 1-891761-07-2
$22.00/$25.00 Canada

The Girls from Hangar B
by Kristin Campbell Nail.
WWII, the union and men are no match for four women when they break all the rules.
ISBN 1-891761-08-0
$22.00/$25.00 Canada

Diamond Lies
by Johann Sorenson.
Once you have found your true love, what do you do when the past shows up?
ISBN 1-891761-09-9
$22.00/$25.00 Canada

Between Two Worlds
by Suzi Prodan.
As the new nation of Yugoslavia rises from the ashes of WWII, rebels learn the price of freedom.
ISBN 1-891761-12-9

AsYouLikeIt - A Goodfellow Imprint

Rozner's Constant
by Jeffrey L. Waters.
Now that you have inherited the
secret of the universe, how do
you stay alive?
ISBN 1-891761-11-0
$19.99/23.99 Canada

An Unobstructed View
by Jenness Clark.
Life's unobstructed views, while
desirable, depend on where
one is standing.
ISBN 1-891761-02-1
$12.99/$13.99 Canada

Coming AsYouLikeIt RELEASES

Midnight Choir
by Richard Clement.
In 1907, a Seattle nurse witnesses
a murder and becomes entangled
with the detective she fears may
be the killer.
ISBN: 1-891761-16-1

The Day the Music Died
by Florine Gingerich.
With the help of an unlikely ally,
a young gypsy woman faces the
horror of Nazi aggression.
ISBN: 1-891761-17-X

Yellow Finch
by Ed Ratcliffe.
Two sisters in Peru, struggle to keep
loved ones together when their
family is fragmented by a terrorist
connection.
ISBN: 1-891761-19-6

Point of Departure
by Doni Pahlow.
Surprised by her ability to embrace
change, a successful forty-two-year-
old explores the secrets of her heart
and soul.
ISBN: 1-891761-18-8

GOODFELLOW PRESS *Professional Services*

Goodfellow Professional Services is dedicated to the education of writers and the promotion of the written word, not only as a vehicle for pleasure, but as a work of art. To this end the following services are available.

- Editing Services
  Editing is done by Pamela Goodfellow, Editor-in-Chief of GP, or by an Associate Editor. All editing is done with two goals: supporting authors to reach their highest potential and aiding them in creating a work of fiction viable in the commercial market.

- Weekend Workshops and Saturday Seminars
  These two to five-day workshops offer students complete immersion in the writing process. Sessions are led by Pamela Goodfellow, GP authors, and a variety of guest speakers. This forum provides both new and experienced authors with a motivational boost. Saturday Seminars are a one day alternative to the weekend workshops.

- Ongoing and Private Classes
  Educational opportunities are available in several formats including: evening classes for groups of six or more, on-going weekly critique sessions monitored by a GP author or editor, and weekend seminars by request for groups of twelve or more.

- Speakers Bureau
  Authors, designers, and editors are available as speakers for classes, seminars, luncheons, and professional societies and conferences. Topics include all aspects of book creation, from writing to publishing.

Goodfellow Press
8522 10th Ave NW
Seattle, WA 98117
(206) 881-7699 / fax(206)-706-6352
info@goodfellowpress.com

GOODFELLOW PRESS 2001
EDITORIAL SERVICES RATE SHEET

Editorial Services   **Rate**

1. Four-sentence exercise. $ 25.00
   This is great for pinpointing a problem area and
   working through it. Make up your own or we can
   assign one specifically for you.

2. One-page stand-alone scene (based on
   300 words per page in 12 pt. type with 1″
   margins, double spaced). $ 50.00
   (Each additional page is $25.)

3. One 5-page scene (1500 words) $125.00
   (Each additional page is $20.)

4. A short story of 10-13 pages (3000–4000 words) $300.00
   (Each additional page after 13 is $35.)

5. A series of five 5-page scenes (each scene 1500
   words, total 7500). $500.00
   (Each additional page is $20.)

6. Editorial Consultation (1-hr minimum):
   with an Associate Editor (face-to-face) $65.00
   with Pamela R. Goodfellow (face-to-face) $175.00

7. Editing of full manuscripts is done on a limited basis by individual review.
   Costs vary according to condition of manuscript.

Please specify what you want done and what you expect from us and send to:

Goodfellow Press
8522 10th Ave NW
Seattle, WA 98117
(206) 881-7699 / fax(206)-706-6352
info@goodfellowpress.com